fire fight

dusk valley — book 1

amanda chaperon

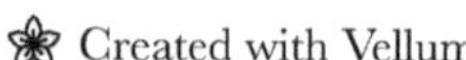 Created with Vellum

content warnings

Dear reader,

Please note that *Fire Fight* contains the following material that may be triggering for some readers: mentions of murder/death by fire, attempted murder, semi-graphic descriptions of burns, drug and alcohol abuse by a main character (off page but discussed), main character dealing with recovering from addiction, on page physical violence, on page abduction, graphic sexual content (bondage, edging, toy play, light breath play), and explicit language.

If you're sensitive to any of these subjects, please use this warning to make an informed decision about whether or not to proceed reading this story.

As always, your mental health comes first. Please take care of yourself.

Xoxo,

Amanda

preface

. . .

FROM: leighlee@email.com
   TO: aspen@mckayinvestigates.com

SUBJECT: Prom Night Arsonist

Dear Ms. McKay,

My name is Leigh Lee. I'm a lifelong resident of a small town in western Idaho called Dusk Valley. On April 24, 1985, my oldest daughter, Victoria, was brutally murdered on the night of her senior prom. Since then, the sick, twisted individual who took my daughter's life has continued to haunt this town, taking more victims at random over the last forty years and leaving more families like my own caught in the throes of an endless tragedy. The press have dubbed them the "Prom Night Arsonist."

I have no idea if you'll ever see this, but I had to reach out on the off chance that you might. My husband and I are getting up in years, and we desperately want justice for our daughter, the other victims, and their families. We can't officially hire you, but we're hoping you might be interested in taking on the case anyway.

Please don't hesitate to reach out if you have any further questions.

Sincerely,
    Leigh Lee

---

prologue

. . .

ASPEN

I WAS a sucker for a sob story.

I'd been taken advantage of once or twice before because of it. But I'd gotten a lot better at recognizing when someone was fucking with me, and when someone was genuinely looking for answers.

Leigh Lee and her husband, Harold, fell into the latter category.

My private detective business was a one-woman show, so I personally monitored all of my digital and physical mail correspondence. My office was in a shitty little building in a borderline bad neighborhood of Denver, and I called the shitty little apartment above it home. Most of my time was spent on the road anyway, making it nothing more than a landing place between cases.

My last one was two months ago, and I've been itching to get back out there ever since.

When Mrs. Lee's email came through, adrenaline shot through my veins.

I'd never heard of the Prom Night Arsonist, but in the two weeks since receiving that electronic missive, I'd done enough research to become well-versed—latching particularly onto the fact that the local police had barely any leads, much less a viable suspect.

This guy was a fucking ghost.

Even before I'd officially spoken with Mrs. Lee, I knew I wanted to tackle this case. The small town wasn't flashy enough to attract national media attention, but the murders were devastating to the people who lived there. With a killer who had been active for decades, it was the kind of case I most enjoyed. There was a lot of meat on its bones, and I was ready to take a big bite.

Mrs. Lee's voice held such…rawness and despair when I'd reached out that my heart damn near cracked in my chest. While I'd long since gotten good at marshaling my emotions and constructing a cage around my heart to protect myself from getting in too deep on my investigations, there was no shielding yourself from a mother still reeling from the loss of her child.

I understood that with stark, unending clarity.

The pain in her voice—it was the same I'd heard in my own mother's for years.

For that alone, I'd find the fucker who'd done this to them.

one

. . .

ASPEN

WHAT AN ADORABLY QUAINT LITTLE TOWN.

That was the first thought I had as I navigated Black Betty, my beat-up, rusted-out old Chevy Suburban, down the main thoroughfare. I had a reservation at the motel back on the highway, but I wanted to get a feel for the place before I settled into my room.

My head was on a swivel as I attempted to take everything in on one pass—a feat I knew would be impossible. My feet itched with the desire to park, get out, and strut up and down the sidewalks, seeing all this map dot had to offer. My nosy, curious nature tended to get the better of me in moments like this. I needed to feel, touch, smell, and taste. I needed to awaken all of my senses and fully immerse myself in the locality.

But I resisted the urge, for now, settling for an optical perusal.

The residents of Dusk Valley clearly took pride in the presentation of their home, because there wasn't any chipped paint to be found, or a decoration out of place, and the streets remained clear of any unwanted debris. The storefronts were an eclectic but somehow cohesive mix of craftsman and brick, each distinguished by a shingle rocking on the gentle breeze, or a merrily striped awning. Flowers overflowed from hanging baskets and window boxes.

The whole facade was quintessentially Small Town, USA.

Unfortunately, it also masked a dark history.

I wasn't delusional enough to think I was capable of tracking down a killer when over forty years of law enforcement professionals hadn't been able to, but something about this one had my bones humming with an unnameable energy.

This guy was living right under these people's noses—a true testament to the duality of human nature as everyone went about their daily errands and jobs like there wasn't a killer walking among them.

I was making it my personal mission to root this fucker out and bring him to justice.

With that thought, I reached the lone stoplight, which didn't shift colors but merely blinked yellow in caution, at the intersection of two perpendicular roads. I glanced in my rearview to confirm no one was waiting behind me, then lifted my phone to plug the address of my motel into my maps app. As soon as I touched it, however, it rang.

Narrowly avoiding rolling my eyes, I answered.

"Hi, Mom."

"Did you arrive?"

No, "Hello, Aspen."

No, "Hi, honey, how are you?"

She cut right to the chase. That was my mother's way.

"Just got here," I lied smoothly. Every time I traveled somewhere new, though my parents hated my job, I had strict instructions to let them know the moment I crossed town lines.

I tended to push the boundaries, mostly because I was thirty-three years old and didn't need them babying me. I'm not sure I *ever* needed that.

They refused to get the memo, though Dad had loosened his

reins a lot more in recent years. Still, it seemed for every inch of control he gave up, Mom picked up a mile of slack.

Frankly, it was fucking exhausting.

And they wondered why I rarely went home to Chicago.

I knew it came from a place of love and worry, but they were fucking suffocating me.

It had been that way ever since my sister died.

My sister, Lola, had been everything I wasn't. Bright and bubbly, never met a stranger, on her way to becoming an incredible pediatrician.

Until the fire that took her from us in an instant, and our entire world crashed down around us.

I was the only child they had left, and I understood wanting to protect me, but I wasn't the sixteen-year-old girl who would crawl into bed with them at night because it was the only way I could stay whole when I felt like half of me had died with Lola. While they'd been dealing with their own grief, they'd still helped me navigate mine, and for that I was eternally grateful.

But that was a long time ago—over half my life had passed since then. They needed to let me live without this dark cloud of guilt and obligation hanging over me.

"You're supposed to call when you arrive."

This time, I did roll my eyes. "Mom, I'm literally still in my car. I haven't even gotten to the motel yet."

"Do you have your taser?"

"Yes."

"Your gun?"

"Yes," I replied, my eyes darting to the hump in the floor between the driver and passenger footwells where my Ruger SR22 was safely stowed in its lockbox.

"And your self-defense keychain?"

"Yes," I gritted out. My jaw ached from clenching my teeth.

She had given me the keychain as a gift a few Christmases back, and it *had* come in handy—mainly to open beer bottles that didn't have a twist off cap. Usually, the infernal thing, with all its bells and literal whistles, remained in the center console of Black Betty, out of sight and out of mind.

I did keep the taser she'd bought me on my person at all times, though. In fact, I carried it even more than my gun. I wasn't above putting someone on their ass if they touched me in an uninvited or threatening manner. After all, I was a petite woman traveling alone. My parents worried needlessly because I wasn't taking any chances where my safety was concerned.

"Don't take that tone with me, Aspen," Mom snapped.

"Sorry," I mumbled without an ounce of feeling behind the word.

"How's the motel?"

I considered the best response and settled on, "Budget friendly."

Mom heaved a sigh that echoed in my ears and settled heavily on my bones. Amazing how she managed to do that, even from fifteen hundred miles away.

"I don't know why you insist on doing this," she said, and I could feel her disappointment like a passenger in the car with me.

"It's my job."

"Come home," she implored me. "Get a *real* job. I'm sure the paper would take you back. You can even live with me and Dad until you find your own place."

"No."

This wasn't the first time Mom had tried to have this conversation with me, and my stance was as firm now as it had been when I left Chicago eight years ago.

Whether they agreed with me or not, I *was* firmly on my feet with a *real* job. I had a sizable savings, and took on frequent cases that paid well enough to cover all of my expenses.

I didn't need much. I was a simple woman who lived a quiet existence, and I liked it that way. I'd already suffered enough heartbreak for one lifetime. Holding myself apart from others saved me from experiencing any more.

Not to mention the fact that I enjoyed what I did. I'd always been a curious person, but it went beyond the norm of human nature, something I didn't fully realize until I was in college. I was studying communications and, in one of my writing courses, we were tasked with picking a topic and writing a research article.

In the midst of the project, I'd gone to a frat party with my roommate and seen some things I shouldn't have. Like a dog with a bone, I dug and dug until I wound up uncovering a massive drug ring within the Greek system.

That was the first time I'd really put myself in the line of fire in search of unearthing the truth, and my professor had taken notice. She told me I would be extremely successful as an investigative journalist, and that I should consider changing my major.

I'd taken her words to heart, ultimately graduating with a Bachelor of Arts in Journalism before working at the *Chicago Sun Times* for five years.

Until everything fell apart, and I left without a backward glance.

I shook those memories off before they could root and fester. I'd worked hard these years to heal from my trauma, and it hurt me that my mother didn't realize how much it pained me when she continued to bring this shit up.

"Aspen…"

"*No*," I repeated, more vehemently this time. "I'm not coming back to Chicago. I'm not going back to the paper. I'm not moving back in with you and Dad. Just…no!"

The silence in the wake of my outburst was deafening.

"Aspen—" Mom tried again, and the way she said my name told me she'd launch into a rant I'd never hear the end of if I didn't nip it in the bud now.

"Sorry, Mom. I have to go."

I hung up, and not a moment too soon as a car behind me laid on its horn. I fumbled to type in the address of my lodgings as I made a right-hand turn.

I knew from my drive-by earlier that it wasn't the nicest place on the planet, but when I actually *stopped* to look at it, the motel was even more depressing. The rooms branched out in two wings that formed a ninety-degree angle, centered by a little enclosed lobby and reception area, the roof of which sagged in the middle. The paint on the siding was peeling, the wood beneath weathered and grey. At least the doors to the rooms appeared to be heavy metal instead of some other flimsy material.

With a weary sigh, I pushed out of Black Betty and approached reception.

The man behind the counter had seen better days, much like his place of employment. His head was pale and shiny, a few wisps of hair from the ring around his skull combed over top. He was pot-bellied and beady-eyed, and he boredly flipped through a *Playboy* magazine, not sparing me a glance as he said, "Name."

"Kay Asplund," I said.

Despite my mother's opinions, I *did* take my personal safety seriously. I never gave places like this my real name, and I always paid in cash.

The man dropped his magazine off to the side and scooted his chair forward until he was belly up to the counter. He tapped the ancient keyboard then finally flicked his eyes up to me.

"Do you know how long you'll be staying?"

"I'd like to pay by the week, if possible."

I had no idea how long this investigation would take, but I knew I'd be here for at least seven days.

His mouth twisted, as though he was considering it, before he said, "That's a higher rate."

"That's fine," I assured him, trying and failing to give him a bright smile. "I won't cause any problems."

He rolled his eyes but muttered, "Better not."

After a few signatures and putting down a four-hundred-dollar deposit for the next seven days—which was highway robbery, if you asked me—he passed an old key across the counter to me. "Room twenty-two, down at the end." He indicated toward the side of the motel that butted up to the road.

I gave him a terse smile and turned on my heel to leave. I hopped back behind the wheel and moved Black Betty in front of my door. I would've preferred a room on the other end, away from the bustle of traffic, but I knew asking the twit at reception would've been futile.

Before lugging my belongings inside, I unlocked the door and entered. At first glance, it appeared clean, if a bit stale. The cream curtains were heavy and blocked most of the light from outside, providing me with a fair amount of privacy. Two full-sized beds dominated most of the space, as well as a dresser on which an ancient, boxy television sat, and a small round table with two chairs in the corner by the window. At the back was a wide counter inlaid with a sink and a large mirror above. The small bathroom contained only a shower/tub combo and toilet.

It suited my purposes fine, despite being far from the most glamorous place I'd ever stayed.

Returning to Black Betty, I pulled out my laptop bag and the old bankers box I used in lieu of a briefcase for files and other pertinent case materials, leaving those by the table in the corner before going back out for the rest of my stuff. It took three trips, but eventually, all of my worldly possessions were in the room with me. I beeped Black Betty locked, then shut the door behind me, flipping the bolt and throwing the security chain.

Sagging against it, I sighed in relief. I'd driven from Denver to Salt Lake City yesterday before coming the rest of the way today, so the drive hadn't been excruciating, but I was still exhausted. Too much time alone with my thoughts, especially on a case like this, had me running a little ragged.

Nothing a good night's sleep couldn't fix.

two

. . .

CREW

AFTER RUNNING my towel roughly through my hair to soak up the excess water, I wrapped it around my waist and padded from the showers toward my locker and a fresh set of clothes. It didn't matter how many times I scrubbed up after a call, though. The scent of smoke was forever a part of my DNA.

In the row over from my locker, I could hear two of my crew members talking in hushed, excited voices.

Childers and Tuck, from the sounds of it.

"She's so hot."

"Who is she?"

"No idea. Obviously not from around here, because I've never seen her before."

"I'd like to see *a lot* more of her, if you know what I mean." I could practically see Tuck's accompanying shoulder nudge and smarmy smile.

"Wanna make a bet?" Childers asked.

"What kind?"

"Let's see which of us can get her number faster."

"You're on."

"What the fuck are you two whispering about?" I asked.

My words were followed by the slam of metal, almost like one of them had startled and slammed into the lockers, and I chuckled.

A beat later, as I was pulling on fresh boxer briefs to cover my junk, Tuck's head peeked around the corner.

"Hey, Cap," he said with a sheepish grin.

Childers, not embarrassed in the slightest, fully entered the aisle and dropped onto one of the benches bolted to the floor. "There's some chick in Chief's office," he said with a sly grin. "Fucking smokeshow."

I knew the expression he wore—had seen it numerous times over the course of the last five years since I'd moved home and became a captain with the Dusk Valley Fire Department. Dude was about to become a fucking problem.

I leveled my finger in his face. "Stay away from her."

Childers gasped theatrically and pressed a palm to his chest. "*Me*? What about this fucker?" He hooked a thumb in Tuck's direction.

"You stay away from her too," I said as I stepped into my pants.

"Ahh, you say that now, Cap," Tuck grinned. "But you'll be singing a different tune when you see her. Take my word for it and get in on the action. I'll bet you guys a hundred bucks I get her digits first."

I shook my head, and Childers protested as droplets of water sprayed in his direction.

"I can't be playing your childish games anymore, Tuck." I paused to pull my polo over my head, tapping at the patches on the lapels of the collar that held my bugles, smiling cheekily. "I'm a big boy now."

"With a big stick up your ass," Childers muttered.

Tuck tipped his head back and laughed, and I dove at Childers, wrapping an arm around his neck and giving him a noogie.

"Lawless!" Chief Madden's shout stilled me, my head swinging around to meet his eyes. "Stop fucking around and get your ass out here."

I let Childers go and straightened. "Yes, Chief."

When he disappeared with an exasperated shake of his head, I stuffed my feet into my boots and saluted the guys. "Duty calls."

We filed out and found Chief standing in the center of the common room, an unfamiliar woman at his side.

Tuck and Childers hadn't been lying—she was a fucking stunner.

Rich, warm brown hair and eyes the color of cinnamon. Full, pouty lips with a light sheen I guessed came from lip balm; she didn't look like a gloss or stick kind of woman.

She was petite, barely coming to Chief's shoulder. So petite, in fact, that with her pert little nose, delicately pointed chin, and high cheekbones, she almost looked like a fairy.

But there was something…hardened about her. I couldn't quite put my finger on why I thought that, though, other than the darkness in her eyes, and the way her smile didn't quite reach them.

Somehow, I knew this wasn't a social call for her, or some fun exploratory mission about bringing her kid in to see the fire trucks and meet some real-life first responders.

"This is Aspen McKay. She's a private investigator looking into the Prom Night Arsonist," Chief said, confirming my suspicions. "She was hoping one of us would be willing to sit down with her and review our incident reports."

"I volunteer!" Childers supplied quickly.

The withering look Chief gave him had Tuck and I coughing into our fists to hide our laughter.

"Appreciate the enthusiasm, Childers, but this is a job for your Captain."

I collected myself, perking up at that.

The woman—Aspen—raised a brow. "*You*'re the captain?"

Shuffling forward a few steps, I extended my hand. "Captain Crew Lawless, at your service."

God, I sounded like a tool.

The corner of that plump mouth ticked up a fraction before it flattened again.

When her hand slid into mine, those slight, delicate fingers wrapping around my much larger and calloused ones, a jolt shot up my arm, like an electrical current coursing through my veins. I barely held myself from yanking back in surprise.

"You're awfully young to be a captain," she said when she released me, and I flexed my hand at my side, attempting to shake off the lingering tingling sensation.

I shrugged. That wasn't the first time I'd heard the sentiment, and it likely wouldn't be the last until I aged another decade or so. "I've been a firefighter for thirteen years, ma'am. I think I can handle myself."

Behind me, one of the guys snorted, and Chief shot them a glare.

"Noted," Aspen said. "Well, if you wouldn't mind letting me pick your brain, I'd love to sit down and chat when you're off shift next."

My eyes flicked up to the large, glowing-red wall clock over our heads, my mind mentally tabulating the hours between now and the end of my shift.

"I'm off tomorrow morning at eight, so how about we meet at the diner for breakfast shortly after that? My treat."

Aspen was already shaking her head, and my brow scrunched in confusion. Aspen laughed. "Yes to breakfast," she clarified. "But it's *my* treat. You're doing me a favor here, not the other way around."

I crossed my arms over my chest, and I didn't miss the way those cinnamon eyes flared as my biceps bulged, like she thoroughly enjoyed what she saw.

Or maybe it was less about the muscles and more about the

sleeve of tattoos that engulfed my left arm. Women loved that shit, right? They loved the thrill of getting with a bad boy, and once upon a time, I was about as bad as they got.

"Tomorrow then," I said, greeting her with a smirk when her attention flew back to my face.

She grinned in response, unbothered that I'd caught her checking me out. "Tomorrow."

three

. . .

CREW

THE FOLLOWING MORNING, I pushed into the diner, wide awake despite not getting any meaningful sleep. Over the second half of my shift, we'd had four calls that had kept us out most of the night. Any time I'd get a chance to rest, the bells would go off again.

Dusk Valley FD wasn't as exciting as shows like *Chicago Fire* and *Fire Country* made firefighting seem. Mainly, it was routine chaos, a mundanity that, after five years, I'd settled into easily.

As the door swung closed behind me, the waitress, Bonnie, who had been working here since I was a kid, approached with a wide, nicotine-stained grin.

"Morning, Crew. You want your usual seat at the counter?"

I shook my head. "I'm actually meeting someone," I said, gesturing to the box of files under my arm in explanation.

"Take your pick then," Bonnie said. "I'll bring over coffee and menus." She curled a brow on the last word, her inflection making it more of a question than statement.

"Menus would be great. Thanks, Bon."

The place was mostly empty; it was that odd time of year between winter and summer tourists when Dusk Valley became a ghost town. The same locals who came in every morning like clockwork were in their usual spots, so I had my pick of tables. Scanning the room, I didn't see Aspen anywhere, so I selected a booth along the exterior, where the windows let in the early-morning sunshine, and slid in with my back to the wall.

When Aspen walked through the door, I was struck momentarily speechless by how beautiful she was. Dark jeans clung to her shapely legs, the hems disappearing into a pair of black, shit-kicking combat boots with a thick sole. She had on a tight black tee tucked into the jeans and a charcoal grey windbreaker thrown overtop to ward off the chill. Chocolatey hair was pulled back into a tight bun at the base of her skull, and she wore no makeup that I could tell.

In a word, Aspen McKay was breathtaking. I knew I had to keep my wits about me with this one.

Bonnie appeared from the back, and I didn't miss the way the older woman's gaze slid up and down Aspen's person, inspecting, though her expression remained bored.

"Can I help you?"

"I'm looking for Crew Lawless?"

Bonnie pointed in my direction, and I stood as Aspen's gaze locked on mine, a small smile curving her mouth as she walked my way.

"Miss McKay," I said when she stood in front of me. "Good to see you again."

"Aspen, please," she told me as she slid into the booth opposite me. "You as well. I'm sure you'd much rather be sleeping, so I appreciate you taking the time to meet with me."

"It's really no problem at all."

She didn't look convinced, but she dropped the argument when Bonnie approached with another mug and carafe of coffee.

"I'll give you a second to look over the menu," she said pointedly to Aspen, knowing I'd had the thing memorized for years.

After offering her a smile, Aspen's attention dropped to the laminated paper, and I mouthed *be nice* at Bonnie.

With an eye roll, the old woman disappeared once again.

"So what's good here?" Aspen asked.

"Everything."

Aspen chuckled. "Helpful."

I hitched a shoulder up. "I've been eating here as long as I can remember. I've tried everything Bonnie has to offer, and there's not a single bad dish."

"Okay…" Aspen said, dropping her menu and resting her elbows on the table to lean toward me, those cinnamon eyes assessing. "Then tell me what you're getting."

I mirrored her pose, dropping my voice. "You want me to tell you what to do?"

Aspen blinked slowly at my tone, but breathed, "Maybe."

"You don't seem like the type, Miss McKay."

"Aspen."

"Aspen," I repeated.

"Yes?"

"Chicken and bacon waffles," I said lowly, almost like I was describing my favorite sexual position.

What the fuck was happening here? I knew we were being lured into dangerous waters, but I couldn't find the energy to pull us from the trance.

Aspen's pink tongue darted out to trace along her bottom lip, and my skin tightened with the action. Wondering how it would look swirling around the tip of my co—

"You two ready to order?"

We snapped apart like we'd been shocked, and when I dared a glance up at her, Bonnie's lips were pursed in my direction, clearly unimpressed. Internally, I groaned. The problem with being a small town boy was that all the old folks treated me like their child. But I didn't need to be mothered. If I wanted that, I'd head over to the ranch and let my real mama fuss over me.

"My usual," I croaked.

"Honey and syrup?"

I chuckled at Bonnie. "Do I ever get it any other way?"

She smirked, but her expression flattened when she turned to Aspen.

But Aspen's eyes were on me.

"Honey and syrup?" she asked, one of those perfect, dark brows raised toward her hairline.

"Honey for the chicken, syrup—"

"For the waffles," Bonnie finished. "He's been doing it since he was a kid."

"That's…a lot of sugar."

I merely shrugged. In general, I took great care of my body, but I liked to indulge every now and then.

Aspen considered that for a second before she said, "I'll have the same. And can I get a bowl of whatever fresh fruit you've got on the side?"

Bonnie nodded, said, "Sure thing, toots," and left again.

"*Toots?*" Aspen asked.

"She's warming up to you."

Aspen snorted. "Well, I hope everyone else in town warms up as quickly."

"Dusk Valley is the best. I'm sure they will."

"Did you grow up here?"

"Sure did. Born and raised."

"How long have you been a firefighter?"

"Since I was eighteen."

"And how old are you now?"

"Thirty-one."

Her eyes widened and brows raised. "Your captaincy is impressive at your age."

"You can't be much older than me."

"Thirty-three," she admitted.

"Exactly."

"So you joined the fire department here right out of high school then?"

I grimaced at the memories her words unearthed. She couldn't know the bruise she'd pressed on, reminding me of a time when I'd been a stupid kid and not the mostly well-adjusted man before her.

"Not exactly," I said. "I applied for the Chicago Fire Department early on in my senior year, and miraculously, my name was drawn in the lottery. After graduation, I moved to Chicago, went through the academy, and worked there for five years."

"And you've been back here since?"

"Nope," I said proudly, popping the *p* dramatically. "I spent almost three years in Northern California fighting campaign fires before ultimately moving home and settling in at the DVFD."

Aspen leaned back in the booth and crossed her arms over her chest. "So you're a hotshot too. Doubly impressive."

I raised a brow. "You know what a hotshot is?"

"Please," she scoffed. "I've seen *Fire Country*."

I couldn't help it; I tipped my head back and boomed out a laugh. This woman—she was something else. And I was only scratching the surface.

Glancing down at myself, I flicked my gaze up to her and smirked. "You comparing me to Max Thieriot?"

Aspen made some dismissive, disapproving sound in the back of her throat. "Definitely not. You look nothing like him."

"You're right," I agreed. "I'm obviously way hotter."

"You're incorrigible. And we're not here so you can flirt with me, Captain."

"Is that what we're doing, Miss McKay? Are we flirting?"

God, I fucking hoped so.

"No," she clipped, far too quickly to be believable.

I grinned but let it drop, shifting gears to the reason for our meeting.

Twisting to the side, I lifted the lid on the box of files and withdrew the one on top, the first label reading 24-APRIL-1985, SUNSET RIDGE CAR FIRE.

"Walk me through what you know so far," I said, passing the file over.

"I'll be honest, not much," she admitted, almost absently as she scanned the incident report. "I was contacted by Vicky Lee's parents. They don't want to be involved, and they aren't paying me, but...I was intrigued enough to reach out via phone. We talked for a few hours, and I knew I couldn't let this one go." Returning to herself, Aspen glanced up at me. "No parent should ever have to bury their child," she said vehemently. "I'm going to do everything I can to bring this sick fucker to justice."

"I appreciate the can-do spirit," I said slowly, choosing my next words carefully. "But what makes you think you can accomplish what four decades of law enforcement hasn't been able to?"

"I'm not saying I can. But I can get in places cops can't thanks to all that jurisdictional and bureaucratic red tape." She placed her hand atop the open file and jerked her chin at the rest sitting in the box at my side. "I owe it to these women and their families to try."

"And man," I said, glancing pointedly at the file under her hand, which detailed the incident that claimed Roger Stanhope's life as well as Vicky Lee's.

"And man," she agreed. "Have you looked at these before?"

"I took a cursory glance between calls last night. As of right now, nothing jumps out at me. But I'm happy to spend as much time with you as you need to go over them and get a grasp on what happened."

"Well, this first one seems pretty cut and dry. Car fire, right?"

I nodded. "But both Lee and Stanhope were dead before the fire was set."

Those curious, red-brown eyes latched onto mine and widened. "The fire didn't kill them?"

"Nope. My brother is the sheriff, and he told me the cause of death for both was a gunshot wound to the head. Buckshot, according to department reports."

"A hunter?" she asked.

I shrugged. "They were up on the ridge overlooking town that's only accessed by a woods road, so it could be. Could be they're not connected to the other ten victims at all. But it was also the first incident of its kind in the area that can't be attributed to some cops-and-robbers-type shit from the twenties and thirties, and the timing is a little too convenient to be a one-off."

"Timing?"

"You're aware of the Prom Night Arsonist moniker." She nodded, and I patted the box at my side. "Each of these incidents happened on a Dusk Valley prom night, including Vicky and Roger's deaths. In fact, they'd both been crowned king and queen that night and were dead a few hours later."

A full-body shudder overtook Aspen. "That's…horrible. Have you ever worked one of these?"

I nodded. "My first year at the department. I was only a lieutenant back then," I said, shooting her a wink. "But it was…brutal. Poor girl was found in the school bus garage. All that gasoline…" I gave into a shudder. "Took us hours to knock it down, and by then she was…well, I'll spare you the details."

I could still remember the distinct scent of burning flesh permeating the air, mixing with the gas and smoke. The odor was so strong, my SCBA had done nothing to filter it out. Unfortunately, I'd been the one to find her, and I'd never forget the sight of her blackened body.

I'd worked some awful fires in Chicago that had claimed lives, but there was a difference when it happened in your hometown and the victim was a girl you knew in that same way everyone in small towns knew everybody else.

"Captain?" Aspen prompted, pulling me from my memories.

"Sorry." I cleared my throat. "Whatever you need, you've got my and the fire department's full support."

"Thanks, Crew," she said, her warm smile quelling my discomfort brought on my bad memories.

My name sounded so fucking good rolling off her tongue. I wanted to hear it again and again—preferably with my face between her thighs.

Returning it, I said, "No problem."

Bonnie appeared with our food then, and while we ate, conversation drifted from the case toward more personal things. I was amazed by how easy talking to her was, and I found myself excited about the prospect of having this woman in town for a while.

I looked forward to rolling around in the sheets with her. Somehow, I knew we'd end up there.

No strings, no drama.

Exactly the way I liked it.

four

. . .

CREW LAWLESS WAS INCREDIBLY easy to talk to.

And even easier on the eyes.

I had to keep my wits about me around that one, lest I let his hypnotic ocean gaze pull me into the deep and never let me go.

That man…he was fucking dangerous. Arguably more dangerous to me than the killer I was chasing.

Two hours passed in a blink, and against my better judgement, we exchanged numbers before parting with the promise that I'd call if I needed anything at all.

The demand was so fucking suggestive, I almost gave in right there. It had been a long-ass time since I had good sex, and Crew gave Big Dick Energy—the kind I somehow knew he'd be able to back up.

Maybe, once I was a little more settled in town, I'd make our acquaintance a little less professional.

He didn't strike me as the type to want more than something casual anyway, so despite the red flags waving in the muscles and the grin and the sexy-ass tattoos, it probably wouldn't kill me to take him for a ride.

Fucking hell, McKay, I silently admonished myself. *Get it together.*

I had a job to do, first and foremost.

After we parted ways, I headed back to my motel room with a copy of the incident reports Crew and the Chief had agreed to give me, spending hours poring over them and taking copious notes. Getting the full scope of the crimes without the police reports was difficult, but I did the best I could. I broke briefly for lunch, then set off on my next errand.

Emboldened by how easily Crew and the fire station team agreed to help me, my next stop at the sheriff's department was only logical.

An artificial bell signaled my entrance when I pushed the door open, and the desk sergeant stood and waved me over.

"Hello, miss," she said, her voice muffled by the sheet of plexiglass between us. "What can I do for you?"

"I was hoping I could speak to someone about the Prom Night Arsonist."

In that detached, cop-like way, she did a quick perusal of my person. Ultimately, she must have assumed I wasn't a threat, because she plastered on the fakest smile I'd ever seen, and said, "Excuse me a moment while I get the sheriff."

She disappeared, and I took a moment to turn about the small lobby, studying the framed photos and accolades on the walls.

My gaze latched onto a photo of an officer in full dress uniform, a shiny star pinned to his chest, surrounded by a crowd of people. There, in the thick of it all, was none other than Crew Lawless. Younger than he was now, face freshly shaved, missing that darker blond stubble that shaded his chin and jaw now. The man filled the hell out of a pale blue button-down shirt and khaki pants.

Which meant the officer had to be his brother, the sheriff.

As though I'd conjured him, the *buzz* of a door being opened remotely sounded from my left, and a hulking man with tattoos engulfing both arms, unlike his brother's single sleeve, stepped through.

By my estimation, the sheriff had maybe an inch of height on Crew, but they were both impressively broad-shouldered and muscular, every bit of them from head to toe exuding strength and masculinity. I wondered which one was older.

This one, I decided mentally after studying his face and the lines branch out from his eyes more closely.

"I'm Sheriff Lawless," he said. "Can I help you, Miss…"

There was an irony to be found in his title, a joke buried somewhere.

"McKay, but please, call me Aspen."

"Alright, Aspen," he said, somewhat warily as he hooked his thumbs into his belt. "What can I do for you?"

"I'm a private investigator," I began, withdrawing my license and ID from my bag. "I'm here looking into the Prom Night Arsonist murders, and I was curious if the department would be willing to let me take a look at the case files."

The sheriff didn't respond, he merely spun on his heel and jerked his head at the desk clerk, who admitted us into the inner sanctum.

The heads of his deputies swiveled toward us, tracking our every step through the bullpen until we reached an office at the back. The sheriff ushered me in and closed the door. Without an invitation, I sank onto one of the guest chairs in front of his desk and waited for him to take his seat.

"Tell me why you're really here," he said once he did, resting his elbows on his desk and leaning forward to study me. Clearly, he and Crew were related. I would've figured it out even if Crew hadn't told me his brother was the sheriff. Their hair was the same shade, eyes a matching crystal blue. But where Crew's entire demeanor was warm and inviting, the sheriff's was closed-off and wary.

"I told you. I'm here looking into the Prom Night Arsonist."

"How do you even know about it?"

"A concerned citizen."

The sheriff's eyes narrowed. "I'd like the name of this concerned citizen."

"Sorry, Sheriff. No can do. That's privileged information."

Like hell was I about to drag the Lees into this when they specifically asked to be kept out of it.

He exhaled harshly through his nose, and I waited for him to stand and start screaming. His hands flexed, his knuckles blanching with each curled fist, highlighting the letters inked on each.

Love free.

Interesting sentiment from a cop.

"Fine," he clipped. "Either way, the answer is no. Those files are, shall we say…*privileged information.*" His smirk was downright menacing as he turned my own words against me.

"Fair enough," I said, rising from the chair and extending my hand. The sheriff straightened to his full height, glaring down his nose at me, ignoring my attempt at cordiality. I let my hand drop. "Thank you for your time."

I was almost to the door when he said my name, and I looked over my shoulder at him.

"This case brings up a lot of bad memories for a lot of people in this town. You'd be better off packing up and leaving matters to the authorities."

I snorted. "While I'd love to"—I didn't, actually, and we both knew it—"it seems to me the authorities haven't accomplished a damn thing in over forty years. See you around."

With that, I flung the door open and exited his office.

I felt his eyes like laser beams between my shoulder blades the entire way out.

THE NEXT NIGHT, I found myself at Dusk Valley's watering hole, also known as The Swallow—the ideal place to learn all the local gossip.

The Swallow was about what you'd expect for a small town bar. The sign out front featured a human hand holding a mug of frothy beer, tipping it into the waiting mouth of a bird—a swallow, obviously. The letters were neon tubing twisted into a bold, no-nonsense font that glowed brightly in the dark. A beacon for wayward souls.

Or private investigators who had been stymied by the police.

When I pushed through the heavy oak door, I was surprised by its spaciousness. Though smoking in public places had been outlawed ages ago, the scent of tobacco still clung to the room. Off to one side was a large area cordoned off by wooden half-walls to create a dance floor presided over by a raised stage. The bar stretched the length of the opposite wall, and a man and woman hustled back and forth behind it.

As I moved deeper inside, weaving through freestanding tables, I could feel several sets of eyes on me, but I didn't pay them any mind. I was used to this particular dance. Afterall, I was fresh meat. The new, shiny thing nobody could take their eyes off.

At last, I reached the bar and managed to, miraculously, locate a free stool. I dropped onto it, and the male bartender approached, expression giving nothing away as he slid a coaster in front of me and gruffly said, "What can I get you?"

"Whatever your local draft IPA is, please," I replied as I withdrew my wallet from my crossbody bag.

With a curt nod, he moved over to the tap, poured my beer, and returned.

"Five bucks."

I handed him a ten and told him to keep the change.

That seemed to loosen him up a bit because after putting my

order in the till and cashing out, he slipped his tip into his pocket and turned to me with a wide grin.

"So what brings you to town?" he asked.

"Little of this, little of that," I said noncommittally, taking a sip of my beer.

"You here alone?"

Dragging my finger coyly around the rim of my glass, I asked, "Why?"

He leaned forward on his elbows and dropped his voice. "Just wondering if I've got any competition."

I tipped my head back and laughed. Amazing, how a five-dollar tip could change a man's mood so drastically. With dark hair and eyes and a reasonably symmetrical face, he wasn't bad looking, though he couldn't be older than twenty-five and thus too young for me.

Still, it made me wonder what I could accomplish with a twenty—or with a different incentive entirely.

"Yes, I'm here alone," I answered, shifting closer like I was about to share a secret. "Actually, I'm a private investigator here on a case."

His eyes widened fractionally, curiosity clearly piqued.

"What kind of case?"

"Murder. Arson. The usual."

He straightened to his full height—which, if I had to guess, was right around six feet—and crossed his arms over his chest. He had two thick bands of dark ink wrapping around his right forearm, but no other tattoos or identifying marks that I could see.

"The Prom Night Arsonist."

"Good guess," I praised. "What can you tell me about it?"

One of his shoulders hitched up in a half-shrug. "I know what the papers tell me. Some sicko has been tormenting our town for decades."

"Did you know any of the victims personally?"

"A few," he answered noncommittally. Clearly, the walls had gone back up, making it unlikely that I'd get anything else out of him.

Still, I pressed. "Are any of the families of the victims still around?"

"Almost all of them, I think. Except maybe the Lees? They typically head south for the winter and haven't returned yet that I've seen."

"And you'd notice?"

"It's a small town, lady. And I work here."

"Fair enough. So let's say I wanted to talk to someone about those murders and the victims, and the sheriff's department is no help. What would you suggest I do?"

Once again, he rested his elbows on the bar, this time more menacing than flirtatious. "You want my honest opinion?" I nodded. "Give it up. You're an outsider, which means the people of this place won't exactly be welcoming or forthcoming when they find out you're dredging up all this old shit. There hasn't been a murder in a few years. I'd suggest letting it go and getting out of town before something bad happens to you too."

My hackles rose. "Is that a threat?"

He shrugged and pursed his lips. "Statement of fact. Have a nice night."

And then he was gone, leaving me reeling.

I hadn't expected to be welcomed with a goddamn parade or anything, but you'd think these people would look a little more kindly on someone trying to *help* them.

In my haste to get away from the bar, I accidentally collided with another body. My beer sloshed all over my bag, hand, and the front of my shirt, immediately suctioning the material to my skin.

A very pissed-off woman, her strawberry blonde hair cut in a severe bob at her chin, glared at me in disgust.

"Watch where you're going!" she sneered, striking green eyes shining with malice. "What is wrong with you?"

"I'm so sorry," I replied, unsure why I was apologizing. The woman appeared no worse for the wear. Her clothes were still dry, drink still full in her hand.

With a huff, she disappeared into the crowd, her friend mumbling an apology to me before following.

In search of napkins, I turned back to the bar, only to find the bartender smirking and shaking his head. I'd find no assistance from him.

The natives had officially turned on me, and I needed to leave—*now*.

Wiping my hands off as best as I could on my jeans, I pushed my way through the crowd and exited into the night.

Goosebumps erupted on my arms instantly as the chilled air hit my drenched shirt, and I plucked it away from my body as I made my way across the packed-dirt parking lot toward Black Betty, cursing the entire way.

In my back jeans pocket, my phone had been spared any damage. I pulled it out and started a Google search for a local laundromat. I'd also need to see about finding a new bag. Mine was likely ruined beyond repair, the dark amber of my beer soaking in and staining the pale canvas fabric.

I never saw the hit coming.

One moment, I was stomping the final ten feet to my SUV. The next, I was belly-down on the ground, my skull throbbing.

Lifting a shaky hand, I probed my skull, my fingertips coming away red.

Blood.

What the fuck?

My bag had landed several feet away when I fell, and I tried to scramble for it and the taser inside. I only managed a few feet before my assailant caught hold of my hair and wrenched me back, my neck craning to an uncomfortable angle. A kick to my ribs had it snapping forward, a crunch echoing from my nose when my face collided with the ground. Pain bloomed, my eyes watering, blurring my vision, and hot liquid dribbled into my mouth.

More blood.

A cold, terrifying laugh made goosebumps rise all over my skin, and another well-placed kick to my side had me gasping for air. I still tried to crawl for my taser, screaming for help, but there was no one around to hear me. Another boot to my ribs yet again thwarted my progress.

The realization of how this would play out hit me with sickening clarity: there would be no escaping.

Confirming my thoughts, there was a jolt, burn, and buzz against my neck that reverberated through my entire body.

Then everything went black.

five

. . .

CREW

THE BLARE of an alarm had me jolting upright in bed. Muscle memory brought me to my feet before I'd fully opened my eyes, stuffing them in my boots and moving from the bunk room to the garage behind the rest of my truck company.

The dispatcher's voice rang out from the PA system as the bells cut out.

"Truck twenty-seven, engine forty-five, ambulance thirty-five. Warehouse fire, Maple and Alder."

Adrenaline coursed heavily through my veins, energizing me better than caffeine ever could, and I donned my gear on autopilot. Mentally, I drew up a map of town, focusing on the area we were headed. Maple and Adler was in the industrial park, so we'd have to be mindful of the other businesses in the area to ensure the fire didn't jump and spread.

As I hopped into the front passenger seat of our truck, the rest of the men loading into the back, something tickled my brain. Something about this night and the location of the call.

"Prom night, ain't it?" Childers asked from behind me.

My blood ran cold as my thoughts cleared, his words catching that thread and yanking it to the forefront of my mind.

I shared a sidelong glance with Tuck, who was our driver. "You think it's him?" I asked, loud enough that my whole crew could hear.

Tuck shrugged, eyes on the road, navigating us from the station at the edge of town and through the sleepy streets of Dusk Valley. "Hard to say until we get there. Been quiet for a few years, though."

"That means he's due," I gritted out, my words mostly drowned by the sirens as Tuck flipped them on once we mostly cleared the residential neighborhoods and were cruising through the business loop of downtown.

As more adrenaline released into my bloodstream, my body began to hum in anticipation. This could've been another run-of-the-mill warehouse fire—I'd fought dozens in my career. But…I couldn't forget the prom night fire I'd worked a few years back, and I didn't believe in coincidences, especially not on this night.

My only hope was we arrived in time to save the poor woman he'd targeted this time.

When Tuck pulled up to the structure, the fire was already fully involved. Flames licked at the window panes along the side, the garage doors on the front glowed orange as they were battered from behind, and fire danced around the frame of the closed side entrance.

This building used to be an auto shop owned by a local family. They'd recently moved to a larger, more modern place they'd built on the other side of town, and this one had been sold to a landscaping company.

We hopped out of the truck, and as the most senior person on the scene until Chief arrived, I took charge of incident command, calling it into dispatch to let them know we'd arrived. Quickly, I ran the perimeter, assessing how and where was best to breach and attack.

"Where do you want us, Cap?" Sutton Rausch, the paramedic in charge at our fire station, asked when I returned to the front, gesturing to herself and her partner, Thomas.

"I want you guys on standby. If we radio out, be ready. I have no idea what, if anything, we'll find in there, but…"

"We got it," she reminded me.

I nodded grimly. Like me, Sutton had grown up in Dusk Valley. She was a few years ahead of me in school and had graduated with my brother, Lane. This also wasn't her first prom night fire.

When I looped around the side of the truck and greeted my men, Burns, the fourth member of our truck crew, held out an air bottle and SCBA for me.

"Tuck, I want you with me going in through this side door. Childers and Burns, I want you to head around to the rear entrance. That door is kitty-corner from this one. This side seems to be where the worst of the blaze is, so we'll breach away from it, assess, do a sweep for vics, and get the fuck out. Understood?"

My men nodded and, faces set in determination, moved to carry out my directions.

The building butted up to a copse of trees, and nearby sat an abandoned pile of wooden pallets.

Kindling.

"Engine!" I shouted, and their lieutenant rushed to my side. "Keep things contained while we do a quick sweep. Douse those pallets, and be mindful of the trees. Snake a line around that backside if you can in case it decides it wants to jump."

"Roger that," he saluted.

"Great, now haul over a line and cover us while Tuck and I go in."

"Davis!" the lieutenant called. "You're up!"

Emergency lights cut through the night as Chief Madden slammed his buggy to a stop at the curb, pulling his helmet on and withdrawing his own SCBA from the backseat before approaching the scene.

"Status report!" he shouted as he approached.

"Tuck and I are heading in," I said. "Engine will cover us. I'm sending Childers and Burns around back."

Chief nodded and yelled, "Let's go, boys!"

Davis from the engine crew raced over, dragging a hose with him. While he positioned himself, I approached the front entrance and turned, bracing my hands against either side of the door jam. The material was hot, even through my gloves, and sweat instantly broke out on my back. I glanced at the engine guy, who gave me a nod.

"You ready?" I shouted at Tuck.

The man gave me an almost feral grin. "Let's rock."

"Three…two…one…" I swung my right leg back forcefully, delivering a perfect donkey kick that sent the door careening open.

I moved out of the way as Davis hollered at his team, "Charge it!"

Across the hard-packed dirt lot, I watched the hose expand with water until it reached the nozzle, and Davis opened it up, shuffling forward, directing the spray at the flames inside.

I came up behind him, one hand resting on his shoulder. Tuck did the same behind me, and as a unit, we moved into the building.

Nothing could ever prepare you for that first blast of a fire, which was a lot like when you opened a heated oven and all that hot air smacked you right in the face—times a thousand. Every time, I had to remind myself to take slow, normal breaths, to not gulp in air like I was desperate for it. As long as the bottle strapped to my back didn't empty before I could exit the building, I was fine.

"The worst of the fire is that way!" I shouted, pointing toward our left, where the narrow hallway we were in opened onto the garage floor. "Hit this stretch and give us some room!"

"You got it, Cap!"

Davis shifted, aiming the hose where I indicated, and Tuck and I shuffled forward through the opening he created in the wall of flame. As soon as we were through, he'd fall back and contain the blaze from outside until we needed to get out.

"You smell that?" Tuck asked, remaining glued to my six as was protocol.

I spared him a quick glance over my shoulder.

"Fuel. Diesel, if I had to guess."

Tuck nodded, but it wasn't a guess. The smell of diesel fuel—there was nothing like it.

"Could be lingering from the shop."

I shot him a look that told him we both knew that was wishful thinking. For starters, the odor was far too strong. And secondly…

I pointed at the floor, the concrete which had once been polished to a high shine that was now sooty and marred by dark scorch marks—obvious signs of an accelerant being used.

Tuck and I both knew the former owners of the shop hadn't done that.

Thankfully, the floor wasn't aflame—the fuel seemed to have burned off—but even through the smoke clouding my vision, the scorch marks ran down the hall in a mostly straight line before veering sharply to the left through an open doorway.

At least that solved the mystery of *how* the fire had started.

Unfortunately, after burning off the diesel on the floor, the fire had climbed the walls, searching for more fuel, and grown tall enough to get into the roof. Eventually, it spread into the trusses and down to the insulation. The temperature had risen high enough to put major thermal stress on the windows, thus blowing them out.

"Follow the Yellow Brick Road!" Tuck urged, nodding at the blackened path.

Staying low, we inched along until the reception area opened on our left, the offices beyond that. Straight ahead was the garage floor.

We continued past the walled-off admin area until the garage opened up. In front of us were the two bays they'd use for larger industrial machinery when the county depot was backed up, and to the right were the smaller ones for personal vehicle maintenance.

I opened my mouth to give an order, but Tuck cut me off. "Don't you dare."

Chuckling, I did it anyway, pointing at the door in the far-right corner. We watched as it popped open, the other two members of our crew appearing in the frame.

"Grab them and clear this area. It'll be faster with the three of you. Then I want you to send them out and around the front before coming back for me."

"You're heading in there, aren't you?" he asked, jerking his head at the offices.

I shrugged. "Gotta clear it."

As their captain—as the one responsible for their lives—I'd rather be the one to do it than force any of them to risk it.

Tuck held his fist out, and I bumped it with mine. "Be safe."

I gave him a mock salute. "Always am."

Three offices branched off the main area. Reception itself held nothing but an abandoned desk that was lit up like a Christmas tree. After checking beneath it, I moved toward the door on the far left.

"Fire department, call out!" I shouted when I opened the door.

The room was completely empty, with nowhere for anyone to hide or be trapped, so I pivoted to the middle door. The fire was growing higher, the smoke getting thicker. I had to clear these last two rooms and bail out *fast* before I got trapped.

The middle room was the same as the first, but I wasn't so

lucky with the third—and neither was the figure lying near the back wall, the flames inching closer and closer by the second.

"HEY!" I shouted.

The figure shifted slightly, and I breathed a sigh of relief.

Rescue, not a recovery.

Not yet at least.

I intended to keep it that way.

Rushing to their side, I realized the person was a woman whose wrists and ankles were bound with zip ties, and a gag was tied around her mouth. Even with the roaring of the fire, I could hear her sobs and muffled pleading as she pulled on her restraints.

"Miss, miss," I said as gently as I could while still conveying the sense of urgency our situation possessed. "I'm going to get you out of here, but I need you to calm down."

She stilled instantly, though her chest still heaved with her rapid breathing. I reached behind her, untying the gag and stuffing it in my pocket for safekeeping. Lane would never forgive me for leaving a potential piece of evidence behind.

"Please," she whimpered, turning her head toward me.

I startled, stumbling back a step.

"Aspen, oh my God," I breathed.

What the fuck? I'd last seen her less than two days ago. What the fuck had happened since then? How had she wound up here?

"Crew?"

I shook my head, getting back into the game. There'd be time for questions later, when we weren't in the middle of a burning building that could collapse at any second.

"It's okay, honey," I placated, the pet name rolling easily off my tongue. Reaching into my coat, I withdrew my small bolt cutter and used it to free her restraints, adding those to my pocket with the gag. She attempted to say something else, but instead inhaled a lungful of smoke and hacked out a cough instead.

Fuck, the smoke was getting worse, and she'd suffocate if I didn't get her out of here quickly.

Groping for my radio, I pressed the call button and shouted, "Got a vic! Office in the bravo-charlie corner! We're coming out, but I need cover!"

The radio crackled to life with a response immediately.

"Got you, Cap!" Davis replied. "Head back the way you went in!"

"Roger that!" I said then turned back to Aspen. "You ready to get out of here?" She nodded, and I grinned, trying to keep her calm. "I'm going to have you loop your arms around my neck and I'll carry you out. Okay?"

Aspen merely nodded. Bending down, I gingerly wedged my hands under her body. An agonized scream left her, and I when I jerked away, I found my gloves covered in blood and…fuck, was that *skin*? As gently as I could, I shifted her over so she rested on her right side and took stock of the damage.

Her clothing was ruined, and my gut churned at the sight of the burnt skin beneath, the fire having eaten right through to flesh. God, how had that happened? Had those burns been intentional?

Still not the time, I reminded myself.

"Aspen, I apologize in advance, but this is gonna fucking hurt." I grimaced when I squatted next to her. Before she could protest, I hauled her up into my arms. She screamed again, the sound fading to the whimpering and hissing of someone trying to breathe through the pain.

"We'll get you fixed up," I vowed to her as I shuffled out of the office and across reception. "Don't worry, Aspen. I've got you."

Her only response was a nod—a quick jerk of her head against my shoulder.

When we reached the hallway, Tuck was waiting.

"Follow me!" he shouted.

I was grateful for the assistance.

I curled my body around Aspen to shield her from further injury, making it difficult to keep my head up. The way out should've been a straight shot, but the air around us was hazy with grey smoke, making it difficult to see more than a few feet in front of us. I focused on Tuck's feet as he led the way.

An ominous creaking sounded from above us, and I dared a look up.

Fuck.

"Trusses are coming down!" I shouted at Tuck. "Move!"

He didn't need to be told twice and broke into a run—going as fast as he could in all his gear. I did my best to match his pace, trying not to jostle Aspen too much. But if we didn't get the fuck out of this building in the next fifteen seconds, we were all going to die.

We reached Davis, and Tuck yanked on his coat as we raced by, pulling him and the hose out with us.

No sooner had we stepped into the night than the roof collapsed with a thunderous *bang*, sending a fireball shooting into the sky. The force of the blast dropped me to my knees, and I barely maintained my grip on Aspen. When I managed to stumble back to my feet, still cradling her, I shouted to the engine crew.

"Scene is clear. Open 'em up!"

The hiss and sizzle of the two elements colliding filled the night air a beat later.

Before I could call for them, Sutton and Thomas were already at my side with a gurney.

"She's alive and lucid," I said as I laid her down on the gurney. "Name is Aspen McKay. Thirty-three, but I don't know anything else about her history. Definite smoke inhalation, and she's got some pretty gnarly burns on her left side."

As Sutton slipped an oxygen mask over Aspen's face, I

removed my gloves and pulled my SCBA off, deeply inhaling the fresh night air.

A hand wrapped around mine a moment later, and I glanced down to find Aspen had reached for me.

"Thank you," she croaked, letting me go as Sutton and Thomas hauled her away.

Tuck approached and settled a hand on my shoulder.

"Nice save, Cap."

I mock-saluted. "All in a day's work."

Tuck only grinned and bumped me with his shoulder.

"Let's go help those engine boys."

After a final look in the direction of the ambulance, sending a prayer up to the universe that Aspen would be okay, I faced the blazing building and got back to work.

six

. . .

ASPEN

THE FIRST THING I noticed upon waking was that my entire body screamed in pain, like I'd been run over by a train.

I'd barely cracked my eyelids only to slam them shut against the light threatening to blind me. On top of feeling like my body was a giant bruise, my head pounded like a jackhammer had taken up residence in my skull.

Breathing deeply, I willed the throbbing in my brain to recede enough to fully open my eyes. My other senses began to pick up on the happenings around me, and I strained my ears, attempting to figure out where the fuck I was and why.

First, I took stock of myself. I lay on my right side on a semi-soft surface, and any shifting around made my left side pull and pulse, like my skin was rubbed raw and blistered. My throat ached, and my mouth felt stuffed with cotton.

Beeping. Low, murmured voices. The squeak of rubber-soled shoes on the floor.

When the searing pain in my skull dulled to a slightly more manageable ache, I attempted to open my eyes again.

As soon as my lids parted, a yelp sounded from somewhere nearby and a moment later, a woman's face filled my vision.

I knew that face well. The same cinnamon-colored eyes set in my own face stared back at me.

"Oh, sweetheart," she breathed.

"Mom?"

"You're okay, honey. You were in a f-fire." She choked on the last word.

My heart stopped, then shattered.

Oh, not again.

Without thinking, I reached for her, but my progress was stalled by the IV plugged into the back of my hand. Forlornly, I let it drop to the bed at my side, but Mom reached for it anyway, clasping me so tightly it hurt, tugging at the catheter buried in my vein. I winced, but didn't let go.

The pain reminded me I was here, still breathing.

Reminded me that my parents hadn't lost their only remaining child—in the same way they'd lost the other one, no less.

My dad appeared behind Mom a moment later. His expression was…haggard, his normally clean-shaven face sporting prickly silver stubble. His skin sagged, and dark circles had taken up residence under his eyes. Warm brown hair, the same shade as mine, was limp and greasy. Mom looked much the same. Worn out and in dire need of some self-care.

Both of them had tears in their eyes, which swam with fear and pain and heartbreak.

Fuck. I hated that I was the reason for them.

"What happened?" I croaked. My throat was ravaged, and I had distant memories of screaming until I was convinced my lungs were bleeding.

I squeezed my eyes shut once more, hoping to stave off the onslaught of images that assaulted me.

Bindings on my wrists and ankles.

A windowless room and a cold concrete floor.

Gnawing hunger pains in my stomach.

Flames and heat.

Searing pain along my side.

Begging for anyone to save me.

And finally, an amorphous mass approaching me through the blaze, and gentle words in a gruff voice soothing me as best as they could, assuring me I'd be okay.

I was grateful the owner of that voice had kept their promise, because I was alive, and that was good enough for now.

"Ah, Miss McKay," someone said from the doorway, and I whipped my head in that direction, wincing as the sudden movement made my brain throb again. "Good to see you awake and alert."

It took a moment for my vision to clear, but when it did, I found a man standing there in a white doctor's coat with a clipboard in hand.

"What happened?" I asked again. "How long have I been here?" My panic rose the longer I went without answers.

This wasn't the first time I'd been injured on the job, but it was the first time things had felt so…bleak.

The doctor approached my bedside, his smile wide and welcoming if unnaturally white. He had warm brown eyes and dark hair that was more grey than brunette.

"You were in an accident last night."

I scoffed, or tried to, but it really came out as more of a choking sob. *An accident* was a…diplomatic and polite way of putting it.

"What day is it?"

"Sunday morning."

Okay, that eased some of my panic. Good to know I hadn't been unconscious for an extended period of time. I'd been at the bar on Friday night, which meant that fucker had held me captive for an entire day before leaving me in that building to die. My memory was so goddamn foggy, I was having difficulty remembering anything but flashes of the last thirty-six hours.

When I didn't respond, my mother asked, "What's the prognosis?"

"In addition to a large contusion on the back of her head that caused a minor concussion"—*that explained the headache*—"Aspen also sustained burns to roughly fifteen percent of her body, localized to her left posterior. They're mostly superficial, medically speaking," he tacked on as I opened my mouth to protest. There was nothing *superficial* about this level of pain. "Meaning, the wounds aren't so wide or deep that grafts will be necessary. I'm not going to lie, you'll have significant scarring, but they'll heal on their own."

"Exactly how bad are they, though?" I croaked. I knew there were levels—degrees—to burns. I'd be marked by this trauma for life, in more ways than one, but I wanted to know exactly how deeply these physical scars would run.

"Mostly second degree with slight areas of third," the doctor said, studying the papers in his hands. "You were very fortunate, Miss McKay."

Funny, I thought. *I don't feel fortunate.*

"So what's the treatment plan?" Dad asked.

"I understand it's not ideal, but we'll be keeping you for a few weeks."

"*A few weeks*?" I screeched.

He nodded solemnly. "This is a very precarious time in your healing journey. We need to ensure you're in a sterile environment and receiving routine and proper care in regards to medication and bandage changes. Plus, there's the matter of the concussion, which we'd like to monitor to ensure it doesn't become more severe. What's your pain level at right now?"

Before I could answer, Mom sputtered, "That's outrageous! She would be much better off coming home with us. Don't you think? Tell her, Donald," she urged my dad.

The doctor merely shook his head. "I understand the desire

to want your daughter under your care, but I'm afraid that's not possible."

"Don't I get a say in this?" I asked. I was growing exhausted by this whole production, my energy rapidly waning.

God, I needed a fucking glass of water, the strongest painkillers this place could legally give me, and to sleep for the next two weeks.

The doctor gave me a sympathetic smile. "Sorry, Miss McKay, but you remaining under our care is truly in your best interest."

"I agree," I said, and my mother inhaled a gasp, as though I'd deeply wounded her by daring to agree with my *doctor*. Then I added, "And my pain level is probably an eight. Now if you'll excuse me, I'm going to take a nap."

I was out before my eyes fully closed.

WHEN I AWOKE NEXT, the sky beyond the window of my room had darkened to that hazy orange-pink before dusk, gilding the mountains in a golden glow that reminded me, unfortunately, of fire.

I gave into a shiver and averted my gaze, then took stock of myself yet again.

The room was silent, meaning everyone had left—including my parents. Likely, they'd gone to freshen up while I rested.

I had no idea how long I'd slept, though long enough that my entire body was stiff from lack of movement. Then again, that could also be attributed to the fact that I was confined to this hospital bed. The pain in my head had dimmed from a sharp stabbing to a dull ache that went a long way to making me feel more alert.

Thankfully, I had the room to myself. The exit was on my left, window to my right, and a small TV was mounted high on the wall directly in front of me. Below was a whiteboard with scribbled notes regarding my condition, as well as a bulletin board tacked with numerous medical announcements and drug advertisements.

My mouth was still so dry you'd think I hadn't even heard the word "water" in several weeks, and the pressure on my bladder had reached painful levels. I was both surprised and pleased I didn't have a catheter.

As gingerly as I could, I shifted until I could reach the remote with the call button that rested on the small bedside table to my right.

Not long after I pressed it, a nurse shuffled in, smiling brightly at me.

"Hello, Miss McKay. What can I do for you?"

"Aspen," I said around my sore throat. "Please call me Aspen."

She winked. "Okay, Aspen. I'm Sonya."

"Nice to meet you, Sonya. I'd really love some water," I wheezed. "But first, I have to pee."

Her laugh as she approached me was a musical little tinkle that settled some of my anxiety. As gently as she could, she drew back the covers and shifted my legs over the edge of the mattress, careful not to go anywhere near my left side. I wasn't sure how far the burns extended, but I could feel the sting of them along my ribs as I moved around. With a deep breath and Sonya's hands under my arms, we managed to get me on my feet.

And I damn near collapsed, my legs feeling as strong as jelly, and only Sonya's support kept me upright.

With aching slowness, we shuffled across the room to the small bathroom in the corner by the door. Modesty went out the window as I gathered my hospital gown around my waist, pulled down the mesh underwear they'd dressed me in, and gingerly lowered onto the commode chair. I hissed as my backside made contact with the seat. Fuck, I even had burns on my ass.

Being an invalid was fucking humbling.

Once that task was completed, we got me settled back into bed, Sonya propping some pillows up against my back to make resting on my right side more comfortable. Then she brought me a small Styrofoam cup of water with a lid and a straw.

"Small sips," she instructed. "You don't want to make yourself sick."

Tentatively, I stuck the straw between my lips and sucked. The cool liquid was heaven on my tongue, and a moan slipped free.

"Good?" Sonya asked with a knowing grin.

"Best water I've ever tasted."

That laugh echoed around us again. "I'm going to go see if I can scrounge you up some soup from the cafeteria. I'm assuming you have no idea when you last ate."

"Please. I don't even know what day it is," I joked.

"Sunday," she said with a wink before she disappeared.

After a few more sips of water, I set the cup on the tray at my side and closed my eyes. The trip to the bathroom had sapped nearly all of my energy, and I doubted I'd be awake when Sonya returned.

But I tried.

In an effort to see exactly where my injuries began and ended, I reached my right arm across my body and gently probed my left side, bending my left arm at an awkward angle that pulled at my skin. From what I could tell, the burns began midway down my ribcage and extended down my thigh, a few inches below the curve of my ass. The bandages felt too hot against my fingertips, like my skin was still on fire. Dropping my arm, I closed my eyes once again. I was so damn exhausted, right down to the very marrow of my bones.

I hovered on the edge of unconsciousness, wondering what kind of mess I had gotten myself into.

seven

. . .

ASPEN

FOOTSTEPS ECHOED in the hall outside my room and paused in the doorway. I didn't bother to open my eyes. Maybe Sonya would leave the soup and go. I could eat it cold, right?

But the tentative shuffle on the floor of my room had them flying open anyway, and I was confronted with the looming presence of a large tattooed man in a sheriff's uniform.

"Miss McKay?" Sheriff Lawless asked gently. "I'm sorry, I didn't wake you, did I?"

"No," I assured him. "I was only resting my eyes."

He nodded. "You must be exhausted," he said. "But if you're up for it, I'd like to get your statement about what happened to you?"

The man standing before me now was a far cry from the burly, take-no-bullshit man who'd sat across from me in his office three days before. The rough edges of the tone he'd used with me before were smoothed and softened, as though I was as delicate as glass, liable to shatter under his previous harshness.

He wasn't treating me like a common citizen or a pest he wanted to be rid of anymore.

Now…I was a fucking *victim*.

I hated that. Hated the pity in his eyes and his tentative movements. I squeezed my eyes shut, face heating with embarrassment as tears leaked out and trailed down my face.

Had I mentioned yet that I was exhausted?

Was I up for an interview? I knew as well as anyone that law enforcement wanted to strike while the iron was hot with these sorts of things, before time warped my memory and tainted my recollection. But the simple truth was, at the moment, I didn't remember much of anything.

"I-I'm not sure," I stuttered.

"I can come back," he said, almost as if he *wanted* to leave. And I couldn't blame him. No one liked hospitals.

My mouth opened to ask him to come back later, but I stopped myself, deciding it was better to rip off the metaphorical bandage and get it the hell over with.

"Okay," I whispered.

The sheriff withdrew a phone from his pocket. "Do you mind if I record this?"

"No."

After tapping on the screen a few times, he held the device to his mouth and said, "Sheriff Lane Lawless interviewing Aspen McKay on April twenty-third at approximately nineteen hundred hours." He moved around to my right side and pulled up a chair, setting the phone on the table between us. "Start from the beginning."

"Like the day I was born, or…"

One corner of his mouth hitched up, but he didn't admonish me. Like he understood I needed to mask my pain and fear with sarcasm. The knowledge had me relaxing slightly.

"How about when you arrived in town?" he prompted.

Okay, that I could do.

"Have you done any background on me?"

Lane shook his head. "Not yet. I prefer to get a feel for a person before I go rifling through their history."

Another point in the sheriff's favor.

"I'm a licensed private investigator, based primarily out of Denver," I started. "About three weeks ago, I got an email about this place, and the Prom Night Arsonist—" I stopped, shivering at the name. Knowing this sick, twisted human had put his hands on me. Had tried to kill me.

The beeping of the heart rate monitor increased speed, and the sheriff laid a hand over mine.

"It's okay, Miss McKay. Take your time."

"I'm staying at that little motel on the edge of town. You know the one?"

The sheriff nodded. "Out by the highway. Yeah, I'm familiar with it."

The way he said it told me the place had a reputation about as good as its accommodations, which was to say…not very.

"I got to town about a week ago and set up shop there. I have a list of people I wanted to interview, but those first few days, I wandered. I got a lay of the land, took the temperature of the townsfolk, got a feel for how easy or difficult they'd make this on me."

"And?"

I shrugged, then winced as the movement tugged on my bandages.

"I was genuinely surprised by their friendliness."

"Dusk Valley is a friendly place."

I snorted. "Maybe to you. But I haven't always been welcomed with open arms. And of course, once word about who I was and what I was doing in town started to get around, they became…chilly."

My throat caught on the final word, and I coughed, pausing a moment to sip some more water. Damn, where was Sonya when I needed her? I could've really used that soup.

"Chilly, how?"

"There was a bartender at the Swallow. Pretty rude guy."

The sheriff chuckled. "Benny. He's always been a bit of an asshat to women who don't want to sleep with him."

That made a lot of sense actually, and I nodded.

"What happened on Friday?"

"Well, first, we need to back up to Wednesday, when I went to the fire station. I spoke with the chief about taking a look at their old incident reports from those fires, and he was more than happy to help me out. Even set me up with the captain to go over them. I believe you know him?"

The sheriff blinked slowly, then cursed under his breath, and I grinned. I was deeply pleased to have caught him off guard—to know Crew hadn't told him about this.

"For the record, you're talking about Crew Lawless?" he gritted out. "My little brother?"

There was nothing *little* about that man, but I was glad I'd guessed correctly that Lane was older.

"The very same. He was on shift on Wednesday, but Thursday morning, we met for breakfast at the diner and spent a few hours going over the incident reports. Then I went back to my motel room and pored over them myself."

"Fucking Crew," he whispered, then blanched when he realized he'd said it on the record. "Sorry. Then what happened?"

"I had lunch, then came to see you."

Succinctly, the sheriff relayed for the record the details of our meeting, giving me a moment to sip some water and attempt to conjure up more of what exactly had happened to me.

Unfortunately for him, I still had nothing for memories beyond leaving the Swallow but a smoking pile of ash.

"On Friday night, Black Betty and I took a ride around town, checking out a few of the crime scenes, and then went to the Swallow."

"Black Betty?" the sheriff interrupted.

"My Suburban."

"Black?"

"What gave it away?"

He shot me a warning look. "We found one with Colorado plates abandoned in the lot at the Swallow," he said.

"Yeah, that's mine. Where did it end up?"

"Towed it to the impound lot at the auto body shop, but you can get it back with no charge once the doctors let you out of here."

I heaved a sigh of relief. The last thing I could afford right now was having to pay a monumental towing bill and impound on top of all the medical bills that would likely wipe out my entire savings.

"Oh fuck," I breathed as another thought occurred to me.

"You remembering something?"

"I had a bag," I explained. "Had my wallet, keys, taser, and other necessities in it. Is it…do you see it around here anywhere? Or maybe my phone?"

God, my head hurt too fucking bad to be worried about this shit right now, yet I couldn't stop.

The sheriff stood and walked around. "No," he said. "Maybe the staff is keeping that stuff elsewhere? Or maybe it perished in the fire?"

"Maybe," I conceded, though there was no conviction in the word. Likely, my attempted murderer had disposed of my things prior to leaving me in that building to die, making it more difficult to identify me in the event I didn't survive, which was exactly what they'd been banking on.

"So anyway," I pressed on, rubbing my fingers over my forehead in an attempt to ease the ache. "I ordered a beer, chatted up the bartender—Benny, you said?" He nodded. "Obviously, he wasn't very forthcoming, and told me to give it up and leave. I wasn't about to do that, but after an unfortunate collision that ended with me wearing my beer, all I wanted was to take a shower and crawl into bed."

"Did someone do that on purpose?" he asked.

"Nah," I assured him. "I accidentally bumped into a woman and wound up dumping my beer on myself."

"Were those the only two interactions you had at the bar?" I nodded, bracing for what I knew came next. "So you left?"

"I tried," I corrected. "Almost made it back to my SUV before someone attacked me."

"Did you see anything?"

"No. They came at me from behind and hit me over the head."

My fingers found the burns on my neck, and I shivered as I tried to remember the assault. How the dark figure had come out of seemingly nowhere. Lying on the dirt, gasping for air, blood from my nose coating my teeth and tongue.

The altercation beyond that was such a blur, and the time between my abduction and waking up in that garage building was completely absent—likely my brain's way of protecting me from the trauma. The harder I tried to bring things from that night into focus, the more other memories appeared.

A different town halfway across the country.

City lights beyond the windows of a white-washed apartment.

A different attacker, more than one, a different set of injuries.

A different hospital, but the same smells, sounds. Same parents crying over the near loss of another daughter.

Pain. Pain. Pain.

Like a morbid, fucked up slideshow, memories from then and now layered over each other.

Barely making it to the phone to call for help.

Calls for help echoing back at me from the concrete warehouse, unanswered.

Around and around they went until I no longer knew where, when, or who I was. My breaths sawed in and out of me, and though I could hear voices calling, repeating a name that seemed vaguely familiar, I struggled to find my way toward it.

My temples pounded, my brain a messy, tangled web of sounds and sensations.

"Sheriff!" someone shouted, cracking through my delirium. "What are you doing to her?"

"Nothing!" came the reply.

"Aspen," a female voice said, closer now. Distantly, I registered her grabbing my hand. "Look at me."

I had no memory of even closing my eyes, but I did as she asked. It felt like my lungs were being squeezed by a fist, tighter and tighter. My pulse throbbed in my head.

"I need you to take deep breaths," she, who I recognized as my nurse, Sonya, commanded, showing me what to do. "In for four, out for six. Let's do it together."

In tandem, Sonya and I counted, the numbers leaving me in gasps, until the obnoxious beeping—which I belatedly realized was my heart rate monitor—stopped, until I could fully inhale once again.

Too embarrassed to look at him, I rubbed my temples and kept my gaze on the wall ahead as I said to Lane, "I'm sorry, Sheriff. Can we do this another day?"

Finally daring to meet his gaze, I scanned the room, finding him standing by the door.

But he was no longer alone.

It's okay, honey.

We'll get you fixed up.

Don't worry, Aspen. I've got you.

"Crew."

eight

· · ·

CREW

AS A FIRST RESPONDER, I'd gotten really good at pulling victims out of fires, leaving them in the care of paramedics, and moving on with my life. That was the job: make the save, then forget about them. Over and over and over. Getting attached was not only frowned upon, but could be dangerous as well. When we were on shift, our entire focus had to be centered on every call.

That wasn't to say a lot of the guys in the department didn't have families, because they did. Chief Madden, in particular, had been married for over twenty years and had a daughter and son. Most of us were younger, though, still sowing our wild oats before ultimately settling down.

Not that I was sure I'd ever reach that point.

All that was to say, something about Aspen McKay had drawn me in the first time I laid eyes on her, and I'd spent every second since that call worried about her.

According to Sutton, she was stable when they dropped her off, but her burns were a concern. Aspen seemed like a tough woman, though, and somehow I knew she'd be okay.

Still, I wanted to see it with my own eyes.

I was damn near itching to get off shift the morning after so I could go visit her at the hospital.

Unfortunately, after shift, I desperately needed sleep. Typically, I worked one twenty-four hour shift with two days off in between, but the lieutenant on first shift—the one that came before ours in the rotation—had to take some unexpected personal time off, so I stepped up to cover him. Doubles were no joke, especially in my line of work, and I was exhausted.

I lived about fifteen minutes out of town, right on the edge of my family's land. When I moved home five years ago and decided I was staying for good, I built my spacious house. Maybe one day I'd fill it with a wife and kids. I'd never really envisioned myself as a family man outside of my mom, brothers, and little sister, but maybe that would change if I met the right woman.

I resolutely did *not* entertain the flash of dark hair and set of peculiar brown eyes that flashed through my mind.

I loved living out here. After spending five years in Chicago, followed by another three working campaign fires in northern California, I savored the peace and quiet. I was close enough to town that it didn't take me long to get to work, and we'd cut a dirt track through the woods ages ago so I could go to the ranch for family dinners without having to go all the way around the craggy hills in between.

My driveway was shaded on both sides by towering pine trees that provided cover year round. The narrow lane approached my house with an attached garage that sat at the edge of a large swatch of field. Hitting the button over my head in my truck, I waited for the garage door to open and pulled inside.

Once I was parked, I turned it off and leaned my head back against the seat, closing my eyes and basking in the stillness broken only by the ticking of my cooling engine.

Finally finding the energy, I got out of the truck and approached the door leading into my mudroom, punching in the code to quiet my security system as it began beeping with the breach.

As I did every time I entered and exited my house, I silently cursed my brother, Trey, for forcing me to install the ridiculous system.

I lived in no man's land, and I could protect myself. I didn't need the bells and whistles doing it for me. Especially not when I knew he could easily access the feed to the cameras he'd set up around the property whenever he wanted.

He was taking the term *big brother* a bit too literally.

Unceremoniously, I tossed my bag through the door into the laundry room, not even having the energy to walk it inside. Then I kicked off my boots and padded down the hall, past the open kitchen-living-dining room and down another hallway to my room.

After stripping naked, I climbed into the cool sheets and heaved a sigh of relief, all the tension bleeding from my muscles as I relaxed into my mattress.

But sleep didn't come easily, my mind still whirring with thoughts of Aspen and that fire.

I had so many questions, not only about her, but about this fucker that had tried to take her from this world.

With each year that passed without a single clue or lead, it felt like any chance of catching the guy slipped further and further away.

But…he'd never left anyone alive before. And Aspen wasn't simply *any* woman—she was a private investigator now personally invested in the case, more so than whatever had drawn her to it in the first place.

Aspen had an admirable sort of tenacity, and I knew she'd stop at nothing to catch this guy, even if it meant putting herself back in danger. The thought didn't sit right with me, and though I knew it was a bad idea for a thousand different reasons, I also knew I'd be keeping an eye on her once she was released from the hospital.

I couldn't quite pinpoint what about this woman had me twisted in knots, but for once, I wasn't questioning it or planning on running from it. Never before had I experienced the electricity that coursed through me when Aspen was near. For once, I wanted to chase that feeling, to run headlong into the storm.

As a rule, I didn't do relationships. While I'd done a lot of work to heal and better myself from my disastrous teenage years, I didn't have the mental or physical energy to devote to making someone else happy. A serious, deeply committed relationship seemed inadvisable when I wasn't sure I was all that happy myself.

With Aspen, I wasn't looking for anything beyond a couple nights—or maybe weeks—spent buried in her tight little body before she left town. That was all I could spare, and I had a feeling she was in a similar boat.

At last, with thoughts of her cinnamon eyes and perfect pink mouth floating at the forefront of my brain, I fell into a deep sleep.

***

WHEN I WOKE AGAIN, the sun had mostly set, and my stomach rumbled insistently. I got up, ate, showered, and headed for the hospital.

Upon walking through the doors of Dusk Valley Memorial, I was reminded how much I hated the place.

I'd been standing in a third floor hallway when I found out my dad was dead.

I'd spent more than a few nights in my youth having my stomach pumped from overindulging in things that were bad for me and nearly cost me my own life.

So many bad memories assaulted me at once, freezing me in place right inside the sliding doors.

I had no idea how long I stood there before my name being called broke me from my trance.

"Crew!"

I glanced up to see one of the nurses, Sonya, waving at me.

Sonya was somewhere in her forties, though with her practically ageless complexion, I couldn't tell for sure. All I knew was she was older than me and beautiful, her ebony hair pulled back in a no-nonsense bun at the base of her skull, her pink scrubs bright against her deep brown skin.

I smiled, her familiar face settling some of my nerves.

"Hey, Sonya," I said as I approached. "Where you headed?"

She hooked a thumb over her shoulder. "Cafeteria. Gotta get a patient some soup."

"Speaking of patients…"

Sonya's eyes narrowed knowingly. "You're wondering about that girl, aren't you?"

I nodded, giving her a sheepish grin. "How is she?"

"That's actually who I'm getting soup for, so why don't you come see for yourself?"

Like a puppy dog, I trailed after Sonya to the cafeteria.

As Dusk Valley was the seat of the county, albeit a small one, we had a serviceable hospital that could handle most major incidents. That Aspen hadn't been transferred up to Boise for additional, more specialized care was a good sign.

Sonya and I chatted about our families while she conned the cafeteria workers into heating up some soup, despite the fact that the dinner window had closed hours ago. Then I followed her up to the fourth floor where Aspen was staying.

All was mostly quiet when we stepped out of the elevator.

"We've only got a few overnight patients right now," Sonya said. "Little Bobby Ma—"

Her words cut off as a loud, insistent beeping filled the hallway. The man standing at the nurse's station glanced at the wall then to Sonya said, "Four seventeen."

"Fuck," Sonya breathed, and I was momentarily startled. I'd never heard her curse once in the entire time I'd known her, which was damn near my entire life.

She shoved the tray of food into my hands and took off running. As quickly as I could without spilling the soup everywhere, I followed after her.

"Sheriff!" I heard Sonya shout. "What are you doing to her?"

"Nothing!" a man yelped—a voice I recognized very well.

It took a moment for my brain to comprehend the scene when I reached the doorway to the room. My brother, Lane, stood in the center, hands raised as he stared at the woman on the bed.

Aspen.

Her eyes were squeezed shut, tears rolling down her cheeks, chest rising and falling rapidly, fingers white-knuckled as she gripped the blankets covering her.

Clearly in the throes of a panic attack.

In the nighttime, I hadn't gotten a good enough look to see the purple bruising and swollenness around her eyes. And if I had, I likely would've assumed it was soot from the fire. In addition to the bandages around her head, she had one across her nose.

God, this fucker hadn't simply tried to kill her. He'd *beaten* her first.

Something primal perked up in my chest, demanding I go to her, cradle her in my arms, and comfort her until she calmed down. The deep-seated protective instinct roared to life, stronger and louder than ever, claiming Aspen as his. I saved lives daily, but that baser instinct had never been so adamant before. It took every single ounce of self-control I possessed to remain rooted in place, on the fringes of Aspen's life where I belonged.

"Aspen," Sonya said gently, reaching for one of Aspen's hands. "Look at me."

Aspen's eyes flew open, locking on Sonya's.

"I need you to take deep breaths," Sonya urged. "In for four, hold for four, out for six. Let's do it together."

Sonya slowed her breathing and counted as she inhaled, Aspen following along, each word no more than a gasp of air. Lane and I stood by, watching as Sonya expertly brought Aspen down from her panic attack.

"What the fuck did you do to her?" I hissed at Lane.

Lane cut me with a side eye. "I was taking her statement."

I growled. "You couldn't have waited a few weeks?"

"You know it's best to do these things as soon as possible afterward."

"Well clearly, she wasn't ready to talk about it."

"I see that now," Lane gritted out.

At last, Aspen's breathing returned to normal. Her fingers trembled as she lifted her hands to rub her temples, gaze fixed ahead, face red—almost like she was embarrassed.

She'd suffered a deep, nearly life-ending trauma, and she was embarrassed? About what? God, I wanted to deck my brother, having no doubt he was the cause of her inflamed cheeks.

"I'm sorry, Sheriff," Aspen said weakly. "Can we do this another day?"

At last, she sought Lane out, though when she found me next to him, our gazes collided and held, her eyes widening.

I could practically see the memories of the night before playing on a loop in her eyes like an old school film projector.

"Crew," she breathed.

"Hey, Aspen."

Some emotion I couldn't name flickered in her expression, those gorgeous cinnamon depths once again welling with unshed tears, a stray slipping free and rolling all the way to the edge of her jaw. Clinging for dear life.

Why was I gripped by the sudden urge to go to her and brush it away?

Before I could do something stupid, a petite woman barreled into the room, shoving me out of the way as she rushed to Aspen's side, followed by a man with hair the same shade as Aspen's.

My eyes flitted between Aspen and the newcomers, deciding these must be her parents.

"What in the world is going on here?" her mom demanded.

"You must be Mrs. McKay," Lane said, having come to the same conclusion as me, stepping forward and extending his hand. "I'm Sheriff Lawless. I'm here to take Aspen's statement regarding the fire."

"Less than twenty-four hours later?" she hissed. "I don't mean to be rude, Sheriff, but that's incredibly insensitive." Mrs. McKay gestured to her daughter, who was visibly upset. "She's clearly not ready."

Sufficiently chastened, Lane bowed his head like he'd been scolded by our own mother, murmuring his apologies.

Then Mrs. McKay's stare landed on me.

"And who are you?"

"I—"

"He's the one who saved me, Mom," Aspen whispered.

"Oh!" Mrs. McKay squeaked, rushing across the room and throwing her arms around me in a hug that was surprisingly crushing given how tiny she was.

Awkwardly, I wrapped my arms around her shoulders and gently patted her back as she sobbed into my shirt. Aspen looked on with a bemused grin. Aspen's father merely gave me a curt nod and mouthed, "Thank you."

I appreciated that much more than I did the woman clinging to my body.

After long, uncomfortable minutes, Mrs. McKay finally let go and swiped the tears from her face.

"Thank you…" she trailed off.

"Oh, Crew, ma'am. Crew Lawless."

A brow raised. "Lawless?" She hooked her thumb at Lane. "You related to this one?"

I fought back a chuckle at her unimpressed tone. "Yes, ma'am. He's my brother."

Mrs. McKay pursed her lips, eyes darting between us, then said, "Well, at least one of you has some sense."

This time, my laughter bubbled free, unbidden, and Lane's face darkened like a thunder cloud.

"I'll see myself out," he said petulantly. "I'll be in touch, Miss McKay."

Aspen weakly saluted him.

"Do you want to walk the scene Tuesday morning?" I murmured to him before he could leave. "I'll be back on shift."

Lane nodded. "Around ten? We can meet at the garage."

"Yeah, as long as no early calls come in."

"See you then," he said, then disappeared down the hall.

Returning my attention to the room, I found four sets of eyes watching me expectantly.

"Is that for me?" Aspen croaked, glancing pointedly at the tray of food I still carried.

"Oh! Yeah," I said awkwardly, moving to her bedside. "Sonya kind of passed it off to me when we heard the commotion."

"Good thing," Aspen said. "I'm starving."

"Small bites," Sonya warned as she walked out, leaving me alone with the McKay family.

"Here, honey," Mrs. McKay said to her daughter but approached me and reached for the tray. "Let me feed you."

"Moooooooooom," Aspen groaned. "I'm thirty-three, not three. I can feed myself."

Mrs. McKay sniffed. "I'm only trying to help."

"You're hovering," Aspen deadpanned. "I'm fine."

Aspen's mother huffed out a disgusted sigh. "We fly across

the country to be by your side while you heal and this is how you repay us? You're terribly ungrateful, Aspen."

"I'm not ungrateful," Aspen murmured. "I'm exhausted and in pain, but I'm still perfectly capable of feeding myself."

Mrs. McKay sighed heavily and opened her mouth to further the argument, but her husband put a hand on her arm.

"Leesa."

All the fight left Mrs. McKay with the utterance of her name, and she nodded at her husband. To Aspen she said, "Okay, honey. I'll just sit with you then. Is that okay?"

Aspen smiled at her. "Of course, Mom."

"Would you like to join us?" Mr. McKay asked, mirroring his wife by pulling up a seat on Aspen's other side.

"Ah, no. That's okay. I only wanted to check on Aspen, and now that I see she's okay, I'm gonna go."

I turned to leave, but Aspen calling my name stalled me in the doorway, and I glanced back over my shoulder at her.

"Thank you," she said, her parents echoing the sentiment.

"Anytime," I promised.

And then I was gone.

nine

. . .

CREW

I UNDERSTOOD TENSE FAMILY RELATIONSHIPS, and Aspen's with her parents was really the least of my concerns, but I couldn't shake off the interaction I'd witnessed. The way both Aspen and her father had quickly diffused the situation told me they'd likely done it countless times before.

Less than thirty-six hours later, as I strode into the station for my next shift, it still played on a loop in my mind. For some reason, I found I genuinely cared how her parents treated her. While I believed her mom meant well, the last thing Aspen needed was stress in the form of overparenting. I'd been in that position myself, and it fucking sucked. Like every single move you made—big or small—was examined under a microscope.

"Sup, Cap," Tuck said when I walked into the locker room.

"I could've used another day off," I grumbled. My sleep schedule was all sorts of fucked up.

"That's what you get for working a double," he chided. "You could've appointed an acting lieutenant for first shift."

I scoffed. "I don't trust any of those fuckers enough to do that."

Tuck laughed. "Fair enough."

I dropped my bag and opened my locker, then began stripping out of my street clothes in favor of my uniform.

I tugged my polo over my head, and a voice called my name. I turned to find Lane standing at the end of the row.

"Sheriff," Tuck said, tipping an imaginary hat to my brother as he left the room.

Lane shook his head. "Amazing that kid became a firefighter considering the number of times I arrested him when I first joined the force."

"You could say the same about me," I pointed out.

"Yeah, but at least you got out of town and made something of yourself."

"Tuck is a hell of a firefighter, Lane," I told him, leveling a finger in his face. "Don't insult my men. Ever."

Blood was thicker than water and all that, and I loved my family fiercely, but my men and I were forged in the fire together. Sometimes, I thought that was a stronger bond than anything else. The trust we had to place in each other to come out of every call alive meant opening ourselves up fully. There couldn't be secrets. Everything had to be out in the open because our—and other people's—lives depended on it.

My brother raised his hands in surrender and said, "Okay. Sorry."

I only gave him a curt nod in response, then asked, "Why are you here?"

"We're walking the shop fire today." His eyes narrowed. "Did you forget?"

Pinching the bridge of my nose, I willed myself not to react to his goading.

"No, I didn't forget, but I just walked in the door." I gestured to my boots, the laces still undone, and my shirt folded up around my chest where I hadn't fully pulled it on. "And I thought we were meeting there."

"I wanted to get a jump on things."

I bit my tongue, holding back my retort. This was so like my brother, to ignore set plans in favor of his own schedule—even though meeting at the site at ten had been his suggestion in the first place.

"I haven't even conducted the morning meeting yet."

Lane turned and gestured to the door. "Then by all means, Captain."

With a grumble, I led the way out of the locker room and down the short hall to our meeting room, where the entire company was already gathered, waiting for me.

Chief Madden was the highest ranking officer in this firehouse, but when I was promoted to captain, he asked me to take over morning meetings. Usually, there wasn't much to say, and I mainly focused on reminding the guys about completing incident reports, making sure they stopped throwing their dirty clothes on the floor of the bunk room, and telling them—again—to clean up after themselves in the kitchen. Scheduled maintenance on the trucks and tools. Housekeeping-type shit.

Basically, I was more of a parent than a fire captain.

But this morning, we actually had some things to discuss, and the crowd silenced as Lane and I strode to the front of the room.

"Morning," I said when I reached the little podium waiting for me in front of a massive whiteboard.

"Morning," everyone murmured back.

"What's he doing here?" Sutton asked, jerking her chin at my brother.

"I need to take statements from everyone who worked the shop fire on Saturday," Lane said, shooting the paramedic a glare.

Ahh, at last, the real reason for his early arrival. It grated on me that he hadn't just said that. He knew damn well we'd cooperate in whatever way we could.

Sutton stuck her tongue out in response, and I choked back a laugh. Those two had long since made an artform of needling each other.

"You'll give the sheriff your full cooperation," I told the room, meeting the gazes of each firefighter and paramedic individually, hoping to put the fear of God in them.

"Aye, aye, Cap," Tuck said, giving me a mock salute.

The rest of the meeting was business as usual, and less than ten minutes later, I dismissed everyone, hanging back so Lane could take my statement first.

I really should've known my brother would give me the third degree—and not about the fire.

"Why were you at Miss McKay's room the other night?"

Fuck.

"I wanted to check on her."

My brother raised a brow. "Since when do you check on your saves after shipping them off to the hospital?"

"Always," I deadpanned.

Lane snorted. "Get real, baby bro. Give me the real reason, no bullshit."

"Like I said, I wanted to check on her."

That much was the truth, if only part of it.

As usual, my brother saw too much.

"There's more to it than that."

Pulling out one of the chairs at a nearby table, I sat down and pushed my fingers through my floppy hair, destroying the work of the pomade I'd put in it that morning to keep it out of my face while I worked.

"I don't know what to tell you," I said at last, because I truly didn't.

Lane sighed heavily, like this conversation with me was the most exhausting thing he'd do all day.

"Fair enough," he said. "But I'm warning you—stay out of this."

I pursed my lips. "I'm already involved, bro. I've responded to two of these scenes now." Rising to my feet, I got in his face. "And *I* made the save that got you your only living witness."

My brother merely blinked at me, not saying anything. Recognizing that there was more going on here if I was getting this worked up about it.

Wisely, he didn't press the issue, only sat across from me and pulled out his phone to record our conversation.

"Sheriff Lane Lawless," he started. "Going on record with Dusk Valley Fire Department Captain Crew Lawless regarding the events of the prom night auto shop fire."

He rattled off the date of the incident, case number, and a few other identifying details before he said to me, "Walk me through what happened."

I'd done this enough times over the years that I was down-right emotionless as I gave Lane the rundown. He'd have my formal incident report to supplement this interview, but he liked to get his information straight from the horse's mouth.

When I finished half an hour later, after Lane asked seemingly incessant probing questions, he let me go and asked me to send Tuck in. For the rest of the morning, we sat around the common room shooting the shit.

Honestly, that was a normal day at the firehouse. Small towns weren't exactly notorious for being busy in general, and the same could be said for the fire department. There had been talk for years of downsizing us to a volunteer outfit, but with the constant threat of forest fires that could travel miles in a blink, the town voted against it every time it came up on a ballot, and for that I was thankful.

I wasn't meant to do anything else with my life but this: fight fires and save people. I wouldn't *survive* doing anything else. And really, what else was there? Join Trey's security firm? Pass. Work on the ranch for Finn or West? Double pass.

No, I wasn't meant for that shit. I was right where I needed to be.

Finally, Lane wrapped up his interview with the last of the crew that had been at the fire, which wound up being Sutton, and followed her out of the meeting room.

"You boys feel like taking a ride to the scene?" he asked, jerking his head at me, Tuck, Childers, and Burns.

The other three men were on their feet before I could even agree. We were all going a bit stir crazy without any calls; the fresh air and doing something useful would be good for us.

We piled into the truck, gear and equipment ready to go in case a call came through while we were out, then followed Lane's sheriff's SUV to the other side of town.

I'd thought the building looked bad that night after we'd knocked down the flames, turning it into nothing more than a smoking husk of its former self against the starry, Idahoan sky.

Nothing could've prepared me for seeing it in the daylight.

"Jesus Christ," Tuck breathed when he pulled the truck to a stop on the curb. "How the fuck did we get out of there alive?"

He'd stolen the words right out of my mouth.

The structure had completely collapsed, imploding in the center, taking the entire roof and the tops of the exterior walls with it. Nothing living could've survived the roof coming down, and considering how close Tuck, Aspen, and I had come to never walking out was terrifying.

But we were alive, and what was even better was knowing that Aspen, the initial target, also still drew breath. For the first time since this killer became active, law enforcement had a witness. I could understand why Lane wanted me to stay out of this—or rather, what he'd really been saying when he warned me off: *stay away from her*.

I'd be damned if I could do that. There was no logical way to explain it except to say there was some larger force at work. While I'd been interested in the outcome of this case before, both because I'd already pulled a dead body out of a fire as a result of this sicko's actions, and because I wanted him to stop terrorizing my town, things felt…different now.

Aspen was different.

But how did I tell that to my brother? I barely knew the girl. Flirting over chicken and waffles then saving her life didn't make me an expert on her—nor did it explain my fascination.

"Alright," Lane said as we exited our vehicles and stood on the concrete drive in front of the building. "Time for a reenactment."

Even though we'd already been through this with my verbal statement, showing Lane exactly what had gone down by walking him around the property was much easier. My brother was a hands-on kind of guy. Entering the structure was a nonstarter, mainly because the roof now rested on the concrete floors. So we walked the perimeter, and the guys and I pointed exactly where we'd gone and when.

"And where did you find Miss McKay?" my brother asked.

I led him around the side toward where the offices had once been. "She was in this office here," I said, gesturing to the badly damaged half of a wall that remained standing. "Tied up and gagged." Fuck, that reminded me…"Hold that thought."

I raced for the truck and my gear. Before reaching into the pocket, I put one of my gloves on then withdrew the cloth and zipties I'd found on Aspen.

Holding them out to Lane when I returned, I said, "Here."

Lane quirked a brow. "The fuck is this?"

"The gag and restraints I removed from Aspen when I found her."

"And where have they been since?"

"My turnout coat pocket."

"Crew…" my brother began, his face turning red as his blood pressure obviously rose.

"If you're worried about chain of custody," I started before he could lay into me, "I literally took them off her and stuffed it in my pocket, where they remained until about a minute ago."

"You're a real fucking pain in my ass."

"Could've been worse. They could've been left here," I argued, gesturing to the destroyed building. "At least now you might be able to get DNA not belonging to Aspen off them."

Lane eyed me warily. "You really haven't touched them with your bare hands?"

"Nope," I said proudly, dangling them in his face, and my guys choked on their laughter.

Finally, he stomped to his SUV and came back with an evidence bag. I slid the cloth and plastic inside, and he sealed it.

"Now, back to business," he said. "Did you notice anything unusual at the time?"

Tuck and I shared a glance, remembering that distinct smell that had lingered in the air.

"The scent of diesel hung in the air like a cloud."

"Could've been lingering from the shop," Lane pointed out.

"I said the same thing," Tuck supplied. "But it was pretty obvious that wasn't the case."

"How do you know?"

"There was a trail," I told him. "The entire structure was burning, of course. Once it climbed the walls and entered the trusses, there was really no saving it. It wasn't a matter of *if* it would come down, but *when*. But there was an obvious path, scorch marks, that led us from the exterior door"—I pointed toward where we'd breached—"to the entrance of the offices. I bet it'd still be visible if we cleared the rubble."

"So you followed it back here?" Lane asked, his jaw clenched in anger over my recklessness.

The instinct to protect ran deep and true in me and my brothers, and even though I'd only been doing my job, Lane clearly hated that I'd put myself in danger.

"Yes."

My voice didn't waver. And put in that situation again, I'd make the same choice—over and over and over.

Big brother didn't get to tell me how to do my job simply because he was older and supposedly wiser. I'd been a firefighter longer than he'd been a cop; he knew I knew what I was doing.

"Why?"

"There was an obvious fucking trail, *Sheriff*," I gritted out. "Like hell I wasn't going to follow it."

"He had backup," Tuck quipped, shrugging when my brother cut him a glare. "I followed him in, Sheriff."

"Then you're both idiots," Lane muttered, moving back around to the front.

Tuck and I wordlessly followed.

"Anybody got a diagram of this place?" he asked when we reached him. "Like, do you have schematics of the buildings in town?"

I shook my head. "Only the ones we deem extremely dangerous and high-risk. But the city planning office would have them."

Lane withdrew his phone from his pocket and tapped the screen a few times, then held it to his ear.

"Hey, this is Sheriff Lawless calling." He paused. "Yeah, I'm good. How are you? The kids?" Another beat. "Great. Hey, look, I'm calling because I'm hoping you could get me the building schematic of Mack's old auto shop." Lane quieted and rolled his eyes. "Yes, that one. Yeah, what happened to that girl was awful, but she's alive, and we're going to find who did this to her. Yes. Yes, I promise. Now how about that schematic?" More silence from Lane, and then his face broke into a grin. "Great. I'll be by to get it in about ten minutes. No, thank you. Yep. Bye."

"Carmon?" I asked with a brow raised.

Lane chuckled and shook his head. "Naturally."

Carmon was the county clerk, and while she was a nice woman and great at her job, she was also a terrible gossip. There wasn't a thing that happened in this town that she didn't immediately know about—which meant everyone else knew about it not long after.

"Alright, you go get that schematic and we'll meet back at the firehouse."

No sooner had the words left my mouth than my radio crackled to life.

"Truck twenty-seven. Multiple vehicle accident on Highway twenty-two. Requesting fire and rescue."

The moment the dispatcher's voice died on my radio, that same scratchy voice relayed the same information through Lane's.

We looked at each other and shrugged, breaking apart and racing for our respective vehicles.

Duty called.

ten

. . .

CREW

THREE HOURS LATER, after extracting multiple injured persons from a pretty gnarly crash out on the highway—no one died, thankfully, but they were all pretty banged up—and clearing debris from the scene, we finally made it back to the firehouse.

After rinsing the grime from my body and putting on clean clothes, I headed into the meeting room to find Chief Madden standing at a table, head bent over the drawing spread across it, Lane at his side.

"About time," my brother grumbled.

I rolled my eyes. "Either you complain about me showering, or you complain about me not. I couldn't win, so I went with the option I preferred."

Chief chuckled and glanced at Lane. "You should be glad he rinsed off, Sheriff. That gear makes us sweat something fierce, and it's a smell unlike any other when it comes off."

I waved them both off as I approached the table, pushing a hand through my wet hair, attempting to brush that one stubborn lock off my forehead.

"I'm going to have Crew take over," Chief said, backing away. "Fight nice, boys."

Lane snorted but wisely silenced any retort.

"Alright, walk me through it."

I tapped my finger at the side entrance. "This is where we breached. Engine knocked down the flames in the doorway to get us through. We noticed the diesel smell when we got into the hall." Moving my finger along the map, I indicated another point. "Tuck and I parted here. I sent him through the back before going inside to clear the main area and the offices."

"Wait, back up. Why did you and Tuck separate?"

"Burns and Childers were breaching the back, so I wanted them and Tuck to clear the bays. There was more space to cover out here"—I swept my hand over the swath of open space on the schematic—"than the offices, which I knew I could handle myself. When they were done, I told Tuck to send Burns and Childers around the front again and come back for me."

"Always gotta be the hero," he mumbled.

Said the cop to the firefighter.

"I was doing my job, Lane. If someone is going to get pinned down in a sticky situation, I'd rather it be me than any of my men. As Captain, it's my job to allocate resources, and I needed the bulk of those *resources* clearing the bays. I got out alive."

Barely, I thought wryly, but he didn't need to know that. He hadn't been on duty that night, so he'd arrived at the scene after the roof had collapsed.

My brother merely grunted in response. "And which one did you find Miss McKay in?"

Lifting an arrow-shaped sticky note from the pack resting on one side of the schematic, I placed it at the edge of the office that butted up to the large bays. "It was completely empty except for her, lying on her side along the back wall. She had that filthy cloth in her mouth, and plastic zip ties around her ankles and wrists. The smoke had grown so thick, I knew we didn't have a lot of time to bail out before things got really hairy. Only after I tried to lift her up did I realize how badly her side was burned."

But how? I wondered. How had she even gotten those burns? When I found her, the flames had been circling, sure, but they weren't anywhere near her body to have caused the damage.

Lane hummed, his eyes having taken on a hazy expression that meant he was listening but also reconstructing the scene in his mind.

"We exited the offices as Tuck came back, and Davis laid down a line inside long enough to get us out."

"Too fucking close, kid," he breathed, clapping a hand on my shoulder as if to remind himself I was still breathing.

I understood the sentiment. None of us Lawless boys, except our oldest brother Owen, had ever been very good at keeping ourselves out of the line of fire. I literally walked into burning buildings for a living. Lane was a cop. Trey had spent eight years protecting a former President of the United States during his two terms, and Finn and West had joined the Army after high school, both becoming highly decorated Rangers.

We'd all settled back into this quiet, small town life, but that didn't mean danger didn't lurk around every corner for us all.

And after we'd lost our dad so unexpectedly all those years ago…well, we still fought. We were siblings after all, and men at that, but I also knew, without a doubt, I'd take a bullet for any one of them and our sister, Aria, and I knew they'd do the same for me.

"Alright," Lane said, snapping us both out of the moment and focusing on the task at hand. "In your expert opinion, what's your read on this guy?"

I considered that for a bit. When I'd been with the Chicago Fire Department, I'd been hungry and eager to learn everything I could about fighting fires, including investigating them. I spent six months in the Office of Fire Investigation, learning how arsonists ticked. Since my return to Dusk Valley five years ago,

I'd dedicated considerable time to reviewing the Prom Night Arsonist files, as well as numerous other closed arson cases, attempting to form some sort of profile.

"He's organized," I told Lane at last. "Disciplined. There's no chaos in his incidents. They're carefully controlled, confined to abandoned buildings where nobody but his victim could possibly get hurt. The vic was *the* target. Full stop."

"You're sure it's a man."

I nodded. "I don't think a woman is capable of disabling these victims and moving them from the abduction point to the crime scene. Not to mention, he has to have some sort of hidey-hole, right? Somewhere he kept Aspen between her abduction Friday night and the fire Saturday. So that's three locations, and three chances to get caught. These aren't crimes of opportunity."

"But Aspen's ordeal kind of toes the line, doesn't it?" Lane prompted, picking up my trail of thought.

"She's an obvious target because she's looking into the case, but I don't think she's been in town long enough for this guy to conduct adequate surveillance and make a solid plan. My guess is he was at the Swallow that night, heard her asking about it, and used that to his advantage."

"Maybe the lapse between the abduction and fire isn't his normal MO, either," Lane mused. "Maybe he needed that day to come up with the ideal way to dispose of her." He withdrew his mini spiral-bound notebook from his pocket and jotted down something, then said, "I want to talk to Benny."

"Like, the Swallow's bartender, Benny?"

"The very same."

"Why?"

"Because, little brother," Lane said, grinning like a fiend, like maybe he was onto something and was excited to see where it went. "He was likely the last person to speak to Aspen before she was taken."

"You don't think…"

"Nah." Lane waved me off. "He's too stupid to be a criminal mastermind, and he's too young to be our guy. But he can at the very least corroborate Aspen's memory of events and tell me if he noticed anything out of the ordinary that night."

I nodded my agreement. "Might as well check the security footage while you're at it. You know Red's got that place strung up like a damn Christmas tree."

Lane snorted. "Already on it."

Narrowing my gaze at my brother, I asked, "What do you think your chances are of being the one to catch this guy?"

My brother pondered that for a moment, and the fact that he was taking a beat to think about it instead of shooting some cocky, off the cuff remark at me told me he actually liked his chances.

Finally, he said, "A lot better now that I've got a living victim."

eleven

. . .

ASPEN

TWO WEEKS LATER

GINGERLY, I slipped my linen pants on, mindful of the bandages that covered much of my left side. Then I slipped on my top, the same color and material as my pants. After several exhausting minutes of trying to shrug it on without pulling at the wounds on my back, my phone rang.

"Hi, Mom," I said when I answered, already exhausted by the call.

"Hi, honey," she said brightly.

Mom was all about cheerfulness these days, ever since she read some health magazine article about how optimism would help me heal faster.

Mostly, it grated on my last nerve.

I appreciated her and Dad, and the week they'd spent here in Dusk Valley with me, reading to me or telling me stories about home while I was suffering through the worst of the healing.

The itching had gotten so bad at one point, I wished I'd died in that fire.

Okay, that was a lie. I was grateful to still be breathing. Especially since I was all Mom and Dad had left.

Hell, my life was all *I* had left.

Before this ordeal, my life had been dictated by two traumatic events: the loss of my sister, and the story that nearly cost me my own life. After Lola died, I threw myself into activities, trying to use my friends and a packed schedule to hold myself together. For a long time, it worked. I survived the rest of high school and college unscathed. There'd be no filling the hole my big sister left in my heart, but distance from her death made it a little easier to breathe every day. Then there was the Bullough story, and the beating I'd taken for looking into it, that had the opposite effect. I withdrew from everyone and everything, quit my job at the *Sun Times*, and moved across the country. Desperate for a fresh start where no one knew me, where I could fly under the radar and live my life in relative peace and silence.

And here I was again, facing down the aftermath of yet another trauma I'd have to carry for the rest of my life.

Maybe this time, I'd find a happy medium.

That started with humoring my mother when she smothered me. Them spending last week here had given Mom the opportunity to dote on me in the way she'd been trying since I'd moved out of their house fifteen years ago. She made it her personal mission to replace my credit, insurance, and ID cards, and had a field day on a trip up to the mall in Boise where she bought me an entirely new wardrobe, even though the only clothes I'd lost were the ones I'd been wearing in the fire.

I'd had to draw the line at her buying me a new phone and adding it to her and Dad's plan. Once I had a new credit card and access to my money —I didn't ask how she managed to send everything here to Dusk Valley when my permanent address was in Denver; I wasn't looking *that* gift horse in the mouth—I ordered a replacement iPhone myself.

Additionally, she'd taken it upon herself to call in a cosmetologist to fix my hair. Before, it had extended halfway down my back, but the fire had taken random odd chunks of it, forcing the woman to cut it to my shoulders. The new length took some getting used to.

At first, I cried. I loved my long hair, and losing it felt like another thing my attacker had robbed me of in addition to unblemished skin. But I quickly realized those were material things, and I still had my life.

The real kicker had been the loss of my sense of safety. Honestly, anxiety had set in the closer I got to walking out of the hospital, knowing I'd no longer be protected by the security system, guards, staff, and well-lit corridors.

"Was there a reason you called?" I asked, wincing at my tone. *Be nice*, I silently admonished myself.

"I wanted to check in," she said. "Wanted to know if the hospital had given you a discharge date yet. We've got your room all set up and ready for you to come home."

Internally, I groaned.

I'd like the record to reflect that I hadn't bothered to stop her helping me for two reasons. First, I knew she needed to feel useful. Second, while I'd been healing, I hadn't really been in a position to stop her.

Unfortunately, that was proving to be an error on my part. Now, she was acting like everything she said was gospel and the fact that I was a grown woman with my own free will didn't matter.

"I'm getting out today, but I'm not coming back to Chicago," I reminded her as gently as I could.

"Aspen," my mother sighed, sounding as exasperated as I felt. "We've talked about this."

"No, *you* talked. I didn't argue because I didn't have the energy. I still don't. But I've made my stance on the matter clear on numerous occasions. You refuse to listen."

"Sweetheart, you need to be surrounded by family right now.

You al-almost—" Her sentence was cut off by a sob, and after some background shuffling, my dad came on the line.

"Sorry, honey," he said. "You know she means well. And truthfully, I'd feel better if you came home too."

I understood where they were coming from. I really, truly did. We all dealt with the effects of losing my sister daily. But I didn't know how to explain it to them in a way that would make sense given all I'd been through. I *needed* to be here. Needed to stay in Dusk Valley and finish what I started.

"I know you worry about me after what happened to Lola—" A lump formed in my throat at the mention of my sister, but I pressed on. "I need you guys to trust me when I tell you I can take care of myself. I'm thirty-three, Dad. You have to let me live."

"I know, I know," he said, sighing heavily. In the background, I could hear Mom sniffling still. "Just…be careful. And check in daily, okay? We know how you get when you're on a case."

"I will," I promised. "You'll tell Mom?"

"Yes you little brat. I'll smooth it all over."

I grinned. "Thanks, Dad. Love you."

"Love you too, honey. Talk soon."

"Bye."

After hanging up, I gathered my discarded hospital clothes—the breathable, soft cotton shirt and sweatpants that I'd lived in for the last two weeks—and stuffed them into the hamper in the corner of the bathroom. I stepped out as a knock came at the door to my room.

My doctor stood there, clipboard in his hand weighed down by paperwork—my file.

"Miss McKay," my doctor said. "Good to see you mobile."

I would've been mobile from the beginning, but you people refused to let me out of bed for longer than to go to the bathroom, I thought wryly.

Actually, I hadn't protested too much. Every step, even on the short path to and from the toilet, had ached fiercely while my body healed. My movements were now easier and more free, if a bit reserved in deference to the shiny, delicate new skin on my back and side.

"Yeah," I said instead, pasting on a fake smile. "Feels great to be on my feet again."

"Good, good," he mumbled, scanning my chart. "Any sharp pains? Burning sensations? Loss of feeling entirely?"

I shook my head. "Just a dull ache in the wounds."

"That's to be expected. Your burns are fully healed over, but the new skin is quite thin. It'll take some time before that sensation fully dissipates."

"As long as I don't have to endure the itching again," I grumbled.

The doctor laughed. "No, we're well past that stage."

"Thank fuck."

Unperturbed, the doctor said, "Well, I wanted to bring your discharge paperwork. Once it's all filled out, you can drop it off at the nurse's station and make a plan for aftercare. Then you're free to go."

"Great!" I exclaimed, sounding more excited than I felt. Before he turned to go, I thought of one final question. "And my bill? I know that's not your area of expertise, but…"

"The ladies at the nurse's station will point you in the right direction." He stepped toward me and extended his hand. "It's been a pleasure leading your care team."

All I could do was nod for a moment as tears inexplicably pricked my eyes and stung my nose. When I collected myself, I said, "Thank you."

"I'd say anytime, but I don't want to see you back here."

With a wink, he was gone.

twelve

. . .

ASPEN

ONCE THE MOUNTAIN of paperwork was completed, I passed it over to the nurses and shuffled to the first floor, where the billing department was.

A woman with bright red hair waved me into her office, the sign next to the door telling me her name was Marjorie and she was the supervisor of the department.

"Hello!" she said brightly when I entered. "What can I do for you?"

"I've been here for the last two weeks, and I was just discharged, but I wanted to discuss my bill before I leave. I'm not local, so I was hoping to enroll in paperless billing and figure out a repayment plan."

"We can absolutely look into that for you. Why don't you take a seat, and I'll pull up your file."

I flinched at the thought of parking my tender skin on the hard wooden chair. "I'll stand, if you don't mind." Tattooed brows creased, and I gestured to my left side, clarifying, "Burns."

Expression clearing, she said, "What's your name?"

"Aspen McKay."

Her fingers flew over the keyboard, but she didn't look away from me. "I'm sorry for what happened to you."

"Thank you."

"Sheriff Lawless is a wonderful man. He'll do whatever he can to bring your attacker to justice."

I barely withheld a snort. My two interactions with the man hadn't exactly been stellar, but the sheriff's department was actually my next stop, so we'd see if the third time was the charm.

"I hope you're right," I mumbled noncommittally.

Marjorie gave me a reassuring smile, her bright pink lips parting to reveal stark white teeth, then returned her attention to her computer.

"Let's see here…Aspen McKay…Huh. That's interesting."

"I'm sorry, what is?"

"It seems your bill has already been paid in full."

"What?" I asked dumbly.

"You have a zero balance," she said slowly, like she was worried I'd also sustained brain damage.

Actually, I had, but the concussion had cleared up, the lingering mind fog and headache lifting a few days ago.

Maybe I wasn't as healed as I thought.

Still, I took my shiny new iPhone out of the pocket of my brand new crossbody bag and navigated to my banking app. Maybe my Mom had used my card to pay it without my knowledge? I had yet to even see a bill, so I had no idea how much I owed, but I doubted the sum had been small enough to be covered by what I had in my checking account.

Regardless, the transaction history didn't reflect any disbursements to Dusk Valley Memorial.

"Does your system tell you who paid?" I asked an expectant Marjorie when I looked up from my phone.

Squinting at the screen and arrowing down a few clicks, she said, "Donald and Leesa McKay—oh! Those must be your parents. Wow, that was so generous of them."

"Yeah, it was something alright," I muttered, then shot Marjorie a wide grin. "Could I have a copy of the invoice for my records?"

"Sure thing."

Five minutes later, sheaf of papers detailing my stay and care at Dusk Valley Memorial in hand, I exited the hospital for the first time in two weeks.

The gentle breeze brushed my skin, cooling my angry red cheeks.

Mom and I were about to have a reckoning, so I took a seat on a little bench in the sunshine right outside the doors and dialed her number.

"Hi, honey!" she crowed. "I'm sorry about earlier. I just worry about you, you know? But I know you can take care of yourself, and as long as you—"

I cut off her rambling with six words.

"Did you pay my hospital bill?"

The air at the other end of the line was dead for so long I pulled my phone from my ear to make sure she hadn't hung up on me. Finding the call was still connected, I said, "Mom?"

"Yes," she said firmly. "Your father and I made the decision to pay your bill for you."

"You had *no right*," I gritted out, my jaw aching from clenching it so tightly.

"We're your parents, and it is our *right* to take care of you, to help you when you're struggling." She heaved a sigh laced with years of exasperation. "Honestly, Aspen, you're taking this whole independence thing too seriously."

I huffed out a disbelieving laugh. "You can't be serious."

"I am. Your refusal to let people help you is only going to end up hurting *you* in the long run. It's likely why you're still single, and why you've never really had a serious relationship."

The words struck me in the chest like a stab wound, catching me so off guard I dropped my phone onto the bench at my side. My mom's voice became a distant squawking.

Losing the one person in this world who understood me better than anyone, who had been my sounding board for all things like boys, fashion, school, or life in general, had taken an obvious toll on me. I was only sixteen when Lola died—at a critical stage of my formative years—and suddenly, my rock vanished, leaving me floating in space.

In all the years I'd been alive, I'd never once doubted my parents loved me. Before, I thought it had been unconditional, but the way Mom had been acting lately…maybe *her* love came with strings, and the fire singed them all away, once again leaving me untethered.

Did I want a family, a husband and children of my own? Eventually, sure. But at this point, I'd spent so long alone I almost couldn't imagine making space in my solitary existence for anyone else.

Clearly, I didn't even have a good relationship with my parents. How could I expect to be happy with a man?

Finally, I picked the phone back up, Mom's words going in one ear and out the other.

"Good to know what you really think, Mom," I said when she stopped speaking. "I don't want to talk to you for a while. I'll reach out when I'm ready."

"Asp—" she started, but I hung up.

Well fuck.

If I sat on that bench and thought about it for too long, I'd likely never get up, so I stood and put one foot in front of the other…as far as the sidewalk, anyway. After that, I had to pull out my phone and see if this town had any sort of public transit system. They did, but it was either wait thirty minutes for the bus or walk the ten minutes to the police department.

The day was gorgeous, and I'd been cooped up inside for too damn long, so I opted to walk.

By the time I pushed inside the department, I was regretting it. My side ached like a bitch, and after two weeks of being sedentary, I was panting like a dog.

Clearly recognizing me from last time, the desk sergeant didn't get up, but she did say, "I'll buzz the sheriff for you. And I'm real sorry for your ordeal, Miss McKay. It's good to see you out and about."

"Thank you," I said, and she lifted the phone, calling back to the sheriff. After a brief conversation, she buzzed me back into the bullpen.

Eyes tracked me across the room once again, my skin crawling with the sensation of having too many people staring at me. When I reached the sheriff's office, the door slightly ajar, I pushed inside without waiting for an invitation and slammed it shut behind me. Then I dropped unceremoniously into the chair I'd been in before, a hiss of pain leaving me when my injuries met the cushion.

His brow was curved toward his hairline when I met his gaze.

"Sorry. I hate people staring at me."

"Understandable. And for what it's worth, I'm sorry for what happened to you. I can't remember if I said it before…"

Before, when the first time he'd tried to conduct this interview sent me into a panic attack.

I waved him off, not needing his sympathy or pity.

"It's fine," I said. "Let's get this over with."

The sheriff looked like he wanted to press the issue, to say something else, but wisely kept his mouth shut. He withdrew his phone, opened the voice note app, and pressed record.

"Sheriff Lawless here with Aspen McKay, second interview in regards to the events of the prom night fire." He paused and looked up at me. While he was a little more rugged than Crew, a little less clean, they had the same eyes, complete with the same fringe of thick lashes. The realization settled me. Sheriff Lawless wasn't here to harm me in any way. He merely wanted to catch whoever had done this to me. "You good?"

Swallowing hard and squaring my shoulders, sitting up as straight as I could muster while favoring my left side, I nodded. "Yeah."

And then I let it all out, remaining as detached as possible. I may have felt significantly calmer this time around, but that didn't mean I wanted to relive the events of that night any more than I did before. The sheriff asked gently probing questions, and I did my best to answer them. There was still a good chunk of time missing—namely the entire day between being abducted and coming to in the middle of that inferno. I had to assume my brain was suppressing the memories for the sake of my mental health.

Still, it irritated me to no end that I couldn't *remember*.

There had to be something lingering in there that would lead us to this guy. I was the key to unlocking the entire thing, and I couldn't get my goddamn mind to cooperate.

"And then I woke up in the hospital," I finished, breathing heavily like I'd run a marathon.

Trauma sure was fun.

The sheriff clicked his pen, tapping it against the desk, then stopped the recording.

"I want to ask you something off the record, if that's alright with you."

"Okay…"

"Your burns," he began. "I talked to Crew, got his statement about the incident, and he didn't seem to think the fire had gotten close enough to you to cause them…"

Unfortunately, I remembered how I'd gotten them with stark, unending clarity. So far, that had been the one thing no one had pressed me on. They'd all assumed they'd been a result of the fire, which wasn't wrong. But they weren't accidental.

That fucker had purposely lit me on fire.

"The time between the Swallow parking lot and waking up in that garage is gone," I started, "but I know the exact moment I came to, and it wasn't when Crew found me. I woke up because I was in the worst pain I'd ever experienced in my life. Took me a few heartbeats to realize I was literally on fucking fire." Tears spilled from my eyes and dripped down my cheeks, and I angrily swiped them away. Then I gave the sheriff a watery, sarcastic smile. "That stop, drop, and roll shit they teach you in school really works."

Lane's face had blanched white, his eyes wide as saucers.

"I stopped when I hit the wall, and surprisingly, the cool concrete actually felt great on my wounds."

"What a fucking nightmare," he said quietly.

I choked on a laugh. "Yeah, you're telling me."

"Thank you for sharing. I know that couldn't have been easy."

"I've been through worse," I told him.

Curiosity appeared in his expression, but that wasn't a can of worms I was opening *ever*, least of all with this man I barely knew. Then again, I wasn't sure it got worse than someone literally setting you on fire in the hopes you'd die.

As if recognizing he'd get nothing further from me, he leaned back in his chair and regarded me. "You're free to go, Miss McKay. I've got your number if anything else comes up."

I rose from my seat and nodded. "I'll be around."

His brows drew together. "Surely you mean that figuratively?"

"Nope. I'll be in town for the foreseeable future."

The relaxed man from a moment ago disappeared in an instant. The next thing I knew, he was on his feet, palms flat on his desk as he leaned toward me.

"I'm going to have to advise against that."

"I'm afraid there's not much you can do about it."

"I could arrest you."

I snorted. "For what, exactly?"

"I'll think of something."

"And I'll slap you with a civil suit for unlawful arrest."

I could practically hear his teeth grinding together as he considered his next move. Likely, he knew he'd never talk me into leaving, but he gave it a final shot anyway.

"You really need to leave, Aspen. Don't give this guy any more opportunities to hurt you."

I shook my head emphatically, my dark hair whipping around my shoulders, slapping me in the cheeks. I looked him dead in the eye, brooking no room for argument as I said, "I can't do that, Sheriff. I'm sorry, but this is personal now. I'm not going anywhere."

With nothing further to say, I left the room, but the sheriff wasn't done, and his murmured parting words found and followed me anyway.

"It's your funeral."

thirteen

. . .

ASPEN

THE MOMENT I exited the police station, I pulled up short on the sidewalk out front and swore healthily.

I still didn't have a car.

And the last thing I wanted to do was walk all over this town in search of the impound lot where Black Betty had ended up.

So, with my tail between my legs, I huffed and walked back inside.

"Did you forget something, Miss McKay?"

"I was hoping you could direct me toward the impound lot? I need to get my vehicle back."

"Oh, sure!" she said, leaning forward and sliding the glass window that separated us open. "It's on Aspen," she chuckled, and it took me a moment to realize she was naming a street and not me. "If you follow this road out front down three blocks and take a right, it's down that way on your left. Can't miss it."

"Great, thanks!"

I turned to leave, but she called after me, and when I faced her again, she brandished a piece of paper.

"You're going to need this," she said. "It'll get your car out of there without having to pay the fees."

"You're an angel," I breathed.

Twenty minutes later, covered in sweat and in dire need of some pain pills, I stood in front of my car and the piece of paper flapping under the windshield wiper in the gentle breeze.

"Did you put that there?" I asked the lot worker who'd walked back here with me.

"No, ma'am. We parked it and left it alone."

Then he tipped his hat and disappeared.

Each step closer to the vehicle weighed heavier and heavier until I stood close enough to reach up with shaky fingers and retrieve the paper.

Everything about this felt inexplicably wrong. I couldn't put my finger on why, only that I knew I wouldn't like what I found when I unfolded it.

Welcome to Dusk Valley, Aspen McKay. We hope you enjoyed your baptism by fire. A shame you survived, though. You should know I don't like loose ends. Until we meet again, little cockroach.

A cold pulse of fear slithered down my spine, raising the hair on the back of my neck. I glanced around, looking for a perpetrator, but found no one.

I was alone, and who the hell knew how long this note had been waiting for me. Had they placed it there immediately after attacking me? No, that wouldn't make sense. Not if they'd intended for me to die in that fire.

That could only mean someone had snuck into this lot and left it there, knowing it'd be waiting for me when I was released from the hospital and claimed my vehicle.

Was this their attempt at driving me out of town? Or was this them merely fanning the flames on my desire to catch them?

Definitely the latter. This person was clearly taunting me.

Well fuck. That.

I would not be toyed with. One day, hopefully sooner rather

than later, I would look this fucker in the eye as I brought them to justice.

Getting behind the wheel of Black Betty, the seat, which was perfectly molded to my ass—a much needed comfort in a day from hell—I put her in drive and shot the attendant a wave as I sped out of the lot, feeling a bit more like myself as I headed toward my first stop: the scene of the crime.

There was no explanation for *why* I wanted to go there. I supposed morbid curiosity made me want to gaze upon the place that nearly claimed my life. To remind myself that I'd made it out.

The sight took my breath away.

What once had likely been a tall, sturdy structure was now nothing more than a blackened husk, the broken walls shooting up toward the sky like jagged teeth. I closed my eyes as I sat there, parked on the curb out front, willing the missing fragments of my memories to return to me.

My eyes popped open when nothing happened, and suddenly, I was so damn exhausted. Nothing sounded better than heading back to my motel and sleeping for the next twenty-four hours.

I supposed that was another thing I had to grudgingly thank my mom for, despite the fact that she'd been lobbying hard for me to move home. She had made it possible for me to have a room to return to after my release.

Unfortunately, the universe—and the shitty ass clerk—had other plans.

"Miss McKay!" the desk clerk—the owner—shouted at me when I exited my car in the parking lot. "A word please."

Grumbling internally, I dragged my feet to the reception desk.

He'd called me by my real name, which didn't bode well.

But my eyes skipped right over the man seated there and landed on a pile of personal belongings stacked in the corner.

My personal belongings.

"Why are my things out of my room?" I barked.

"I'm afraid we're completely booked. Since you've been… gone," he said, putting undue emphasis on the word, "we've had to empty out your room to accommodate paying customers."

I hadn't been *gone*, I'd been fucking *taken* against my will and nearly died.

My blood boiled.

"I just spoke with you this morning!"

"Things have changed."

My gaze narrowed, and a lightbulb illuminated in my brain.

The fucking sheriff.

Gritting my teeth, I attempted to quell the rage coursing through me.

"Can I at least go in and make sure you didn't miss anything?" I asked.

He shook his head. "Sorry, there's someone now renting that room."

I cursed colorfully in his direction, glaring pointedly at the parking lot, empty save Black Betty and a piece of shit Nissan, which I assumed belonged to him.

Undeterred by my outburst, the rat's smile was greasy as he said, "Would you like some help loading your things in your vehicle?"

Instead of a verbal response, I shot him the middle finger and moved around behind the counter, collecting all of my bags and carrying them to Black Betty in one trip.

My skin crawled, knowing that man had been through my stuff, had his fingers all over my personal effects and files.

Angrily, I threw myself behind the wheel, fuming in the quiet of the car. I was so pissed off, I didn't even feel the pain in my side anymore. My tires squealed as I peeled out of the lot.

What a fucking *prick*. Both the owner of this roach motel and the goddamn sheriff.

After I'd spilled my guts about how I obtained my wounds, he had some fucking nerve telling the little rat to kick me out.

I had half a mind to murder him, but that'd only provide a legitimate excuse for my arrest.

Okay, Aspen. Think. This isn't the end of the world. You've been in worse situations before.

With a sigh that I hoped would expel all the furious energy brewing beneath my skin—spoiler: it didn't—I pulled into the first parking lot I found, withdrew my phone, and clicked into the Airbnb app.

Ten minutes later, I had a new place booked, and I smiled smugly as I headed toward the adorable little cottage on the edge of town. The directions took me back by the impound lot, and I realized how truly small this town was.

I'd never lived somewhere with such a tiny population, where you could drive end to end of the city limits in under ten minutes. After nearly a month in Dusk Valley and the shit I'd endured, staying in this one longer than I had to wasn't likely.

I was halfway to the new rental when my phone dinged with an email.

Reservation Cancelled

"What the fuck…"

Steering Black Betty to the shoulder, I put her in park and read the email.

We regret to inform you that the host has cancelled this booking…

I didn't bother looking at the rest, merely sent it flying toward my trash folder and booked another one.

After three more attempts with the same result, I finally gave up.

It seemed the sheriff had covered his bases.

Unbidden, hot, angry tears spilled from my eyes, and though I tried to wipe them away and pull myself together, they morphed from the silent kind to body-wracking sobs in an instant.

God, I was so fucking tired.

I'd had a good life once. A beautiful apartment looking out on Chicago's Mag Mile and Lake Michigan beyond it, a job I loved, amazing friends, and parents who respected me.

The version of me from five years ago wouldn't recognize the woman I was now. Somehow, I thought that was for the best. *That* version of Aspen McKay would be horrified to learn I now called home a five hundred-square-foot apartment over my office, though I basically lived out of my twenty-year-old vehicle. That I rarely wore makeup, nothing in my wardrobe contained a designer label, and I hadn't gotten a manicure in years.

I let it all out. The hurt, the anger, the sheer exhaustion. I refused to be run out of this town so easily, but I'd be damned if the way these people shunned me didn't sting an awful lot, like salt in an open wound.

A rap on my window snapped my eyes open, and I startled enough to smoke my head off the roof. After cranking the window down a hair, I said, "Can I help you?"

"I was going to ask you the same thing."

The woman was likely in her mid-fifties, with strawberry blonde hair chopped above her shoulders, an AirPod resting in one ear, and an excited dog pulling on the leash in her left hand. A sizable square-cut diamond glittered on her finger. She looked like the portrait of a quintessential suburban housewife.

"I'm okay," I assured her. "Just having a rough couple of days."

"If you're sure…" she trailed off, eyeing me suspiciously.

For the first time since I'd parked here, I took in my surroundings, realizing I'd stopped in front of a cute craftsman home in the middle of a quiet neighborhood. Along the street, curtains on front windows twitched as the residents checked me out.

"I'm sure," I promised. "I was just leaving."

The woman merely nodded and took off at a brisk jog in the

direction opposite of which I faced, though I didn't miss her glancing over her shoulder periodically until I pulled away from the curb and turned a corner.

A few more random turns had me back on the main drag, and I slammed to a stop in front of the cafe, an idea forming in my mind. A visit to a certain firefighter was exactly what I needed to distract me from the hellscape my life had become.

The bell above the door tinkled soothingly as I pushed inside, an intoxicating blend of sugar, coffee, and freshly baked bread wrapping me in a warm hug.

"Welcome to The Spout," the younger girl working the register said. "What can I get for you?"

"I'm looking for a cake."

***

TWENTY MINUTES LATER, I pulled up to the fire station, and everything in me seemed to settle when I laid eyes on Crew.

He was out on the apron, clipboard in hand, as a few of the other guys moved around the truck and called out things to him. None of it made any sense, though I had to guess they were taking inventory of their tools and supplies. Instead of approaching, I took a moment to lean up against the side of Black Betty and watch him work.

Crew had a natural charisma about him, and emanated that kind of big dick energy that alerted anyone around that he was the top dog, the alpha male, in any given situation. His men followed him without question, and I couldn't blame them. Crew was physically imposing, of course. Tall, broad-shouldered, muscles for days. But he had an easy smile that disappeared quickly when things turned serious. Those sky-blue eyes were able to cut through the bluster and bullshit. And to be a fire captain so young? Obviously, he was great at his job. There was a magnetism to him, impossible to ignore.

My inconspicuousness disappeared when one of those men spotted me.

"Well, well, well," he said, grinning and socking Crew on the shoulder. "Look who was finally sprung from the joint."

I rolled my eyes. "I wasn't in prison."

Crew smirked as he approached me. "Hospitals aren't much better."

"Food is probably better in prison," I admitted.

His expression morphed into a wide grin, and I couldn't help but match it.

"What're you doing here?" he asked, instantly dousing my good mood.

Shrugging, I dragged my toe through the dirt, eyes darting everywhere but at his. Suddenly, I couldn't look him straight on for fear he'd see all my weaknesses and anxieties written across my face in stark, black letters.

"I was bored."

Crew chuckled. "I can fix that."

Roughly, I cleared my throat and turned away, lest he see the blood heating my cheeks with the seductive promise in his words. I yanked open the passenger door of Black Betty and withdrew the cake.

"Actually, I wanted to bring you this."

Crew accepted it, one of his dark blond brows curving in amusement.

"'Happy birthday, Timmy'?"

I winced. "Sorry. It was the only one they had on short notice."

"You mean to tell me you stole some little boy's birthday cake for me? I can't accept this, Aspen. That's just…mean."

"No!" I shouted, backpedaling, though his little smirk told me he was messing with me. "No, it's not like that. Apparently, there was a mix-up with the theme and his parents ordered a new one. They were going to throw this one away at the end of the day, so really, I was doing them a favor."

"Lawless," a deep voice said from behind him, and I glanced over Crew's shoulder to see Chief Madden had joined his men outside. "It's all good."

Crew turned back to me with a grin, now aware of something that had gone right over my head. The guys chuckled as well, and I crossed my arms over my chest, waiting for someone to clue me in.

"Timmy is Chief Madden's son," Crew explained, taking pity on me at last. Then he jerked his head in the direction of the station. "How about we go inside and enjoy a slice?"

"Sure," I said, happy to have something to do with myself that didn't include wallowing and eager to spend more time around Crew. I knew coming here would be a good idea. This man had, after all, saved my life. It made sense I'd feel safe and calm in his presence.

Plus, nothing bad could happen to me at a fire station.

We headed inside and gathered around the long table that took up half the space in the common room. Plates and silverware were passed around, the cake was cut, and we all dug into our slices in celebration of Timmy Madden.

"So when did you get out of the hospital?" Crew asked quietly, leaning his head closer to mine. With his attention wholly focused on me, I felt like the only person in the room—hell, the *world*.

"This morning," I said around a mouthful. "Then I went to the sheriff's department and spoke with your brother. Got my car back, got kicked out of my hotel..."

I added that last part as nonchalantly as I could despite knowing he wouldn't let it go that easily. But maybe, deep down —or *not* so deep down; I *was* effectively homeless at the moment —I was hoping he'd find a way to help me.

"Your brother wants me to leave town—" I continued.

"You're planning on staying?" he asked hopefully, cutting me off.

"I *was*…until the sheriff blacklisted me at every hotel, motel, and short-term rental in the county."

Fuck, what was I going to tell Mrs. Lee?

Sorry, ma'am. I couldn't find your daughter's killer—the man who targeted me too—because the sheriff ran me out of town.

Crew placed his hands flat on the table and began to push to his feet, but I wrapped one of mine around his wrist and yanked him back down.

"I'll kill him," Crew seethed. "Who gave him the right?"

"To be fair, he is a cop, and I suppose in a fucked up, misguided way, he's trying to look out for me."

Crew scoffed. "You can look out for yourself."

My heart expanded in my chest with some unnameable emotion.

How long had I been waiting for someone to say that to me? To remind me of that fact? To look at me and see someone who didn't need to be babied and sheltered from the world?

"You're right. And that starts with finding somewhere to stay. Maybe you can talk to Lane about lifting the ban? Convince him I'll be okay?"

Crew's murderous expression quickly shifted into one of mischief. "Actually, I've got a better idea."

At this point, I was willing to accept all the help I could get, so I folded my fingers over my palm in an *out with it* gesture.

"You can stay with me."

fourteen

. . .

CREW

"*YOU CAN STAY WITH ME.*"

Aspen's fork clattered to the table, the guys around the table going silent like a gun had gone off.

She shook her head. "No, I can't ask you to do that."

"You're not asking me to do anything," I promised. "You need a place to stay, I have a spare room. I'm happily offering it up to a friend in need. We're…friends, right?"

One of the guys snickered—likely Tuck—but I didn't look away from Aspen's face to glare at him. Having this conversation in front of my men wasn't ideal, but Aspen moving in with me would become public knowledge quickly, spreading through town like wildfire.

"You've already saved my life, Crew," she whispered. "You can't do this for me too."

"Saving your life was me doing my job. This I'm doing because I want to. *Please.*"

I wasn't above begging, and I offered her what I hoped was a reassuring smile while I waited for her response.

My brother would surely shit a brick when he learned what I'd done, but there wasn't a single cell in my body that gave a fuck. There was something happening here with Aspen, some string in the loom of fate being tugged, and I knew I'd be a fucking moron to ignore it.

I couldn't let her leave without giving us the chance to explore this thing that sparked to life and hummed beneath my skin whenever she was near.

"Are you sure?" she asked, eyes darting across my face as though searching for an indication that I was about to withdraw the invitation.

She wouldn't find it.

I hadn't been this sure of anything in a long fucking time.

"Positive. In fact," I said, rising from my seat and pulling her up with me, that inexplicable electrical current coursing through my body at the contact. "Follow me."

I led her through the station until we reached the locker room. Opening mine, I fished around in my bag until my hand closed around my keys, and I handed them over.

"Take my truck," I told her as I rifled around the top shelf in search of the stack of sticky notes and a pen. I quickly jotted down the code to my security system and pressed that into her palm. "The opener will get you in the garage, this key"—I indicated a silver one—"will let you into the house, and that code will disable the security system long enough for you to get settled. Then you can arm it again."

"What kind of firefighter are you?" she asked, glancing up at me.

"One with a brother who owns a private security firm."

Aspen eyed me suspiciously. "How many brothers do you have?"

"Five," I said, ushering her back out of the locker room and toward the side exit of the building.

"There are *six* of you?"

"And a baby sister."

"Jesus Christ," she muttered as I pushed her along, my hand

on the small of her back, the heat of her skin seeping into my palm through the thin material of her shirt.

I chuckled. "Jesus had nothing to do with it."

We reached my truck then—a brand spankin' new Chevy Silverado 2500HD, completely blacked out with a tool box in the bed—and Aspen spun toward me, placing her hands on my chest to halt my progress.

Curl your fingers into my shirt, darlin', I silently urged. *Pull me closer.*

She didn't, and I'd be damned if I wasn't a little disappointed. Aspen simply let her hands linger, staring up at me. "What's your brother going to say?"

"Fuck my brother."

"Crew…"

"Aspen."

"Be serious."

"I am being serious. Lane doesn't get to dictate your life because he's the sheriff. You have as much right to be here as anyone else, and if the rest of the town won't welcome you in, I'm making it my job to fix that."

Gently, I settled my hands on her hips and shifted her out of the way, then opened the driver's door for her. Even with the running boards, she was so petite it would clearly be a struggle for her to get inside, so I took pity on her and lifted her into the seat myself.

"Fire it up," I said, indicating the button to start it. "Foot on the brake."

After inching the seat forward so she could reach the pedals, she did as I asked, the engine roaring to life. God, I loved that sound.

"Now what?"

"Tap into the GPS and punch in my address." I rattled it off, and that creepy robotic voice filtered through the speakers, telling Aspen where to go first. "It's a bit out of town, but you'll be safe there. Make yourself comfortable. There's only one guest room because I use the other as my office, so I'm sure you can figure it out. Now give me your phone and keys."

She did as I requested, and after pocketing the keys, because I'd have to take her SUV home when I got off shift, I punched my number in her phone, then sent myself a text to make sure I'd have hers.

"Text me if you have any issues. I'll be home around eight thirty tomorrow morning, and I'll likely sleep most of the day. Once I'm up, we can figure out what's next."

Aspen narrowed those gorgeous cinnamon eyes on me. "Why are you being so nice?"

Because, inexplicably, I care about you.

But there was no fucking way I could tell her that, not when this was effectively the second legitimate conversation we'd ever had.

"You've been through enough," I said instead.

"Thank you, Crew," she whispered.

Fuck, my name on her lips had blood stirring in my groin, and I had to let her leave before I did something crazy like haul her into the backseat and make her say it with a lot more volume and pleasure behind it.

Shaking my head, I croaked out, "No problem," and stepped out of the way so she could close the door. Then I stood there like a schmuck and watched her drive away.

"You've got it baaaaaaaaaaaad," someone said from behind me, and I whirled to find Tuck standing there, leaning against the side of the building with his arms crossed over his chest, a smug expression on his face.

"Shut the fuck up," I muttered, pushing past him, his answering cackle following me inside.

ASPEN'S CAR was a fucking death trap.

The thing rattled and hummed concerningly as I drove home, and I breathed a sigh of relief when I pulled to a stop in front of my garage. Both because I'd survived and because I couldn't wait to crawl into bed and sleep for the next seven hours.

We'd had five calls overnight, which was admittedly a lot. But with the weather warming up and school getting closer to ending, stupid kids were getting bolder.

And that boldness led to recklessness.

I grabbed my bag from the passenger seat and got out, moving to the garage door and punching in the code to let me in. Once it closed again, I let myself into the house, dropped my bag in the laundry room as always, and padded down the hall.

Everything was undisturbed, almost like no one but me was there. But I could sense the charge in the air, alerting me to the fact that I wasn't alone. Letting me know that down the hall, Aspen lay sleeping.

As I made my way toward my room, I paused outside her door and cracked it open to check on her. She was on her stomach, limbs starfished across the mattress, her hair a dark fan across the pillow. The swelling around her eyes had gone down completely, and the bruising around them was now a faint yellow tinge versus the horrific purple it had been in the hospital. Her breath snuffled softly, and with sleep slackening her features, she looked much younger than her thirty-three years. Like all the hurt and hardness she carried melted away until her true, gentle nature shined through. I found myself deeply pleased that she appeared to be resting comfortably, and I was grateful I could be the one to give her this soft place to land.

Reluctantly, I forced myself to walk away and go to bed before she caught me staring at her like a creep.

As I drifted into the land between slumber and awake, my phone chimed.

SHERIFF

Outside. NOW.

Shit.

Yes, I had Lane saved in my phone as "Sheriff," much to his annoyance, and it looked like my big brother found out what I'd done sooner than I planned. I had hoped to at least get some sleep before he showed up to rip my head off.

And honestly, who the fuck showed up at someone's house, unannounced, at eight o'clock in the morning?

I dressed quickly, cursing Lane the whole time, before heading out of the front door and meeting him on my front porch.

The door was barely closed behind me before he exploded, not even bothering with a greeting before launching into his tirade.

"Are you out of your fucking mind? She's the only witness in this case. Ever, Crew. The only woman who has ever survived. I'm not going to let you fuck it up so you can get your dick wet."

"Fuck you," I spat at him. "That's not what this is about. This is about the fact that you had her blacklisted from every hotel and short-term rental in this town!"

He at least had the wherewithal to appear remorseful. "And I'm sorry for that. But I'm trying to keep her safe by getting her to leave."

"Then you don't know her very well."

"Neither do you!" he shouted. "You met her two weeks ago, and suddenly you're giving her a room in your house? This is so unlike you."

I gritted my teeth against the endless retorts I had lined up, attempting to marshal my temper. "Trying to keep someone safe is *very* like me, actually. And with this fucker still at large, Aspen is very much still in danger."

"I want her gone, Crew."

"That's not up to you."

"Why are you being like this?"

"Why are *you*? You said it yourself, Lane. She's the only surviving victim. And she's a private investigator. Seems to me you could benefit from working together."

"I don't work with civilians," he said through clenched teeth.

"Maybe you should start. Have you even bothered to look into her?"

"No…" he said, scuffing the toe of his boot through the gravel to avoid looking at me.

"Do that," I told him, turning away to head back into the house. "Then come talk to me."

Before I got too far, his hand clamped onto my shoulder, halting my progress and spinning me back around. "I'm warning you, Crew. You fuck up this investigation, you interfere in any way, and I won't hesitate to lock your ass up. Understood?"

I nodded. "Whatever you say, Boss Man. Keep me updated on the investigation."

"That's not how this works, little bro."

"Of course it is. Whatever happens to her is my business now."

"Only because you made it your business, you dumb fuck."

I grinned but it was all teeth. "You love me."

Lane sighed sharply through his nose and wrapped his arm around my neck, giving me a noogie before I pinched his side and he released me with a yelp.

"Get back inside you little shit. Keep an eye on that girl."

Trust me, I thought. *My eyes aren't going anywhere else.*

With a mock salute, I pushed back inside, crawled into bed, and promptly passed out.

WHEN I WOKE several hours later, after the kind of deep sleep that momentarily disoriented me, the first thing I noticed was something smelled good.

Really good.

But…why?

And then I remembered: Aspen.

Aspen McKay was in my home, *living here now*, and apparently, whipping up something delicious in my kitchen.

I took the fastest shower of my life and slipped into some sweats before I went out to greet her.

Aspen wore nothing but a long, oversized tee, her shapely legs and the bottom curve of her ass on display when she reached overhead to dig in my cupboards. Her burn marks peeked out from beneath her black cotton panties, the edges raised, shiny, and bright pink.

In my line of work, avoiding burns was impossible, and I'd sustained a major injury back in Chicago about ten years ago. The scar that would never go away stretched nearly six inches along my left forearm was the reason I got my first tattoo—ultimately leading to the full sleeve.

On silent feet, I approached the island and leaned against it. She hadn't heard me come in, and I was content to watch her for a moment. Her hair was shorter than it'd been—likely thanks to the fire—brushing the tops of her shoulders instead of trailing down her back like it had before. Somehow, I enjoyed this version of her more. While visions of wrapping the length of it around my fist as I pounded her from behind were no longer viable, I was adaptable. She looked like a sexy little pixie I wanted to put in my pocket and keep safe forever.

I loudly cleared my throat.

She whirled on me, tugging the hem of the shirt down to make sure it covered her panties.

I was happy to report it failed—miserably.

"Oh my God," she breathed, face blushing deeply. "I'm so

sorry. I was looking for coffee. I thought you were still sleeping. I'll just—" She moved around the counter and disappeared down the hall, her door slamming shut behind her a moment later.

Whatever she'd been cooking was still bubbling on the stove, so I lifted the lid on the pot to find some sort of soup with tomatoes, hamburger, and rice bobbing on the surface.

A moment later, she reappeared…wearing pants. I bit back a groan.

"I'm so sorry about that," she said as she moved toward the stove, shoving me out of the way to stir the soup. Her cheeks were as red as the tomatoes, and I loved that I flustered her so much. "I'll start remembering to put pants on. I'm so used to living alone, you know?" She glanced up at me. "I haven't had to share space with someone in a really long time, and—"

I cut her off with a finger to her lips, a dangerous touch that singed my skin. "It's fine, Aspen. Really. This is your home now too. Do whatever makes you comfortable."

And it *was* fine…even if I'd be fucking my fist later to nothing but the memories of her sexy, silky-smooth legs, and the idea of how they'd feel wrapped around my waist—or my head.

I really had to get my shit together.

fifteen

. . .

ASPEN

CREW CLEARED his throat and he shuffled away from me, giving me some much needed distance from his…*everything*.

"So, what're you making?" he croaked.

Tipping my face away from him, my lips tilted up in a small smile. Knowing I flustered him as much as he did me was a powerful realization.

"Tomato, hamburger, and rice soup. It's a simple dish, but one of my ultimate comfort meals. I thought it would make me feel better, after everything, and you had all the ingredients…" I trailed off as I shot him a sheepish smile. "Sorry. I should've asked before rifling through your shit."

"What did I just tell you?"

The words were practically a growl, emanating from deep in his chest.

"To make myself comfortable?" I said, though my inflection at the end phrased it as more of a question.

"Exactly." He leaned forward and sniffed as I stirred. "And this smells fucking amazing."

My cheeks were damn near flaming now.

I was used to living alone and spending the bulk of my time

on my own. Even on a case, I was a one-woman show, a solitary operation. It had been nearly fifteen years since I'd lived with my parents, and roughly twelve since I had any sort of roommate. I was operating on an outdated playbook regarding cohabiting etiquette.

Crew hadn't seemed to mind, though. I hadn't missed the way his eyes heated as he'd taken me and my bare legs in earlier. There was such…*desire* in that look. Despite my embarrassment, it made me feel good. Reminded me that I was alluring, that someone found me attractive.

I was simply having a hard time wrapping my brain around this tattooed, action-figure-come-to-life, literal hero being the one.

Then again, he didn't know my story. Crew could easily look at me and see something other than the broken girl I'd considered myself since my sister died.

While I added the finishing touches to the soup, Crew withdrew half of a baguette from the pantry, sliced, buttered, and topped it with thick-cut mozzarella before putting it in the oven broiler.

Honestly, his kitchen was a dream. Hell, the entire house belonged on the cover of a lifestyle magazine.

When the soup was done, we carried bowls and the tray of bread to the island and sat side by side to eat.

The silence was surprisingly companionable as we tucked in. I didn't feel any sort of compulsion to fill it with pointless babble. Crew was easy to be around. There were no frills about the man. So far as I could tell, he was a what-you-see-is-what-you-get kind of guy, but I also had a feeling there was more to him than met the eye.

When we finished, the tray of bread nothing but crumbs and our bowls practically licked clean, Crew wordlessly gathered our dishes and brought them to the sink, rinsing them before loading them into the dishwasher.

I added that to the mental list of things I liked about him. For all intents and purposes, he was a bachelor, but by the state of his home, you'd never know it. Everything was clean but cozy, not a thing out of place.

"Do you have a housekeeper or something?"

He glanced at me over his shoulder, brow creased, and despite having those gorgeous blue eyes focused wholly on me, I found myself instead distracted by the broad expanse of his back and the muscles shifting beneath his thin tee.

Living with this man would be a lesson in self-control.

"No, why?"

"Your house is…impressive. And very clean."

Crew hitched up a shoulder, drying his hands on a tea towel that he draped haphazardly over his shoulder before turning to face me fully, leaning his hips and palms against the counter behind him.

"My dad died when I was young," he began, and I gasped.

"I'm sorry."

He waved me off. "It's okay. It was a long time ago." Despite his nonchalance, his voice cracked a little bit, like the words were still hard to say out loud. "Mom was trying to raise this crazy brood of children, you know? Both Owen and Trey, my two oldest brothers, were gone by then, and Aria was a little girl, so Lane, the twins, and I picked up the slack where we could. Admittedly, we were hellions as we got older, but we did what we could to make her life as easy as possible at home."

There was a hauntedness that took over his expression as he spoke, and I hated how well I understood the emotions swirling within him behind it.

I understood that kind of loss all too well.

"What was it like growing up with so many siblings?"

"Loud," Crew said with a laugh. "And smelly."

I chuckled with him. "How old is your sister?"

"Twenty-four."

Almost the same age Lola had been when she died, though my sister would've been forty by now. Would she have a family of her own? Would I have a brother-in-law and nieces or nephews running around? All the what-ifs and what-could've-beens haunted me daily.

Oblivious to the fact that doing so pressed on an old wound, Crew asked, "Do you have any siblings?"

A pang echoed in my chest. I didn't blame him for the question, but I hated talking about it, hated how, after all these years, it still felt like my heart was being ripped out of my chest anytime she came up in conversation. I missed her more than I could ever accurately express, the pain similar to that of a phantom limb I'd never get back, but talking about her only made it worse.

I owed Crew something though, especially after he shared about his father, so I said, "I had a sister."

"Had?"

"She died." Then I choked on a disbelieving laugh. "In a fire, of all things."

Crew blinked slowly, as if filing this information away and fitting it into the picture he saw when he looked at me. Thankfully, there was no pity in his gaze, only assessment—like he was peeling back my layers to reach my soft center. Unearthing more of me until he found the woman I was buried beneath my hardened shells.

I didn't have the energy to be picked apart, though—not now, not ever—so I got to my feet and asked, "Is there somewhere I can spread out my files and get some work done?"

Crew gave his head a little shake as though coming back to the surface after falling into a trance. With a jerk of his chin, he led me down the hall to his office, the only other room I'd bothered to explore when I arrived yesterday besides the common areas and the guest bedroom.

One side of the space contained built-ins that housed a collection of books and framed photographs. They were painted a deep green that contrasted beautifully with the creamy color of the rest of the room. Along the opposite wall was a large wooden desk with an Apple monitor and a closed laptop resting in the center. A map of what appeared to be Dusk Valley hung beside it, random locations highlighted in red. A whiteboard next to it had random dates and notes that made no sense to me.

I moved closer, curious about the map.

"What is this?" I asked Crew.

"Dangerous buildings in town. The city has been working for years to demolish them and rebuild, but the townsfolk are stubborn about their tax dollars being used for something that doesn't directly benefit them. As a firefighter, I have to know where all of these buildings are in case we get called to a scene at one. It changes our approach."

"But why have it in your home?"

One corner of Crew's mouth twitched. "My job doesn't stop when I'm off shift, Aspen."

"Fair enough," I said, appreciating his dedication to keeping the people of Dusk Valley safe.

Then I returned my attention to the map.

Honestly, I had no idea what I was looking at. I hadn't spent enough time here to truly grasp the layout of the town and recognize landmarks in nothing but a line drawing, but I knew where my accident had occurred. My eyes traced the streets until I found the building.

"It had recently sold," Crew said suddenly, his words tickling the back of my neck. He'd moved closer without me realizing, standing over my right shoulder.

I tapped the map. "The…place?"

He hummed in agreement, knowing what I meant. "The owners of the shop relocated to a larger building on the other side of town."

"The place with the impound lot?"

"Yeah. They're the only shop in town unless you want to

drive the hour up to Boise, so they were able to expand. The structure of the old place was sound, but a purposely-set fire is a beast, especially with diesel fuel. Took us hours to knock it down after the roof collapsed."

His statement pulled me up short. "The fire was started by diesel?"

"You didn't know?"

I scoffed. "I'm only a vic. No one tells me anything."

I rotated slightly so I could look at Crew out of the corner of my eye, and his palm came up to cup and scratch at the back of his neck—a nervous gesture if I ever saw one.

The question was, what did he have to be nervous about?

"Are you sure we should be discussing this?" he asked.

Oh.

He was worried about hurting me, dredging up trauma I'd rather leave buried.

But I learned a long time ago that the only way around it was through it, and while nightmares plagued my sleep, I knew I'd survive this like I'd survived everything else life had thrown at me if I just kept moving.

"I'm going to keep chasing this fucker," I replied, a vehemence behind my words that surprised even me. "Don't sugar-coat anything for the sake of my feelings. This might be personal now, but I won't let that get in the way of doing my job."

Crew sighed, as if weighing his next words.

"Yes, the fire was started by diesel. When my crew and I entered the shop, there was a trail from the door that led me right to you. From the smell of it, we ultimately deduced diesel fuel was used."

"Have you managed to run down any leads?"

Crew shook his head. "Unfortunately, that's not my jurisdiction, and my brother isn't exactly the most forthcoming man on the planet."

I snorted. "Understatement of the century."

He grinned and said, "Let's grab your files and get you set up."

Wordlessly, I followed him out, and ten minutes later, I was set up in front of his desktop computer, the fire department's reports and my notes from the Vicky Lee and Roger Stanhope incidents spread out before me. As a firefighter, Crew had access to some government servers I didn't, and it allowed me to get a bit more background on the two than what Mrs. Lee and the newspapers could provide.

As a former journalist, this killer not being national news was a wonder. Being active for over forty years was…impressive, to say the least. I wasn't about to give the guy any props, but the fact that he'd managed to elude law enforcement for so long told me a number of things, namely that he was both highly intelligent and highly organized.

When I ran out of leads I could follow from the desk, and my eyes swam from staring too long at the computer screen, I got up, stretched, and headed to the guest room to change. After throwing on another pair of linen pants and a loose-fitting tee—my injuries wouldn't be able to handle tighter or rougher materials for a while yet—I went in search of Crew.

I called his name, but received no response. He wouldn't have left without telling me, so I strained my ears for any hint of him.

I felt more than heard bass pulsing through the floor. Moving around the living room and down the hall toward the mudroom, I followed the beat as it grew louder until I stood in front of a door open at the top of a descending staircase. The words became clear then, some old Breaking Benjamin song providing the backdrop to whatever Crew was doing down there.

The sight I found when I reached the bottom stole my breath.

Crew Lawless.

Shirtless.

Dripping sweat.

Pumping a barbell over his chest in time with the drumbeat of the song.

Mesmerized, I could only stand there like a creep and watch.

Fuck, he was glorious. Every inch of his body was honed and lined with strength. His biceps, shoulders, and pecs rippled deliciously with each movement. The muscles of his abdominals were carved out beautifully, and I counted eight before they flattened and disappeared into the waistband of his shorts, along with a thin trail of hair, the same shade as the dusting on his chest. I was gripped by the sudden urge to approach him, straddle his lap where his obliques cut into that sexy ass V at his hips, and lick him clean.

Shaking my head to clear those filthy images—ones I could never act on—I called his name.

He quickly racked the bar and sat up, huffing and puffing but eyes scanning me for any sign of danger or distress.

"Are you okay?"

"I'm fine. I was just coming to tell you I'm going to head into town."

"For what?" he asked, lifting a towel that rested at his bare feet, and—Jesus Christ, he worked out barefoot? Why the fuck was that so sexy?—used it to wipe his face.

"I want to go to the library and look through yearbooks and old editions of the newspaper. Get a better feel for the victims and what else was going on in town around the times they were murdered."

"Do you want company?" He stood, his chest level with my eyes. With a jolt, I noticed one of his nipples had a silver hoop glinting in it.

This man was a goddamn wet dream, and I had to start looking for other accommodations immediately. There was no way I had enough control to keep my hands to myself if I was forced to live with him for any length of time. Not when I'd been celibate for as long as I had.

My toys got the job done fine, thank you very much, but I knew even one night in bed with Crew Lawless would ruin me for anyone and anything else forever.

"No, I'm good," I said quickly. "I was thinking I'd stop at the store and pick up groceries before I came back? Restock what I used on the soup."

"You don't have to do—"

I cut him off before he could finish. "I want to. Just text me a list."

Then I hightailed it out of there before I did something we'd both regret.

***

THE DUSK VALLEY PUBLIC LIBRARY was a gorgeous brick building attached to the high school by an enclosed walkway. More spacious than I expected, the entire back half was dominated by a media lab that had study corrals, laptops people could check out for use, and a bank of desktop computers. Row and rows of books filled the front half, the shelves pristine white and open to allow plenty of airflow.

An older woman—mid-sixties, if I had to guess—sat behind the help desk wearing a sweater and skirt set in a soft pink shade that made her creamy skin appear like porcelain. A name tag pinned to her chest read *Ginny*.

"Hello dear," she said warmly when I approached. "What can I help you with?"

"I was hoping to look at microfiche of old newspaper articles."

"Are you looking for something specific?"

I nodded. "I'm Aspen McKay—" I began, ready to launch into my spiel of who I was and why I was there, but Ginny stopped me.

"Oh dear," she breathed. "I am so sorry for what happened to you."

"Thank you. So that's why I'm here. I'm looking into the case, and I was hoping to comb through old coverage on the previous incidents and victims. And I was also wondering if it'd be possible to look through old yearbooks dating back to the first victims."

Without a word, Ginny came around the counter and wrapped me into a warm, floral-scented hug. Inexplicably, my nose stung with the warning of tears, and I sniffed loudly as I hugged her back.

This sort of comfort was something I'd been sorely lacking in recent years, and it amazed me how much better such simple contact from another human being made me feel.

When she pulled back, she cupped my cheeks and said, "Whatever you need, dear. Follow me."

She led us into the media lab and over to an iMac in the corner. "This is where we keep all the *Gazette* issues," she said proudly as she pulled out the chair for me. "Dating all the way back to its conception in nineteen twenty."

A low, deeply impressed whistle escaped me. "That's incredible."

"It hadn't been easy," she said with a chuckle. "It took me probably ten years to track down every single issue, and another two for us to digitize them. But I'm very proud of the work we've done. Not many towns can say they have these kinds of records."

I nodded in agreement. "I used to work at the *Sun Times*, so I can say with certainty even big city papers aren't as meticulous as this."

Ginny positively beamed. "Get yourself settled, dear. Feel free to print anything you need. When you're done, I'll have those yearbooks waiting for you at that table over there," she promised, indicating a spot across the room.

"Thank you for your help, Ginny. I really appreciate it."

"Whatever it takes," she assured me. "I've lived in this town my whole life, and I'm tired of being afraid I might be next—or one of my daughters or granddaughters."

Then she disappeared, leaving me to my work.

From my backpack, I withdrew my notepad that had all the dates of the murders written down. Starting with the first back in 1985, I was greeted by the front page of the *Dusk Valley Gazette* with an impossible-to-miss headline.

PROM KING AND QUEEN BRUTALLY SLAIN

Accompanying the story was a photo of the car in which Vicky Lee and Roger Stanhope had died. It had been so badly burned, I couldn't discern the color or even the make and model. A quick scan of the article revealed it to be an AMC Pacer, and it had belonged to Roger. The car was a two-door compact, and Vicky and Roger had been found wrapped around each other in the back seat. I also knew from Crew that the two had sustained bullet wounds to the head which ultimately killed them.

Giving in to a brief shiver over the knowledge that this same person had their hands on me, could've easily ended *my* life, I printed the article and kept moving.

After that, the MO of the killer changed, first moving from the car—which I now recognized as a crime of opportunity—to house fires they tried to pass off as accidents, eventually graduating to abandoned commercial buildings. Seemingly random incidents save for a single similarity: they all happened on prom night.

There was something strange about that to me. Why would this person so obviously connect their crimes together when altering the date of their attacks would've kept the police off their trail entirely?

By the time I reviewed the coverage for the final victim before myself—Erica Hughes, murdered three years ago at the age of twenty when she'd been home from college for the weekend—a headache was building behind my eyes, and the sky beyond the windows of the library had turned hazy and golden. Checking my watch, I realized how late it had gotten.

Gathering my things, I headed back toward the information desk, where Ginny bustled around, preparing to lock up for the evening.

"I'm so sorry I made you get all those yearbooks out for nothing," I said sheepishly as I shifted my bag around in search of my wallet.

"It's really no problem dear. You can come back anytime. I'll set them aside so they're ready for when you do."

I took a ten out of my billfold and stuffed it into the tip jar. Though for her kindness alone, I owed her much more.

"Why are you being so nice to me?" I blurted.

The woman was already as grandmotherly as it got, her entire countenance softened further with my question.

"Everyone deserves a helping hand, dear. I'm sorry to hear the people of this town have been…shall we say, less than welcoming? But I promise, you'll find nothing but support here."

Before I could stop myself, I reached for her, hugging her as tightly as possible while mindful of her frailty. Something told me Ginny was stronger than she looked, though.

"I'll be back soon," I promised when I pulled away.

"I look forward to it."

Then I moved toward the exit. Thanks to my ordeal, I was more than a little wary about exiting buildings alone this close to nightfall. Sunlight still painted the horizon, but the shadows were lengthening, so I withdrew my taser from my bag as I crossed the lot to Black Betty.

I only relaxed fully when I was behind the wheel, doors locked and on my way back to Crew's.

sixteen

. . .

CREW

I WAS damn near climbing the walls by the time tires crunched on the drive. Rushing to the window, I breathed a sigh of relief when Aspen got out of her car. But I wasn't going to let her off the hook that easily, and I met her at the mudroom door, hands on my hips and a scowl on my face.

"Where have you been?"

Her forehead scrunched in confusion as she said, "I told you I was going to the library."

"You've been there the whole time?"

"Yes…"

"Aspen, you've been gone for like four hours, and you didn't text me to check in. I've been worried sick."

Her expression smoothed, and she tucked a lock of hair behind her ear, clearly uncomfortable. "I'm sorry. I was going through old news articles and lost track of time."

"I'm not begrudging you your job, but proof of life would've been nice."

"I'm sorry," she said again. "I'm used to working alone, but I'll be better next time."

My breath left me in a huff, and without thinking twice, I

closed the distance between us and pulled her into my arms, needing to feel her vitality against my skin.

I had no fucking idea what was happening with me, but whatever it was, I knew I wouldn't be okay if something happened to her.

Shockingly, she melted into me, her arms coming around my waist and fisting my tee. There was something so easy about it, something so…*perfect* about the way we fit together. Though she was over a foot shorter than me, I loved the way her head tucked under my chin, making it easy to rest there, to completely mold ourselves together.

Though she remained pressed against me, she tilted her head back to look up at me. All I would have to do was bend slightly to capture that gorgeous mouth with mine.

"What're we doing, Crew?" she whispered.

"I have no idea," I answered honestly. "All I know is I want to keep you safe."

"I can take care of myself," she reminded me.

"I know, but you shouldn't have to. Not all the time, anyway."

A shiver passed through her, almost like she'd been waiting a long time to have someone say that to her, and with it finally breathed into existence, she could shake off some of the weight she'd been carrying.

I'd carry it all for her if she let me.

Aspen's movements seemed reluctant as she peeled herself away from me. We both knew that sort of physical contact was a bad idea, and I was glad she'd been the one to break it.

I wasn't sure I could've ever let go, and I immediately mourned her loss. Mourned the warmth of her against me, the feeling of having someone—but especially *this* someone—wrapped in my arms again. My palms itched with the desire to haul her back in. It'd been a long damn time since I allowed myself any sort of intimacy, and I found myself ready to break all my rules for Aspen McKay.

There was a spark here, and I wanted to hold a piece of kindling to it and watch it ignite into an inferno.

"I didn't stop at the store. By the time I left the library, well… I didn't want to chance being out after dark," she admitted, avoiding my gaze.

"That's okay," I assured her, tucking a finger under her chin to tilt her face up for inspection. As expected, her cheeks were stained red. "And you don't have to be embarrassed. In fact, I appreciate your vigilance. I would've been even more mad had you risked it when you didn't feel safe."

"I never used to be afraid of the dark."

"And you're not now," I said. "You're rightly afraid of what lurks within the darkness because someone used it as a tool to hurt you."

She gave me a thin smile. "That's a good way to look at it."

I winked. "I'm full of good ideas."

Aspen huffed out a laugh, then kicked off her boots and followed me into the kitchen.

When she rounded the corner, she gasped.

"You can cook?" she asked, and I chuckled at the incredulity in her tone.

"Of course I can. I feed myself just fine, thank you very much. *And,*" I added as I led her to the dining table, where steaks, potatoes, and a tossed salad sat ready and waiting, "we take turns cooking at the firehouse when we're on shift."

Aspen took the chair I pulled out for her, a bemused expression on her face as she looked up at me. "And captains aren't exempt?"

"Hell no," I chuckled. "Especially not when I'm the best cook there."

"How?"

I moved around the table and sat across from her. "Lots of time in the kitchen with my mama growing up."

"Thank you," she breathed as I placed a sirloin on her plate. "But…what were you going to do if I didn't come home?"

Home. She'd only been here a few days, but I loved how easily that rolled from her lips. Clearly, she felt safe here, and internally, I puffed my chest out like I was the reason and not the simple fact that she had somewhere to stay at all—somewhere with, admittedly, an impressive civilian security system.

"I would've left all this shit here and gone looking for you," I answered bluntly.

Aspen hummed thoughtfully, though the skin of her cheeks turned bright pink beneath the dining room lights, and continued loading up her plate.

At least this time, the flush was from appreciation—I hoped.

Her movements were precise and confident as she cut off a piece of the steak and brought it to her mouth. I watched raptly as her lips closed around the fork, and a moan escaped her.

I felt that sound all the way to my cock, and I shifted uncomfortably in my seat, hand going to my crotch to adjust myself. Aspen, with her eyes closed, remained oblivious to the desire that was surely written all over my face.

Her eyes popped open, and she whispered a single word.

"Damn."

Yeah, I understood the sentiment. That was likely how I'd feel if I ever got to taste her sweet pu—

Cut it out, Crew.

"You can't help yourself, can you?" she said conversationally, and my brows pinched together in confusion.

Had I said something out loud?

"With cooking?" I asked dumbly. "I mean, no? I have to eat…"

Aspen giggled, a high, girlish sound I never would've expected from her, and shook her head. "No. Although, this is amazing. I mean the whole savior and protector thing."

I shrugged. "It *is* my job."

She leveled her fork at me. "I think there's more to it than that."

I hated how easily she pegged me, and while I'd never shared much of my story with anyone outside of my family, I felt like Aspen deserved to know at least some of it. After all, I'd seen her in her darkest moment. It seemed fair I reciprocated, if only to explain why I was the way I was.

"For lack of better phrasing, I was a bad kid. I finally started to turn myself around when someone sat me down and basically put the fear of God in me. That man gave me a second chance, and I owe him my life. Since then, I've made it my personal mission to pay it forward."

That person had been Lieutenant—now Chief—Madden, and I owed him everything. Chief had always hung out on the fringes of our family. Secretly, I thought he had a crush on my mom, but that woman would never move on from Dad as long as she lived. Eventually, Chief found a wonderful woman, married her, and had two kids of his own. But with Dad gone, and me going off the rails entirely once I started high school, he'd been there to pull me back from the ledge on more than one occasion. We had a running joke that I had been the trial run for when he had his own son to raise.

Everything I was—the man and firefighter I'd become—was thanks to him.

"You're a good man, Crew Lawless," Aspen said, and I relished the way my name fell from her lips. What a beautiful sound. "You saved my life, and I'll never be able to repay you for that."

"It was nothing," I said, the words coming out hoarse.

"Yeah, yeah," she replied, reaching for the bottle of wine I'd opened for her, "you were just doing your job."

I grinned, and she briefly returned it before focusing on pouring herself a glass then offering the bottle to me.

"Want some?" she asked, scanning the table for my glass.

She wouldn't find it.

I shook my head. "Nah. I don't drink."

A brow raised. "Ever?"

"Not anymore."

As if sensing something in my tone, Aspen wisely didn't press the issue.

I had no doubt I'd tell her someday, but today was not it.

That was a can of worms that needed to stay sealed for as long as possible.

AFTER DINNER, we retired to the living room. I turned on reruns of *Criminal Minds*, which was, unsurprisingly, Aspen's favorite show, while she brought me up to date on what she'd found at the library.

"There's not a lot in here that I didn't already know," she admitted, her tone edged with frustration as she shuffled through the printouts of old news articles. "But I was hoping you could take a look and see if anything jumps out at you."

I accepted the sheaf of papers. "Of course. And what about the yearbooks?"

"I didn't get a chance to go through them. Ginny was very helpful and said I could come back whenever I wanted, but she was getting ready to close by the time I finished with the newspaper stuff, so I didn't want to press my luck."

"Ginny still works there?"

"You know her?"

"It's a small town," I shrugged. "I know everyone. And she was the librarian when I was in school. She's basically a permanent fixture in that place."

"I'm a big fan of hers. She's the first—" She halted, eyes flicking up to me then back to her lap. "*Second*," she corrected, "person to show me any sort of kindness since I got here."

The realization that the townsfolk of Dusk Valley had given her such a hard time since her arrival—and after what she'd suffered at the hands of one of our residents—had a complex swirl of emotions taking up residence in my chest. Warmth, because she saw me as someone safe and sympathetic, someone who would go to bat for her, protect her. But also a pang of pain and guilt that the list of people willing to offer her a helping hand consisted of only two names.

"You'll always have a friend in me," I vowed.

Aspen's eyes met mine again, a small smile playing on her mouth as she took a sip of Cabernet, a bead of dark red liquid lingering on her bottom lip before she swiped it away with the tip of her tongue.

I hated how badly I wanted to be that droplet of wine.

Then she returned her glass to the table and said, "I was hoping you'd say that, because I need a favor, and friends do each other favors, right?"

I knew damn well she didn't mean it suggestively, but my brain took off like a wild horse, dredging up all kinds of ideas for what these *favors* would entail.

Every last one of them involved getting us both naked.

I marshaled myself enough to say, "I have a feeling I'm not going to like this."

She let out a little laugh, shaking her head. "I'm afraid not, hotshot."

I made an *out with it* gesture. "Lay it on me then."

"I need you to talk your brother into handing over the police reports from each incident."

I groaned. "It's not that simple."

"It really is," she argued. "As simple as asking the question. Pull the brother card. Call in an old debt."

"You obviously don't know the sheriff very well if you think pulling the brother card would work."

She giggled. "He is a bit of a hardass, isn't he?"

I quirked a brow. "A bit?"

"Fair," she said. "All I'm asking is that you try."

"I will, but…" Briefly, I went back and forth on whether or not to share Lane's early morning visit with her, ultimately deciding I didn't want to keep secrets and that she deserved to know. "You should know he stopped by here this morning because he found out you're staying with me."

"Damn, news travels fast."

"You have *no* idea," I grimaced. "But he basically told me I was an idiot for getting involved and that you'd be better off leaving town. I suggested he work *with* you instead of *against* you, but…"

"But he's a stubborn asshole," Aspen finished for me.

"Precisely."

"I'm prepared for him to say no. But we won't know unless we ask. Please, Crew," she begged. Inexplicably, a shot of adrenaline raced through my veins with the word, spoken so like that night in the fire when she was pleading with me to save her. I supposed for her, and for other residents of this town, whether or not Aspen got access to those files could be a life or death situation.

"I–I need this," she pressed on. "I need to help these families. Help *myself*. Find my strength again. Regain what I've lost."

My goddamn heart melted into a puddle. There was such pain in her eyes, such fear. Was it fear that whoever had done this to her was still out there, lurking in the shadows? Fear of failure? Fear of never being able to move past this, of forever feeling like a victim?

If I had to guess? Likely a combination of all three.

Reaching across the couch, I captured one of her hands in mine, squeezing it tightly for a few heartbeats before relaxing.

Our gazes collided and held.

"You *are* strong, Aspen. One of the strongest women I've ever met. You're like a literal goddamn phoenix, risen from the ashes of a fire. Made even stronger because you built yourself back up from the very thing that tried to take you down. Don't ever forget that."

Her eyes had gone glassy, and she offered me a watery smile, sniffing back tears before they could fall.

"Thank you," she whispered.

"Anytime. And I'll talk to Lane. I'll get you those files."

I'd do it too. Even if I had to break into the fucking department and steal them.

For her, I'd do whatever it took.

seventeen

. . .

CREW

IT TOOK a week for my brother and I to cross paths, and only because I pulled up to the station at the exact moment he walked outside one afternoon, making a point to wake up earlier than I normally would after spending the previous day on shift.

"Where are you going?" I asked as he came down the concrete path toward his cruiser.

"To interview a suspect."

He had that shifty countenance of someone who didn't want anyone—least of all me—asking too many questions, which is exactly why I continued to pry.

"In the arsonist case?"

"Yes," he gritted out.

"Perfect," I said happily, throwing myself into his passenger seat when he beeped the SUV open. "That's what I wanted to talk to you about, so I'll ride along."

Lane's sigh was exasperated, like I was the most infuriating person he'd ever come into contact with, but he got behind the wheel anyway.

"This isn't a fire department case."

"I disagree. Rooting out arsonists is part of the job description, big bro, and you won't find anyone in the county more qualified than me."

He grumbled but wisely didn't argue because he knew I was right. Chief Madden had some experience, but not as much as I'd gained working with the CFD.

"So where are we heading?"

Lane's teeth still ground together as he spat, "Chris Taal's place."

I blinked in surprise.

"He's still dealing?"

"Is the sky blue?"

I made a show of looking out the window.

"Yep."

"I've spent a lot of time over the last week going over the reports, and it seems my predecessors thought he was good for it but could never make anything stick. So I'm going to see if I can be the one to shake something loose."

"Like what? A confession? He's gotta be in his sixties now, Lane. Don't you think he would've come clean already if he was the guy?"

"I think that little weasel will do anything to save his own ass." He glanced pointedly at me. "Including throwing a seventeen-year-old under the bus."

I couldn't help wincing at the memory, but the blame for that incident couldn't rest strictly on Chris's shoulders.

I'd been there. Been an active participant.

But he'd made me the fall guy for the whole thing instead of taking responsibility for his role in it all.

That was the night everything changed for me, and if Chief Madden hadn't pulled me out of that twisted hunk of metal that had once been a car, talked some sense into me in the aftermath while I'd been laid up in the hospital with a shattered tibia, I wouldn't be having this conversation with Lane.

I likely wouldn't have made it to my eighteenth birthday

without that accident. Wrapping that car around a tree had been the best thing that ever happened to me.

Memories continued to plague me, anxiety rooting in my chest at the prospect of confronting this demon I thought I'd banished.

"Maybe it's a bad idea for me to come with…"

"Nah," Lane said, his blinker filling the space between us while he navigated through town, toward the trailer park. "I think it'll be good having you there. Might make him a little more forthcoming."

I snorted in disagreement but kept my mouth shut.

Once upon a time, Chris and I had been…*close*, in the way that all drug addicts were close with their dealers. Now, I doubted he'd recognize me. I was so far removed from that spiraling teenage boy, those events may as well have happened in a different lifetime.

Dusk Valley's trailer park, aptly named Mountain View Estates because it did afford residents a gorgeous backyard look at the lower peaks of the Owyhee Range, was a well-kept neighborhood. The people who lived there were mainly single parents who worked hard for their money as laborers, waitresses, and nurses.

On two streets perpendicular to the trailer park sat Dusk Valley's version of the slums. The rows of houses were rundown and falling apart, with broken furniture, vehicles that no longer ran, and other detritus littering the lawns.

Pulling up to Chris's shack—there really was no other word for the dilapidated two-story that leaned precariously to one side—was like stepping into a time warp that transported me back sixteen years to the very first time I'd been here. I knew without going inside that nothing had changed. The main floor was an open concept kitchen and living room, constructed before such things were fashionable mainly to cut costs on putting in more walls, and a small bathroom with an ancient clawfoot tub, overhead shower, and cracked toilet that somehow still ran. The upper level held the bedroom. Both the front and back yards were postage stamps that Chris kept clean, mostly to not give law enforcement any reason to come knocking at his door—even if they all knew what went on behind it.

The tick of the cooling engine after Lane turned the car off was damn near deafening as he waited for me to move.

I wasn't sure I could. Walking back in that house…there were inevitably things about a past version of me, the man Chris had known but who existed no longer, that would be thrown in my face. That would stir up all kinds of bad feelings and memories, both for me and my brother.

"I'm sorry," Lane said quietly. "You don't have to do this. I didn't really think it through, what it'd be like for you coming back here."

That was quite possibly the most sensitive and empathetic thing any of my brothers had ever said to me, and somehow, it gave me the courage to get the fuck out of the car.

Wordlessly, I opened the door and climbed out, and Lane followed my lead.

The grass out front was slightly overgrown along the path, brushing my boots and the hem of my jeans as we made our way toward the house. Lane climbed the two crumbling concrete steps and pounded on the peeling door, the damn thing so flimsy, a stiff wind could easily knock it down.

Beyond, footsteps creaked against the floor before the sounds of several locks, chains, and deadbolts disengaging reached us, the door cracking open a moment later.

I staggered back a step.

Even back in my wild youth, Chris hadn't been in the best shape, but the years since I'd last seen him had been even less kind than I anticipated. He was rail thin, his skin hanging off his bones, making him appear at least twenty years older than he actually was. His watery grey-blue eyes squinted into the harsh sunlight, sizing us up.

"The fuck you want, pig?" he asked my brother.

"Got a few questions about prom night, Mr. Taal. May we come in?"

Chris's gaze shifted to me, the fog seeming to lift momentarily.

"Well, well, well. Look who found himself on the right side of the law after all."

"I'm not a cop."

"Nah, but you still got the stink."

I rolled my eyes. *Whatever that meant.* "Can we come in or not?"

Chris shifted out of the way, opening the door wider as he went. "Be my guest."

Lane went ahead of me, and it took everything I had to lift my foot and place it down on the other side of that threshold, like I was crossing some invisible demarcation line between the old me, the life I'd left behind, and the one I lived now, which I'd worked my ass off to build for myself.

But now, I was stronger mentally. I wasn't some kid searching for any high that would take me from my reality, and this visit to the past wouldn't change that.

Chris's grin was positively feral as I moved past him, like a lion welcoming prey into its den. Little did he know, I was no longer a lamb.

The place hadn't changed a bit in the last fifteen years, other than falling even further into disrepair. I guaranteed I could walk into the kitchen and easily locate cups and bowls, silverware and plates.

The air was hazy with weed smoke, the pungent scent stuffing itself up my nostrils and burrowing deep so I knew I'd smell it for hours after we left. Despite the odor, there wasn't any paraphernalia lying around. I glanced at my brother. Sure enough, his eyes scanned the room with that cop's assessing gaze, searching for anything he could use to pinch this guy and at least bring him to the station for formal questioning. Chris had been at this for a long time though, and he wouldn't allow a random drive-by compromise his business. The house was littered with hidey-holes.

Chris was always high as a kite on weed, but he never dabbled in the harder stuff. Claimed it "muddled his senses." I snorted at the memory, and both heads snapped toward me.

"Somethin' funny, pig?"

"I'm not a cop," I said for the second time, kicking an empty beer can out of my way so I could wade deeper into the room.

"But I am," Lane said. "You mind if we ask you a few questions?"

"About what?"

"Prom night," my brother repeated.

Chris groaned. "Why is it when some bad shit goes down in this town, you people always think it's my fault?"

"Because you're the perfect suspect," my brother sneered, pointedly scanning Chris up and down.

"Not helping," I murmured.

Ignoring me, Lane cut straight to the chase.

"Where were you the Friday night before prom?"

Chris scrunched his eyes, clearly thinking hard. "Meeting a…*client* at the Swallow."

That pulled Lane up short, and he reached into his pants' pocket to withdraw his phone, the device emitting soft clicking sounds as he tapped around on the screen, pulling up a photo of Aspen. Then he held it up in front of Chris's face.

"Do you recognize this woman?"

Chris's expression never changed as he studied the photo. There was no spark of recognition, no fear that he'd been caught. Obviously, he had no idea who she was.

Unfortunately, he was already too stupid to play dumb.

Lane seemed to agree but continued to press anyway.

"What about the following evening, the night of prom?"

"Working."

"At the school."

"I am a janitor there, so yes, at the school. Cleaning up after all those little brats."

"Why would you be working *during* the dance?" I asked, chiming into the conversation for the first time. "Isn't that something you'd do the morning after?"

"Well, I uhh…" he sputtered dumbly, eyes darting everywhere but at me and Lane.

Huh, I thought, considering the abrupt change in demeanor. *Maybe not as stupid as I thought.*

"I uhh wasn't working, exactly," he continued, brushing his hand through the air and giving me and my brother a cocky little smirk like, *you know how it is*. "I forgot something in the office, so I swung by to get it."

"What exactly did you forget?" Lane asked.

"Uhh…my lighter."

Lane and I shared a look, both of us then sweeping the room, noting the multiple lighters strewn across multiple surfaces near half-smoked packs of cigarettes.

"You wanna try that again?"

As though his legs had given out, Chris collapsed into the armchair behind him, which creaked loud enough I was certain it'd fall apart right under him. Resting his elbows on his knees, he scrubbed a hand over the top of his shiny head. "Look, man, I didn't hurt no one. Sometimes, I go to the school when there are dances. You know, relive my glory days."

A disgusted sound came from deep in my throat at the same time my brother made a similar one.

"We've had numerous reports about you over the years, Mr. Taal. You creep the young girls out. And I've heard several rumors that you deal to those kids too. That's what you were really doing there that night, isn't it? Dealing."

Chris exploded out of his chair so fast, I barely saw him move. Next thing I knew, he was damn near nose to nose with the sheriff—or as close as he could be given Lane had a good five inches on him. Normally, the sight would make me laugh. This guy was a fucking loser, the scum on the bottom of society's shoe. My brother was a highly decorated police officer and the youngest sheriff this county had ever seen, not to mention twice as wide as Chris, his biceps as big around as the dealer's head.

Under normal circumstances, it would be no contest.

But apparently, Chris didn't like being called a creep, because he held a shiny silver knife to the underside of my brother's jaw, a crazed look in his eyes as he silently dared Lane to make a move.

In the end, I was the one who moved first, not even thinking as I threw myself at Chris and tackled him to the ground, flipping him face first into his rank ass carpet and driving my knee into the center of his back to keep him pinned.

By the time I'd collected his wrists and brought them together, Lane was holding his cuffs out to me, which I slapped on Chris and hauled him to his feet.

"I didn't do nothin', man! What the fuck!" he shouted as we marched him outside.

"You threatened a police officer with a knife, you dumb fuck," Lane said, shaking his head as if he couldn't believe the audacity of this guy. "*With a witness.*"

"Police brutality!" Chris shouted as I practically carried him across the lawn, his body going limp as he tried to halt our progress. "This is police brutality! Help!"

I snorted. He wouldn't find any assistance in this neighborhood.

"I'll remind you once again, Chris," I said as I stuffed him in the backseat of Lane's cruiser and bent close. "I'm not a fucking cop."

Chris continued to scream obscenities—at me, at Lane, at the goddamn government, at anything he could think of—once I slammed the door in his face.

When I faced my brother, his tattooed arms were crossed over his chest, an amused smile tipping the corners of his mouth.

"What's so funny?"

He tipped his head in Chris's direction.

"Bet that felt good."

The realization of what I'd done barreled into me, and I swayed slightly on my feet.

I'd helped arrest one of my abusers.

I wasn't a saint back then. The drugs, the booze, the sex—I'd been a willing participant in all of it.

But after I'd gotten out, and with the help of my therapist, I understood Chris had taken advantage of me. He'd preyed on my pain and used my naivete and the fact that I didn't have a legitimate father figure in my life to get close to me. Plainly put, Chris Taal was a predator, and I had been one of his victims. My brother was right, but *good* was a woefully inadequate way to describe how I felt in that moment.

Elated was more like it.

A wide grin stretched across my face, a matching one appearing on his as we got in the car and headed toward town.

When we arrived back at the station, Lane handed Chris off to a couple of deputies, but before he could follow them in, I held him back.

"I never did get to ask you what I came here for."

Lane's eyes narrowed. "You said it had something to do with this case?"

I nodded. "Aspen is hoping—actually, both of us are—that you'll give us a copy of the case files for review."

"Crew—" he started, clearly readying to deny me, but I held up a hand.

"It's the least you could do for trying to run her out of town."

At least he appeared chastened by the mention of his dick-headed actions. "She's a civilian."

"She's a PI," I corrected.

"She does have a pretty impressive closure record from the few cases I could find…"

"Ahh, so you finally ran a background check."

"Only so I could assure myself you weren't living with some sort of psychopath."

I rolled my eyes. "You're so goddamn dramatic. She's five-two and probably a hundred and twenty pounds soaking wet. She's not going to stab me in my sleep."

"It's exactly those types of women you gotta look out for. Especially ones with faces like hers. They're sirens waiting to lure you into the deep and drown you."

I snorted. Lane would know all about that.

"Whatever. Are you going to give us the files or not?"

My brother tapped his chin thoughtfully, pondering, leaving me hanging for long enough that I was about to storm off when he finally said, "Fine."

I eyed him suspiciously. "You mean it? You're actually going to help?"

He nodded. "Against my better judgement, yes. But I trust you. Those files don't leave your house once you take them to Aspen, got it? And lock them down when you're not home."

I held up three fingers like the Boy Scout I never was. "Scout's honor."

Lane cuffed me over the head. "You're such a little shit."

"You love me."

"God knows why." He turned to go, then paused. "Give me a day or so and I'll have a copy of everything we've got for you."

I saluted him. "Take your time. See you at dinner tomorrow?"

"Considering Mom would kill me if I missed it? Yeah, baby bro, I'll be there."

The mention of our mother had some puzzle pieces clicking together in my head, and I said, "Hey…she and Dad were in school around the same time as Vicky and Roger, right? Have you ever asked her about them?"

Lane's eyes widened in surprise. "Bring the girl to dinner. We'll tug on Mom's heartstrings a bit."

With a chuckle, I waved goodbye, and we headed in our separate directions. My mom didn't need any help in the emotionality department, but I could get on board with bringing Aspen to my ancestral home and introducing her to the whole family.

Inexplicably, the idea of Aspen meeting my mom and brothers didn't feel like a one-off. It felt…momentous. Like the start of something new and enduring.

The thought was pure insanity.

We barely knew each other.

She wasn't staying.

And yet…

I couldn't help hoping.

What a dangerous, silly emotion.

eighteen

. . .

ASPEN

CREW HAD BEEN GONE for hours, and I was beginning to understand his worry and anxiety when I'd lost myself at the library the week before, because I was a bundle of stress by the time I heard the garage door open later that afternoon.

I was about to get up from the desk in his office to greet him when my laptop pinged with an incoming email.

FROM: imwatchingu@email.com
TO: aspen@mckayinvestigates.com

SUBJECT: Can you help her?

The first is the key
Crowned the prom queen
Face forever locked in a scream
But who could the killer be?

A shiver sluiced down my spine like a trickle of ice water as I stared at the four lines, the words blurring together as my mind tumbled over possible explanations.

What did they mean?

Who were they from?

Were they…a clue?

Was someone trying to help me? Or was it merely a taunt?

"Aspen?"

Crew's voice came closer as he continued to call for me, though it sounded like a distant echo as the world spun out around me.

And then he appeared in the doorway, and everything snapped back into focus in time with me slamming my laptop shut.

"Hey you," he said, though the wariness in his eyes belied his warm greeting.

"Hey," I said quickly, practically leaping from the chair.

"You okay?" he asked, that shrewd blue gaze not missing a thing.

"Fine!" I said, both too quickly and too cheerfully.

I was so far from fine we weren't even in the same country, but I wasn't about to dump my shit on him. This man had already done more than enough for me; he didn't have to take on this creepy emailer either. Not to mention, the way I was trying —and failing—to deal with my trauma. Somehow, though, being near Crew settled everything for me, made it easier to think and to move forward. Already, the tension in my body eased.

"Are you sure? You're acting kind of weird…"

"I'm sure, Crew. You don't know me well enough to know if I'm acting weird or not," I gritted out, immediately regretting the tone when he blinked in surprise and yielded a step, as though I'd slapped him.

I couldn't take the words back though, especially because they weren't even a lie. Letting me sleep under a roof didn't give him the right to…hover. I had my very own helicopter parents for that.

Parents I wasn't currently speaking to for that exact reason.

"Sorry," he said, raising his hands in surrender. "Just checking."

I sighed roughly through my nose and squeezed my eyes shut for a beat, willing myself to calm down.

"Where have you been?" I asked, scanning his face. His expression was tight, lips flattened into a thin line, the normally clear blue of his eyes hardened. "Are *you* okay?"

"I'm fine. I was with Lane. I went to go ask him about those case files and ended up riding along to a suspect interview."

Instantly, I perked up. "For this case?"

He nodded. "Drug dealer named Chris Taal. He's a janitor at the school and has been long enough that he would've been around the night Vicky and Roger were murdered."

"And?" I prompted, practically vibrating now, my mood doing an impressive one-eighty, cryptic email momentarily forgotten.

"Decades of cops seem to think he's good for it, but they've never been able to pin him down. The interview was kind of a bust, but he ended up holding a knife to my brother's neck, so at least Lane can hold him on that for a while."

"Holy shit," I breathed. "Is Lane okay?"

That was the first time I'd called his brother by his given name instead of "Sheriff," and it felt funny on my tongue. Like I was doing something I shouldn't be—like I was claiming an intimacy between me, this man, and the members of his family. I wasn't sure I deserved it, or that there'd ever be anything between us beyond working this case together, but I couldn't deny how much I liked it. Like Crew and I were discussing the daily happenings in our lives instead of talking through the first interview in a murder investigation.

Crew snorted, oblivious to my mental gymnastics. "He's fine. My big brother is invincible."

"I want to talk to this guy."

"No," Crew said quickly, and I met his eyes quick enough to see what looked like fear pass across his face, there and gone so fast I wasn't entirely sure it'd been real.

"What do you mean, 'no'?"

"I mean, no, you can't. He's in police custody, where he'll likely stay for a while. Maybe when he's out, but…he's a bad guy, Aspen. A long-time drug dealer who associates with the bottom dwellers of this town. I don't want you anywhere near him if I can help it."

My blood pressure rose instantly.

"That's not your decision to make. I need to interview him for my own investigation, and I'll do so with or without your permission."

"Aspen…"

"No," I said, backing away from him, down the hall and toward the guest room. I could feel the walls closing in around me, suffocating me. I thought Crew had been doing me a favor by giving me a place to stay, and that he understood the kind of woman I was—the kind who could stand on her own two feet. But maybe I'd been wrong.

Him standing in my way now combined with the email had my hackles raised, and the urge to *run* flooded every one of my senses until I could barely think or breathe around the desire. "You don't get to make those kinds of decisions for me. You don't get to make *any* decisions for me. Maybe this was a bad idea."

Crew frowned, the corners of his mouth turned down, bottom lip jutting out slightly.

The expression shouldn't have been sexy, but I'd be damned if I didn't want to pull that lip between my teeth, or feel that mouth glide across my skin.

What a conundrum I'd found myself in. Unwilling and,

honestly, unable to let this man care for me how he wanted, yet wanting to rip his clothes off and ride him into the sunset every time I looked at him.

The duality of women, ladies and gents.

I really needed to find a fucking therapist.

"What was a bad idea, Aspen?"

"Me moving in here. Maybe I should go."

Without another word, I retreated into my room, though I didn't bother to shut the door, knowing he'd follow me. This was his house, after all.

Before I could get too deep inside, he caught my wrist and jerked me back, spinning me to face him and pinning me against the nearest wall.

Like two puzzle pieces slotting together, our bodies aligned perfectly, his thigh parting my legs, the tips of my breasts brushing his upper abdomen, right below those juicy pecs. His hands came up to rest on either side of me, completely caging me in.

Fuck, I liked it.

Loved it, in fact.

Loved the heat flaring in his eyes, turning them the ice blue of a white hot flame. Loved the way his jaw muscles fluttered as he ground his teeth together, his entire body vibrating with the final shreds of his self-control.

I knew because I felt it. Not because of his rapid breathing or pulse jumping at the base of his strong, sexy neck, but because I felt the same.

There was a bed *right* there.

I wanted to give in to this push and pull, and I was confident he did as well. But that was a terrible idea for so many reasons. We both knew that.

Still, he seemed content to play with fire, because he leaned closer, the tip of his nose brushing against my hair as he brought his mouth to my ear.

"You're not leaving."

"You can't stop me," I said on a breathy exhale.

"Fucking watch me, Aspen."

"What're you going to do, tie me up? Been there, done that, got the scars to prove it."

Crew wasn't cowed by the reminder of what I'd endured. And God, I appreciated that so much—was deeply pleased by the fact that he didn't treat me like a victim. That he didn't act like I was made of glass and could easily break at any moment.

The dichotomy between him wanting to take care of me and knowing I could take care of myself made my head spin—much like his proximity.

He bent closer, his lips brushing the shell of my ear, as he said, "Only if you ask nicely."

An entirely different kind of shiver raced down my spine, and I sucked in a breath that had him chuckling darkly.

"Pass."

I barely managed to choke out the word, and it tasted thirty different types of *wrong*. We both knew under the right circumstances, I'd climb this man like a fucking tree. If I molded our bodies tighter together, Crew would take that as the invitation it would be. I'd find myself naked and on my back in seconds.

He shifted away, only far enough to bring his face in front of mine, our lips nearly pressing together, more the suggestion of touch than actual contact, his breath fanning over my mouth when he spoke.

"One day," he said, his words a sensual promise that skittered across my skin. "One day you'll give in."

And then he pushed off the wall and disappeared, leaving me with a swirling mind and wet panties.

Only to return a moment later.

"Before you distracted me," he said, leaning in the door frame with those beefy arms folded over his chest and legs crossed at the ankle, "I was coming to invite you to dinner at my mom's house."

My heart rate kicked up for an entirely different reason.

Poorly, I attempted to play it off, to act like a hoard of butterflies hadn't taken up residence in my stomach.

"You want me to meet the family? Moving awfully fast, hotshot."

Crew smirked, those blue eyes flaring, the tension from before bleeding away, only to be replaced with a different sort of charged energy between us.

Vague talk of sex was one thing. Introducing me to his family in *any* sort of capacity was entirely different.

"My mom was in school with Vicky and Roger," he explained. "Lane and I thought it might be a good idea to pick her brain about them and their friends and everything else going on around town when they died."

"That's…genius."

"I do have good ideas on occasion," he said. "We do family dinner once a week, which happens to be tomorrow night. We'll leave about five thirty, so make sure you're ready by then."

I gave him a mock salute, and he left me to my own devices.

"SO WHAT EXACTLY SHOULD I EXPECT?" I asked from the passenger seat of Crew's truck the next day.

The thing was so large, I had to use the running boards and leverage myself with the *oh shit* handle to get inside. I hissed through my teeth as the strain pulled on my burn marks. They bothered me a lot less lately, but the skin wasn't anywhere near fully healed.

My face heated as my mind flashed back to the last time I'd been in it—when Crew made me drive it home. I could still feel the ghosts of his hands on my hips, the way adrenaline had spiked my bloodstream at his touch. Everything about the man elicited a reaction from me on some chemical level I couldn't control if I tried. Simply sitting beside him now, with only the center console separating us, had my internal temperature rising. His scent filled the cab, masculine and fire smoke, until I couldn't take a breath of Crew-free air.

God, I was in a bad way. Maybe the attraction wouldn't be so strong if I had gotten laid sometime in the last five years.

Having forgotten I'd asked a question, lost in a thousand-yard stare locked on his gorgeous, broad hands, his voice startled me.

"Well, my whole family will be there. Mom always makes an impressive spread, despite the fact that she cooks breakfast for the ranch hands every day. We always tell her she doesn't have to go through the trouble, but she says she likes doing it because it gives us an excuse to all be together, and because then she knows we're at least getting one home-cooked meal a week."

"That's sweet," I said absently, mind turning to my own family as endless fields passed by the window. We sped down a gravel road, rolling right up to the foothills of the mountain range that bracketed the town.

I hadn't heard either of my parents' voices since the call the day I got out of the hospital. Surprisingly, my mother had respected my wishes for space. Dad, on the other hand, had taken to texting me periodically, something he'd *never* done before. Telling me he loved me, he missed me, and he hoped I was doing okay. I assured him I was but didn't go any deeper than that. I wasn't about to put him in the middle of my shit with Mom.

Now that I'd had a little time to cool off, I could—grudgingly —see where she'd been coming from, and I could understand their desire to want to take some of the burden off my shoulders after everything I'd been through. But maybe this reckoning was the best thing to happen for us. Maybe now, she'd give up her quest to dictate my life and bring me back to Chicago.

I hadn't been back for years, with good reason. There were too many memories there for me, and not only the ones that featured my big sister.

Even growing up, though, with only the four of us, and seven years between me and Lola, we rarely had consistent, sit-down family meals. We were at very different stages of our lives, Lola with her school extracurriculars and me devoting myself entirely to making a career out of dancing.

That all changed the day she died, and I hadn't danced since. After her loss, I couldn't bring myself to do the things that had once brought me joy any longer, not when she'd never get that chance for herself again.

Maybe, in a way, I'd been punishing myself.

Maybe I still was. Leading this quiet, solitary existence was my way of atoning for living when she hadn't.

Thoughts of the past floated away on the breeze when Crew rolled the windows down as we approached a gate leading down a long gravel drive. Two logs as big around as telephone poles stood sentinel on either side while another rested across them, a dangling, shiny metal sign that read "Lawless Rescue & Dude Ranch" swaying in the wind.

"A rescue *and* dude ranch?" I asked. "How is that even possible?"

Crew chuckled. "We've got a lot of land, for starters."

"How much is 'a lot'?"

"About a hundred thousand acres."

I whistled low. "Damn. And how long has it been in the family?"

"Since the mid-eighteen hundreds."

I gaped at the vast expanse surrounding us as we rolled down the drive. I couldn't imagine this kind of legacy. Sure, both of my parents had grown up in Chicago, but that wasn't the same as a single family working this exact land for nearly two hundred years.

"How come you didn't join the family business?"

He shrugged. "Never wanted to. And that's the great thing about my parents. They encouraged us to do whatever we wanted instead of making us feel obligated to work this land like our ancestors."

"Did any of you stick around the ranch then?"

"Finn and West. The twins," he added when my forehead pinched in confusion. Honestly, there were so many of them and I had no frame of reference for anyone outside of him and Lane at this point, seeing as they were the only two I'd met.

Although, I supposed that was about to change.

"So do they handle all of it together, or…"

"Nah," Crew said, guiding us around a bend. "Finn handles the rescue side of things, and West manages the dude ranch. But they both work with the animals we use for byproducts."

"Byproducts as in…meat?"

"We stopped slaughtering animals a long time ago, about the time my dad took over. After growing up here when it had been a working cattle ranch, he couldn't stomach it anymore. Thankfully, that happened before any of us came along, so this is all we've ever known. We have dairy cows, chickens for eggs, and goats for cheese."

"Quite the operation."

"Dad did an incredible job building a solid foundation for us, and when he died, it ran relatively smoothly for years until Finn and West settled down and started the rescue and dude ranches."

I found myself hanging on every word as he described growing up here, running amok through the fields with his five older brothers, learning to ride horses and milk cows, rock climbing on the sheer cliff faces and jumping from the top into the random lakes that dotted the property.

Before long, we pulled up to the most gorgeous house I'd ever seen. Standing two stories tall, it featured white clapboard siding, the bottom three or so feet accented with smooth, medium-sized river rocks ranging in color from dark grey to light beige. The entire front facade consisted of windows, and I could imagine they let in a ton of natural light—especially with nothing to obstruct the view, though towering maple trees dotted the surrounding yard, providing some shade.

On the opposite side of the driveway, the land gently sloped away to barns and corrals in the distance. Horses and ranch hands moved around outside. There was a white, low slung barn and a taller red one. In the fields beyond, cows grazed.

Crew took a deep breath as he turned the engine off and looked at me.

"You ready?"

I quirked a brow. "You worried?"

"I love them," he said, flicking his gaze toward the house. I followed to see a woman emerge, her grey-blonde hair piled into a messy yet stylish bun atop her head. She wore a bright red apron overtop jeans and a simple tee, a matching dish towel slung over her shoulder, and a wide grin. Crew groaned and finished, "But they're a lot."

"I'm sure they're amazing," I said, reaching over and squeezing his hand. We lingered in that touch for a moment before I gave his fingers a final pulse, let go to unbuckle, and hopped out of the truck.

nineteen

. . .

ASPEN

"YOU MUST BE ASPEN!" the woman crowed as she hurried down the white-washed steps of the wraparound porch to greet me.

"I am," I said, thrusting my hand out. The woman—who could only be the Lawless matron—swatted it away and drew me in for a hug. Everything about her was warm, from her skin to her scent to her voice.

I loved her immediately.

When she retreated, though her hands rested gently on my upper arms, I said, "It's great to meet you, Mrs. Lawless."

She waved me off. "Please, call me Birdie. All my friends do," she added with a wink.

"Hey, Mama," Crew said as he rounded the front of the truck.

"Baby boy," she said softly, letting me go to greet her youngest son.

The size difference between the two was comical. If I had to guess, Birdie couldn't have been more than a few inches taller than me, which meant Crew had an entire foot on her. Still, he bent low and wrapped his arms around her waist, scooping her up and swinging her around. By the time he returned her to her feet, she was red-faced and laughing, though she swatted at him with her towel.

"I'm too old for that shit," Birdie gasped.

Crew grinned. "No such thing, Mama."

"Well, c'mon then. You two are the first ones here, which means you can help me set the table."

Birdie bounded up the steps with a hell of a lot of energy for a woman who had to at least be in her sixties, and Crew crossed over to me, muttering, "Lucky us," as he took my hand and led me inside.

I couldn't find it in myself to pull away. It seemed as though we'd crossed some sort of boundary last night, and casual touches were now encouraged. I didn't mind one bit, loved the sense of belonging it gave me to have his rough, calloused palm against mine. Holding me down. Keeping me safe.

The exterior of the house was stunning, but the interior was even more breathtaking.

The ceilings of the entrance soared, a catwalk bridging the two sides of the second floor. The walls of the foyer were lined with hooks and cubbies where the kids must've once hung their coats and stored their filthy boots in all seasons. Straight ahead was a narrow hallway, off to the left an archway that led to a stunning formal dining room, and to the right was an ascending staircase with a living space beyond. A gas fire burned in the hearth, and I flinched, tensing at the sight.

Crew caught on quickly and paced across to a dial on the wall, extinguishing the flames.

Birdie's hand flew to her chest. "I'm so sorry, Aspen. I wasn't thinking."

"It's okay," I said with a weak smile. "Just…unexpected."

I wasn't sure the day would come where I wasn't terrified of an open flame. Trapped safely behind the grate of the Lawlesses' hearth, logically, I knew it couldn't hurt me. But even the mere suggestion of fire brought too many memories to the forefront of my brain, dousing me in panic for a threat that didn't exist.

Her eyes remained locked on me for another heartbeat before she nodded and turned on her heel, leading us to the left.

"I can't believe you grew up here," I hissed at Crew as we followed her past the long dining table and through a swinging, saloon-style door into an equally impressive kitchen.

Honestly, what the fuck? This place looked like the set of some cozy western television show about the trials and tribulations of a big fictional family.

On second thought, that was exactly what this place was, only there was nothing fictional about it. This family had celebrated wins and mourned losses together within the walls of this home. They'd laughed and cried, argued and loved. I could practically see the messy boys racing through the foyer, Birdie yelling at them to kick off their dirty boots and bring their filthy clothes to the laundry room. I bet it had been loud and so full of life—a stark contrast to the tomb my own home had become after my sister died.

"It didn't always look like this," Crew snorted, once again pulling me from my inner turmoil. "We expanded right around the time Owen signed his first brand deal."

"Which one is Owen?"

"The oldest," Birdie supplied, picking up a heaping platter of what appeared to be pulled pork. "And the reason we survived losing Jase."

I shot Crew a quizzical expression.

"Jase was my dad," he supplied, then he murmured that he'd explain the rest later, picking up a tray of rolls that had been cut open. I grabbed a bowl of salad and followed him and Birdie into another room off the back of the kitchen.

Clearly, this was where the real, ordinary family meals took place. The center of the narrow room was dominated by a long oak table flanked down each side by two benches. The wood was heavily scarred with nicks, dents, and scratches. Some burn marks even marred its surface. Pot holders sat waiting for food, and several places were set with plates, silverware, and glasses.

The ceilings in here were lower, though still plenty high in deference to Crew's height. After having met Lane, I had to assume each of his brothers were equally as tall, and I had to wonder about the baby sister. Did she get the literal short end of the stick like her mother, or would she tower over me too?

"Ma?" someone called.

Birdie's head whipped toward the door before she checked her watch.

"Ah, that'll be the twins."

"Both of them?" I asked, wiping my suddenly clammy palms on my jeans. They were the nicest pair I owned—unless you counted the frilly wardrobe my mom bought me in Boise. Dark-washed and tight enough to give me the appearance of curves. I had worn one of the tops Mom got, though, because it seemed perfect for the occasion: a gauzy, pale blue blouse with cap sleeves that fluttered against my deltoids and a lacy hem that hit the waistband of my jeans. When I'd stepped out of my room earlier and Crew studied me, his eyes had darkened in that way I was coming to associate with desire—or rage, but the circumstances obviously had me leaning toward the former—telling me I'd done well.

"Baptism by fire," Crew said, then winced. "Shit, sorry."

The stricken look on his face had me chuckling. "It's fine, hotshot. Phoenix risen from the ashes, remember?"

His shoulders relaxed, and he reached up to tuck my hair behind my ear, fingertips lingering on the piercings lining the shell. I'd been forced to take them out while in the hospital—actually, the emergency staff had done it for me—and putting them all back in a few days ago had been cathartic, going a long way to making me feel like my old self again.

"Well then, little phoenix"—he shifted away and turned sideways, gesturing grandly for me to go ahead of him—"into the flames you go."

Squaring my shoulders, I marched back into the kitchen… and immediately pulled up short.

Jesus Christ, did all the men in this family look like models?

The twins were…well, I didn't exactly have words for it, but suffice it to say I wouldn't have been surprised to find them starring in Calvin Klein commercials and posing on the covers of magazines instead of running a ranch in western Idaho.

Crew was handsome in a rugged sort of way, which was generally the type of male attractiveness I gravitated toward.

Finn and West—I had no idea which was which at this point —were beautiful. One of them had his hair shorn closer around his ears while the rest was longer, sort of like a toned down mullet that I had to admit was sexy as hell. The other's hair brushed the tops of his broad shoulders. Standing side by side, they were clearly identical, both of their mouths stretched wide in matching grins as I approached.

Birdie pointed a wooden serving spoon at them before she dug it into a dish of delicious-smelling macaroni and cheese and lifted it off the counter.

"Be nice to our guest, heathens."

Ignoring their mother, the one with shorter hair stepped forward, hand extended. "Finn Lawless, ma'am. Gotta assume you're Aspen."

"I am," I said, accepting his handshake. Pulses of electricity didn't race up my arm like they had the first time Crew and I touched—and every time since. All I felt was a weird, familial sort of warmth.

Finn released me and moved back so his twin could greet me.

West, apparently, wasn't nearly as formal, because he bent down and swept me right off my feet in a hug so tight, my back cracked. But again, I experienced no unwanted emotions beyond the same inexplicable and immediate fondness I felt for Finn.

The easy display of affection was jarring—but not unwelcome—for someone as touch starved as me, though I did hiss through my teeth when his arm banded across the middle of my burns.

"Shit, I'm sorry," he said, hastily setting me back on my feet. "I'm a hugger."

I gave him a smile I hoped conveyed it wasn't a big deal, despite my side throbbing slightly.

"It's okay," I assured him. "I'll live."

West nodded like he understood. "You've been through worse."

A short chuckle left me. "Understatement of the century." Glancing between the twins, I added, "Well, I'll admit I wasn't sure what to expect, but it certainly wasn't *that*."

"What *did* you expect?" Finn asked, raising a brow, eyes darting between me and Crew.

"Not all of my brothers are assholes," Crew gritted out, and I glanced at him to find his arms crossed over his chest, eyes narrowed at the twins, that muscle in his jaw jumping as he ground his teeth together.

Was he…*jealous*?

The idea sent a thrill through me, and I grinned knowingly at him. He continued to pout.

"Let me guess," Finn started, sharing a look with West. In unison, they finished: "Lane."

"Someone say my name?"

Speak of the devil…

I didn't recognize him at first in his civilian clothing, and it took me a beat to connect the voice to his face.

"Sheriff," I greeted.

"Miss McKay," he replied, tipping a proverbial hat. "Good to see you."

I snorted, and Crew said, "Don't act all welcoming now, asshat."

West rubbed his hands together excitedly. "What did our esteemed sheriff do this time?"

"Tried to run me out of town," I said flatly, eyes narrowed on Lane.

"You did *what?*" Birdie gasped, choosing that moment to re-enter the room.

"Oh, you're in for it now," Crew whispered as Birdie approached, stopping toe-to-toe with Lane and somehow managing to look down her nose at him despite the height difference.

God, I wanted to be her when I grew up.

"Lane Roderick Lawless," Birdie said, punctuating each of his names with a finger to the chest. I doubted he felt it through his thick muscles, but it had to be embarrassing to be reprimanded by your mom like you were a child.

"Oh shit," Finn hissed. "She full-named him."

"Need us to get the shovels, Mama?" West asked. "I've had the perfect spot to bury him picked out for years."

The guys snickered as Birdie, ignoring their commentary, demanded Lane explain himself.

"I asked her to leave," he said at last, his eyes darting everywhere but at his mother.

"No," I corrected. "You made it impossible for me to stay by blacklisting me at every hotel, motel, and short-term rental in the entire county."

Birdie let out a disgusted sound and turned away from Lane, like she couldn't stand to look at him. "I thought I raised you better than that."

"I was trying to protect her!" Lane shouted.

"That's not your call to make," I shot back.

"So that's how she ended up staying with you," Birdie said to Crew.

"Yep," he said proudly.

"Good boy. You get an extra piece of pie after dinner. You can have Lane's."

"What?" Lane sputtered. "C'mon, Mama. That's cruel and unusual punishment."

Birdie whirled on him and planted her hands on her hips. "A punishment befitting the crime, my boy. Now grab those beans and get your ass to the table."

Lane hung his head and mumbled, "Yes, ma'am," as he did what he was told, his brothers' laughter following him out of the room.

I moved after them, but Crew caught my wrist and pulled me back. When I faced him, his eyes darted between mine, concerning shining in them. "You okay?"

"I'm great," I answered, giving him an honest smile.

And I meant it. These people—they didn't know me. As far as they were concerned, I was nothing more than an interloper. On the surface, it probably looked like I was taking advantage of Crew's obvious kindness and that deep-seated sense of protectiveness he felt over everyone and everything around him.

Still, they welcomed me with open arms, easily folded me into the family like I belonged there.

I hated how much I loved it, how much I wanted this fantasy of a life at Crew's side I was stupidly building in my head to become a reality.

After a few more trips, Birdie's feast was laid out before us on the table, and the twins immediately grabbed their plates and began loading them up.

"Shouldn't we wait for everyone else?" I whispered to Crew.

"Nah," he said, handing me my plate before lifting his own. "They'll serve themselves up when they get here."

No sooner had the words left his mouth than did another man come strolling through the door, rounding to the opposite bench from the seats Crew had selected for us.

There were only two brothers I had yet to meet, so I took a stab in the dark.

"Owen?"

The man laughed, then winced. "Christ, do I look that old? Nah, honey. I'm Trey."

"Don't call her that," Crew snapped.

"Why not, baby bro?" Trey asked, shit-eating grin on his gorgeous face.

Yeah, *gorgeous*. I mentioned all these men looked like models, right? Even the asshole, Lane.

"Because she's not your honey."

"How about we stop talking about me like I'm not right here?" I said sweetly, though I glared daggers at Crew, who held up a hand in surrender.

"Got him on a tight leash already," Trey said, holding out his fist for a bump. I ignored it.

"I can take care of myself."

Fucking hell, I was getting tired of repeating those words to the men of this family.

Trey nodded. "I don't doubt that, *honey*."

Crew's plate fell to the table, the tower of green beans tipping to the side and spilling over as he jerked like he was going to leap across and throttle his brother.

I had no doubt he could take him. Height wise, they were evenly matched, but Trey was leaner than Crew. Muscular, but in a slimmed down way.

Still, I placed a hand on Crew's forearm, and he stilled.

"Relax," I whispered. "It's not that big of a deal. I'm fine."

His eyes met mine, those blue depths darkened in anger. "You sure?"

"Positive. Let's just enjoy this meal."

He gave me a curt nod and dropped onto the bench, patting it for me to join him.

"So where is Owen?" I asked.

"Michigan," Finn said around a mouthful of pulled pork.

My brow furrowed as I glanced at Crew.

Taking a big gulp of water, he said, "Owen used to play professional football for the Detroit Mustangs."

"Holy shit," I breathed.

As a born and bred Chicago girl, I'd grown up going to Chicago Grizzlies games with my family.

The Mustangs were a division rival of Chicago in the NFC North, and for nearly a decade, we'd been plagued by two losses a year at their hands.

All thanks to their star quarterback, who never once lost a game against us.

Owen Lawless.

As though he'd seen the light bulbs illuminate in my brain, Crew grinned and nodded.

"That's my big brother."

My God, this family was impressive.

"Anyway," Trey said, picking up the thread for Crew. "Once he retired, he decided to stay in Michigan. Bought a club up in the northern part of the state, remodeled and opened it, and has continued to expand his business empire there. He got married last November, and his wife is pregnant with their first child."

"I'm planning on flying out there for a month or so in the fall, once the baby is born," Birdie said proudly. "My first grandbaby."

Happy tears lined her eyes, and my heart swelled with emotion.

"That baby is lucky as hell to have so many uncles," I said hoarsely.

"And aunts," Lane piped up. "Delia, our sister-in-law, has four sisters of her own."

"And you can't forget yours!" a feminine voice called from the doorway, and a young woman came bounding into the room.

"We could never forget you, baby Ari," West cooed.

So *this* was Aria.

Well, any hopes I had of her being on my level height wise immediately went out the window. She was tall and lithe, her hair a long, wavy blonde curtain that swished around her shoulders, brighter than her brothers' sandier shades. But the eyes were the same, as was the smile. I'd seen variations of it on all the faces in this room.

"Where were you, young lady?" Birdie asked.

"Grooming Scamp," Aria said, not bothering to look at her mother as she dished food onto her plate.

"All afternoon?"

Aria giggled. "Don't be silly, Mama. Of course not. First, we took a ride."

Six near-identical groans filled the air over the table, and the men began to talk over each other, scolding their baby sister, before Birdie silenced them all with a hand raised.

"We've told you a thousand times not to ride alone, honey."

Aria rolled her eyes. "I'm twenty-four, Mom, not a baby anymore. And I know this land like the back of my hand."

"That doesn't mean shit," West said. "You could've gotten hurt, and you know there's hardly any cell signal out there."

"Please. I've been riding Scamp since I was a kid. I know how to handle her."

"There's also a killer out there, Ari," Crew said quietly from beside me.

The reminder of what had happened to me, and twelve other people sobered Aria quickly.

"I won't do it again," Aria replied quickly. "Promise."

Crew nodded and reached behind me to give her shoulder a squeeze. "Thank you."

My attention had been so wholly focused on Aria during the exchange that when I returned my gaze to the table at large, I was surprised to find all eyes on me.

"We're real sorry for what happened to you, Aspen," Finn murmured.

"Thank you."

"Speaking of…" Lane started, and the whole table groaned.

"You know the rules, Lane," Birdie reminded him, and I had to assume she meant they weren't allowed to talk business at the table. "You're already on thin ice as it is."

"Fine. After dinner then."

After dinner, I thought. *Hopefully then I will have some answers.*

twenty

. . .

CREW

TRUE TO FORM, I was disgustingly full by the time we finished eating dinner—though I made sure to save enough room for both my and Lane's pieces of Mama's apple pie. I made a real nice show of vocally enjoying it while my brother looked on petulantly, a grimace tilting his lips down and murder in his eyes.

The best piece of pie I'd ever had.

After we cleared the table and helped Mama load the dishwasher, Aria disappeared upstairs, and Finn and West headed out to their respective homes on the property.

That left me, Mama, Lane, Trey, and of course, Aspen to enjoy a nightcap—with ulterior motives.

I'd been unsure about tonight, mainly because I knew how exhausting my family could be, and I was worried Aspen would run screaming in the opposite direction as they all started filtering into the house.

But she continued to surprise me.

She held her ground with all of my brothers, and spent most of dinner in deep conversation with Aria about music, which happened to be my sister's favorite topic.

Though we told her several times that guests didn't help with

170

cleanup, she refused to listen, up to her elbows in soapy water alongside my mom as they cleaned the dishes that had to be hand washed.

Then we retired to the den. With Aspen's permission, we turned the gas fireplace back on, dispelling the chill that tended to set in this time of year once the sun went down.

"I know Finn said it at dinner, Aspen, but I speak for all of us when I say how sorry I am for what happened to you," Mom started.

Aspen gave her a twitch of a smile. I knew she hated being the center of attention, and neither wanted nor needed the sympathy and pity.

"You were in school with Roger and Vicky, right?" Lane asked, cutting right to the chase and saving Aspen from having to respond.

Mom nodded. "They were two years behind me and your father in school."

I softened at the mention of my dad in the way I always did. My parents had been high school sweethearts, graduating and choosing to stay right here on the ranch, knowing they'd already found their forever in each other and wanting to start their family as soon as possible. As the story went, Mama was already a few months pregnant with Owen when they got married. All she ever wanted to be was a mom, and I was fucking grateful she was mine.

A weaker woman would've given up on me a long time ago, but she never once wavered in her support.

Aspen reminded me of her in that way—they both had that fierce strength.

"What can you tell us about them?" I asked.

"Good people, from what I remember. Vicky was smart as hell and planned to go to UCLA for school. I can't remember what she wanted to major in, but I have no doubt she would have excelled in college. She was on every damn committee you could think of, from yearbook to student council, debate team, Key Club, on top of playing basketball in the fall and running track in the spring. She was…impressive.

"On the flip side, Roger was a goof. The class clown, if you will. One of the funniest guys I'd ever met, and had a personality way too big for this tiny town. On paper, he and Vicky shouldn't have worked, and maybe they didn't entirely because they spent a lot of time off and on. And when they were off, he…"

Mom paused and shook her head, opening her mouth, apparently about to skip over what she'd planned on saying, but the cop in Lane perked up.

"Tell us, Mama."

"I don't want to speak ill of the dead."

"It's not ill if it's the truth," Aspen added quietly. "And if there's anything you can tell us to help figure out who hurt them, who hurt *me*, then you owe it to us to do that."

This was why Lane had wanted Aspen here. Mama had a backbone of steel but a bleeding heart, and she'd already taken a strong liking to Aspen. My girl obviously wasn't opposed to using that to her advantage.

Mom took a deep breath, eyes locked on Aspen as she said, "Roger got around. When he wasn't with Vicky, he was with… everyone else. I doubt there was a girl in the high school that he hadn't been with."

"Even you?" Trey blurted.

Mom leaned forward and swatted at him. "No, not me, you little shit. I've been head over heels in love with your father since the day I first laid eyes on him."

Mom and her family had moved to town over the summer before their freshman year of high school. That first day, they laid eyes on each other, and the game was over for them both. They dated until they were eighteen, got married at twenty, and had Owen shortly after. Their love story was the shit of fairy tales.

My heart squeezed painfully at her use of the present tense, though. Dad had been gone for twenty years, but she'd never moved on. Not for lack of trying on our part. Our old ranch foreman, Cyrus, had always held a torch for mom. After Dad died, he'd stuck around another five years until we all managed to get back on our feet. When he retired, we encouraged Mom to go out with him—or anyone—but she never listened. She always claimed she only had room in her heart for one man, and that man had taken it with him when he died.

Fuck, I wanted a love like that. Their time together had been cut short, but my parents were the blueprint. The standard I held every single one of my own relationships to…which was why they'd been few and far between.

Like Mom said: she knew the first time she looked at him, and I hadn't experienced that yet.

Or maybe, I had, and simply wasn't willing to admit it to myself.

"Okay, so Roger was a slut," Lane muttered. "Not helpful, but good to know anyway I guess?"

It seemed odd to me that Lane, the literal fucking cop who had been trained to peel back the layers of what people weren't saying and expose the truth underneath, couldn't see this potential lead that was staring him right in the face.

So I was forced to do my brother a solid.

"Who else was he hooking up with at that time, Ma?"

Lane's head jerked in my direction so quickly, his neck cracked, and Aspen shot me a proud grin.

Jackpot.

"You don't think one of them could've—" Lane started, but Mom cut him off.

"Honestly, he always had a few girls in rotation. And at that point, I'd been out of school for a few years and was busy being pregnant and a new wife. You'd be better off asking some of their other classmates."

Lane withdrew his damn notebook and flipped through it, scanned a page, then said to Mama, "What about Angela Mickelson?"

"Why does that name sound familiar?" I mumbled.

"She was the third victim," Aspen replied softly.

"The name rings a bell," Mama admitted, "but I can't say for sure whether she had any sort of relationship with Roger. I don't remember her being in high school when Jase and I were."

"Besides," I pointed out, "Angela is dead. It's not like she's the killer."

Lane huffed out a laugh. I knew my brother well enough to understand he was trying to save face, because he was embarrassed I'd jumped to the obvious conclusion before he had. "You don't think this killer is a woman, do you?"

"Of course not," I told him honestly. "There's no way a woman could do all this."

Trey nodded. "I'd have to agree that a woman couldn't have done this." He looked at Aspen. "I mean, you're tiny, but you still weigh over a hundred pounds, right? There aren't a lot of women that could handle lugging deadweight around like that, and not a single one of them lives in Dusk Valley."

"What I do think, though," I continued, giving Trey a nod of approval for having my back, "is that there could be another guy on the other side of these relationships who was caught in the crossfire, either because of Roger fucking around or because he carried a torch for Vicky, and they're taking their aggression over the situation out repeatedly on innocent women."

Lane huffed an irritated breath out through his nose. "When did you become a cop?"

"Learned from the best…"

"Aww," Lane grinned, sinking back into his chair. "That's sw—"

"Trey," I finished.

Trey wasn't technically a cop, but he had spent nearly a

decade in the Secret Service and the bulk of his time since in private security. Basically the same thing, right?

Plus, nothing made me happier than busting Lane's balls.

Trey, Mama, and Aspen burst into laughter, but as quickly as he'd reclined, Lane shot to his feet.

"I'm leaving."

"Oh, c'mon, princess," Trey cooed. "Don't be so dramatic."

"I have to work early," he grumbled, then bent to kiss Mama on the cheek before stomping out of the house.

"I do too, actually," I said, rising to my feet and looking down at Aspen, extending my hand. "You ready?"

Before she could reach for me, her mouth opened on an impressive yawn, giving me my answer.

I helped her up, electricity shooting up my arm at the contact. It brought me right back to the night before in her room, when I'd had her pressed against that wall.

Fuck, I'd wanted to taste her. To lick my way up the column of her throat, capture that perfect mouth with mine, and show her exactly what my lips could do to her other set.

She wanted it too. Her cinnamon eyes had darkened, pupils blown wide.

But I wasn't in the habit of taking something I wasn't offered, and *when*—not if—I finally got Aspen naked and willing beneath me, it would be because she asked for it.

As Lane had done, I folded myself over Mom and pressed a kiss to her cheek, murmuring good night, then stepping back so Aspen could bid her farewell.

Mama got to her feet and hauled Aspen into a hug, saying something in her ear too low for me to hear. When they pulled apart, Aspen nodded, took my proffered hand once again, and let me lead her out to the truck.

The sun had sunk completely below the mountains by then, but it lingered somewhere behind them, silhouetting the peaks and turning the sky a pretty, bright pink. Aspen stopped in the middle of the drive, pulling me up short with her, to admire it.

"This place is breathtaking," she said softly.

"My favorite place in the world," I agreed.

"How come you don't live on ranch land like Finn and West?"

I grinned as I tugged her the rest of the way to the truck and helped her in, my hand lingering on her hip for longer than was strictly necessary, slipping down the length of her thigh as she buckled herself in.

"I do," I said. "A hundred thousand acres, remember?"

"So all the way over there"—she gestured in what she thought was the general direction of my house—"is still your family's land?"

"A hundred thousand acres is roughly a hundred and fifty square miles, so yes. Trey and Lane have houses on the land too."

"You guys really love it here." It wasn't a question, and I didn't treat it as such, especially not when she continued, her eyes sparkling and teeth glowing inside a grin in the dashboard lights. "I can see why."

I hoped that meant she was falling in love with it too. That maybe, when this was all over, she'd want to stay.

"What did my mom say to you back there?"

Aspen's hand came up to cup my cheek. "She told me to take care of you."

I scoffed. "I'm a grown man."

"We all have scars, Crew. Even you."

I couldn't argue with that, and now was not the time or the place to get into the gritty details of my personal trauma. With a curt nod, I moved out of the way and gently shut the door. I'd taken one step toward the driver's door when someone called my name.

Lane sat behind the wheel of his personal SUV, window down and staring at me.

"What?"

"Got a present for you in the back."

Curiosity piqued, I opened the hatch and found several boxes, each labeled with an assortment of letters and numbers. Instantly, I knew what they were.

Lane met me at the back to help me load them into the bed of my truck. When he finished, he clapped a hand to my shoulder, stalling me in place as his fingers dug into my flesh.

Retribution for earlier, no doubt, but also a reminder that if I fucked this up, there would be hell to pay.

"Be careful. This killer is operating in the shadows, and getting close to Aspen could paint a target on your back. I can't —" Lane cut himself off and cleared his throat. "I can't add you to the victim list."

"Aww, big brother!" I crowed, socking him on the shoulder so he released mine. "You care!"

He hooked an arm around my neck and ruffled my hair. "You tell anyone, and I'll kill you. Just like I'll kill you if these files wind up in anyone's hands but yours and Aspen's."

Laughing, I shoved him away and made for the driver's side of my truck. "Love you too!" I called as I popped the door open.

"Yeah, yeah," he grumbled before speeding off.

"What was that about?" Aspen asked when I settled behind the wheel.

For some reason, I wasn't quite ready to share my bounty with her. Maybe I was worried she'd take the files and run, cutting me not only out of the investigation but out of her life.

So I did what I had to: I lied.

"He was getting rid of some old weights and asked if I wanted them."

Aspen snorted. "You don't have enough in that basement of yours?"

I hitched a shoulder up. "You can never have too many. Plus, I'm getting stronger." In the dashboard lights, I made a show of flexing and patting my bicep, and Aspen giggled. "Gotta increase my weights if I don't want to lose muscle."

"Trust me," she mused. "I don't think you're in danger of that happening anytime soon."

"You been checking me out, little phoenix?" Flashing her a grin, I put the truck in drive and rolled away from the house.

"Yep," she answered proudly.

"Good," I said. "Me too."

"You've been checking yourself out?" she quipped.

"Woman…" I warned.

A deep, throaty laugh filled the cab, and I couldn't help joining her.

"Please. You know you're hot."

"All that matters is that you think so."

And speaking of *hot*, had it gotten warm in the cab, or was that coming from us?

twenty-one

. . .

ASPEN

WHEN I WOKE the following morning and Crew had left for work already, I could admit, I was a bit forlorn. I'd come to rely on his presence, not only to make me feel less alone, but also because having him around made me feel safe in a way few things else ever had. Secretly, I didn't love being here without him, without his warm presence filling the cold, dark spaces. I knew nothing bad could happen to me even with him gone, not with his impressive security system, but I wanted *him*, not technology.

How quickly I'd come to rely on him in such a short amount of time was staggering and terrifying.

I really enjoyed his company—more than was probably wise, considering I'd be leaving this town in the rearview when this case wrapped up. Still, I intended to savor these days with him. Even if all I got from him was friendship, that would be enough.

Though I desperately wanted more, namely his hands on my body, making me feel things other than *safe*. Something about Crew Lawless made me want to be reckless, a controlled environment in which to unleash myself.

Without any leads to run down at the moment, I decided to

have myself a spa day in the hopes of a distraction, trading in the serviceable but small tub in the guest bath for the huge soaking one with jets in Crew's master. I located some bubble bath in the linen closet, attempting to convince myself his sister kept it there instead of believing it had been left behind by an old flame.

I didn't want to think about Crew with other women.

I only wanted to think about him with *me*, even if in my head was the only place we'd ever exist that way.

For over an hour, I soaked in the bath, my favorite true crime podcast set at a low volume keeping me company. I even went so far as to shave my legs and my pussy, luxuriating in the smooth skin I exposed beneath the overgrown hair.

Also in the interest of self-care, I couldn't hold back from pleasuring myself with the vibrator I'd brought with me.

Switching off my podcast in favor of some sultry music, I picked up the toy and turned it on, the low hum of the vibration filling the room and tightening my skin with anticipation. I'd spent a long time alone, which meant getting good at turning myself on and getting myself off with the help of my toys. This one was one of my favorites—bright pink and about five inches long with a slight curve to it that nestled itself right against that spot inside that always had my legs shaking uncontrollably when I hit it. It also had an external stimulation feature, two little "bunny ears" that hugged the sides of my clit and made my orgasms that much stronger.

First, I pressed it to my nipples, arching my back into the sensation. I was a member of the itty bitty titty committee, and Crew's massive palms would likely be able to entirely dwarf my chest, but I still wondered what it'd feel like to have his calloused hands scraping against my delicate skin. How his hot, wet mouth would feel on the tight peaks, drawing my nipples between his teeth and applying light pressure.

I liked a little pain with my pleasure, and I had a feeling Crew would know exactly what to do with me. He'd rough me up a bit, gripping me tight enough to bruise, leave bite marks all over my body. But also he'd know when to pull back, when to be gentle. When I needed the slow rocking of his hips and when I wanted him to pound relentlessly into me.

Moving the toy to my mouth, I ran my lips along it, tongue darting out every so often before slipping it in and closing around it, hollowing out my cheeks and sucking hard. I pretended it was Crew's cock, like he was standing next to me, outside the tub, rocking himself in and out of my mouth. I imagined the sounds he'd make, the way he'd fist my hair and fuck my face while I stared up at him, eyes pleading for more.

Soon, my clit throbbed insistently, demanding attention, and I dragged the toy down my abdomen and between my lips. Working it back and forth, I let the blood heat in my veins as I toyed with myself. The vibration against my clit was maddeningly delicious, drawing a soft moan from my throat as I lingered. The pressure in my core coiled tighter and tighter the longer I held it there—only to pull it away right before the wave of release crested and crashed.

I liked edging myself.

I liked it even better when a man did it for me.

Damn, I'd bet all the money I had that Crew was a knockout in bed.

Unable to stand it any longer, not with thoughts of him at the forefront of my brain, I thrust the toy inside myself. My back arched against the intrusion, and I shifted my hips and the vibe around until the tip hit that hidden spot.

Then I flicked on the bunny ears on the lowest setting, a cry leaving me as they strummed my clit. The toy was good, I'd give it that, but I could guarantee Crew's touch on my sensitive bud would feel so much better.

When I was comfortable, when the toy was exactly where I needed it, hitting all the right pressure points and pleasure spots, I cranked it all the way up.

Instantly, my toes curled against the porcelain beneath my feet, my head falling back to rest on the rim of the tub. Gasping moans and whimpers left me as the vibrator did its job, working me higher and higher, taking me apart from the inside out.

My orgasm came on faster this time, spurred by the filthy images I conjured of Crew in this tub with me, his fingers buried deep in my pussy as he held me above the surface of the water and flicked my clit repeatedly with his tongue. I squeezed my eyes shut and pictured his strong, tattooed arm bunching and flexing as he fucked me with his hand. That quickly morphed into thoughts of him sinking into the water and pulling me onto his lap, where my pussy, drenched in arousal, would allow me to easily impale myself on him, riding his cock like it was my fucking job. Eyes still closed, I rocked forward onto my knees and gripped the end of the toy with one hand and the edge of the tub with the other, holding myself upright while pumping it in and out in an approximation of what I'd do with Crew.

I detonated with a loud cry, my release scattering me into a thousand little pieces as I called his name, the word echoing back to me from the tile walls in the cavernous room. Water sloshed over the edges and onto the floor as I bore down on the toy, my climax sending wave after wave of pleasure through me.

At last, I stilled and drooped, boneless, back into the water, a satisfied smirk on my face.

twenty-two

. . .

ASPEN

IN THE TWO days since my bathtub play time, I'd hardly seen Crew. Admittedly, he'd slept most of the day before when he got off shift, but now that he was restored, he was still suspiciously MIA. For some reason, he'd been locked in his office. But *why*? Had I done something wrong?

Oh, God. Had he somehow learned what I'd done to myself in his tub with his name on my lips?

No, that wasn't possible. The house may be wired, but there was no way in hell he'd have cameras in his private spaces.

Unfortunately, I was going crazy being cooped up, and I needed to let him know I was leaving.

I lightly tapped the door with my knuckles. "Crew?"
"Yeah?"

His voice was muffled, and I waited, listening, but only silence greeted me. He made no move to greet me face to face.

I sighed, suddenly irritated. Ever since dinner at the ranch, he'd been acting cagey and weird.

"I'm going to run into town. I want to run to the library again, and I'll pick up something for dinner. Anything you want?"

"Nah, I'm good. Be safe!"

"I always am," I grumbled under my breath as I walked away, making my way through the house, purse slung over my shoulder and keys in hand.

Since I'd been staying with him, Crew had been kind enough to let me park in his garage, and I'd been more than a little grateful for it. Now, I wouldn't have to worry about any more jump scares in the form of creepy notes left under my windshield.

At least, not while I was home.

My head would be on a swivel while I was away, though.

When I reached town, I headed straight for the library. I was greeted like a celebrity, Ginny excitedly shuffling out from behind the info desk and sweeping me into one of those warm hugs.

"Oh, it's good to see you, dear," she said, clasping my hand and leading me back into the meeting room. "I kept those yearbooks stashed away for you. Take a seat, and I'll be right back."

"Oh, I can help, Ginny. You don't have to do that."

"Nonsense," she insisted, waving me off. "Get comfortable. I can handle carrying a few little books."

I wasn't about to argue with her. Little old ladies like her were stubborn, and there'd be no talking her into letting me assist.

A few minutes later, she returned with a stack of yearbooks—then left again and came back with another. After two more trips, I had probably forty of them on the table before me. Damn, this woman was stronger than she looked.

"This is…more than I was expecting," I admitted.

"I pulled them for each of the years those girls were in school," Ginny said proudly. "To really give you the full scope of their high school careers."

I glanced up at her with a grateful smile. "Thank you so much, Ginny. You are truly a gem."

"It's no problem, dear. Old ladies like me like to be useful."

"So far, you're the most useful person I've met in this town."

A blush flooded her deeply lined cheeks, a pleased smile gracing her lips.

"Thank you. I'll leave you to it, but let me know if you need anything."

"Will do. Thanks, Ginny."

With a final squeeze to my shoulder, she disappeared.

I took my time flipping through the yearbooks, starting at the beginning with Roger and Vicky, smiling at any pages I came across that featured Birdie and her late husband, Jase. Despite being grainy and sepia-toned, I recognized his sons in his face easily. They'd all taken after him in one way or another—the height, the broad shoulders, the muscular build. The smile. The lack of real color to the pictures didn't offer any confirmation, of course, but I could guess his eyes were blue, his hair the sandy shade each of his sons sported in variation. Birdie was still gorgeous, but she'd been a knockout when she was younger. Aria was a dead ringer for her mother.

Vicky had been as vibrant and involved in school activities as Birdie had said. I could hardly flip a page without her face appearing in a photograph.

She reminded me so much of my sister, my heart thumped painfully in my chest every time I looked at her. Was it her dark hair? Or maybe the way her energy seemed to leap off the page, making me feel surrounded by her spirit despite the fact that she was long gone?

Whatever the reason, I found myself lingering on her photographs, wanting to feel close to my sister in this fucked up way.

"I miss you," I whispered, hoping Lola, wherever she was, could hear me.

By the tenth yearbook, I was scanning for victim number four, a girl who had been twenty at the time of her death, home from her sophomore year of college, kidnapped on her way home from the store. The second my gaze locked on her face, the wheels in my brain started spinning at warp speed, and a pattern emerged.

Suddenly, the weird ass email I'd gotten the other day made a lot more sense.

I spared far less time on the remaining eight victims, only going so far as flipping to the individual photos of each student from each grade to locate the girls before moving onto the next.

I knew what I'd find; I merely needed confirmation.

After glancing through the final one, I left them on the table in five neat stacks, collected my things, and rushed out to Ginny.

"Thank you so much again," I told her. "I left them on the table because I'm not sure where they go. I can absolutely help you put them away, but—"

"You run along, dear," she said, gently halting my rambling. "I can tell you're fired up about something."

I gave her a quick hug and sprinted for the door.

Once safely behind the wheel of Black Betty and punching the doors locked, I checked my phone for the first time in hours to several texts from Crew.

HOTSHOT

Pizza sounds amazing. You don't mind, do you?

Aspen?

Goddamnit, Aspen, text me back.

We've been over this.

If you don't respond in the next two minutes, I'm coming to find you.

And you won't like what I have to say when I do.

The last two came in as I was reading the first ones, so I quickly tapped out a response.

ME

Promises, promises 😏

HOTSHOT

You are a goddamn pain in my ass.

ME

You love it.

HOTSHOT

Please tell me you got caught up at the library again and aren't being held somewhere against your will

ME

…again

HOTSHOT

ASPEN

Cackling, I told him I was fine, that I was going to grab pizza and head home, then dropped my phone in the cupholder and set off. There was only one pizza joint in town, and luckily, they had take-and-bake pizzas with a variety of topping combinations, so I picked out a classic pepperoni and a loaded supreme, paid, and headed back onto the street.

At this time of day, when people were getting off work and running errands before heading home, downtown Dusk Valley bustled with people, the bulk of parking spaces along the street full. I'd managed to slide Black Betty into one a few blocks up, so with an extra pep in my step, I started that way. When I reached the first street corner, I paused for traffic, but as I was about to step into the crosswalk, the hair on the back of my neck rose.

In my line of work, I'd long since honed my sixth sense, and the ability to know when someone was watching me had become second nature, easy as breathing.

As if on cue, keeping in time with that creepy-crawly feeling sliding down my spine, my phone pinged with an email.

My hands shook as I withdrew it from my pocket.

FROM: wudntulk2no@email.com
    TO: aspen@mckayinvestigates.com

No Subject

I see you, but so do too many other people. Broad daylight is such a bummer. I much prefer darkness illuminated by the glow of a flame. But don't worry, little cockroach. Soon enough I'll catch you alone, and I can finish what I started.

My fingers trembled so violently, I could barely hold onto my phone, so I stuffed it in my pocket in favor of studying my surroundings. Sweeping my eyes around the area, I took mental snapshots of all the people in my vicinity.

The man holding his young daughter's hand.

The woman in a smart suit, phone pressed to her ear as she ate up the sidewalk.

The two women, clearly mother and daughter, exiting the diner with take-out containers in their hands.

The man standing on the corner a block ahead, hat pulled low over his face, shoulders hunched as he waited for a car to pass so he could cross the street.

I stepped into the street, the blare of a car horn barely penetrating my haze as I rushed to the other side, eyes locked on the man who passed from view around the side of a building.

By the time I got there, though, he was long gone, seemingly vanished into thin air.

I spun in a slow circle, searching for any sign of him, but to no avail. Eventually, I gave up and got behind the wheel of Black Betty to head home.

Too freaked out over the email and disappearing, I skipped right over the part where I started thinking of Crew's house as *home*.

The man himself waited for me on the front porch when I pulled up to the house, so I stopped in the driveway, hands on his hips and a pissed off expression on his face. I hopped out of my car, grabbed the pizzas from the back, and walked toward him.

"Oh, come on," I groaned. "You can't be that mad."

"All you had to do was text me. I was about to send out a goddamn search party."

I rolled my eyes. "I'm fine, hotshot. Ginny pulled like fifty yearbooks, and it took me ages to go through them all. Honestly, what could be safer than a library?"

"The house, for starters," he grumbled as he followed me through the living room and into the kitchen. "Libraries have no security at all."

I sighed. "You're exhausting."

"And you're a brat."

I'd barely slid the pizzas onto the counter when he grabbed my shoulders and turned me to face him.

That worry in his eyes was back, the same expression I'd seen the last time I'd gone MIA for a few hours.

I fucking hated that look—had seen it on my parents' faces too many times over the last seventeen years. The last thing I wanted was to stress anyone out unnecessarily.

Before he could start raging at me, I stepped forward and wrapped my arms around his waist, sinking into his warmth, as well as the freshness of his detergent layered with the smokey scent that always clung to his skin. I was growing far too familiar with that particular blend, and after the filthy things I'd mentally conjured to get myself off in *his* tub the other day, this hug was likely the worst idea I'd ever had. But when his arms banded around my shoulders, somehow pulling me even closer, I couldn't find a single cell in my body that cared.

Since my ordeal, mostly all physical contact had pained me. I wasn't a fan of unwanted touch in particular, as it reminded me too much of the worst offenses I'd suffered at other people's hands.

None of that bothered me with Crew. I *liked* having his hands on me, more than I cared to admit. Not only because I knew his hands were that of a protector, and that he'd *never* raise them against a woman in anger, but also because he calmed me. My negative thoughts and horrific memories quieted when he touched me.

"I'm sorry," I murmured against his shirt, which was so soft against my cheek, I could damn well curl up there forever.

Crew relaxed against me, his rough exhale brushing against the top of my head.

"It's okay. I just want you to be safe."

"I get that," I said, pulling away. "But you can't fly off the handle every time I take a bit to respond to a text. You have to remember I've spent a long time on my own, and I'm still navigating having anyone give a fuck where I am or what I'm up to."

"Your parents do."

"That's different."

The change in his expression with those two words was subtle, but I was watching closely enough to see it happen. The slightly furrowed brow smoothed out, his dark eyes cleared, the tightness around his mouth relaxed.

And I knew why: he'd heard my silent admission.

He was different.

My parents were genetically predisposed to care what happened to me—and my mom, in particular, usually took it about twenty steps further. Like because she'd given me life, she could also control it.

Crew Lawless did not fall into that category. He cared because he chose to, because he worried about the woman he knew, the woman I was *right now*, not the amalgamation of every version of Aspen McKay I'd been all the years I'd been alive.

Silence stretched between us as we stared into each other's eyes, and I angled my head to the side.

The answer to an unspoken question and a silent invitation.

The corners of his beautiful mouth twitched, as though he was amused by me, and he started moving closer. Slowly, clearly trying to give me the chance to back out, to back down.

I stood my ground.

His lips brushed faintly against mine, a teasing taste—and then a beeping rent the still air around us.

Crew leapt back like he'd been electrocuted, scrubbing a hand through his hair as he turned away, looking everywhere but at me.

"Oven timer," he explained, then set about removing the pizzas from their shrink wrap so he could get them cooking.

I blinked in confusion, having no idea what happened. Why was he suddenly acting like kissing me would be the biggest mistake of his life?

I sighed. *Men.*

Needing to get away from him and the cloying awkwardness that hung in the air around us, I let him deal with the food while I disappeared to my room.

For every investigation, I kept a notepad of random thoughts, odd bits of information, and seemingly innocuous occurrences that may wind up being important later. Tucked in the back of this one was that note I'd found under my wiper the day I'd picked Black Betty up from impound, and I spent a few minutes detailing my findings at the library, then jotted down a couple paragraphs about the email, the people on the street, and the disappearing man.

A light knock came at the door as I closed it and returned it to the drawer of my bedside table.

"Yeah?"

"Can you come out?" Crew asked. "I want to show you something."

"I guess," I sighed, quiet enough that I knew he wouldn't hear, and went to meet him.

When I opened the door, he jerked his head in the direction of the office.

"Oh, are you finally going to show me what had you locked in here all day?" I asked, awkwardness forgotten in my excitement as I followed.

"Yes, ma'am."

I wrinkled my nose. "Don't call me 'ma'am.' I'm thirty-three, not sixty-three."

Crew chuckled. "Fine. Then little phoenix it is."

Little phoenix.

I turned it over in my mind for the few seconds it took us to reach the office door and couldn't find fault. It made me feel powerful and strong. Reminded me I was a survivor, not a victim.

Reminded me of the man who ensured I continued to draw breath.

Crew stopped in front of the still closed office door, hand gripping the knob.

"You ready?"

"Yes!"

With a grin and a flourish, he twisted the knob and pushed, then reached in to flick the light on.

At first, I couldn't make sense of what I was seeing.

The far wall, which had once been home to the maps of the city and a corkboard, was now lined with paper. Stepping closer, my hand flew to my mouth as I gasped.

"You got the case file," I breathed.

"Lane gave it to me the other night."

I turned and smacked him. "Gym equipment, my ass. Why did you lie to me?"

"I wanted to look it over first—and I wanted to do this."

"My very own murder board." I grinned at him, ire over his untruth instantly soothed.

He remained silent, allowing me the opportunity to study the spread. It would take me a few days to read all the reports and interview transcripts, but the same thing that had jumped out at me at the library was even more obvious now.

As though he sensed the wheels in my mind turning, Crew moved closer, the heat of his body and his intoxicating scent wrapping around me.

"What do you see?" Crew asked quietly.

I fingered the dark strands of my hair. I wasn't entirely surprised by the discovery, but to see it laid out so plainly like this…my heart raced faster with the knowledge.

That while I'd obviously been targeted for my desire to solve this case, there was more to it than that.

"I see an awful lot of brunettes."

twenty-three

. . .

CREW

I SEE *an awful lot of brunettes.*

My fist slammed harder into the bag, sending it careening toward the concrete wall of my basement workout space.

Once Aspen had uttered those words, I'd needed to collect myself. I managed to sit still and keep my cool while we ate pizza and chatted about nothing, but the second the plates were cleared and the leftovers were in the fridge, I bolted downstairs.

Obviously, she'd been targeted because she was working the case and hoping to find the piece of shit tormenting my town, but to see all the victim's faces lined up side by side, to recognize she'd also happened to fit the physical profile?

The realization had something ugly twisting in my chest, the constant desire to *protect, protect, protect* morphing into something far more dangerous.

I'd burn the fucking world down for Aspen McKay, destroy anyone who tried to hurt her, and that scared me more than anything.

Did she feel the same? Would she give her life to protect mine in the same way I felt compelled to do for her? Not that I'd ever ask that of her. I'd do everything in my power to ensure she never had to. But we'd had a moment in the kitchen. Before we'd been saved—or maybe damned, if the way my cock still refused to soften was any indication—by the oven signal, I'd been centimeters away from kissing her like she deserved, not that weak-ass, glancing touch I'd given her. Like a planet helpless to resist the gravitational pull of the sun, I'd been drawn into her orbit, and I didn't see a way out.

Hell, I didn't *want* a way out.

I'd never really been in a *real* relationship. I'd had a high school girlfriend before the accident that sent me into a tailspin, and once I got my shit together, I was too busy moving across the country, then with the fire academy and starting my career, to worry about also keeping a woman happy. Sure, I'd had flings; I was a red-blooded male. I scratched the itch when needed. But there'd never been a woman I could see myself with long term.

And then Aspen McKay blazed into town, setting my entire world on fire, and suddenly, I was picturing forever with a woman who, in the grand scheme of things, I hardly knew.

But I wanted to change that. I wanted her to become someone I knew better than anyone, wanted the kind of relationship I remembered my parents having—where we could exchange whole conversations with a simple look. Where we woke up together every morning, and fell asleep curled around each other every night.

Fuck, I wanted to get married and fill this house with babies.

And I wanted all of that with *her*.

With that thought, I punched the bag so hard, my knuckles stung through the tape I'd wrapped them in, and I leaned my forehead against it for a beat. I was breathing so damn hard, my thoughts so loud, I almost missed my phone ringing across the room.

Rushing over, I found Lane's name on the screen.

"You're calling awfully late," I said in lieu of greeting.

"There's been a fire."

"What? Where?" I dropped the phone on the bench and put it on speaker, quickly unwinding the tape from my hands.

"Dumpster behind Mozzy's."

The pizza place…where Aspen had been earlier, picking up dinner.

"Do you think—"

"I don't know," he said before I could finish. "I *hope* it's not connected, but I can't be sure. I wasn't even going to call you, but—"

"You knew I'd be pissed if you didn't. I'm coming down to check it out. Give me ten minutes."

"You live fifteen miles out of town."

"And?"

Lane's sigh echoed through the speaker. "Be careful."

Then he hung up, and I rushed upstairs.

Aspen was in the office, her laptop on the desk in front of her. The end of a pen was stuck between her teeth, and a notebook balanced on her bent knees as she stared at the murder board.

I could practically hear the gears in her mind turning as she tried to make sense of it all.

Not wanting to scare her, I lightly rapped my knuckles on the open door, and she spun toward me.

"Hey."

"Hey," I replied. "So, Lane called."

She bolted upright, the notebook and pen falling to the ground, instantly forgotten.

"Another fire?"

I nodded. "I'm going to check it out, so I'll be back lat—"

"I'm coming with."

"No."

So many emotions flashed across her face with the single

word, I couldn't grasp any to make sense of them. Finally, she settled on annoyance.

"I'm coming with," she repeated.

I approached her, placing my hands on the back of the chair and ducking until we were eye level.

Too close, my body warned.

Fuck, she smelled good, like some floral shampoo and vanilla. And…mint? Her lips had a slight sheen, and I guessed that was her lip balm.

I hated how badly I wanted to taste it.

"Please, Aspen." Unbidden, my hand moved up to cup her face, thumb stroking her soft cheek. "I can't be focused on my job if I'm worried about you. Please stay here where I know you're safe."

I was admitting a lot with the demand. I might as well have cut my heart out and laid it in her palm.

Bracing myself, I waited for her reaction.

At last, she softened, her shoulders dropping away from her ears, eyes fluttering closed as she leaned into my touch. "Okay," she agreed.

All the tension bled from my own shoulders, and I shifted my palm to cup the back of her neck, pulling her in to press a kiss to her forehead. Aspen inhaled sharply at the contact, but her hand found the front of my shirt, grasping it and holding me there longer than was probably wise.

"Thank you," I murmured against her skin.

She pulled away enough to look up at me, and God, with her mouth *right there*, I wanted to close the distance and finish what we'd started earlier.

But I wouldn't—not like this.

When I finally made Aspen mine, it wouldn't be as I was rushing out the door. She wasn't the kind of woman you kissed and ran from.

Aspen was the kind of woman you worshiped all night long.

"Be safe," she whispered as I let her go.

I grinned. "Always am, little phoenix."

THE STARS SPARKLED OVERHEAD as I pulled out of the garage and navigated down my long driveway. The days were getting longer, but at eight thirty at night in early May, the sun had already disappeared, leaving that spring chill in the air. I'd stowed the extra set of gear I kept at home in the backseat of my truck and pulled on a thick fleece jacket over my tee, legs still clad in the sweats I'd worked out in.

I drove pedal to the metal all the way to town, making what should've been a twenty minute drive in half the time. The scene was awash in red and blue emergency lights from a lone fire truck, Lane's sheriff SUV, and a few patrol cars.

After a quick assessment, I noted the fire was already out, so I left my gear in the back and approached my brother.

"You really didn't need to come down," he said, not bothering to face me as he stood with his arms crossed, surveying the first responders clearing debris and taking photos.

"Too late now. Any idea what happened?"

"Likely a dumb kid causing trouble. As far as I can tell, there's no connection to our guy. No one was injured."

"What started it?"

"Smells like lighter fluid, Cap," one of the third shift guys said from nearby.

"Not diesel fuel?"

He shook his head, then turned back to overhaul.

"So probably not connected," I said, "but the timing is a little too convenient if you ask me."

Lane hummed in agreement. "We're kicking up dust by

digging into this thing, especially with Aspen around. For now, I'll treat it as a one-off."

"Well, in the interest of full disclosure, you should know Aspen was here earlier getting dinner. Might mean something, might not."

Lane swore, rubbing his hand over his face. "We'll check the cameras in the area and see if anything pops."

"Do any cameras even face the alley?"

"Not the city-operated ones," he said, pointedly glancing around at the light posts where such things would be mounted. "But we might be able to catch the perp arriving or high-tailing it out of here. And most of these businesses have private security systems."

"Trey?"

"Trey," Lane confirmed, pulling out his phone to shoot a text to our brother.

Glancing up and down the alley, I mentally mapped any potential escape routes the perp could've used. Mozzy's was in the middle of the block damn near dead in the center of what was considered city limits, which didn't provide a lot of immediate cover. But…

"I can hear your mind working," Lane said, tossing me a smirk. "What're you thinking?"

"Shouldn't I be the one asking you that?" I teased.

"Quit being a pain in my ass and tell me."

"This alley runs all the way through town, perpendicular to Cassia, right?" I started, naming the main street all of these businesses faced. "At this time of night, the perp wouldn't be able to shuffle onto Cassia and blend in with the foot traffic. And people don't normally walk down alleys in the dark. Which means…"

Lane jerked his head to the other side of the alley, where residential homes began to mingle with the businesses, where the street lights became fewer and farther between. "They had to have gone that way. They could've snuck through yards until they were far enough away to book it."

"Exactly."

"Deputies!" he shouted over the commotion, and the five guys he had on scene all turned his way. "Set up a canvas. I want a five by five block radius on the south side of Cassia, and the same to the north. Ask residents if they saw or heard anything suspicious."

Murmurs of, "You got it, boss," floated back to us as his deputies set off in different directions to carry out his orders.

"What do you need from me?" I asked my brother.

"Nothing else right now." With a glance back at the fire crew still working the scene, he settled a hand on my shoulder and steered me away. When we reached my truck, he added, "Have you had a chance to look at the case file?" I nodded. "Anything jump out at you?"

"You mean other than the fact that the women are all white, brunette, and in their late teens or early twenties?"

Lane blinked slowly, processing that information.

"Sounds an awful lot like a profile."

"Seems like something your brethren should've figured out sooner."

The corners of his mouth turned down, the skin around his eyes tightening—whether in anger or shame, I didn't know.

"Not gonna lie to you, little bro. My predecessors were…lazy, for lack of a better word. This killer lay dormant for long enough stretches that things would go cold before the next strike, and they didn't work hard to keep the fire burning, if you know what I mean."

"That's not going to be the case with you."

He didn't treat it like a question because it wasn't one. If nothing else, Lane was a hell of a cop, and I knew he'd run down every possible lead and keep turning over rocks until something crawled out. That, and I'd be on his ass every day, not letting him forget.

"Aspen doesn't exactly fit," he said after a moment.

"She's white and brunette," I pointed out. "Her age doesn't really matter in the grand scheme of things. Hell, her physical appearance doesn't really either if you think about it."

We all knew why Aspen was targeted, and it had everything to do with *why* she was here, not who she was or what she looked like.

"No, I suppose not." He squeezed his eyes shut and popped them open, and I noticed for the first time how exhausted he looked. This case had to be taking its toll on his department, and I probably could take it a little easier on him. "Well, keep her safe, and let me know if anything else sticks out."

With a salute, I left.

But instead of heading home, I went to the fire station, unsurprised to find Chief Madden's personal vehicle parked out front.

At nearly ten p.m., those not currently out on the call ambled around, clearly getting ready to catch some shut eye. I nodded at everyone I passed as I beelined for Chief's office.

"What're you doing here, Lawless?" he asked when I appeared in the doorway.

"Just came from the dumpster scene."

"And?"

"Nothing much to report. Seems like a standard kid fucking around type situation."

Chief smirked. "And you'd know all about that, wouldn't you?"

I groaned. "God, don't remind me."

"It's good to remember how far you've come."

Well, he wasn't wrong there.

"*Anyway,*" I said, moving deeper into his office. "That box of incident reports I'd gone over with Aspen that one day—would it be possible to take another look at them? Lane gave me copies of all the police files on each victim, and it'd be nice to cross reference some things."

"You really want to find this person, don't you?"

"Of course. Don't you?"

"To prevent them from taking another life, sure. But I think there's more on the line here for you."

Internally, I cursed. This man had always been able to see through me like I was a window instead of the iron vault I wanted to be.

"That obvious?"

One of his shoulders hitched up. "I know what being in love looks like, and you're on your way there, son."

"So is that a yes on the files?" I asked hopefully.

Chief chuckled and jerked his head toward the corner, where the same box still rested from when I'd set it there several weeks ago, after that very first meeting with Aspen.

But I pulled up short when I reached it, then turned back to Chief.

"You wouldn't have some time to sit down and go over these with me, would you?"

That was really why I'd come to the station, anyway—to get his opinion.

His mouth spread into a smile.

"I'd love to. It's been a while since I've done any investigative work." He rose from his desk and ambled over to me. "But you're not allowed to stay past midnight. You're on shift in the morning."

"Aye aye, captain."

He snorted. "That's Chief to you."

With a mock salute, I followed him out.

SHORTLY AFTER MIDNIGHT, I quietly let myself into the house. Chief had come to many of the same conclusions as me while we pored over the reports. This killer was organized and intelligent, and we'd need a major break, for them to make a colossal mistake, in order to catch them.

Aspen had left the kitchen light on for me, which I appreciated as I tiptoed through the room and toward the hallway.

Alarm shot through me when I found her bedroom door open and her bed empty, and I willed my heart rate to slow. She'd probably fallen asleep on the couch watching a movie, which she'd already done a few times since moving in with me. I needed to change out of my workout gear, which was really starting to stink, and then I'd carry her to her.

When I walked into my room and flicked on the light, I found her asleep in my bed. Well, she *had* been asleep, but I'd unintentionally woken her up, and she lifted her head to squint at me.

I was by her side in a few long strides.

"What are you doing in here?" I asked softly, kneeling beside her and brushing her hair back from her forehead.

"Had a nightmare," she said sleepily, her eyes remaining closed. "And then I heard some weird noises when I couldn't fall back to sleep. Without thinking, I ran to you, but…"

"I wasn't here." I was on the bed in a flash. Pulling back the covers, I wrapped her in my arms and curled us together in the center of my mattress. "I'm so sorry."

"You don't have to apologize for doing your job," she said. "I don't even know why I came looking for you anyway."

Yet she made no move to pull free and leave, and I found myself holding her tighter.

"I saved your life. You see me as someone who can protect you. I bet you'd feel the same about anyone in my position."

Not for a second did I believe those words, and they felt like glass scraping my throat on the way out, but I had to put it out there. Had to see how she'd react to me trying to downplay whatever was happening between us.

I felt more than saw her shake her head. "No, Crew. No, this is…" She placed her hand over my heart, which, despite her proximity, thumped evenly. She was the one who needed comforting, and had come to my room in search of it, but I also knew *I* was safe here with *her*. Holding her like this was right where I needed to be. "This is all you."

I grinned into her hair, then pressed a kiss to the top of her head. Shortly after, her breath evened out as she drifted back to sleep. Not wanting to move and risk waking her again—and because I didn't want to let her go—I remained where I was.

Thinking.

About all the ways this could go wrong. The danger of us getting close like this, both physically and emotionally.

But I couldn't deny how badly I wanted her, and the fact that the first place she'd run to when she had a bad dream was the one place in this house where she could feel closest to me told me she felt the same.

If we wanted to be together, we'd find a way to make it happen. Of that, I had no doubt. So with that thought, and a smile on my face, I followed Aspen down into unconsciousness.

I WAS JOLTED from sleep some hours later at the insistence of some sort of alert blaring from my phone. Damn, my alarm for work already?

Next to me, Aspen grumbled something unintelligible and shifted onto her other side while I rolled toward my nightstand. Slapping my hand down on the device, it instantly silenced… only to start back up again.

Bleary-eyed, I squinted at the vibrant red alert screaming at me from the home screen. Unlocking it, I clicked into my security system app to see what all the fuss was about.

Unnaturally high temperatures detected at garage door.

What the fuck?

Careful not to wake Aspen for the third time, I slid out of bed and padded through the house until I reached the garage. With the press of a button, the door began to lift, and I knew before it opened fully what the problem was as a cloud of smoke greeted me.

Aspen's car was on fire.

twenty-four

. . .

ASPEN

CAUGHT in that land between awake and asleep, I was only distantly aware of Crew getting out of bed—then returning in a rush sometime later.

I rose further from unconsciousness when he started speaking with someone on the phone.

I came fully awake when he shouted, "Lane, Aspen's car is on fucking fire in my driveway! Get your ass out of bed and get here *now*."

Fire.

Aspen.

Car.

As the word coalesced into a coherent thought, I bolted upright, barely registering I was still in Crew's bed—and that we'd spent all night cuddling.

"My car is on fire?" I croaked.

Crew winced. "Yeah. I'm sorry." His hand lifted to cup the back of his neck. "But hey, at least you weren't in it?"

He phrased it as more of a question, and I choked on a laugh. I appreciated the dark humor, actually. If I didn't laugh, I knew I'd cry, and I was done giving this crazy fucker my tears.

There was no other explanation, and while I knew it'd be difficult to confirm, I refused to believe the person who attacked me wasn't also behind this.

"I want to see."

"Aspen…"

"It's my car, Crew. I deserve to see it."

"Okay, but I'm warning you, it's not pretty."

Throwing the covers back, I crawled out of bed. I was on my feet before I remembered I wasn't wearing pants, and even in the room only dimly lit by the light from the rising sun, I didn't miss the way Crew's eyes darkened.

"No pants?" he asked hoarsely.

"You're just now realizing this?" I asked, awkwardly squeezing my thighs together and tugging on the hem of the oversized tee I favored for sleeping. "I'm sorry. I wasn't thinking. I didn't plan on, you know…staying."

"Never apologize for…*this*," he said, gesturing at me. "My only regret is that I don't have time to explore what's underneath."

A shiver of excitement raced down my spine, morphing into desire that pooled in my core. We'd been dancing around this thing between us for weeks, neither of us ballsy enough to cross that line and say what we'd both been thinking.

Until now.

"One day," I replied boldly, though my voice was barely above a whisper.

One side of Crew's mouth twitched up in that sexy little smirk I was coming to crave from him. "One day," he agreed. Then he dipped into his closet, returning a moment later with a pair of sweatpants and hoodie I'd likely drown in. Still, I slipped the pants on and pulled the string as tight as it would go, rolling them several times at the waist before cocooning myself in the hoodie.

Crew shot me a crooked grin as he helped me roll the sleeves up.

"You're cute."

"I look like I'm playing dress up in my dad's clothes," I murmured.

"I'm not your father, Aspen," he said softly, then leaned closer, his lips brushing the shell of my ear, "but I can definitely be your daddy."

Choking on a laugh, I shoved him away.

"Let's go assess the damage to my poor baby, you freak."

"Oh, honey, you have no idea," he chuckled as he gestured me out ahead of him.

Right when we stepped outside, a sleek black SUV pulled to a stop on the outskirts of the drive, giving a wide berth to my smoldering Suburban. Not far behind came another vehicle, this one I recognized as Lane's.

Trey got out of his and ambled toward us.

"Got the alert," he said. "Came as fast as I could."

Crew must've caught my confused expression because he said, "Trey owns a private security company and is responsible for all the systems on all of our homes. So when something goes wrong here, or at the ranch—"

Trey wiggled his phone. "I get an alert too."

"That's…handy."

Trey snorted. "They frequently call me Big Brother, which isn't the insult they think it is since I am, quite literally, their big brother."

"You are also, *quite literally*, a pain in my ass," Crew muttered.

"Takes one to know one."

"Fight nice, children," Lane said as he joined the group.

"You're younger than me," Trey reminded him.

"And yet I'm the only one with a badge."

"Not technically true," Crew piped in.

Rubbing my temples, I blurted, "Can we not?"

Though I'd spoken softly, I may as well have shouted for the way the three of them stopped dead like they'd been frozen in time.

They all opened their mouths to start speaking at once, but the blare of an emergency vehicle horn cut through the air, and a fire truck rounded the bend into the driveway.

Completely unnecessary, in my opinion, as the fire appeared to be out.

"Did you put that out?" I asked Crew.

He nodded. "I keep some equipment handy in the garage, but I'm going to have to replace my extinguisher now."

"Thank you."

"No thanks necessary, little phoenix."

The fire truck pointed itself at the husk of my car, lights illuminating the area so they could work to ensure the fire was completely out. One firefighter pointed a hose at it, dousing the entire thing from end to end a few times, and we all stood in silence as it hissed and cooled.

When the smoke cleared, and my eyes caught on the scorched garage doors, my blood ran cold. Unbidden, my feet propelled me forward until I stood only a few feet away.

"Aspen!" someone hollered from behind me. "What the fuck are you doing?"

The gravel of the drive crunched beneath fast approaching footsteps, and I knew by the way my nerve endings charged like they'd been plugged into an electrical socket that Crew had joined me.

We stood in silence as we read the words painted across his garage door in a deep red, gravity pulling the letters down grotesquely.

YOU CAN RUN...

"Fucking hell," the sheriff muttered when he joined me and Crew.

"Is that…blood?" I whispered.

Lane pulled on a pair of nitrile gloves and approached the words, swiping a finger through the Y and bringing it to his nose.

"Spray paint."

"Was that there when you got home?" I asked.

Crew shook his head, jaw clenched tightly. "No. What time did you have your nightmare?"

"Eleven twenty-four." Lane raised a brow. "I looked at my phone when I woke up."

"I got home at midnight," Crew said, then whirled on Lane. "This is your fault, you know."

Lane snorted. "How do you figure?"

Crew stalked toward Lane, pushing right up into his personal space, wagging a finger in his face as he began shouting.

"It's your job to find this fucker! Now my goddamn house is a crime scene, and Aspen is still in danger!"

Noticing his boss was caught in the middle of an altercation —though perhaps not understanding it was more a feud between brothers than anything else—a deputy stepped between them and shoved Crew back.

"Mind your manners, smoke eater," the deputy said.

Like a train crashing into a school bus on the tracks, I was as unable to look away as I would've been to stop what happened next.

Crew grinned—a full on, terrifying bearing of his teeth—at the deputy.

Then he swung his fist right into the center of the deputy's face.

"Crew!" I shouted at the same moment blood spurted like a faucet from the deputy's nose.

"Trey!" Lane yelled as he grabbed the deputy a moment before he could lunge in retaliation.

Trey waded into the fray, hauling Crew backward with his arms hooked around Crew's elbows, speaking to him too low for me to make out.

The deputy was belligerent, shouting about arresting Crew, pressing assault charges, and a bunch of other shit I had no doubt Lane would quash as soon as possible.

In the commotion, I hadn't noticed the ambulance appear until a paramedic approached the deputy where Lane had sat him out of the way, on the top step of Crew's porch.

"Sutt," Lane said, surprised. "What're you doing here?"

"Heard the call over the radio," the woman said. "Thought I'd come check on everyone. Seems I arrived right in time."

She turned and raised a brow at Lane, who snorted, giving me the first good look at her face.

Though my memories of that night were hazy at best, her features crystalized and sharpened the longer I stared at her until it finally clicked.

"You were there that night," I blurted.

I didn't need to explain which one, and the paramedic nodded.

"Sutton Rausch," she said in introduction. "Good to see you on your feet, Miss McKay."

"You can call me Aspen."

"Well, Aspen, I'm happy to see you mobile."

"Thank you for your help that night."

"Just—"

"Doing your job," I finished for her with an eye roll.

Sutton laughed. "You've heard that before, I take it?"

I hooked my thumb in Crew's direction. "Seems to be his favorite mantra."

She nodded. "I've worked alongside him since he moved home, and you won't find a firefighter better at their job, or a man more protective, than him."

Lane scoffed next to me. "What about me?"

Sutton didn't look up from where she mopped the blood off the deputy's face. "It runs in the family, that's for sure."

The way she said it didn't make it sound like a good thing where Lane was concerned.

After cooling down enough to be allowed near people once again, Crew approached and pulled Lane to the side. Wanting to be included, I followed them down the drive and out of earshot of the first responders milling around.

I joined the guys in time to see Lane smack Crew upside the head.

"You're fucking lucky I'm the sheriff and can bury this, you dipshit. Otherwise I'd have to arrest your ass for assaulting an officer."

"He had it coming."

Lane sighed and wisely dropped it. We could both tell he wasn't getting through to Crew, not right now, and not like this.

Clearly desperate for a subject change, Lane asked, "Notice anything weird when you were knocking it down?"

"Diesel."

"I was afraid of that."

"They're fucking taunting her now," Crew ground out, his jaw ticking as he looked at me. There was such…*rage* in his eyes. I knew it wasn't directed at me, but it still had me yielding a step. Correctly interpreting my movement as fear, he blinked, replacing it with wariness and worry. Then he reached for me, and I let him take my hand, allowing the contact to soothe us both.

"That's why I'd like to take her into protective custody."

"Absolutely fucking not," Crew spat at his brother.

"I'm afraid you don't have a choice," Lane said.

"The hell I don't. She's safest here with *me*."

Lane raised a brow, glancing pointedly between us and the burned out husk of my Suburban. "You sure about that?"

"She's not going anywhere with you and your useless fucking deputies," Crew snarled, getting in his brother's face. "Definitely not with Johns involved."

"I heard that, you stupid fuck!" the deputy—Johns, presumably—shouted.

Crew shot his brother a look as if to say, *See what I mean?*

Before things could get out of hand, or before Crew could assault another cop tonight, I squeezed his fingers tightly. His attention turned to me instantly, menacing expression softening to concern.

"How about we let me decide what I want to do?"

Lane glanced at me, blinking slowly, as if remembering I stood right there while they'd been talking about me like I didn't. "I suppose that would be the humane thing to do."

I snorted. "You think?"

The sheriff pursed his lips and crossed his arms over his chest. "And I'm sure I can accurately assume you're going to stay here."

I nodded, tucking myself into Crew's side. "It's like he said: I'm safest with him."

Lane tipped his face toward the sky, squeezed his eyes shut, and sighed heavily. Then he looked at Crew. "Would you at least let Trey run a check and make sure everything is working properly?"

Crew nodded. "That's fine."

"Did I hear my name?" the third Lawless brother asked, strolling up to our little powwow.

Beyond the house, the sky had lightened considerably while we'd been out here, no longer that bruised purple right before dawn but a soft golden getting brighter by the minute.

Between this and the nightmare I'd had late last night, this had already been an especially long and emotionally draining day. I was ready to crawl back into bed.

The thought of my nightmare combined with the words on the garage triggered something else in my memory, and I blurted, "Did the firefighters find any sort of timing device?"

Their conversation about Crew's security system died, and three pairs of eyes turned to me, two of them narrowed in confusion, the third wide in understanding.

"The weird noises you heard last night," Crew said, thankfully remembering my off-handed comment from when he'd found me in his bed.

"What weird noises?" Lane asked.

I screwed my eyes shut, willing myself to recall those dark, quiet moments that had been interrupted. "Scuffling noises, I guess. I thought it might've been an animal of some sort, but there were also a couple bangs. Not loud. More like…muffled. Those happened right as I was on the edge of sleep, though, so I could've imagined them."

Lane withdrew his little notebook from his pocket, quickly jotting down what I'd said. "Where in the house were you?"

"The guest room at first, and then after the second time I heard it, I went to Crew's room."

"Because it's furthest from the doors," Lane said with a nod, as though that explained everything.

Crew and I shared a secret smile, neither of us correcting him.

Whatever was happening between us wasn't anyone's business but our own, especially not while we were still figuring it all out.

Lane continued to scribble as Crew paced away, pulling one of the firefighters aside. After a moment, the firefighter walked back to my car, which was recognizable as nothing other than a melted and blackened frame. He got on his hands and knees, using the metal tool in his hand to sweep underneath, both along the undercarriage and the ground, brushing any debris out into the gathering light.

The second the little black square appeared, and Crew swore loud enough to be heard from thirty feet away, I knew.

I'd known before, of course, but now I had confirmation.

The fire had been set intentionally.

Another deputy produced an evidence bag, dropped the square inside, and handed it off to Crew, who walked it back to us.

"You ever seen anything like this?" he asked Trey.

Trey took it from him, pressing the plastic tight to the device to get a better look at it, running his fingers over the surface through the bag.

"It's an incendiary device controlled by a remote," he confirmed. "One this size would cover a relatively small area, but combined with the gas and oil in the car, we got—*that*."

That being my totaled vehicle with a blast radius several feet wide around it.

Fuck, I was stranded here.

The thought made my skin prickle with anxiety, that desire to run taking over. My breaths came quicker, my sight going a little hazy around the edges.

"Aspen?"

My name barely registered, but then warm hands were on my upper arms, a handsome face ducking into my field of vision.

"Breathe, little phoenix."

That nickname penetrated the roaring in my ears, bringing me back to the surface enough to gulp down air.

"Is she okay?" another one of the guys asked.

A female voice piped in. "She's having a panic attack."

"Jesus Christ," someone else swore.

"Aspen," the voice attached to that gorgeous face I was coming to adore so much said softly. "Breathe with me."

I matched the cadence of his inhales and exhales, and gradually, my breathing returned to normal, heart rate lowering considerably.

In the aftermath, when the excess adrenaline vacated my system, I was shaky and drained. Crew's arms wrapped around me, and I was too weak to protest as he swept me into his arms. I buried my face in his neck, keeping my eyes closed and letting his scent soothe me.

"I'm going to take her inside. You guys do what you need to do out here, and I'll touch base with you later. I'm on shift today, so maybe swing by the station later."

"I'll need to get inside to check the system," Trey said.

"You know the code," Crew said. Then, quieter, added, "You set the damn thing."

Even in my exhaustion, I chuckled softly into Crew's shirt.

Once we were inside and the blissful quiet of the house converged around us, Crew brought us back to his room and once again settled us in the center of his bed. For a long while, we were content to sit in the silence, both of us working through the events of the morning in our own way.

"I need to get a new car," I croaked eventually.

"Let's not worry about that right now."

"Why not?" I asked, peeling my face from the crook of his shoulder to peer up at him.

"Because you're not going anywhere alone until we catch this fucker, so I don't see any reason why you need a vehicle right now."

Oh.

That's how he wanted to play this.

I threw myself from his arms and was on my feet in a flash.

"That's not how this works."

"Not how what works?" he asked, rising to stand as well, though he wisely maintained several feet of space between us. "Me wanting to keep you safe? Me wanting to ensure some deranged killer doesn't have the opportunity to finish what they started?"

I sighed. "I know you mean well, Crew. But you can't keep me locked up here like some damsel in distress. I'm a grown woman."

"I know that. And I know you can take care of yourself. But please, just...*please*."

I'd been prepared to stand my ground and press him on this until he relented, but his pleading tone took all the fight right out of me. I'd known from the very start the kind of man Crew was. One who carried the weight of the world on his shoulders in the form of wanting to protect everyone he held dear.

I knew he didn't think me incapable of watching my own back. He knew I could. He simply *wanted* to look after me, and I was fucking honored to be someone he cared about so much.

"Okay," I whispered at last.

He deflated, closing the distance between us to wrap me in an embrace. In his arms, cocooned in his warmth, was the safest place I could imagine.

"I know I've said it before, but I really couldn't take it if something happened to you. Only until we catch this fucker, and then you can go wherever the wind blows you."

The words were...almost resigned. Like he hadn't even gotten me yet and was already bracing for the day I'd leave.

Because that's exactly what would happen. We'd crack this case, put this sicko behind bars, and I'd be gone. Off on my next great adventure.

There'd be another small town. More families to save and more justice to serve.

But there'd never be another Crew Lawless.

This man...he *was* this town. His entire family was here, his roots ran deep into the ground beneath our feet. I knew there was nothing I could do or say to convince him there was a big world out there worth exploring.

A world he should explore with *me*.

We had to content ourselves with having an expiration date, so maybe there was something to be said for the fact that we hadn't yet crossed any physical boundaries beyond hugs and handholding.

It'd make it that much harder to walk away when the time came.

twenty-five

. . .

ASPEN

A FEW HOURS LATER, Crew left for work, leaving me once again alone in his big house. After all the excitement from the morning, I crawled back into his bed, his intoxicating scent surrounding me, and promptly fell to sleep.

When I woke again, a glance at my phone screen told me it was nearing three p.m. For the first time in a long time, I felt well rested. My scars weren't bothering me, and bad dreams hadn't chased me from sleep.

I got up, showered in Crew's massive, glass-walled shower, standing way too long under the head that mimicked rainwater, letting it wash over me, soothing me.

Once I was dressed and set the coffee to brewing, I squared my shoulders and strolled outside to assess the damage.

I wasn't sure whether to be happy or sad that my car was gone, leaving nothing but a wide, misshapen scorch mark in the center of the concrete pad I'd parked on. The garage doors had also been cleaned, though the once-pristine white paint now sported a pink tinge as a reminder of the words that had been there before.

You can run...

A shiver wracked my body, and I rushed back inside, slamming the door and triple checking that the lock was bolted, the security system armed—then made my rounds of the rest of exterior doors and windows to ensure the house was completely secure.

My stomach was still too unsettled to eat, despite the fact that I couldn't name the last time I'd consumed a meal, so I took my mug of coffee into the office, sitting in front of the murder board and thinking while I sipped.

What were we missing?

After another hour, my coffee was gone, and my eyes were gritty from staring so long at the wall, willing a clue to jump out at me.

I knew what I'd normally do in these situations: go for a walk. That always did wonders for my peace of mind, both from a stress standpoint, and because allowing my thoughts to wander was the perfect brainstorming activity.

Walking Crew's property without anyone nearby should something happen was a terrible idea, doubly so because I had no idea where I was going. But I was already getting a mean case of cabin fever after only a few hours cooped up inside. I needed fresh air. I needed to feel the sun on my skin and hear the whisper of the leaves on the trees rustling in the wind.

What Crew didn't know wouldn't hurt him, right?

With that thought, I brought my mug back to the kitchen, rinsed it and loaded it in the dishwasher, then retreated to my room to change into a pair of leggings and a comfy tee, pulling a fleece overtop that I could remove if I got too warm.

My taser was stuffed in the pocket. I wasn't *that* reckless.

Stepping outside instantly improved my mood. Like the band that had been holding my lungs hostage finally slipped free, allowing me my first full intake of breath since…God, I didn't know when. Maybe since before I'd been abducted.

Crew's property was stunning. The house itself was shaded

by a few maple trees, and a long dirt path cut off the main drive into a field that went on what seemed like forever until it butted up against a thick stand of pine trees in the distance. I walked along one of the narrow tracks made by years of tire treads, the tall country grasses swishing around my calves.

And to think, this and what I'd seen at the Lawless family home were only small portions of the ranch land. I found myself wishing to explore all of it, to take an ATV and ride along tracks like this one that likely crisscrossed the acreage. I wanted to learn how to ride a horse, hear more about the rescue and dude ranches, pick Trey's brain about his security company. Listen to Aria sing for a crowd. Get Birdie to tell me more stories about her late husband and the son who didn't live here.

I wanted *everything* when it came to this place.

I stumbled a step, that thought pulling me up short.

For the first time in way longer than I could remember, despite the fact that I had a crazed serial killer after me, I was at peace. This place, these hills and valleys, the people.

Crew.

All of it had settled me in a way I'd never found before, not even in my own home. I loved my parents, but I'd never been very good at living up to the high standards Lola had set, and when she was gone, well…I couldn't compete with a dead girl. I missed my sister with every fiber of my being, and I wished more than anything she was still here, giving me nieces and nephews and growing old alongside me. Instead, she was frozen in time as that perfect girl about to graduate college at the top of her class, forever setting the bar out of my reach.

I knew Mom and Dad loved me, and maybe they didn't mean to, but they constantly made me feel like I was never good enough. Like everything I did fell short of the woman they expected me to be. And that included when I'd landed the *Sun Times* job right out of college. Instead of "We're so proud of the woman you are," I often heard "Why can't you be more like Lola?"

After the ordeal that ultimately had me giving up my life in Chicago in favor of running as far away as I could, I stopped trying to meet their expectations, though they still refused to give up the fight. Mostly Mom. Dad was happy one of his daughters still drew breath.

I didn't understand why that couldn't be enough for Mom. Even now, after I'd almost lost my life *again*, she hadn't been able to let the impossible standards go, nor had she given up trying to micromanage my life despite my constant protestations.

After leaving Chicago, getting my PI license and bopping around the country had been fun—in theory. But I'd never felt the pull to put down roots any deeper than the shallow ones I'd planted in Denver.

That was nothing compared to the way I felt about Dusk Valley.

A lot of that had to do with my sexy-as-sin, tattooed, over-protective roommate.

I spent a few hours wandering the property, and while nothing in regards to the case jumped out at me, I felt recharged when I returned to the house.

Until I walked inside and was greeted by the faint strains of music.

Someone was in the house, and I knew it couldn't be Crew. He'd texted me a bit ago from the station to check in.

Wrapping my fingers around the taser in my pocket, I prowled down the hall from the mudroom, pausing to peek around the corner into the kitchen.

I found Trey at the stove, humming softly to himself while he stirred a pot of something bubbling, steam wafting into the air around him and scenting the room with a deliciousness I couldn't name.

"What the fuck," I breathed.

Trey whirled on me, grin on his face. "Nice walk?"

"How did you—" I cut myself off, mentally smacking myself in the head. "The cameras."

He nodded. "They're placed sporadically around the property to keep an eye on things."

"Someone should've told me."

"Where would the fun be in that?"

I grumbled in response, then withdrew my phone to call Crew.

"Hey, little phoenix," he said in greeting, and the nickname had warmth blooming in my chest.

"Why is your brother here?"

"I asked him to come check on you."

"So now I'm a captive *and* I need a babysitter?"

"You just took an unsupervised walk on my property," he reminded me. "You're hardly being held captive."

I snorted. "*Unsupervised* my ass. You had eyes on me the entire time."

In the background on his end, an alarm blared, and Crew cursed under his breath.

"I have to go, but we'll talk later."

"Don't bother," I said, hanging up.

All the peace I'd found on my walk evaporated in an instant, replaced by a fury so consuming, I was genuinely shocked smoke didn't pour from my ears.

I whirled on Trey, about to tell him to get the fuck out, but he held up a hand.

"I'm not leaving, so you can give up on that little crusade right now. I made you dinner, so you can sit down and eat with me like a good girl, and *maybe* I'll leave you alone afterward."

"Fuck you."

"Only if you ask nicely."

Groaning, I clenched my fists at my sides, pressing my nails into my palms until the sting grounded me. Otherwise I'd do something insane like take a swing at him.

"Really, I don't need you here. Your fancy security system will keep me safe until Crew gets home in the morning."

"No can do, little one." He pointed the wooden spoon, stained red from the sauce he'd been stirring, at one of the island stools. "You might as well sit and enjoy the meal."

Knowing there was no way I was getting rid of him, I reluctantly slid onto the seat. "I'll eat because I have to, but I can assure you I won't enjoy anything about this."

Trey tipped his head back and laughed. "I like you."

"The feeling is not mutual."

With a grin, he returned to the stove, and I texted Crew.

ME

I hate you.

HOTSHOT

C'mon, little phoenix. You don't mean that.

ME

Okay fair. But I do hate your brother. I don't need a babysitter, Crew.

HOTSHOT

I know you're miserable, and I'm sorry, but please do this for me. If it makes you feel better, he's a hell of a cook—and maybe I'll make it up to you later.

That got my attention.

ME

I'm listening…

HOTSHOT

We'll discuss when I'm home 😉

ME

You're a menace.

HOTSHOT

See you in the morning 😇

I cursed and dropped my phone face down on the counter. Trey chuckled, his back still to me. "I take it that went well."

"I'm stuck with you until tomorrow."

"I promise I'm a good time when you get to know me."

Truthfully, I didn't doubt that, but Trey wasn't the kind of good time I was interested in. It did, however, make a certain amount of sense to get to know him platonically if I was going to be sticking around and becoming a permanent fixture in Crew's life.

But that was putting the cart before the horse. I hadn't even talked to Crew about the epiphany I had on my walk. I couldn't get ahead of myself.

Trey moved around the kitchen like he knew the layout as well as he knew that of his own home, and I had to guess he spent a significant amount of time here. Despite the way they antagonized each other, the brothers were obviously close.

My eyes practically glazed over as I stared at him, my mind a million miles away.

To me, having a vehicle had always equated independence. As long as I had wheels and enough money for gas, I could go wherever I wanted, and no one could stop me. I'd gotten my license only a few weeks before Lola died, and I used to drive around in her car, blasting the mixed CDs she kept stowed neatly in a case in the center console, crying and missing her.

Now, I was effectively trapped here like a princess in a tower, and I *hated* it. Hated Trey for invading our space—yes, *our*, and no, I wasn't going to examine that word choice too closely. Hated this killer for putting my life in danger and dragging Crew and his family into it.

Most of all, I hated myself. For not being stronger. For not being able to find this guy already. For being taken down so easily outside the bar that night, and for giving this fucker the chance to continue terrorizing this wonderful town and its residents because I couldn't remember a goddamn thing about the day I'd been held captive.

"You're thinking awfully hard over there," Trey said without looking at me as he plated the pasta dish, then withdrew a bottle of wine from the pantry.

"Want a glass?" he asked.

I shook my head, knowing I needed to keep my wits about me where this man was concerned.

And damn was I grateful I had as the next twenty minutes played out.

Once he'd poured himself a healthy serving of the Cabernet, he grabbed the plates of food and inclined his head to the table.

"Come eat."

"I'm fine here."

Like hell was I sitting at that table with him like this was some sort of friendly meal.

As far as I was concerned, Trey was an interloper, and interlopers didn't get cordiality.

"Fine," he said tersely, his unflappable attitude was starting to wear thin.

Unceremoniously, he dropped the plate in front of me, and I grinned at the shift in his mood. Maybe I could piss him off enough to make him leave.

Not interested in carrying on a conversation or even acknowledging his presence, I dug into the food.

I barely silenced the moan that wanted to escape me.

First Crew, then Birdie, and now Trey? Was there anyone in this family who was a bad cook?

"You can say it," he chuckled softly. "It's amazing, isn't it?"

I swallowed the mouthful and spared him a quick side eye. "It's…fine."

"Keep fighting it," he said, and I saw his mouth stretch into a grin in my periphery. "But you know that's the best pasta puttanesca you've ever had."

Not bothering to respond, I shoved another forkful into my mouth.

Yeah, equally as good as the first.

And maybe I'd been teetering on the edge of hangry, because the more I ate, using the thick, crusty slice of homemade garlic bread to mop up any lingering sauce on my plate, I almost softened toward Trey.

At the very least, I came to tolerate him enough to not be outright hostile when he asked me questions. Unlike with Crew, though, I kept my cards close, giving him clipped answers.

For the entire meal, he tried and failed to engage me in a meaningful conversation. Honestly, I should've bolted to my room the second the last mouthful passed through my lips, but I remained rooted in place.

Which gave Trey the perfect opening to do something really fucking stupid.

He put his hands on me.

One of his massive palms slid up my thigh, pinky arcing dangerously close to the apex, and I scrambled to my feet, knocking over the stool in my desperation to get away from him.

"What the fuck are you doing?"

"C'mon, Aspen," he grinned. "We're all alone in this big house with nothing else to do. Why not pass the time getting lost in each other?"

"Because I want nothing to do with you," I spat.

"No, you want my brother. But newsflash, Aspen. You've been living in this house with him for over a month and he hasn't made a pass at you." I nearly made a noise of protest, but I wasn't giving Trey the satisfaction of being right. He smirked. "You don't know my brother like I do. He's too fucking noble to cross that line with you because he sees it as taking advantage of a woman in a vulnerable state. And he's spent his entire career protecting women and removing them from such situations."

Was that really how Crew saw me? A legitimate damsel in distress who couldn't take care of herself?

No. I shook my head, throwing off Trey's words before they could settle and burrow beneath my skin.

Trey may think he knew his brother, but he didn't—not really.

Crew wasn't locking me in this house because he didn't think I could take care of myself, and he hadn't asked Trey to keep an eye on me because I *needed* a babysitter.

Trey was here ensuring my safety because if something *did* happen, he didn't want me to be alone. He wasn't worried I wasn't strong enough to handle whatever was thrown at me. He was worried about something happening to me and him not being here for me. Like my nightmare last night when I ran to him and he was gone.

Siccing his brother on me was the next best thing.

Still, that little niggling doubt wormed into my brain and wouldn't let go.

Why *hadn't* he made a move yet? There was no denying the physical connection between us. And for all his teasing and flirting and filthy promises, we *hadn't* crossed that line, though clearly we both badly wanted to.

Lost in my inner turmoil, I hadn't noticed Trey closing the distance between us until his hands snaked around my waist.

Instantly, my knee came up to his balls, and he dropped to the floor.

"What is wrong with you?" I hissed. "He's your *brother*."

Trey wheezed from the fetal position, looking up at me through watery eyes.

"Just checking the temperature around here," he managed to gasp out, unfurling slightly from the ball he'd been curled into and resting on all fours.

"What the fuck is that supposed to mean?"

He was silent for a long time while he marshaled himself, and I couldn't help but grin down at him. It seemed all my self-defense lessons paid off because I'd gotten him *good*.

At last, he sank back on his heels and scrubbed a hand over his face, sucking in gulps of air that eventually steadied.

"Crew is obviously into you," he started, staring up at me, his face beet red as he struggled to regain his composure. "And now, I know you're into him and can't be swayed otherwise. I think maybe you two should stop dancing around it, and I just gave you the push you needed."

"What happens between me and Crew is none of your business."

"Keep telling yourself that, *little phoenix*. But my little brother has never once had an extended house guest, nor has he ever brought a girl to the ranch...until you. If you're going to be around, you're all of our business."

"He's doing me a solid by letting me stay here," I protested weakly. "And he didn't want to leave me alone."

Trey shot me a look as if to say *get real* as he gingerly rose to standing, hand cupping his junk to adjust himself—or maybe to protect himself from further assault.

"If I never have children, I blame you," he groused as he gathered our dirty dishes and his empty wine glass from the island and took them to the sink, where he rinsed then loaded them into the dishwasher.

"You'd have to find someone willing to sleep with you first," I shot back. "And I'm not going to hold my breath."

Trey chuckled. "Yeah, you'll fit in just fine around here."

I didn't press the issue because truthfully, I was done with the conversation—done with Trey. So instead, I watched as he cleaned.

Like his brother, his movements were efficient and confident when he wiped down the counters and returned the kitchen to its original state. Where Crew only had a single sleeve of tattoos engulfing his left arm, Trey had one and a half, the ink on his right arm stopping right above the crease of his elbow. If it wasn't for the fact that Trey was slightly taller and leaner, telling him apart from Crew, and even Lane and the twins, would be difficult.

He was, objectively, good looking. All the Lawless boys were beautiful. But my blood didn't heat at the sight of any of them the way it did with Crew.

Trey making a pass at me had forced my hand, and Crew's as well. As irritated as I was, I could almost appreciate it. He knew I'd tell Crew what happened, and Crew would either put up or shut up.

Still, I held my ground, watching him head for Crew's room where he'd be sleeping.

I almost begged him to switch, but that would only make matters worse. So I let him go, staring at his retreating form, eyes darting up to his gaze when he paused at Crew's door and turned back to me.

"You could do a lot worse than my brother, Aspen. And you could do a lot worse than calling this town home."

With that he disappeared.

I know, I wanted to say.

I figured that out already.

twenty-six

. . .

CREW

WAITING for the third shift lieutenant to come in and relieve me the next morning was pure torture, like watching the clock tick down on those final seconds before summer break back in high school. I hadn't heard from Aspen since our texts the night before, and I'd have been worried if my brother hadn't stayed with her overnight.

Then again, where Trey was concerned, maybe I should have been worried anyway.

No, I mentally scolded myself. *She's into you. And even if she wasn't, she* definitely *isn't the kind of woman that would hook up with your brother under your own roof.*

The moment the lieutenant walked into the firehouse, I was off like a shot, racing down the halls and outside to my truck.

"Someone is in a hurry!" Tuck called after me.

"Yeah, I'm…exhausted!" I called back.

Tuck and the guys snickered behind me and my lame-ass excuse.

"Or maybe you're just pussy whipped!"

Turning toward them, I flipped Childers the bird before throwing myself behind the wheel of my truck. I peeled away, tires squealing, the guys cheering me on. I drove too fast through town, but I couldn't find a fuck to give.

I was paused at the stoplight when my phone started ringing, and I answered via my truck's Bluetooth.

"Morning, Sheriff."

"You leave work yet?" Lane asked.

"Yep. On my way home."

"Turn around and get your ass to the station."

"Has there been a break?"

Lane hummed. "You could say that."

Checking both directions to make sure nothing was coming, I whipped a U-turn in the middle of Cassia and sped back in the opposite direction. Thirty seconds had me parked in front of the station. I hustled inside, the desk clerk buzzing me in before I could utter a word.

"Hey, Cap," one of Lane's deputies said. "He's in interview two."

The smaller of the interview rooms, I noted, wondering what that could mean.

Unfortunately, I knew the layout of the police station about as well as anyone who worked there did, and it wasn't thanks to a previous lifetime as an employee.

I'd spent numerous hours across those metal interview room tables from law enforcement, being scolded and questioned about one incident or another.

Spent a decent amount of time in the holding cells in the basement of the building too, drying out after a bender.

My knock preceded me into the room, but I didn't bother to wait for an invitation. On one side of the table sat my brother in full uniform. Across from him sat a teenage boy, with floppy, dishwater blond hair and pale skin. Even sitting down, I could tell he was tall and lanky. It'd be a few years yet before he grew into his limbs.

"Captain," Lane said, nodding in my direction.

Ahh, we were using official titles. Okay then.

"Sheriff," I replied.

"This is Parker Abrams," Lane said. "Parker, this is Captain Lawless with the Dusk Valley Fire Department."

The kid may have been young, probably fifteen or sixteen by my guestimation, but he wasn't dumb, and he easily put the pieces together.

"Lawless?" he asked. "Like…"

"The captain is my brother, yes," Lane conceded. "But that's not why he's here. Our departments frequently work together on arson cases, and we understand you've got some information for us regarding last week's dumpster fire."

Parker leaned his elbows on the table and bent over them, steepling his fingers under his chin. "First, I want some assurances."

With Parker's advance, Lane reclined into his chair, and I pulled up one next to him, flipping it backward so I could rest my arms across the back.

"What kind of assurances?" my brother asked.

"That I won't be charged for this."

Lane snorted. "You know that's not possible, Parker. You deserve some sort of consequences for your actions."

"Then give me community service. Just…not juvie. My mom and sister won't survive if I'm sent away. Not with…*him*," he spat.

There was true fear in the kid's eyes, and I had to wonder what kind of life he'd been living if he was concerned about leaving his mom and sister with this man.

"Tell you what," Lane said, matching Parker's body language. "I'll let you off with a warning if you tell us everything you know."

"Done."

I snorted, and Lane cut me with a glare. Beneath the tattoos and the gruffness, the man was a fucking softy. Always had been.

"Tell us what happened then," I urged.

"I was walking home from school the other day. Normally I cut through the park down on Elm because sometimes I like to go there and chill before I gotta head to the house." His expression remained impassive as he added, "My stepdad is a prick."

Ahh, the infamous *him*.

Parker didn't elaborate, but I could guess "prick" encompassed a whole lot of shit that would get the authorities involved in Parker's life in a way he clearly didn't want.

"I was sitting on the swings, minding my own business, when this person approached me. Dressed head to toe in bulky, black with one of those ski mask things covering their face."

"What did they want? Could you tell if they were a man or a woman? Height? Weight? Age?"

Lane was practically vibrating, and his little notebook made its appearance. I settled on hand on his shoulder, silently urging him to chill the fuck out.

"Easy, Sheriff," Parker said with a grin. "I'm getting there."

"Then *get there*," Lane gritted out.

"Bro," I hissed. "Get it together."

Lane exhaled sharply through his nose and gestured for Parker to proceed.

"They asked me if I wanted to make five hundred bucks. And I don't know about you guys, but five hundred bucks? That's life changing money for someone like me. I've been working hard at saving up so I can get the fuck out of here after graduation, and that money would go a long way."

"So you said yes."

Parker raised a brow, eyes darting between us. "Wouldn't you?"

I shrugged. "Fair enough."

"I asked what I had to do, and they told me all they needed was for me to set fire to the dumpster behind Mozzy's that night.

They gave me two fifty then, and I'd get the rest when the job was done."

Lane was bent over the table, scribbling, and didn't look up when he asked, "Any identifying features?"

"Tall-ish?" Parker phrased it almost like a question. "Probably a few inches shorter than six feet. No idea if they were a man or woman, though. Their voice was all jacked up, like they were using some sort of device to distort it. Like Batman or some shit."

I couldn't help but chuckle. This kid was really growing on me. His act of arson notwithstanding, he appeared to have a really good head on his shoulders.

"Why did you turn yourself in, Parker? You've lived here your entire life, so you have to know we didn't find anything on the cameras or our door to door canvas."

"I've been doing some thinking, and I've come to realize this has to be connected to the Prom Night Arsonist, right? Like…the person that paid me is likely the killer?"

A shiver wracked his body as he spoke, and I understood the feeling. Coming face to face with someone who had murdered twelve people and almost took a thirteenth out would make anyone's skin crawl.

"Yes, Parker. We think the dumpster fire is connected," I said.

"Do you have the money by chance?" Lane asked.

Parker leaned to the side and dug through the backpack resting at his feet, withdrawing the thin stack of bills and sliding them across the table to my brother. Without a word, Lane got up and left the room, returning shortly thereafter with an evidence bag, a pair of nitrile gloves covering his hands.

"We'll send this up to Boise for fingerprinting and other diagnostics," Lane said as he slid the bills into the bag.

"They were wearing gloves both times I met with them," Parker said. "I doubt you'll find anything."

I had to agree with the kid, and I was sure Lane did too.

Only Lane had gone completely still, the only movement of his body his eyelids slowly opening and closing.

"You met with them twice?"

"Yeah," Parker said, clearly confused by the question. *That made two of us.* "Once when they approached me in the park, and then after the fire when they gave me the rest of the money."

Lane sealed the evidence bag and swept it off to the side, then peeled the gloves off and returned to his chair, pen poised over his notebook once again.

"Where'd you meet the second time?"

"In that little field on the backside of the school gym."

For another ten or so minutes, Lane pressed Parker for more information, asking Parker to recount every minute detail he possibly could. I had to admit, I was impressed. The kid had incredible recall, and though the person who'd approached him didn't give much in the way of identifying information, Parker handled each of Lane's questions with poise. Finally, when there was nothing left to say or ask, Lane let Parker go with only the promised warning.

We followed him out and when Parker turned right toward the front of the building and the exit, Lane and I headed left toward his office.

The door slam behind us was heavy, and Lane's carefully crafted facade began to crumble right before my eyes.

"This guy has evaded capture for forty years," Lane said. "This kid is the first solid lead we have—"

"And Aspen," I cut in.

"—and the fucker made certain to completely mask his identity."

Without warning, Lane's fist shot out and slammed into the wall, punching a hole clear through it. Dust floated around him, and several pictures fell, shattering on the floor.

"Woah!" I shouted, grabbing his arm a second before he landed another. "What the fuck?"

Lane pulled away from me and stalked behind his desk, resting his palms on the surface and bending over.

"I fucking hate this guy, Crew. Anytime we get close, he takes off running. It's like he's forty steps ahead, and no matter what I do, I can't close that distance."

I moved to his side and placed a hand on my brother's shoulder. He was tense as a statue, and I didn't envy him this job that made him feel like he carried the weight of the world on his shoulders.

Hell, I understood that feeling better than anyone.

"We're going to catch him, Lane."

Without looking up at me, he simply nodded and exhaled harshly.

For the sake of my own sanity, I had to believe that was true.

"You good?" I asked. "I'll stay if you need me, but—"

"Fuck," Lane breathed. "You've gotta be exhausted. Go home. I'm fine."

I eyed him. "You sure?"

"Promise," he nodded. "Gonna be fun explaining to the city why I need to allocate funds to fix my office wall, though."

I chuckled as I headed for the door. "Knowing you, I think they'll understand."

twenty-seven

. . .

CREW

I PULLED into my driveway as Trey exited the house through the porch door. My brother didn't stop to chat, merely waved and hopped into his truck before peeling out in a cloud of dust as I navigated into the garage.

Weird.

But I didn't stop to give it much thought in my desperation to get inside and see Aspen.

After the ordeal with her car, I wasn't taking any chances, and I closed the garage door before I got out of my truck, then ambled into the house. After kicking my boots off, I headed for my room, ready to curl around Aspen and fall asleep.

Only, my bed was empty and the door to the guest room was closed. Had Trey slept in here instead? I supposed that made sense. There wasn't anything happening between me and Aspen, *yet*, and she likely wouldn't want to draw attention to the distinct lack of *something* by asking Trey to sleep in the guest room.

Still, I hated that my sheets wouldn't smell like her when I eventually crawled into them.

But after the interview with Parker this morning, I was too keyed up to sleep. Plus, I'd managed a decent stretch between calls last night anyway. I showered quickly, changed, then headed to the kitchen, got coffee brewing, and started on breakfast.

The smells must have enticed her out of bed, because a few minutes later, Aspen appeared.

"Hi," she murmured as she slid onto a stool right as I placed a mug of coffee in front of her.

"Morning, gorgeous."

Aspen's cheeks pinked, and she hid her grin behind the cup as she sipped.

She pulled the mug away slowly, staring down at it as if it were a puzzle she wanted to solve.

"Something wrong?"

"You know how I take my coffee," she whispered.

I grinned, immensely pleased with myself. "We've been living together for over a month, little phoenix."

"I wasn't aware you'd been paying attention."

Holding her cinnamon gaze, I spoke my next words confidently and without hesitation.

"I've done nothing else since I met you."

The gentle, healthy glow turned to a full blown blush that crept up the collar of her shirt and into the apples of her cheeks. She ducked her head, hair falling in a curtain around her, blocking her from view.

My smile remained as I turned back to the stove and finished our omelets.

Once our food was done, I placed our plates side by side and climbed onto the stool next to her.

"Between you Lawless boys and your mom, I've been incredibly spoiled by food since getting out of the hospital," she said as she dug in.

"Told you Trey was a good cook."

"Yeah, he's…something."

My fork paused halfway to my mouth as I noted the subtle discomfort underlying her tone.

"What did he do?"

She waved me off. "It's nothing. Tell me why you got home so late."

I quirked a brow, my brother momentarily forgotten. "You noticed?"

"You're not the only one who's been paying attention."

The way she said it told me she was embarrassed, and that was the last thing I wanted.

"I like that you've been watching me," I assured her, nudging her with my elbow. "Makes me feel like I'm not alone in this."

"You're not," she said, glancing at me sideways for a beat before returning to her food.

We ate in silence, and I practically inhaled my eggs. Though I'd managed some decent sleep last night, I couldn't remember the last time I'd eaten, and I hadn't realized how starving I was until we sat down.

Although, once the hunger pains in my stomach were satisfied, I still found myself ravenous.

And it had nothing to do with food.

Side by side, Aspen and I cleaned up the kitchen, then retreated to the living room so I could tell her about my morning and the interview with Parker.

"Brave of him," she said when I'd finished.

"I thought so too."

"He's taunting us now. The killer, I mean."

"Yeah," I agreed. "Looks that way."

She didn't respond, merely stared blankly at the wall, and I'd do anything to bring her back to me. I couldn't imagine what was swirling around in that brain of hers, but I was desperate to find out. Her sudden silence drew me back to the way she'd responded when I brought up Trey earlier, so I decided to poke that bear again.

"How was Trey? What'd you guys do?"

"Oh, he made a pass at me," she said absently.

Then as if realizing what she'd admitted, and so carelessly at that, she slapped a hand over her mouth and stared at me, eyes wide in horror.

"He *what?*" I exploded, coming off the couch and damn near flipping the coffee table over.

"Fuck," she breathed, standing and putting her hands out as though to steady me.

But there was nothing steady about me, nothing calm in the way my blood roared through my veins.

Trey had made a pass at Aspen?

My Aspen?

That stupid fucker.

I was going to kill him.

"Were you even going to tell me?"

"Of course I was. I was working my way up to it."

"Why?"

"Because I knew you'd react like this! And frankly, I don't see what the big deal is."

"The big deal? *The big deal?*" I roared. "Why are you acting like it's *not* a big deal?"

After everything we'd shared, how was she being so cavalier?

Had I misread the situation that badly?

Completely disregarding the rage obviously coursing through me, Aspen stepped closer. Right into my personal space. Wrapping me in her goddamn intoxicating scent, making it difficult to breathe.

"Why wouldn't I?" she asked. "I'm not in a relationship. In fact—"

My hand came up to her face, squeezing her chin between my thumb and forefinger.

"Do *not* finish that sentence."

Her palm pressed to my chest, tiptoeing her fingers upward to the curve of my shoulder, around the back of my neck and into the short hairs at my nape.

Everything within me and between us moved, like a seismic shift of the very foundation we'd built our friendship on. Because that's what we were—friends. Through the late nights and early mornings, long talks about life, this fucking serial killer, and the weeks spent sharing this space, a friendship had blossomed between us.

Now, I wanted to be so much fucking more than her goddamn friend, I thought I might go insane with the force of it. Genuinely might lose my mind without an outlet for how badly I wanted her.

In a flash, my anger became desire, the heat licking at my veins morphing into the need to own her.

"There's nothing happening here, Crew," she pressed, though I noted with no small amount of satisfaction that her chest was heaving, her small, perky tits brushing my upper abdomen with every inhale.

"The fuck there isn't," I growled.

Then I crashed my mouth to hers.

There was nothing soft and sweet to be found in that kiss. I was savage and claiming, my tongue shoving carelessly into her mouth, teeth dragging over her lips, opening her wider. I fucking *moaned* with that first taste of her, coffee and something so purely *Aspen*, a heady combination I hungrily drank from her lips.

Gripping a handful of her hair, I tugged, angling her where I wanted her. She whimpered into my mouth, her tongue meeting each stroke of my own.

Fuck, I loved that sound. I wanted to see what other ones I could get her to make. Wanted to see if she'd make it again with my tongue buried in her pussy.

My blood damn near boiled, my skin tightening. I needed to have her. Now. Right here in the middle of this fucking living room. I'd fuck her into next week bent over the back of the couch.

We were all hands and savage teeth, sighs of pleasure and

moans of desperation. I'd never had a kiss like this, one so all-consuming it seemed to sink deep into my bones and root there.

A kiss could make a man crazy, and hers had set me on fire.

Aspen was an addiction—and for once, I wasn't afraid of getting hooked.

I peeled my mouth from hers, and Aspen gasped for breath, but I didn't let her go. My hands remained at her waist and in her hair, fingers digging into her skin. I was too far gone to give a fuck about hurting her. I *wanted* to see my marks on her skin. Remind her exactly who the fuck she belonged to.

"How do you feel now, Aspen?" I asked, resting my forehead against hers. "Still think there's nothing happening here?"

She tilted her face to nip at my jaw. "Take me to bed, Crew. Make good on everything you just promised me with that kiss."

I hauled her over my shoulder before she'd fully finished speaking, carrying her down the hall, though I took a quick detour into the guest room where she'd been sleeping.

"What're you doing?" she asked, her voice floating up from somewhere around my ass. God, I was fucking feral for this woman. The fact that she was letting me manhandle her like this? I was a fucking goner.

I didn't answer her, simply rifled through the drawer of the nightstand until I found what I was looking for, then continued to my room, slamming the door shut behind me before I dumped her in the center of my mattress.

Aspen lifted onto her elbows, those cinnamon eyes darkening as she watched me twirl her vibrator over my fingers.

Girls like her always had a vibrator. Likely because no man had ever fucked her good enough to make the toy obsolete.

That was, of course, because she'd never been with *me*.

"You wanna play, Aspen?"

"I'd rather have the real thing."

I chuckled darkly. "All in good time, pretty girl." I palmed myself through my sweats. "You'll get this all day long. In fact, by the time I'm through with you, you'll be begging me to stop."

"Promises, promises."

"You know I'll make good on them."

Aspen rose and crawled to the edge of the bed, then sat back on her feet, toying with the hem of her shirt. Finally making a decision, she gripped it and pulled it over her head.

Leaving her topless and looking like every fucking fantasy I'd ever had come to life.

Her body was gorgeous. Pert little tits with dusky rose-colored nipples. Trim waist and a flat abdomen shadowed by muscle. Thick, delicious thighs that strained against her silky pajama bottoms.

"Goddamn," I breathed. "You are…stunning."

She grinned shyly, and as she shifted slightly to hide her left side, suddenly it occurred to me why.

Her burns.

"Don't hide from me," I said softly, moving closer and lifting one of her hands from her lap before placing it on my forearm.

Aspen gasped as her fingers traced the skin that was marred beneath my tattoos—the reason I'd started getting them in the first place.

"What happened?"

"I've got all kinds of these. Hazard of my job. But this one was my first, and it's the worst. It was the first major blaze I'd worked after finally moving up from candidate to full-fledged firefighter. There was a woman trapped in a room, and I thought I could get to her. Went in way too cocky. Half the ceiling ended up collapsing on me."

"And the woman?"

I shook my head. "She didn't make it, and I spent a few weeks in the hospital and another four rehabbing until I could go back to work."

Moving to her side, I reached out and trailed my touch over the fresh pink skin spanning her left side.

"The point I'm trying to make here is your scars don't determine your worth." I met her gaze. "In fact, I think you're even more beautiful because of what you've endured."

"Little phoenix," she whispered.

Grinning, I nodded. "Exactly. So don't hide from me. Let me explore all of you."

"Okay."

I relaxed, grateful she felt so at ease with me to give in so quickly.

"Now where should we start?"

"I took a bath in here a few weeks ago, you know," she said, almost conversationally, nodding at my en suite then the vibrator. "Brought that guy with me."

"This puny thing?" I said, waving the toy through the air.

Aspen smirked. "It got the job done."

"What'd you think about?" I asked as I flipped it through my fingers like some sort of baton. "All alone in *my* bathtub." *Twist.* "Naked." *Flip.* "And soaking wet."

"You," she said simply. "Imagined what your hands would do to me." She reached for me, palm rubbing against my cock where it tented the front of my sweatpants. "How well this cock would fill me."

My answering grin was downright feral. "Wicked girl. I'll make every one of those daydreams a reality."

Aspen tipped herself back on the bed and slipped out of her pajama bottoms, the silky black fabric sailing across the room. That left her in only a pair of pale pink panties that wedged between her pussy lips as she spread her legs for me.

"What do you want, Aspen?"

"You. All of you."

The answer was immediate and final.

"Then that's what you'll get," I assured her, moving until my knees bumped against the foot of the bed. "But make no mistake, little phoenix. The second I fit myself between those pretty thighs and get my first taste, there's no going back."

Her hair swished against my comforter as she shook her head.

"I don't want to go back. I only want you."

And that was enough for me.

So I dropped my pants and shed my tee, leaving me entirely naked before her.

"Fucking hell," she breathed. "You can't possibly be real."

"I'm very real, baby. *This* is real."

"I'm about to become a real big slut because of you," she mused. "That nipple ring gives me all kinds of dirty thoughts."

With my free hand, I reached up and toyed with the hoop pierced through my left nipple, pinching and tugging it. "You can be as slutty as you want, baby. But only *here*. Only with me."

She grinned. "Deal. Now show me what you got."

I still gripped her toy, so I wrapped my other hand around my cock and held them side by side, wanting to see how I compared to the thing she'd been using to get off.

Aspen choked on a laugh.

"You better not be laughing at me," I warned, palm rasping up and down my shaft once. God, even that one simple touch was almost too much. I felt like a teenager again, ready to combust with a single tug.

"Of course not. Your cock is beautiful, hotshot. I'm laughing because I have no fucking idea how it's going to fit after I've been using *that* for so long." She gestured toward the vibrator, the bright pink silicone dwarfed by my broad palm.

And, yeah, next to my dick? I hadn't been lying earlier when I called it "puny."

I grinned. "Don't worry. You can take it." Finally, I crawled onto the bed and laid down on my stomach, my shoulders pressing her thighs wider as I came face to face with her cunt. "But how about we warm you up first?"

"God, please."

"Not God, little phoenix. Just Crew."

"Please, *Crew*." She squirmed closer as I lifted the toy and brushed the blunt tip through her sex, the silicone coming away glistening. Her eyes were glued to me as my tongue darted out and worked around the toy, tasting her arousal for the first time.

My eyes closed and a moan fell from my lips. "You taste incredible. But next time, I'm taking it from the source."

Aspen reached down and hooked her hands behind her thighs, spreading herself wider.

"Now, *please*."

"Fuck, you're so pretty when you beg. You want me to eat while I fuck you with this little thing?"

She bit down on her bottom lip and nodded. "You can tease me. I…I like to be edged."

"Aspen…" I groaned, her name a prayer.

I'd met my match with this one.

Too many of my previous partners had rushed or wanted to skip foreplay entirely, but I fucking loved it. Loved toying with women until they were panting, sweaty messes desperate for my cock. Until my dick was weeping with the desire to fill them. I had…urges that maybe went beyond what was normal. Somehow, I didn't think Aspen would balk or judge me for them. I had a feeling this woman would be down for whatever I threw at her —and would come back for more and more and more.

The toy buzzed in my hand when I powered it on, but I ignored it for the moment in favor of bringing my mouth to her flesh, groaning when her taste exploded on my tongue.

I wanted to make this good for her, wanted to drag it out until she was clawing at me, begging for release, but I wasn't sure I had it in me to wait. Especially not when I inserted a finger into her and felt how hard she clamped around me.

"Fucking hell, woman. This tight little cunt is going to destroy me."

"Crew," she whimpered, wriggling her hips and grasping at the sheets. I'd barely touched her and she was already strung out.

Good, I thought. Now she experienced a fraction of the hell I'd been in since the first time I laid eyes on her.

Withdrawing my finger, I lifted up on my elbow and brought it to her lips.

"Suck."

Aspen's eyes widened but she opened up, and I shoved into her mouth. Her lips and teeth closed around the digit, tongue swirling as she lapped me clean—and moaned.

"See how good you taste?" I asked when I pulled free. "Now you'll understand why I'm happily going to die right here between your pretty thighs."

My name fell from her lips, begging me to touch her, and at last I relented.

Bringing the toy to her sex, I ran it up and down her seam, coating it in her arousal before slowly inching it in, flipping backward so the little bunny ears designed to stimulate her nub rested against her taint.

Her clit was mine, and as I began to work the vibe in and out of her, I flicked my tongue against it. The skin was silky smooth and I sucked it between my lips, working it against my teeth and tongue. That sharp scrape had Aspen's hips bucking against me.

"That's it," I murmured, pulling away slightly to speak. "Ride my face."

Tentatively at first, trying to find a rhythm that worked combined with my mouth and the toy, Aspen's hips swiveled against my face. But she settled in quickly, the easy undulation timed perfectly to each flick of my tongue and pump of the vibe.

Soon, she was riding out my ministrations like I hoped she'd ride my cock—roughly and with abandon, like the only thing that mattered was her orgasm.

And to me, it was…which is why I quickly jerked the toy free and removed my mouth from her body.

twenty-eight

. . .

CREW

"CREW!" she growled in frustration, her chest heaving. I could tell from the way her pussy spasmed that she'd been close to coming. She pulsed like she needed something to grip and a little bit more pressure to get her there.

"Patience," I said, turning the vibe off and tossing it across the room. "I promised I'd take care of you, and I will. Don't you trust me?"

Despite her obvious annoyance and the eyeroll I wanted to fuck right off her face, she nodded.

"Good girl."

Roughly and without warning, I shoved three fingers in her cunt, and Aspen's back bowed off the bed.

"Fucking hell," she breathed.

"Gotta stretch you out." Jesus, even full of three of my long, thick fingers, she was still incredibly tight. I was going to make her come like this, then I knew I couldn't wait any longer to replace my hand with my cock. Pressing my pelvis deeper into the mattress, the pressure against my dick was the only thing keeping me from coming before I got inside her.

"That's…a lot," she whined, but slowly relaxed around me,

enough so I wouldn't hurt her as I began to move. Not thrusting in and out but curling my fingers repeatedly inside her, rubbing against her inner walls experimentally until her legs started to shake.

And then I was merciless, curling them faster and faster against that spot as I lapped at her clit like a man starved. Aspen's whimpers grew in volume until she was screaming for me, hands buried in my hair and tugging the strands.

"Yes, little phoenix," I growled against her. "Get there."

With a final crook of my fingers and the sealing of my lips around her clit, sucking it deeper into my mouth, my girl fucking *shattered*.

My timing perfect, I withdrew my hand and replaced my mouth with my fingers on her clit, rubbing quickly as she soaked my face. Her entire body shook with the force of her climax as I wrung her out, the wave continuing to roll through her, her spasming endless and beautiful.

I stilled only when her fingernails drew blood on my arm.

"I—" she gasped, unable to finish the thought from lack of oxygen.

I grinned as I rose up and leaned over her to my nightstand where I kept my condoms, withdrawing an entire line of squares and tossing them next to her.

"I don't think I can," Aspen said softly, almost embarrassed.

"You can, sweetheart," I told her, bending to pepper her face with kisses before settling on her mouth. In deference to how hard I'd made her come, I was gentle, a slow, sensual slide of my lips against hers, tongues lazily tangling. It did nothing to let her catch her breath, but she was grinning dreamily at me when I pulled away.

"Okay," she said, wrapping her legs around my hips and urging me closer so the tip of my cock brushed against her. "But no condoms."

I blinked in surprise. "Are you sure?"

"I don't want anything between us, Crew. I'm on birth control, and I haven't been with anyone in a long time. I trust you, and I want to feel you."

This woman was truly going to be my undoing, and I didn't even care. I was running headlong into the mayhem, knowing I'd come out an entirely different man on the other side.

Reaching between us, I gripped my dick and ran it through her lips, coating it in her cum and spreading it down the length. "For what it's worth," I told her as I notched my head at her entrance, "I also haven't been with anyone in a long time, and I had a physical at work a few months ago. Everything came back clear."

Aspen hooked her ankles together at the base of my spin, and my tip slid inside. The pressure against my crown was fucking unreal, and I dropped my head to her shoulder, moaning as she said, "Then I'm yours, hotshot."

I thrust home on a single long pulse, and I swear to God, stars exploded across my vision.

Something irrevocably changed within me in that moment, like the entire foundation on which I'd built myself cracked and shifted into something different. I stilled, momentarily unable to move. She took me perfectly, but the connection was more than that. I'd never been this close to someone in my life. By welcoming me inside her body, Aspen had cracked the door between our souls, allowing them to merge into something else entirely.

For the first time in my life, I felt…whole.

Aspen clung to me, her fingertips dancing paths up and down the expanse of my back, and she lifted her head to flick my nipple ring with her tongue.

"I know," she whispered when I pulled back to look down at her, seeing everything I felt reflected in her cinnamon stare. "*I know.*"

The first few pumps of my hips in and out were slow, careful.

Taking the time to watch the spot where I disappeared into her body. I'd been right to assume she'd fit me like a glove. Tighter, in fact. The squeeze of her pussy around me bordered on pain. But I'd be damned if it wasn't the most exquisite torture.

"Nothing has ever felt better than you," I murmured. "Fuck, you fit me so perfectly. We were fucking made for each other."

"Crew," she whispered after a few more gentle strokes.

"You okay?"

"Better than," she grinned. "But I need you to do something."

I stilled. "Yeah?"

"Fuck me. I'm not going to break, hotshot. I can take it."

"You want hard and fast, little phoenix?"

"I want whatever you like."

I chuckled. What a loaded statement.

"We'll work our way up to that," I promised, pressing a hard, claiming kiss to her mouth.

With her permission, I unleashed, my hips setting a relentless pace as I pounded into her. The bed creaked beneath us with every advance and retreat, and Aspen's moans turned from breathy to full-throated screams as I branded that spot deep inside her recklessly. Holding myself upright with one palm on the bed next to her head, I gripped her hip with the other, holding her down as I pistoned in and out. Her nails dug into my shoulders, scraping down my back, hanging on for dear life as I drove us right to the edge of that cliff…

And sent us careening right off. Aspen's arms and legs fell away as she spasmed beneath me, her entire body quaking as she thrashed against her climax.

Goddamn, she was a sight to behold, her hair a dark corona around her head against my pale blue sheets, her eyes squeezed shut, mouth parted in ecstasy as she chanted my name over and over.

I followed her right down, my back bowing, limbs going rigid, her name breathlessly falling from my lips as I spilled hot and long inside her.

When we stilled, I brushed her hair off her face to check on her, greeted with a fully sated smile that had my own lips spreading into a grin. Then I pulled free, shifted from between her thighs, and landed on my back. I gathered her to my side, rubbing soothing circles across her back as she ran her fingers through the smattering of chest hair between my pecs, her breaths fanning over my skin, our legs tangled. Even an inch of space was too far away from her now.

The silence between us stretched, but not uncomfortably. Simply *being* with Aspen, basking in the afterglow of our joining was the easiest thing I'd ever done.

This thing between us was quickly becoming *everything* to me.

"I think you just altered my brain chemistry," I said when I had enough breath to do so.

Aspen propped her chin on my chest to look up at me, delight twinkling in her eyes. "Crew…you made me *squirt*."

She hissed the last word like something dirty, and I barked out a laugh, hauling her over me so I could reach her lips for a kiss.

Scars and all, we belonged together. I'd known it for a while now, but the way our bodies fit together so perfectly only further confirmed it.

"Has it ever been like that for you?" she asked.

I tucked her hair behind her ears, wanting to fully see her beautiful face.

"Never," I promised. "There's something here, isn't there?"

Without missing a beat, Aspen nodded.

"I don't know what it is, and it terrifies the shit out of me, but…yeah."

Rolling so I once again hovered over her, I said, "You're not the only one who's scared, Aspen. But we're in this together. I'm not going anywhere."

"I don't know what happens after this," she admitted, and I knew she didn't mean our fucking mind-blowing sex, but the case that had brought her to town in the first place.

"We don't have to have it all figured out right now. Can we agree to take things one day at a time?"

She nodded, and the anxiety that coiled in my chest every time I thought of her leaving dissipated.

I pressed another gentle kiss to her lips, then her nose, before sinking back on my haunches and hauling her into my arms and climbing off the bed.

"Where are we going?" she asked, though she sank deeper into my hold, slinging her arms around my neck and resting her head against my chest.

"To get cleaned up. Bath or shower?"

"Bath," she said quickly. "My legs are fucking jelly."

I grinned. "Damn straight, baby. And there's more where that came from."

Aspen gave me an eye roll, but it did nothing to dampen her answering smile.

There was no way I'd ever be satisfied where Aspen McKay was concerned. My sexual appetite had always been voracious, but everything was different now.

I was falling in love with her, and that changed everything.

twenty-nine

· · ·

ASPEN

CREW FILLED the tub with borderline too-hot water—the way I liked it—and some eucalyptus-scented bubble bath that had been hiding under the sink. When the water reached the perfect level, he stepped in and relaxed against the edge, then helped me in after him. I reclined with my back to his chest, cocooned in the warmth of his body and the water surrounding us.

"A girl could get used to this," I mused as I ran my fingertips over his kneecaps which jutted above the surface. The tub was massive, likely custom made to fit his big body, but with his long legs bent, they still extended past the lip.

"Sex so good you can't walk?" he asked, brushing my hair off my shoulder to bend and press a kiss there.

"That too," I giggled as he hit a particularly sensitive spot right above my collarbone. "I meant *this*." I gestured to our current situation. "Being taken care of. A man giving me life-altering orgasms followed by him relaxing in the bath with me."

I could get used to a lot of things where Crew Lawless was concerned. The camaraderie, the care he showed me both in and out of the bedroom, the safety I'd found in his arms.

The sex too, but while I'd spent the time since I'd met him knowing without a doubt it would be explosive between us, it had also been tender in a way I hadn't expected. He was gruff and commanding, wringing pleasure from my body like wringing water from a rag, but he never pushed for more than I could take. With him, I knew I could take even more than he'd given me. And I wanted to explore all of that, find out exactly what he meant when he said we'd work our way up to what he liked.

But I wanted more from him that went beyond being physical. For the first time since my sister died, a future where I wasn't alone stretched out before me. I no longer wanted to punish myself for something that hadn't been my fault.

I still had secrets, and I wanted to share them with Crew. Wanted to unburden myself for the first time since I'd left Chicago in the rearview nearly a decade ago.

"We agreed to one day at a time," he said, almost like he was reminding himself more than me, "but I'll give you whatever you want for as long as we're together."

"Ditto," I managed to choke out around the emotion suddenly clogging my throat.

His lips continued to ghost along my skin as he murmured, "Tell me about your sister."

With the warm water lapping around us and the heat of his skin on mine, I couldn't remember the last time I'd felt so protected. So I opened my mouth and talked about my sister in a way I hadn't done with anyone ever.

I told him about growing up with Lola as my idol. We were nearly seven years apart in age, my parents trying for years after she was born to have another until finally, they got pregnant with me as they were about to give up.

"She wanted to be a pediatrician," I said, smiling. "And I have no doubt she would've had a whole brood of her own children. Secretly, I think a lot of that stemmed from growing up with a sister so much younger than her. She was almost like a third parent. By the time I reached high school, she was nearly done with undergrad. She was the first person I'd gone to for advice, the first call I made when something good or bad happened." I swallowed hard, trying to get through this next part. "And then she was…gone. Caught in a fire in one of the older buildings on campus and I never saw her again. Never got to hear her voice, or hug her and tell her I loved her. I never even got to say goodbye."

Tears streamed down my cheeks, and Crew shifted me around to cradle me against his chest, swiping at my face with his thumbs.

"She was so badly burned we had to have her cremated," I choked out. "My parents couldn't even visually identify her. They had to use her dental records."

"Fuck," he breathed, pressing a kiss to my hair. "I'm so sorry."

"It was a long time ago," I whispered, trying to play it off if only to regain my composure. "I shouldn't still be crying about it."

"Hey, no," he said, turning my face until I looked up at him. I wanted to drown in the blue depths of his eyes. "You're allowed to feel sad. And cry about it. Grief isn't linear. My dad has been gone since I was ten, and it still fucking hurts to think about."

"I'm sorry you lost him."

"I think he would've liked you," Crew said with a soft smile. "I'll have to go visit him soon and tell him about this girl who turned my world upside down."

Craning my neck, Crew caught my drift and met me for a kiss. "In a good way, I hope."

"In the *best* way."

"What was he like?"

"He was the hardest working man I've ever known, and that's as true today as it was the day he died. I still don't know how he and Mom did it, balancing running the ranch with having seven kids, but they made it look easy. He'd be gone before we even got up for school in the mornings, but he was always home for supper at night. He wasn't the kind of man that made my brothers and I feel bad for having big feelings. He showed us it's okay to cry, or to be so happy you felt like you could burst with the force of it. And most of all, he allowed us to dream."

"He sounds amazing."

Crew swallowed hard and nodded. "He was. Admittedly, I'm the lowest man on the totem pole when it comes to the pecking order in my family, but even with my oldest brother, Owen, he never forced him into anything. Owen realized at a pretty young age he was good at football, and obviously, his talent only continued to grow the older he got. Mom and Dad made it possible for him to chase the NFL dream, never guilting him into feeling like he had to stay behind and run the ranch. The rest of us were free to do what we wanted with our lives too. My dad was the best man, and I miss him every day."

"Is he buried in town?"

Crew shook his head. "Nah, he's buried on the ranch. Mom couldn't bear to have him too far away, so we set up a plot along the edge of his favorite stretch of pasture. It's a short horse ride from the house, and she goes out there at least once a week. One day, she'll rest there beside him."

My heart ached for Birdie, knowing she had to spend the rest of her life without the other half of her heart.

"We spread Lola's ashes on the shores of Lake Michigan. But she's always with me anyway," I said, tapping my chest right over my heart.

"You could get a commemorative tattoo," he smirked. "Really make it permanent."

I scoffed. "And before you know it, I'll look like you."

"Tattoos are addictive," he agreed. "But really, I know a guy. I'll hook you up." He reached around and ran his hand over the burn scars on my left side. "You could get these covered too…if you wanted."

"I'll think about it."

Against my backside, I felt Crew's dick start to stiffen, and I giggled.

"Really? Talk of tattoos turns you on?"

"Baby, there's nothing about you that *doesn't* turn me on, but the thought of your body all covered in ink? Yeah, I like that *a lot.*"

I rose up out of the water enough to kiss him again, cupping the back of his head and holding him to me, nibbling at his lips, his tongue stroking a lazy path across mine.

When I pulled away, I said, "I like *you* a lot."

Crew's answering grin was bright and carefree, giving him a boyish air I'd never seen before. "The feeling is mutual, little phoenix. Why don't you let me show you how much?"

My toes curled in anticipation. "Do your worst, hotshot."

Wordlessly, he flipped me around so my back was once again to his chest. His cock speared between my ass cheeks, and I wriggled around, loving the smooth slide and the way Crew's breath hitched.

"If you don't stop that," he ground out, "I'm going to fuck that hole, and I don't think either of us are ready for that."

I shivered in response but said, "How do you want me?"

"My favorite words," he murmured into the back of my neck as he leaned forward, shifting my body with him. "Hands on the edge of the tub." He placed them exactly where he wanted them, so I was bent slightly forward, then gripped my ankles and put my feet next to his quads, pressing them against the sides of the tub so I couldn't move. His legs stretched out flat beneath me so I hovered over his lap. Then he reached under the water and between us, and the bubble bath had cleared enough for me to see him fist his cock. It brushed against my slit a moment later, and I twitched against the contact.

"Think you can ride me like this, little phoenix?"

I peeked over my shoulder at him and shot him a smirk. "Only one way to find out."

His cock slapped my seam, and then he held it at my entrance. "Sit down then."

Yes-fucking-sir.

As I sank slowly onto him, my head fell forward as a moan escaped me. God, he was huge. By far the biggest cock I'd ever seen or been with. All the edging earlier had been necessary to fit him inside. Now, aided by the water and knowing I could take him, we only met a little resistance as I took him into my body.

When I was fully seated, my ass resting against his thighs, he reached for me. With a hand around the front of my neck, he pulled me backward, bending me so he could kiss me.

My spine arched, contorting me into a position that should've been uncomfortable but wasn't.

Honestly, I'd let Crew break me in half and still come back for more with the pieces that remained. *That* was the kind of hold he had on me.

Not unlike his massive palm spanning my neck, which pressed on my windpipe with enough pressure that I knew he could crush it if he wanted. I didn't care; he'd already proved I could trust him with my life.

"Move."

With aching slowness, I used my quads to lever myself up, dropping my ass back to his lap quickly. Then again, and again, spearing myself on his cock over and over.

I found a rhythm after only a few strokes, and Crew pumped his hips upward every time I came down, forcing himself impossibly deeper. No man had ever hit that spot before, the one I'd only ever been able to locate with my vibrator.

The vibrator I'd have to throw away because if it wasn't Crew's cock, I didn't want it.

"Fuck, look at you," he groaned, thrusting up into me, then

shifting his hand off my throat to hook his fingers into one side of my mouth. I bit down on them, swirling my tongue over the sting, eliciting another rumble from his chest. "You feel so fucking good. I swear my cock was molded specifically for your pussy, little phoenix."

"I'm so full," I agreed, the words coming out slurred and garbled around his fingers.

"Told you."

"Told me what?" I asked, though it sounded more like, *toe me wha?*

"That you could take it."

I glanced back at him in time to see him wink at me.

Then he let go of my face to grab me, his massive palms easily wrapping around my upper arms as he held me in place and bucked up into me.

There wasn't anything I could do but enjoy the ride, unintelligible words and sounds of pleasure falling from my lips as he fucked me. My orgasm shimmered, just out of reach.

"More, more, more," I chanted.

Understanding what I needed, Crew gathered both of my arms in one hand, using his other to reach around me and find my clit.

"Oh, shit, fuck," I swore as he touched me, glancing pressure at first that felt so fucking good but still was not quite enough.

"You wanna get off, Aspen?"

"*Please.*"

"Beg for it, baby. You can do better than that."

The longer he toyed with me, the greater a mess I became.

"Please, Crew. Please," I begged, moments away from tears in my desperation to climax. "Please let me come."

He pulled me back further, angling me to better access that bundle of nerves, and I felt his thighs tighten beneath me as his toes flexed into the end of the tub, anchoring himself in place. I writhed atop him, panting, desperate for more friction.

"Who fucks you this good, Aspen?"

"You do."

"No one else but me."

"No one."

"This pretty pink pussy and this tight little body are mine now. Understood?"

"Yes!"

"Good girl," he said, picking up the pace of both his hips and his fingers. My quads burned as I leveraged myself up and down on his length, driving us both to the brink. Water splashed everywhere, slopping over the sides of the tub and into my face.

I didn't care. The world could've been ending beyond this room, and I wouldn't have noticed as my pleasure arced higher and higher and higher.

At last, the wave crested and fell, dragging me into the deep where my entire body went rigid before breaking apart in spasms. From head to toe, I shivered and thrashed against Crew's hold as he continued to work me. Roaring his own release moments later, his cock pulsed inside me, prolonging the aftershocks of my own.

That orgasm went on for hours—no, *days*.

My brain was wiped entirely clean when I returned to myself. Not a single thing in the world penetrated the afterglow save Crew when he slipped free from my pussy and I collapsed against him.

He banded his arms around me, burying his face in my neck.

Neither of us spoke, but my stomach emitted a loud growl, and Crew chuckled.

"Since you like me taking care of you so much, let me feed you," he said, palm sliding down to rest on my abdomen. "And then, I need to get some sleep."

"Oh my God!" I yelped, shoving out of his grip and stumbling out of the tub. My legs wobbled, about as useful as two pieces of licorice. "Why didn't you say something?"

A brow curved toward his forehead, then raised his hands in

front of him, lifting one higher than the other. "Fucking you…or sleeping. The choice seems obvious to me."

With a huff, I stumbled to the linen closet and withdrew two of the fluffy white bath sheets, wrapping one around my body before returning to him.

Crew smirked at me, which only raised my ire.

"What're you laughing at?"

"You," he said simply.

"Get out of the tub, Crew, and stop dicking around."

"Oh, I'll show you dicking around," he grinned, reaching for me.

"No!" I said forcefully, dancing out of the way, even stomping my foot a little to make my point. "I can feed myself. You get out and get into bed right this instant."

"You're kinda bossy."

"You have to be exhausted," I groused, moving to the other end of the tub and pressing the lever to release the drain plug. Water gurgled as it coiled down the pipes.

"It's a good kind of exhausted," he said, finally standing and accepting the towel I held out to him.

I tried, I really did, but I couldn't keep my eyes off him. From head to toe, the man was the pinnacle of masculinity. Sandy blond hair, the longer strands on top damp and spiky from my hands brushing through. His perfect face, those high cheekbones and jaw so sharp it could cut glass. The crystal blue eyes I learned darkened when he was angry or aroused, the straight nose, the full mouth that said the wickedest things but could be so gentle on my body. The broad shoulders and chest, arms roped with muscle, the chiseled abs and obliques that cut in at his hips. The long, muscular legs. Hell, even his feet were perfect.

The tattoos and the smattering of hair on his chest and lower abdomen turned what would be a pretty boy into the most gorgeous, rugged man I'd ever laid eyes on.

And the fact that his muscles weren't only for show? And that the tattoos covered scars he'd gotten saving lives?

I damn near fell to the floor at his feet and begged him to keep me forever. To know of all the women in the world, this man—this gorgeous, intelligent, overprotective man—wanted *me* was surreal to say the least.

"What's that look for?" he asked as he wrapped the towel around his waist.

"Trying to figure out how I got here."

"You rolled into town in that piece-of-shit car, were taken hostage by a crazed serial killer arsonist, and had that gorgeous ass saved by the hottest firefight in the world."

His grin was cheeky, and he stepped close to me, wrapping my own towel around my shoulders and hauling me into his chest.

My entire body sagged in relief, like one touch from Crew was all I needed to unwind.

"Never been more grateful for a near-death experience in my life."

Crew fisted my hair and peeled my head off his chest so he could bend and capture my mouth. I fucking loved the way this man kissed—with his whole body, wrapping himself around me and injecting the slide of his plush lips against mine with every emotion swirling within him. When he pulled away, I was panting, ready to go for another round.

I was officially *insatiable* where he was concerned.

Those gorgeous blue eyes held mine as he said, "Let's not have a repeat of that, okay?"

As he'd said it before, it went without saying this time around. In the way he kissed me, the reverence with which he held my body, how he played with me until I was a writhing mass of pleasure until I came so hard I forgot my own name, I knew. But also in the small, quiet ways he took care of me: knowing how I took my coffee, wanting to stay awake to feed me, hell, even asking his dumb older brother to stay with me when he was on shift.

I knew how he felt.

He wouldn't survive it if something happened to me.

And I understood because the feeling was mutual.

I'd barely survived losing my sister.

I didn't think I could do it again if something happened to Crew.

thirty

. . .

CREW

MY ALARM PULLED me from the hottest fucking dream I'd ever had in my life.

Only when I slowly blinked my eyes open to the dimness of my room did I realize it wasn't a dream at all.

Instantly, my hand found Aspen's hair as she bobbed her mouth up and down on my cock.

"Fuck, baby," I rasped, voice still thick with sleep. "My filthy little slut."

Aspen only flicked her gaze to me and hummed around my length as she took me deeper and deeper until my head bumped the back of her throat. I was fucking obsessed with her little gag, and how her eyes watered, the sharp inhale through her nose. How none of it deterred her from taking me another inch.

Her hand chased her mouth as she pulled off, the other one fondling my balls in a way that had them drawing up. The base of my spine tingled with impending release.

"How do you want it?" I asked.

Over the last four weeks, since the first time we'd slept together, Aspen had given me more blowjobs than I could count, and her mind was always changing on where she wanted me to unload. I fucking loved how she kept me on my toes. We hadn't worked our way entirely up to my…rougher appetites, but she'd taken everything I'd thrown at her in stride, greeting it all with equal fervor.

She was making it damn hard not to fall completely ass over boots in love with her, and honestly, I didn't give a fuck. As far as I was concerned, Aspen McKay would be the last woman I ever fucked, and my dick would be the last one she ever let in that tight pussy of hers.

"Inside me," she said, scrambling on top of me and reaching between us to shift her panties out of the way and sink down on my length. Both of us groaned, and I gripped her hips hard enough to bruise as she rolled them back and forth, working me in and out of her warmth.

"Fucking hell, little phoenix," I moaned as the sounds of her pussy sliding over my cock filled the room. "I love how wet you get for me."

Aspen hummed in pleasure as she rocked faster, her short nails digging into my chest as she rode me. This was without a doubt my favorite position. Her perfect little tits bounced in time with her movements, her mouth opened in ecstasy as she chased her orgasm, the nub of her clit rubbed against the root of my cock. Watching her unabashedly take what she needed from me was so goddamn sexy.

I knew she was getting close when her inner walls closed even tighter around me, milking me, so I bucked up into her. She cried out and let go, collapsing against me at the same moment my release barreled through me, and I emptied into her while she quivered in my arms.

Our chests heaved in unison as we came down from the high. When my breathing returned to normal, I brushed her hair off her face and planted a kiss on her forehead, which prompted her to tilt her head back and give me a real one.

"Morning," she murmured.

"And what a good fucking morning it is," I grinned. "Unfortunately, I really do have to get up for work now."

She clung tighter to me, arms banding around my chest as if that could keep me here in this bed with her.

"You can't leave me."

"Trust me, there is nowhere else I'd rather be than right here with you. But—"

"We can't leave the citizens of Dusk Valley without their hottest firefighter," she parroted, and I laughed, digging my fingers into her sides to elicit that giggle I loved so much.

The words had become a bit of a running joke between us over the course of the last month. The first time, two days after I'd first taken her, she'd been the one to utter them. Saying that, despite how badly she wanted to keep me here with her, she knew she couldn't prevent me from doing my job.

I hated leaving her as much as she hated to see me go.

"It's twenty-four hours," I promised, like I did every time. "Twenty-four hours, and we'll be right back here."

"I'm counting on it, hotshot."

With a final kiss, I rolled her off me and got out of bed, knowing she'd fall back to sleep while I showered and got ready.

After getting dressed and packing my bag for work, I made a travel mug of coffee for myself and set another one up so all she'd have to do when she got up was press a button. I even went so far as to leave a little note for her.

I miss you already. Text me when you're up.

Xo,
Crew

Was it cheesy? Hell yeah.

Did I give a fuck? Absolutely not.

By the time I rolled to a stop outside the fire station, I was damn near walking on air. Even four weeks into this thing between us, the shine had yet to wear off. We were in the honeymoon phase, and it wouldn't always be sunshine and roses, but I was thoroughly enjoying our time together.

I didn't only mean in bed, either.

We'd been to the ranch for family dinners three more times, and my mom, sister, and the twins fell more in love with her every time they saw her. Lane, of course, was keeping her at arm's length while the investigation was still ongoing.

As for Trey, well…he was fucking lucky I didn't bash his face in the first time I saw him after Aspen told me what he'd done. He kept his distance, being sure to sit as far away from us as possible at dinner and never speaking directly to Aspen or I was liable to growl at him.

The whole charade annoyed the shit out of Mama, but I wasn't ready to forgive him for making a pass at my girl *under my own roof.*

The discord between us wasn't all bad, though. I'd used it to con him into upgrading my security system for free so Aspen felt safe enough to stay there alone at night when I was on shift.

Things on the Prom Night Arsonist had been quiet since the dumpster fire. The lack of any movement on the case would lull normal people into a sense of security, like maybe the killer had decided to go dormant, but people like Aspen, Lane, and I knew better.

Something was coming, and we'd be ready to greet it when it arrived.

"Hey, lover boy," Tuck cooed as I walked into the firehouse and made my way toward the locker room.

I rolled my eyes, shoving him playfully as he got all up in my personal space, making kissy noises at me. "You're so annoying. It's no wonder you're still single."

Tuck scoffed. "I'm single because I *want* to be, not because I don't have options."

I snorted. "Keep telling yourself that, kiddo," I said, ruffling his hair like I would a little boy's.

Tuck ducked away from me then put up his fists in a fighting stance. "You wanna go, old man?"

"I'm three months older than you."

"You started it by calling me 'kiddo,' and you're still *old*er," he pointed out. Then he dropped down on the bench while I got changed and put my bag inside. "But in all seriousness, man…it's good to see you happy."

"Thanks, brother. Appreciate it."

Truthfully, I was still getting used to the idea myself. Before Aspen came along, I had been happy enough—with my family, my job, life in general. But having her by my side made everything better.

Suddenly, I understood what love songs were all about, and why women were obsessed with romance novels.

I wanted to be that kind of boyfriend for Aspen.

Though, the word "boyfriend" pulled me up short because we hadn't exactly slapped labels on anything yet. An oversight I vowed to correct the second I got home tomorrow morning.

She couldn't deny me when I was giving her orgasms, right?

THE FIRST TWELVE hours of shift absolutely slogged by. The only call we got was for the ambulance, which had to respond to a single car accident out at the county line.

The guys and I sat around, twiddling our thumbs, playing endless hands of poker, using jelly beans and M&Ms as chips.

Around ten, with nothing better to do, we decided to tuck in and catch some shut-eye while we still could.

That proved to be wise, because some hours later, the alarm cut through the silence, pulling us all instantly from our slumbers.

The dispatcher's voice rang out when the bells dropped off.

"Truck twenty-seven, engine forty-five, ambulance thirty-five. Residential fire, two hundred block of Willow."

We geared up and headed out, our sirens and lights a noisy, animated procession through the otherwise still night. Everyone in town would be awake now, and they'd all be migrating in this direction to see what all the fuss was about.

"I fucking hate residential fires," Childers said. "You never know what you're going to find."

I nodded my agreement, adrenaline flooding my system. At this late hour, the chances the house had been empty were extremely slim, and I had to hope the residents had awoken and escaped unharmed.

As usual, we were the first on scene, and I shoved my helmet on my head as I hopped out of the truck and took stock of the situation.

The blaze from the two-story house lit up the night sky like a candle in a darkened room. The exterior of the structure glowed red, which indicated the fire was already in the walls. Flames poured from the blown-out windows, licking at the siding and gables of the roof. What I was sure had once been a gorgeous, welcoming front porch was now charred and leaning dangerously to one side, likely minutes away from pulling away from the house and collapsing entirely.

Chief's buggy screeched to a halt at an angle across the street, blocking any through traffic. He exited, grabbed his gear, and approached me.

"What've we got?"

"Looks fully involved," I said, indicating the haze of dark

smoke that blanketed the air above the house. "Haven't gotten in yet, so right now, that's all I know."

"I've got IC," Chief said with a nod. "Take your team and do a *quick* internal sweep. Two start in the basement, two start upstairs, and meet in the middle." He eyed me warily, knowing I tended to go a little cowboy on calls like this. "I'm talking five minutes tops. Understood?"

I gave him a mock salute as I paced away, grinning. "Aye, aye, Chief."

His lips moved with mumbled words, though I was too far away to hear them. Likely talking shit, which only made me smile wider.

"Twenty-seven!" I shouted, and three men appeared out of the smoke and shadows to line up in front of me. "We're going in, so mask up. We're going to do a very quick sweep to clear it of any potential victims. Childers and Burns, I want you two to start in the basement. Tuck and I will take the second floor. *Do not split up*. Eyes on your partner at all times. Got it?"

My men nodded, already strapping their SCBAs to their faces. I donned my own, then followed the three of them up the pathway to the entrance. We breached with a well-placed donkey kick from Tuck, bumped fists, then headed inside.

God, the temperature was excruciating. In an instant, I was dripping with sweat, my base layer clinging to my skin beneath my turnout gear. Even with the mask providing me coverage and fresh air, I could still feel the heat on my face.

"Fucking hot!" Burns shouted.

"We've likely got even less than five minutes! Be quick!"

Childers and Burns nodded before heading around the corner in search of the basement staircase. At my six and with his hand on my shoulder, Tuck and I proceeded up, testing each riser before fully putting our weight on it. The last thing we needed was to end up in the basement with Childers and Burns.

At the top of the stairs, I led us toward the left, figuring we'd start at the end of the long hall which three rooms branched off and work our way back. Thankfully, all the doors were open, and Tuck and I shuffled into the first. He knelt to check under and around the bed while I moved to the closet. In fires, those were the two most common places people would hide to try to protect themselves. There wasn't anyone in either, so Tuck and I moved onto the next room, clearing it and the third in record time.

As we descended to the main floor, Childers and Burns reappeared.

"Perfect timing," Childers grinned. "Find anything?"

Tuck held out his empty hands. "Obviously not, dipshit."

Childers held his own up in surrender. "Just checking."

"Stop dicking around and do your jobs!" I shouted, shoving Tuck forward toward the little hall that jutted off the living room. At the end was another enclosed room that appeared to be some sort of office. There wasn't a bed, but Tuck looked behind the two armchairs on one side while I approached another closet.

When I swung the door open, a wall of flame leapt out at me, and muscle memory had me dropping to the floor as it shot over my head.

"Fuck!" Tuck yelled. "Cap, you good?"

His face appeared in my vision, hand outstretched to help me up when I waved that I was fine.

"Fucking hell," I said. "I thought that was gonna take my head off."

Tuck choked out a laugh. "I thought it did. Closet is clear, though. Let's get the fuck out of here."

"Status report," Chief's voice crackled over the radio.

"Upstairs and basement are clear. Main floor is nearly clear and then we're heading out."

"Good job, boys. See you out here."

After a final pitstop to check behind the shower curtain in the small bathroom and receiving confirmation from Childers and

Burns that the living, dining, and kitchen were clear, we pushed out into the night.

"Open those lines up!" Chief shouted as soon as we appeared, and a heartbeat later, the distinct hiss of water hitting flame filled the night.

Sutton and Thomas approached, handing each of us water bottles. After we removed our masks, Tuck and Childers dumped theirs over their heads while I settled for sipping mine and slipping off my turnout coat.

Police sirens cut through the night, and I watched as my brother and another patrol car pulled up, Lane and two of his men approaching the scene.

I was grateful Johns wasn't one of them. That guy had always been a prick, even when we were in school together. I'd grown up, and grown out of my bad habits, but he refused to let it go. The punch I'd delivered to his face outside my house had been a long time coming.

"Sheriff," Chief Madden said when my brother reached our sides.

"Chief, Captain," Lane replied, nodding at both of us, then to my men. "Boys."

Childers, Burns, and Tuck all jerked their chins in greeting... then promptly found somewhere else to be.

"We cleared the structure and didn't find anyone. Looks like the owners are out."

My brother lifted a hand, urging him to stop. "I could've told you that."

"You know who owns this place?" I asked.

"Yeah," Lane said, scrubbing a hand down his face. "And you're not going to like it."

"Spit it out, Lane," I ground out through gritted teeth.

My brother cut me a glare, but heaved a sigh as if psyching himself up and said, "This house belongs to Harold and Lee Leigh."

I swore under my breath as Chief said, "As in…Vicky Lee?"

"Her parents," Lane confirmed.

"Fuck!"

"Knock it off," Lane warned. "We're in public."

I got in my brother's face, anger coursing hot and heavy through my veins, not giving a single fuck that the entire second shift of the Dusk Valley Fire Department stood somewhere behind me. "Can't you see this fucker is taunting us now?" I shouted, then dropped my voice before dropping a bomb on Lane. "The Lee family is the one that reached out to Aspen. They're the reason she's here."

"*Fuck*," Lane breathed.

"Cap!" someone shouted before I could say anything further, and I whirled to find Childers standing at the perimeter, a few feet off the smoldering front porch. With two hoses, the engine crew had made quick work of knocking down the blaze, and we were about to start overhaul.

"Yeah?" I called back.

"We've got accelerant. Smells like diesel."

A string of colorful curses flew from my mouth.

Always the level head in any situation, Chief settled a hand on my shoulder and said, "Take a walk, kid. Get your shit together, then come back and lead your men."

Before he'd finished speaking, I was pacing away, peeling off my gloves. When I reached the truck, I grabbed my phone off the dash and called my girl.

"Crew?" Aspen said sleepily when she answered.

"Hi, baby."

"Are you okay?" she asked. Sheets rustled on her end, and if I closed my eyes, I could see her sitting up in bed—*my* bed— brushing her hair behind her ears and rubbing her eyes. "You never call me from work. And it's the middle of the night."

No, I didn't. But I needed to talk to her, both to calm myself down and to remind myself that she was safe at home.

"I'm sorry for scaring you," I said. "But I'm fine. Just on a call and wanted to hear your voice."

Shit. That had been the wrong thing to say. The last thing I wanted to do was worry her, but I was freaking the fuck out, and my mind to mouth filter was busted.

"What's going on?" she asked, completely alert now.

With a resigned sigh, I said, "We got called out to a residential fire."

"Is everyone okay?"

"Yeah, everyone is fine. Engine knocked it down, and we did an interior sweep to make sure it was empty."

"Okay…"

"The house, Aspen." Fuck, I really didn't want to tell her, but I ripped of the bandage. "It belongs to the Lees."

Aspen gasped loudly, the sound followed by a gentle thud.

"Aspen?" I asked. "You okay?"

When she answered, her voice sounded far away and small, and I decided she must have dropped her phone. "That family has been through enough, Crew."

"I know, baby. The upside is they weren't here, so no one got hurt."

"I fucking hate this guy," she choked out, her tone watery, like she was on the verge of tears.

God, I wished I could hold her. I wanted to comfort her, to wrap her in my arms and assure us both that everything was going to be alright—even if I didn't entirely believe it at the moment.

"We're going to get him," I vowed. I didn't know how, but I knew I wouldn't stop until this fucker was dead or behind bars. Honestly, I didn't have a preference, and I doubted Aspen or anyone else in this town did either.

Aspen sniffed and said, "Okay. Be safe, hotshot. Come home to me."

"I will," I promised.

We hung up a short while later, and I walked back to Chief and my brother.

"You good?" Lane asked.

"Yeah."

I wasn't. None of us were. But I had a job to do.

"I'm going to send some deps out on interviews with the other families that are still local," Lane said. "And I'll be putting in calls to the rest."

"Why?"

"I want to make sure the local ones are aware this is something that could happen. I don't want to see anyone else lose their home or their life on my watch. As for the families that have moved, I want to see if anything funky has happened to them, or if it's only happening here in town. It'll give us an idea of if the perp is mobile or not."

Thumping my fist into my brother's shoulder in an understanding gesture, I said, "Keep me posted, yeah?"

"In the interest of full disclosure, there's something else I should tell you."

"Yeah?"

"We let Chris go late yesterday afternoon."

"What do you mean, *let him go*?"

"He finally made bail thanks to his flunkies, so we cut him loose." Lane shrugged. "Do with that what you will."

Was he…?

Nah, not possible.

There was no way Lane was giving me permission to go off book here, right? He was the *sheriff*, the paragon of justice and doing the right thing and following the letter of the law.

But still, as I caught his gaze, something glimmered there, and I picked up what he wordlessly conveyed to me.

With a sharp nod, letting him know I understood, Lane saluted me and Chief, then walked back to his cruiser, where his deputies had gathered.

"What was that about?" Chief asked.

"I'm not sure," I lied.

Chief's attention was a brand on the side of my face, but I didn't dare look at him. Instead, I focused on the scene, making a mental plan before approaching my guys to execute it.

"Stay out of trouble," he warned as I moved away.

I spared him a glance over my shoulder. "Always do."

His disbelieving snort followed me all the way across the yard.

thirty-one

. . .

CREW

IN WHAT FELT like the blink of an eye—but was really more like four hours—the crew and I trudged back into the firehouse. Once the engine guys had knocked down the blaze, we all spent some time on overhaul, meaning we walked through the structure to ensure the fire was entirely extinguished and made sure the house itself was stable enough to stand until the Lees decided what they were going to do with it. An insurance adjuster would need to come out, photograph it, and process a claim. Plus, I was sure that, if anything inside *was* salvageable, the Lee family would want to go through and take what they could.

My limbs were heavy with exhaustion, but my veins hummed with electricity as I made my way toward the locker room for a shower. The second my shift was up, I had somewhere to be.

Unfortunately, crawling into bed with Aspen, which was where I desperately wanted to be, would have to wait a few hours.

ME

Gonna be late getting home this morning.
Wanted to give you a heads up. Miss you.

Aspen's response was almost immediate despite it being six a.m.

LITTLE PHOENIX

Miss you too. Everything okay?

ME

Yep. Just have to take care of something.

LITTLE PHOENIX

A case-related something?

ME

Mhm. I'll fill you in when I'm home

Two hours later, the second the third shift lieutenant was through the door, I was racing for my truck, shouting a hasty goodbye to Tuck and the rest of the guys.

I didn't bother to turn on the radio as I drove across town, knowing it would only add to the mess of thoughts already at full volume in my brain. My anxiousness had my fingers drumming on the steering wheel as I rolled down the path I'd taken count-less times before.

When I stopped in front of the shitty house, more grey now than white thanks to years of neglect, I wondered if I was making a mistake. This place had been the sight of so many lost nights for me, and while I was over a decade past the boy I'd been, it would be too easy to trip and fall back into old habits.

I'd seen it happen too many times, and I worked too long and too hard, both in therapy and for years avoiding any sort of trig-ger, to go back.

There was no "recovered" for someone like me. You were either recovering—a lifelong process—or you were an addict. Knowing how thin the line between the two was put my confi-dence on shaky ground.

Still, it had to be done.

With a fortifying breath, I got out of the truck and approached the front door, deciding how I wanted to play it. I could go in guns blazing, or I could sit him down and try to talk some sense into Chris.

Ultimately, he made the decision for me.

No sooner had I reached the top step of his porch than did Chris appear in the doorway, a fucking knife in his hand, pricking the skin of my abdomen.

"The fuck you want, pig?"

God, I fucking hated this guy.

In a smooth move, thanks to years of training with Finn and West, who had taught me all kinds of shit they'd learned in the Rangers, I had the blade knocked out of his hand. Shoving him inside, I kicked the door closed behind me, then pressed him into the nearest wall with my arm barred across his windpipe.

"Where were you last night?"

"Here," he choked out, slapping at my bicep to get me to lay off.

I did, but only enough that he could draw air slightly more comfortably. I couldn't have him passing out before I got answers.

"Can anyone vouch for you?"

"Tito was here."

Fucking Tito. I should've known.

Tito, or Timothy Tost, was a washed up high school athlete who turned to drugs after an accident ended his football playing career. He was my age, had never left this county as far as I knew, and was as big a piece of shit as the man in front of me. Tito was considered Chris's "muscle," meaning he knocked around junkies on Chris's behalf when they didn't pay up.

Forearm still braced against Chris's neck, I sent Lane a text, asking him to track down Tito to confirm. Not that I trusted these guys not to lie.

"You sure you two didn't get doped up and go start a fire?"

Chris's beady eyes narrowed. "The fuck you talkin' about?"

"Residential fire last night," I gritted out. "The family home of one of the Prom Night Arsonist's victims. Happened right after the sheriff cut you loose. Seems convenient, doesn't it?"

"It wasn't me," he gasped.

"I'm not sure I believe you," I said, almost conversationally, completely masking the hatred coursing through me. This man…he'd taken advantage of me. Preyed on me when I was in a delicate situation, used both my mental and physical struggles against me until I became another one of his willing little mules.

I *knew* Chris Taal, better than most, which is why I'd never trust a single word coming out of his fucking mouth.

"C'mon, man," Chris said, grinning to expose each of his decaying teeth and equally rotten breath. "You know fire ain't my style. I like to be a little more up close and personal."

The tip of another blade once again pressed against the skin of my stomach, this time with enough pressure to draw blood, and I swore internally.

How could I have forgotten he always kept two on him? The man was a moron, but he took his personal safety seriously. In my angry haze, I'd failed to notice the flailing he'd been doing with his arms was really him trying to reach the second knife.

I inhaled shallow breaths, trying to keep my stomach from expanding too much lest I drive the blade deeper.

"You know murder ain't my style either."

That was also true.

Evidenced by the tip digging into my flesh, Chris enjoyed carving people up as a way of keeping them in line, a few slashes here and there to remind them he meant business.

I had a few on my back to prove it.

But he'd never killed anyone—at least not at the end of his blade.

All the anger coursing through me dissipated in an instant,

leaving nothing but exhaustion in its wake. *I'm free*, I reminded myself. And this man couldn't hurt me any longer.

Curving away from the blade, I removed my arm from his neck and took two healthy steps back.

"Do you know anything?" I asked him. "Anything that can help us. You cooperate, and it'll go a long way toward easing your current legal problems."

"I don't know shit," he spat.

I nodded, turning for the door. My work here was done, and I didn't want to spend a single second longer in this nightmare from the past.

My hand was on the knob when he said, "Okay…maybe I know a little."

I looked at him over my shoulder. "How much is a little?"

"Missy Plano," he said. The knife blade retracted with a *snick*, and he stuffed his hands into the pockets of his baggy cargo shorts, backing away from me. "That's all I got."

Better than nothing, I thought as I escaped at last, dialing Lane before I was fully settled behind the wheel of my truck. I peeled away from Chris's house in a cloud of dust and burning rubber.

"You're alive," my brother said in greeting, "so I'll take that as a win as long as Taal is too."

"He's still breathing," I confirmed. "Fucker actually managed to get the drop on me."

"You okay?"

"Yeah, I'm fine."

"Good. I haven't tracked down Tito yet, but I've got deputies out looking for him. What've you got?"

"Name Missy Plano mean anything to you?"

Under his breath, Lane mumbled the name to himself over and over. "Ahh! Shit, yeah, it does."

I waited for him to go on, but he didn't. The line was silent save the *scritch-scratch* of what I could guess was Lane's pen against his notebook.

"Lane? Care to share with the class?"

"Right, sorry bro."

"So Missy Plano?"

"Missy Plano is, for lack of a better term, the town whore."

Holy shit.

"Damn," I breathed. "I never knew her last name."

Lane snorted, the scratch of his pen replaced by the *click-clack* of computer keys. "Neither did I. Doesn't help that she goes by Mel now either. Or she tries to, anyway."

"What else do you know about her?"

"Nothing off the top of my head," Lane admitted. "But I ran her through the system and got a DOB."

"She got a sheet?"

"The usual shit given her…proclivities," my brother chuckled. "Solicitation. Couple distribution charges, but nothing has ever stuck."

I rolled my eyes. "Wonder why."

"DOB puts her in high school at the same time as Lee and Stanhope though," Lane said. "Maybe we should pay another visit to Mom."

"I'm not opposed to the idea. We can run it by her at dinner this week."

"Deal. See you then, baby bro."

The line went dead, and as I drove home, my mind swirled with all kinds of ideas. Truthfully, I couldn't wait to see Aspen. Not only because it had been over twenty-four hours since I last had but because I couldn't wait to tell her everything I'd learned and see what she thought of it all.

"Aspen?" I called as I padded down the hall from the mudroom.

"In here!" she replied from the living room.

I made my way toward her, not bothering with verbal pleasantries as I hauled her off the couch and into my arms, crushing her body against mine as my mouth captured hers.

Fuck, she tasted good. Like coffee and something that was purely her. I skated my hands down her sides and found her bare thighs, lifting her off her feet. Her legs came around my hips and, mouths still fused, I walked us through the house toward my bedroom.

With her still in my arms, I climbed onto the mattress and settled us in the center before I finally broke free.

"Hi," I grinned down at her.

"Hey, hotshot." She leaned up to press a kiss to the side of my neck, inhaling deeply. "God, you smell so fucking good. Especially after a call. All smokey and sexy."

"Maybe I should quit showering before I come home," I mused.

Aspen shook her head. "I don't want the sweat. Just the smoke."

I chuckled. "Whatever you want, baby."

"How was the call?"

"The Lees house is a total loss, but luckily they weren't home."

"They're in Arizona with their other daughter and her family."

"You keep in touch?"

Aspen shimmied her shoulders. "Here and there. They were planning on coming home for the Fourth of July." Her face fell. "Now I guess they'll stay in Mesa."

Rubbing my hands up and down her arms, I pulled her back to my chest. "I'm sorry, little phoenix."

"It's not your fault," she whispered. "But I don't want to talk about this anymore."

"What do you want?"

"*You.*"

This fucking girl.

"Nice shirt," I said, toying with the hem briefly before sliding my palm higher against her smooth skin to cup one of her tits.

"This old thing?" she said coyly, sitting up and forcing me back on my heels.

The tee had once been black but had faded to more of a dark grey thanks to the number of times I'd worn and washed it. DUSK VALLEY FIRE DEPARTMENT was emblazoned on the front, CAPTAIN was written across the shoulders on the back.

"Yeah, *that old thing*," I replied. "Looks a hell of a lot better on you."

"You know where it'd look even better?" she asked, a wicked gleam in her eye.

I leaned forward to nip at her neck, her ear, whispering, "Where?"

Aspen shoved me away and said, "Your floor."

Then she whipped it over her head and sent it floating to the carpet, leaving her clad in nothing but a pair of panties.

"A goddamn wet dream," I murmured, reaching out to gently trace my fingers over her collarbones and down the line of her sternum before veering over to her nipples.

Aspen sighed as goosebumps erupted over her skin.

Then she stilled, pulling my attention to her face.

"What's wrong?"

"Sorry," she said sheepishly. "But I remembered you had something to tell me."

"What happened to not wanting to talk about this anymore?"

One of those naked, slender shoulders hitched up. "I changed my mind."

Sighing, I ran a hand over my face. I wanted Aspen to know every single part of me, jagged edges and all. And that meant baring myself fully to her and hoping she still wanted to be with me afterward.

"I'll tell you," I said, "but you've gotta put that shirt back on. I can't talk to you when your perfect tits are staring me in the face."

Aspen giggled as I climbed off the bed and retrieved the tee from the floor. I tossed it to her, but she made no move to catch it, instead staring at me, mouth open in shock.

"What?" I asked.

"Crew…you're bleeding."

I glanced down at my torso to a thin line of blood and a small hole decorating my shirt where Chris has cut me.

"Fuck," I breathed, pulling my shirt off and heading into the bathroom. Aspen put hers back on and followed, turning my back against the counter and inspecting the wound. "Antiseptic is in the closet."

She grabbed the bottle and a cotton ball, and I hissed as she dabbed the liquid on my skin. "What happened?"

"Paid a visit to an old friend."

Aspen quirked a brow. "All your friends treat you like this?"

"Just the ones who used to be my drug dealer."

Aspen sucked in a shocked breath, and I was grateful I couldn't see her face. I didn't know what I'd find there, but with my few previous relationships, when we got to this point where I spilled my darkest secret, they always ran. Like the man I was suddenly reverted into the piece of shit I'd been, and they couldn't stand to look at me anymore.

I considered it a good sign, at least, that Aspen made no move to get away from me.

She bent to blow on my stomach, drying the peroxide before stepping back. "I don't think it needs a bandage."

Then she turned on her heel and retreated into the bedroom.

As we'd done countless times over the course of the last month, I gathered her in my arms and reclined us against the pillows, the top of her head tucking perfectly under my chin as she fit herself into my side.

Like she was made to be there.

"Remember how Lane and I interviewed that Chris guy a while back?"

"Yes."

"I went to see him again. Lane told me he finally made bail yesterday and was released. The timing was too convenient."

"And? Was it him?"

"No. Chris…that's not his style."

"What happened? How did you…"

She didn't finish the question, but I knew what she was asking.

"I had an accident when I was fourteen. Finn, West, and I had always been hell-raisers, and it got worse after Dad died. That day, we'd been out in one of the pastures dicking around. I got the dumbass idea to ride my horse by standing on his back. No helmet, no reins, nothing to protect me. I managed to stay up for a while…until my horse got pissed and took off into a nearby copse of trees. Naturally, I fell and shattered my fibula and tibia."

Reaching for her hand, I bent my knee and lifted my pant leg, pressing her fingertips to the silvery scars crossing the shin of my left leg. The intervening years had smoothed them out considerably, but they were still slightly raised.

"It required a few surgeries and a lot of pins to fix, and I got hooked on painkillers in the process," I continued flatly, Aspen's touch giving me the courage to plow ahead. "At first, I really had been taking them for the pain, but after a certain point, I craved the numbness they gave me."

Aspen laced her fingers with mine, curling our hands together and placing them over my wildly thumping heart. I'd gotten through the hard part and she hadn't bolted, which settled me in a way that told me this thing between us was forever.

Two months in was surely too soon for such wild thoughts, but it came and stayed nonetheless. We'd walked through fire together, and now, there was no way in hell I'd ever let her go without a fight.

From there, the exploits of my teenage years poured out of me. How I ran pills for Chris when he needed an extra hand— and was always paid in the form of whatever drug I was pedaling. I'd tried pretty much everything, and only getting hooked on pills versus cocaine or meth had been a miracle. How I fought people because he asked me to, barely graduated high school because I was too caught up in the thrill and emptiness of my addiction to give a fuck about anything else. How badly I broke my mother's heart for all those years, and how nothing and no one could pull me out of the spiral until it had almost been too late.

"My addiction was bookended by accidents," I said. "The one that drove me to drugs, and the one that drove me away."

"What happened?"

"I was almost seventeen at the time. Chris and I were making a delivery on the outskirts of Boise, and things got out of hand. We made the drop, and he decided to stick around for the party. Got caught up in enemy territory, meaning a rival dealer had claimed that particular area as his. Chris had known, didn't give a fuck, and hadn't bothered to clue me in. All hell broke loose. I was high as a kite and wasted off my ass, but Chris made me drive to get us the fuck out of there. And…I crashed. Wrapped his junked-out Honda around a tree."

I shivered, remembering. Even through the haze of pills and booze from that night and the patina of a memory, I could still feel the blood slicking my hands, the shards of glass cutting into my flesh, my shallow, rattling breaths from my collapsed lung, and the sheer agony of my broken leg—the other one that time.

"That's why you don't drink," she said softly.

"It's a slippery slope," I admitted. "Addiction is a deep, dark hole I almost didn't crawl out of."

"But you did. How?" She shifted to look up at me, and I searched her face for any sort of disgust or pity.

I found none of it. All that radiated from her expression was understanding and acceptance.

"Chief Madden," I said, smiling as thoughts of my long-time mentor and friend assaulted me. "After that accident, he took me under his wing. Got me help and gave me a purpose by letting me help out around the firehouse."

It hadn't been easy. Not on me, my family, or Chief himself. I spent the first month of my senior year of high school in rehab, doing double the work to get myself back on track while still hoping to graduate in time. When I got out, I spent any free moment I had at the firehouse with him, learning the tricks of the trade.

"Thanks to Chief, Mama let me apply for the CFD. She hadn't been keen on the idea of me entering the fire service, not when I'd just come out of a fire of a different sort. But after some long and emotionally draining conversations, she gave in. We all knew it was a long shot. People get selected for the CFD via a lottery, and the chances of my number ever coming up were slim. But we decided the chance was worth it if it meant I could get out of Dusk Valley and away from all the reminders of the things I'd done. If it hadn't panned out…I probably would've left anyway."

"You being selected was a miracle," she said.

"Yeah," I replied, shaking my head. Some days, I struggled to wrap my head around it all. I was the luckiest son of a bitch in the world, as evidenced by the woman wrapped in my arms. "It saved my life."

"I'm glad it did." Aspen swung her legs around so she straddled my lap and cradled my face in her hands. "Otherwise, you wouldn't have been able to save mine."

"God, you would've hated that version of me. I wasn't a great guy back then, Aspen. I wasn't worthy of you, and I'm not sure I am now, either."

My secret shame and my greatest intrusive thought: that I didn't deserve all the good in my life because of the kid I'd been.

"No, Crew," she assured me, gripping my shoulders fiercely, like she was going to shake some sense into me if I didn't see reason. "You're a good man. The *best* one."

"I've done bad things to good people," I protested. "And you better believe if it comes down to it, I will stop at *nothing* to keep you safe You're…everything to me." Fuck, it felt good to get that off my chest, even if emotion clogged my throat, my body stiffening, bracing for her reaction. "If that means I have to put a bullet in the head of the fucker responsible for this"—I brushed my fingers along the material of her tee over the burn scars on her back—"make no mistake, baby. I'll happily do it and sleep like the dead afterward."

Aspen tiptoed her fingers up my chest, her entire palm coming to rest against my cheek. "You're pretty sexy when you get all murderous like this."

My hand continued down her side, over the curve of her ass, and she shifted onto her knees so I could grab a handful. "Oh yeah?"

"*Yeah.* Gets me all hot and bothered. Makes me wanna do naughty things to you." Leaning in, she pressed a kiss right over my heart. "And for what it's worth," she continued, pulling back to look me in the eye. "I wouldn't survive if something happened to you. This"—she gestured between us—"is everything to me too."

A low grumble emanated from my chest. Fuck, this woman turned me on something fierce, both with the dirty talk and emotional vulnerability. I slipped my hands under the hem of the tee, once again peeling it off her body. Then I scooted us to the side of the bed and put Aspen on her feet. Naked again save her panties, she stared at me in confusion.

I merely smirked at her, sliding off my pants and boxer briefs. Aspen's eyes widened, and the tip of her pink tongue darted out to trace along her bottom lip, as though she could sense where I was going.

Despite my emotional purging, I was hard as a fucking rock, and I hissed at the pressure when I gave my shaft a few tugs.

"Get on your knees and show me then."

thirty-two

. . .

BEFORE I LAID eyes on Crew's, I thought dicks were ugly as hell, but his was as beautiful as the rest of him. Long, thick, the broad, blunt crown flushed a deeper red than the rest of the pink shaft, hearty veins running along the length. I fucking *loved* his cock, and I was falling hard for the man attached to it too.

I placed my hands on his thick thighs and leaned in for a teasing kiss, using my tongue to trace his lips instead of giving him real pressure. I angled my head to brush my mouth over his stubbled cheek and jaw, the dark blond hair rasping deliciously against my delicate skin.

"I like this," I said, cupping his other cheek with my hand, rubbing my thumb over the beginnings of his beard.

"Beards are too itchy."

"This length is perfect," I promised. "I want beard burn on my thighs and pussy next time I let you eat."

Crew choked on a laugh. "Then that's what you'll get."

I continued my path south, nipping and sucking the strong column of his neck. Laving my tongue over his collarbones, deeply satisfied when he shivered. Lower and lower until I reached his pecs and tight brown nipples. Sinking my teeth into the muscle on the right side, I soothed the sting with a lick before drawing his nipple between my teeth, flicking it once, twice and letting it go. Crew was *vibrating* against me as I shifted to the other side, clamping his nipple ring between my teeth and tugging. His head dropped forward, chin to his chest, and he fucking *moaned*, a breathy, pleasure-filled sound that sent a rush right to my core, my thighs slickening with my arousal.

"I can't tell you how sexy this is," I said, lifting a hand to toy with the hoop.

"A remnant of my wild youth."

"I like you wild," I admitted. "But only in here. Only with me." I glanced up at him. With him reclined on the bed and me standing flat on the floor, he was still taller than me, but I leaned close to meet his eyes. "Promise me."

"Only with you," he assured me.

"Good boy," I praised. "And good boys get rewarded."

Finally sinking to my knees, the high pile of the carpet cushioning my bones, I slowly inched my hands upward from right above his knees to the indents at his hips, tracing them with my fingers, following the path to the creases of his thighs. I leaned in to press kisses to his skin, close to but never quite where he wanted me.

Crew's hand darted out, attempting to grab a fistful of my hair, but I tutted and arched out of his reach.

"No, baby. No touching."

"Yes ma'am," he rumbled, resting his palms on the bed at his hips.

I leaned in, sucking and nipping kisses along the insides of his thighs, torturing him the way he liked to do to me. His hands tightened, fisting the comforter, bleaching his knuckles as he tried to hold himself back.

By the time I let my tongue trail over the slit at his head, cleaning up the precum beaded there, Crew was barely leashed, and his moan was a deep exhalation. Fuck, I loved the sounds he made. His saltiness exploded on my tongue, and I closed my eyes, savoring.

Wrapping one hand around his base, I closed my lips around him at last. I dove in with gusto, as willing to please him as he was me. I rubbed my thighs together, feeling the wetness gathering there, desperate for friction.

"Look at you," he murmured as I took him deep, his head bumping the back of my throat. I gagged and swallowed around him, taking him a bit deeper, and my eyes watered. "So fucking beautiful, all turned on by choking on my cock."

Humming around him, I pulled off with a *pop*, chasing my mouth with my hand, loving his velvet smoothness, so contradictory to the hard steel beneath. Going back down, I bobbed on his cock, hollowing my cheeks out, sucking and swirling my tongue.

Crew groaned. "I'm going to come if you don't stop that."

All I did was suck him harder, milking him, letting go of his shaft to fondle his balls, rolling them in my palm in that way I knew drove him crazy. His hips jerked up into me, his cock branding my throat. Goddamn, he was sexy like this. Out of control, unable to help himself because the pleasure was *too good*. I relished the fact that I was the only one who got him like this.

The protector letting someone else take care of him.

I felt like a goddess in these moments, and though I was the one on my knees, I knew Crew worshiped me like I was one.

Breathing deeply through my nose, I fought off another gag, taking more and more of Crew's length into my mouth, my throat, until the short, clean cut hairs at the base of his cock brushed against my nose.

When I swallowed again, Crew had apparently had enough, because he pulled me off his dick, and I landed in a heap in the center of the bed.

Crawling between my legs, he rose onto his knees and towered over me. The feral twist to his mouth should've scared the shit out of me, but it didn't. Maybe with another man, in a different lifetime, but not here. Not with Crew. There was nothing he could do to chase me away. I was *safe* here, maybe for the first time ever. Not only sexually, but outside these walls too. No harm would come to me as long as he had something to say about it.

My core pulsed in time with my heavy breaths as I waited for his next move.

"You're wicked, little phoenix. Don't you know it's dangerous to play with fire?"

I grinned. "I've already been burned, hotshot. What's a little more damage?"

He blinked, his expression clearing briefly. "You know I'll never hurt you, right?"

Reaching for him, I gripped his hand and twined our fingers together. "I know, baby." I brought them to my chest, slinking mine out from his so he could feel my heart thumping wildly. "This isn't fear," I promised him. "This is *excitement.*"

He nodded once, his shoulders relaxing, then his touch retreated.

"I want to try something with you."

My heart skipped then picked up speed, anticipation-fueled adrenaline coursing through my system.

"You finally going to show me what you're really into?"

Crew's eyes glinted with mischief. "Hold that thought."

He raced from the room. The sight of his bare ass, several shades lighter than the tan skin of his back and lower legs, had me giggling. A few minutes later, a door slammed, and Crew's footsteps grew closer and closer until he stood framed in the doorway, one hand behind his back while the other nervously pushed that stubborn lock of hair off his face.

Rising onto my elbows, I stared at him. "Whatcha got there?"

He approached tentatively, as though afraid I'd bolt at any second.

"Before I show you, I need you to know you absolutely do not have to go along with this. You can say no, and I'll still fuck you into next week."

A shiver wracked my body at the promise in his words, because I knew he'd make good on them.

"Let me see."

Slowly, he withdrew his hand and presented me with what he held: a coiled length of black rope.

As soon as the rope appeared, I flinched, unable to school my expression. My mind went back to the day of the fire, to being restrained. The last thing I wanted to do was hurt this man, or make him feel like I was judging him for any reason. That wasn't it at all, and I tried like hell to tamp down my panic.

Unfortunately, he knew me too damn well. Crew noticed everything when it came to me, and he definitely didn't miss the way my entire body went rigid.

The ropes fell to the ground, and he cursed creatively as he crossed the room and scooped me into his arms.

"I'm so sorry," he breathed into my hair. "I didn't even think."

I shook my head. "It's okay."

"It's not," he said. "The last thing I ever want to do is hurt you."

I smiled weakly as the way his words echoed my thoughts.

I pulled away far enough to look into his eyes. "Can't you see, Crew? You're not hurting me. Being in this town, being *here*, being with you—it's *healing* me."

And it *was*, especially being at his side. I didn't have nightmares anymore, not since I'd exclusively started sleeping in his bed, even on the nights when he was on shift. Being surrounded by his things, by his scent, soothed me and allowed me to rest fully for the first time in years. This house, this roommate situation…it had all started out as temporary. Then somehow, I blinked, and now it felt like a home, a life, and forever with Crew.

On an exhale, most of the tension in his shoulders dissipated, and he pressed a soft kiss to my mouth. "Still, I could've been more sensitive."

"You took me by surprise," I agreed.

"We don't have to," he said quickly, trying to shift me out of his hold so he could take the ropes back where he'd found them.

My hand darted out of its own accord, keeping him in place. My thoughts raced a thousand miles a minute as I tried to make sense of what I was feeling.

"I'm not scared," I told him. "Not of you. *Never* of you."

"Okay…"

Maybe this was a chance to right some wrongs. I could think of no better person to guide me through that process than the man holding me, like *I* was *his* lifeline despite the memories he'd unintentionally dragged up for me.

God, I loved him.

A sobering thought, and one that should've terrified me, but all I felt was peace. Safety, comfort, unwavering support, and yeah, his love too. There was no way he didn't love me right back, not if he felt even a *fraction* for me what I did for him.

I gnawed on my bottom lip, downcasting my gaze. But Crew wouldn't let me hide, and my head tipped up a moment later thanks to the rough pad of his pointer finger under my chin. "Say it."

I mustered all the bravery I could. "I think I'd like it. To replace that memory of pain with one of pleasure."

"Are you sure?"

I nodded. "I know you'll take care of me."

"Always. You are the most precious thing in my life."

Then he let me go to retrieve the ropes.

Anticipation was a steady hum beneath my skin.

I was mesmerized by the way his hands moved as he unwound the lengths, how his forearms flexed, his tattoos on the left rippling like waves. The material didn't appear to be rough or rigid; it looked soft, like it would gently caress my skin instead of biting into it.

Likely rope he'd purchased for exactly this purpose, and I couldn't help but wonder how many other women he'd done this with.

So I asked.

Crew stilled his approach, staring down at me from the side of the bed.

"Two," he answered honestly. "But it's never mattered. Not like this does. Not like *you*."

"Okay," I murmured.

"Do you trust me?"

"With my life."

My man grinned. "Sit up and bend your knees."

I did so, and he began coiling the rope around my body. Each pass against my skin had goosebumps pricking up all over. First, he crisscrossed it over my chest, under and above my boobs, around between them, then up over my shoulders and back around front, knotting it above my belly button. Two lengths of rope were left, and he lifted one, instructing me to place my hand next to my knee while he wound the rope from my shin and around my thigh, then looping my wrist before tying the end next to the knot at my stomach. Once he repeated the process on the other side, he stepped back to survey his work.

"How do they feel?"

I gave an experimental tug. In this position, any shift I made with my arms only widened my legs, and my wrists were locked in a position that made it uncomfortable to draw my knees together, awkwardly shifting my shoulders forward. The ropes themselves were soft and pliant, as I expected, and he'd wrapped them with enough tension to keep me in place and make it impossible to break free.

I was wholly at his mercy.

"Amazing," I breathed, surprising myself.

Crew's answering grin was wicked.

"Hold onto that thought."

I had no idea what to expect from him now. He could have me any way he wanted, and I'd be unable to stop him. The thrill of having control completely taken away from me was heady and intoxicating.

Crew joined me on the bed, settling between my thighs and leaning over me, forcing my back down onto the bed.

"Think I'll start here," he murmured against my lips, then captured them in a savage kiss. He didn't tease before diving his tongue into my mouth, exploring every hot inch, tangling with mine. I moaned into it, meeting him fervently, nipping at his lips. I hated not being able to run my fingers through his silky hair, and I strained my neck, desperate for more when he backed off. My bottom lip was trapped between his teeth, and he let it go with a growl, altering his course.

I threw myself back down with a huff of frustration.

"Relax, little phoenix," Crew said as his mouth skated down my neck and over my collarbones. "I'm just getting started."

With that, he licked a path down my sternum, along the edges of the ropes, and trailed his tongue over the tight peak of my breast. Swirling his tongue around it like I was a damn ice cream cone on a hot summer day, I arched into him, which only made him pull away.

"Oh yes, baby. You're going to be a goddamn writhing mess by the time I'm done with you. That pussy will be fucking dripping, ruining my sheets."

Leave it to this man to draw out every ounce of pleasure he could from simply playing with my nipples. The teasing licks turned to gentle nips of his sharp teeth, which morphed into those perfect lips closing around the aching bud and drawing it deep into the warmth of his mouth. My back bowed off the bed, and a rush of desire zapped straight to my clit.

After he'd repeated the same torturous process on the other

side, I was going insane, and he hadn't even made it below my belly button yet. A sheen of sweat covered my body, the ache between my thighs unbearable.

"Crew," I whimpered.

His only response was a dark chuckle.

Fuck, this man was going to ruin me.

And I'd happily beg for more.

He ran his mouth over every inch of flesh on my stomach exposed by the ropes, arcing closer and closer to my throbbing core. Dipping his tongue into my belly button, licking a trail across my bikini line, nibbling on my hip bones. All of it carefully designed to drive me mad in the best possible way.

At last, he flattened to his stomach, his face level with my pussy as he settled those broad palms on my soft inner thighs and pressed my legs wider.

Crew exhaled, blowing a stream of cool air right across my soaked pussy, and my legs quivered. I was so keyed up from unspent pleasure that him simply swiping a finger against my entrance to collect my desire damn near set me off. I watched through heavily-lidded eyes as he sucked it into his mouth and sighed, like my taste was exactly the thing he'd been craving for so long.

"Fucking delicious."

I thought that would be the moment he'd take pity on me and fuck me with his tongue and fingers—but I was wrong.

Instead, he leaned in close to my clit, only to veer off course at the last second and lick paths up the creases of my thighs, right next to my lips. A growl of frustration left me, my chest heaving madly and pulse thrumming erratically. I was so turned on, I thought I might burst out of my skin at any moment, and I was liable to come the second Crew touched me with any kind of intent. A glorious, beautiful torture.

"You okay?" he asked as if sensing the direction of my thoughts.

"No."

Crew only laughed. "You wanna come, little phoenix?"

"*Please.*"

"Well, since you asked so nicely…"

Finally, he sealed his lips around my clit and sucked it into his mouth, and as his tongue flitted against my nub, I detonated.

With my arms banded to my legs, my body folded the way Crew wanted me, I could do nothing as I broke apart but pull futilely at my restraints, shaking and screaming as the pleasure flowed and ebbed, slamming into me over and over and over. My vision danced with stars, and I squeezed my eyes shut against the onslaught until Crew decided I'd had enough and freed my clit.

I collapsed, limp, breath sawing in and out.

"So fucking beautiful," he murmured. "Think you could give me one more?"

"No," I whined.

He ignored me, starting his ministrations over before I had a chance to fully collect myself, this time with glancing licks of my clit, fingers only inserted to a single knuckle and pumped too slowly to drive my pleasure higher. I swiveled my hips against every intrusion, desperate for more, but he always backed away. The man was a sexual sadist, taking immense pleasure from the pain of denying me orgasms over and over and over.

I neared the end of my rope when he unceremoniously thrust three fingers inside me and curled them against that spot that drove me fucking mad.

When I came, my vision went entirely dark, my brain going blissfully empty as he took me apart. I screamed, my words unintelligible. All I could do was ride out the storm that had my body thrashing in the center of Crew's bed.

By the time I stilled, I was aware Crew had begun the process of taking the ropes off me, and I was far too limp and sated to help. With each inch he removed, his lips found my flesh, running over the marks they'd left, soothing me. My skin was damp, my hair had fallen in my eyes, and my entire body felt boneless.

Crew's face entered my vision, and I gave him a smile that wobbled at the edges.

"You good?" he asked, brushing my hair back and pressing kisses to my forehead and cheeks.

"I'm fucking great," I replied hoarsely.

His cock bobbed against my thigh, hard as granite, the tip weeping. "Think you can take this?"

Wordlessly, I lifted my arms and wrapped them around his shoulders followed by my legs around his waist. My entire body trembled in the same way it did after a particularly strenuous workout, but I wanted that connection with him. Needed to draw him into my body and make sure he found his pleasure too.

I nipped at his ear. "I can always take your cock, hotshot."

Crew laughed softly as he gently pressed into me, slowly rocking in and out. In short strokes, he had me clawing at his back, urging him faster, begging him to drive us both off that cliff into oblivion.

And my man gave me exactly what I wanted.

I was once again weightless, floating on a cloud somewhere in the sky, lost in pure euphoria.

thirty-three

CREW

"SO…" Aspen began as we curled up in bed, both fully sated after the most transcendent sexual experience of my life. Watching Aspen come apart under my touch over and over, seeing her bound in *my* rope, that fact that she'd let me explore that with her?

I was a goner.

Completely fucking ass over boots for this woman.

I loved her.

But I didn't think I could tell her, not yet, not if I wanted any chance at keeping her.

"When you got home, we got…distracted before you could really fill me in on the call at the Lees."

Home.

I loved the way she said it, like this place was hers as much as it was mine. Like we were building something here together. And goddamnit, I hoped we were. I wanted that more than my next breath.

I snuggled her closer. After driving her to her third orgasm—though I'd teased her long enough that the force of them probably made her body feel like she'd climaxed three hundred times

—we cleaned up and tugged on comfy clothes before crawling back into bed. I had yet to sleep, but we did need to talk about the fire first.

"Have you told anyone besides me who contacted you?" I asked.

She shook her head, her hair scratching against the stubble on my chin. "Not that I can think of. I've spoken to Ginny a decent amount about the victims, but nothing in detail. When Lane asked, I told him it was privileged information. Do you think…"

Her body stiffened, and she jolted upright.

"What is it?"

"Do you think the killer has my phone tapped or something?"

My breath stalled in my chest, and I rolled my lips between my teeth as I considered that.

"Where's your phone?" I whispered.

"The living room," she replied at a normal volume, and I relaxed.

The last thing I wanted was some creepy fucker listening in on Aspen and I having sex. But…this was only one of many times, and her phone hadn't always been in another room.

A shiver wracked my body, a matching one racing through hers as she came to the same conclusion. Fuck, what a disgusting invasion of privacy.

"I'm going to call Trey," I said. "Have him come check it out."

Aspen nodded, seeming a million miles away as I got off the bed and sifted through the abandoned clothing on the floor in search of the pants I had on earlier. I found them, and thus my phone, and dialed my brother.

"Shouldn't you be sleeping?" Trey asked.

"I needed to unwind after a long night first."

My brother snorted. "*Right*," he said knowingly.

I wasn't about to give him the satisfaction of confirming his suspicion, not when I was still irritated with him for making a pass at Aspen. But I needed his help, so I bit the bullet and plowed ahead.

"Can you do me a favor and come over? There was a fire at the Lees' place last night, and, well…it's a lot to explain. I'll fill you in when you get here, but we need your tech skills."

"Sure. Give me thirty."

When I turned back to the bed, I blinked slowly in confusion to find Aspen wasn't there. Instead, she paced back and forth at its side, gnawing on the skin around her thumb.

A habit she reverted back to when she was extremely stressed, and I only knew because she'd told me so, not because I'd ever witnessed it firsthand. Things had never been this bad, not since I'd pulled her out of the fire. Her car was replaceable, the dumpster an obvious taunt, but burning down the Lees' family home was on a whole new level.

This fucker was escalating, wearing both of us down, my girl most of all.

Crossing the room to her, I placed my hands on her shoulders to stop her.

"Hey, hey, what's going on?"

"I wish I could remember that lost day," she growled out in frustration. "If I could remember…*something*, we might have already caught this guy."

"Baby, it's not on you to find who is doing this."

"Maybe not," she conceded, looking up at me. "But I want to help. I'm the only living victim, Crew. I owe justice to the ones who didn't get to live."

"Have you talked to Lane about it? Maybe there's some sort of interview technique he's got in that cop repertoire of his that he can try."

Aspen snorted. "Lane never wanted me here in the first

place." Her gaze dropped again, hair falling in her face as she said, "Maybe he was right. Maybe it's time for me to go."

"No."

Final answer.

"Crew," she sighed. "Me being here has dredged up all this shit for you, your family, and the residents of Dusk Valley. The Lees just lost their house! The place where Vicky had grown up." Her voice cut off as she choked on a sob, tears instantly pouring from her eyes like someone had turned on a faucet. "A teenage boy nearly got arrested. You've been forced to confront your demons, and this entire town is on edge. That's on me." She swiped angrily at her cheeks. "Everything that's happened the last few months is my fault."

"No it's not. You can't shoulder the blame for any of it, and you can't give up. We're so close to catching this fucker. We wouldn't be this close without you."

"Yeah, but as long as I stay around, he'll never leave me be. Maybe if I left, things would go back to normal."

I shook my head. "What is normal anyway? All of us constantly looking over our shoulders, wondering if our daughter or sister is going to be next? No, little phoenix. You blowing into town and disrupting this guy's MO is exactly what we needed, don't you see that? He's getting careless now. Taking chances he hadn't been before."

"I think things would be better for everyone if I left."

"I refuse to accept that."

She offered me a sad smile. "I'm afraid you don't have a choice in the matter."

"The hell I don't."

The look she gave me was pure venom, and I could practically see those walls going back up in her eyes as her spine straightened. "Just because you're fucking me doesn't give you the right to make decisions about my life."

Oh, little phoenix. My girl was lashing out because she was hurting, not because she actually believed the shit coming out of her mouth.

"We're doing a lot more than *fucking*," I growled.

"Doesn't seem like it to me."

"Then how about because I love you?" I said softly, with a calm I didn't feel. "Does that give me the right to weigh in on your choices?"

Aspen stilled, and all the air around us seemed to evacuate.

Fuck, what had I done? I meant it, and I wouldn't take it back, but the middle of an argument was absolutely *not* the time to say it.

"You don't get to love me," she whispered.

Oh God. Did that mean she didn't feel the same?

"Why the hell not?"

"Because I'm not staying!" she exploded, pacing across the room, away from me. "Whether I leave tomorrow or whenever —*if* ever—we catch this guy tormenting me, this was always going to be temporary. This thing between us was nothing more than the result of me almost dying and you saving me from that fate. We got swept up in the investigation and heightened emotions because I nearly died. You'll always be special to me because you brought me back to myself. But that's all this is."

No, that wasn't how she felt at all. I knew it in the way she curled in on herself, in the way she refused to look at me. Aspen was lying to herself—and me.

She was crying again, and I understood why. She was trying to cut ties and run before things got too deep.

Well, newsflash, baby. I was already in as deep as it got, and I wasn't going anywhere anytime soon.

"Is that really how you feel?" I pressed, taking a tentative step toward her. When she didn't move, I took several more until I was right in front of her, my hands cupping her cheeks. I brushed the moisture leaking from her eyes away with my thumbs.

So fucking stubborn, my girl.

"Answer me, Aspen," I demanded when she remained quiet. "Is that really how you feel? Do you really think this is just a fling?"

"No," she squeaked out at last, crying in earnest now. "But I can't see how this will work. I don't…" She trailed off, as though unsure how to finish that.

"You can run your business from anywhere."

"Yes, but—"

I pressed a finger to her lips, silencing her. "So don't use that as an excuse. Don't make that the reason you leave. Please, baby. Let me be the reason you stay. Let *us* be the reason you stay."

"I don't know if I can," she said, though she sagged against me, letting me wrap my arms tightly around her.

"You can," I assured her. "Be brave for us, Aspen."

"I want to be," she murmured into my chest.

"Now is a good time to start."

Her shoulders rose and fell with a deep inhale and exhale, and then she said, so quiet I almost didn't hear her, "I love you too."

Wrapping my arms tighter around her, I pressed my lips to her hair. "I know, baby."

"I don't know how this works, or where we go from here."

She lifted her head to look up at me, and I bent to kiss her. Her mouth was salty and sweet, the kiss soft but claiming. When I pulled away, I said, "One day at a time, okay? That was the agreement."

Aspen nodded, then backed out of my arms. "I'm going to shower and freshen up before Trey gets here. I'll be out in a bit."

With a final kiss and a pat on her ass, I let her go. "I'm going to get Lane over here too."

She murmured her agreement, and the moment the bathroom door closed behind her, I sent Lane a text, then hightailed it to the guest room.

Aspen spent every night in my bed—even the ones when I

wasn't here. Now that I knew she loved me, that meant my room was now officially *our* room.

My girl liked to take long showers, and after the morning we'd had, I knew she'd been in there for a while, allowing the hot water to soak into her limbs and ease any lingering tension, so I had plenty of time to complete my task.

Surprisingly, Aspen had taken the time to unpack her things, even going so far as to hang clothes up in the small closet. That made it easy to lift them all right off the rod and move them into the walk-in attached to my bedroom. Her tees and jeans looked perfect next to my work pants and shirts. Next I cleaned out the drawers of the hutch I used as a guest dresser, unceremoniously taking piles of my own clothes out of my dresser to replace with hers.

Lastly, I went to the bedside table, knowing from my previous foray into the drawer to get her vibrator that there were a few more personal things she'd stuffed in there. Medication she liked to have close by, lotion and lip balm, a dog-eared paperback by Susan Elizabeth Phillips. A spiral bound notebook.

I took it all out and laid it in a pile in the center of the bed, then stood hands on hips to survey the room, making sure I hadn't forgotten anything.

Not that it mattered. She was only moving down the hall, not across the country. If there was something I'd missed, she could come grab it.

Satisfied with a job well done, I turned back to the bed to gather her things. The notebook I'd taken from the drawer had flopped to the side off the stack, its pages spread open.

I tried like hell not to look, but ultimately curiosity got the better of me, and before I could stop myself, I was lifting it to read what Aspen had written.

At first, I thought it was a diary of sorts, but as my eyes scanned the pages, it read like more of a logbook, detailing the ins and outs of Aspen's work on the Prom Night Arsonist case.

I ate up her words like they were my new favorite story, but the more I read, the angrier I got. She'd poured so much onto those pages that my eyes swam with the words, barely making sense of it all, but still, some managed to permeate my brain.

Threatening email.

Note on my car.

Someone was watching me.

I saw red, and before I could fully think through my actions, I was storming down the hall and into my bathroom. Aspen was getting out of the shower, her lithe, naked body on display, but my cock didn't so much as twitch. I was too pissed off.

Not at her, *never* at her. But at the fact that she'd been shouldering all of this alone. That she felt like she couldn't share it with me.

Aspen grinned when she saw me, but it quickly fell as her gaze darted between me and the notebook I brandished.

"Where did you get that?" she snapped.

"Figured it was time you officially moved into my room, so I was getting your things and clearing out the guest room. Want to tell me what the fuck this is?"

"I think you know."

"You're right," I nodded. We were past the point of explanations. "Then let me try again: want to tell me why the fuck you *didn't* tell me about all this shit going on?"

Aspen's movements were jerky as she lifted one of the plush white bath sheets off the shelf in the linen closet and wrapped it around her body. Instead of answering me, she stomped right past me into the bedroom, beelining for the closet.

At least she was taking the whole me moving her shit into my room thing in stride.

Like a little puppy dog, I followed her, leaning against the doorframe with crossed arms as she got dressed in black leggings, a sports bra, and one of my tees, which hung to her knees. Logically, I knew Aspen was her own person and not my property, but

I'd be damned if that feral beast in my chest didn't growl *mine* at the sight of her in my clothes. The need to claim her was almost unbearable, so I clenched my fists against the onslaught of desire and waited her out.

Finally, she faced me and mirrored my body language, though she lifted her hand and crooked her fingers at me. "Let's hear it."

"Why didn't you tell me?"

"Because it wasn't your business."

"It damn well is my business!" I shouted. "You're being *stalked* Aspen. How is that *not* my business? At the very least, Lane deserves to know."

Aspen snorted. "Fuck your brother."

"I don't disagree, but he *is* a cop."

The fight left her in an instant, like a switch flipped, and she deflated. I crossed the distance between us and pulled her into my arms, where she sagged against me. "I'm tired, Crew."

"I know," I murmured, rubbing circles across her back.

I was tired too. Tired of this fucker lurking in the shadows, tormenting my town. Dragging innocent people—kids—into this mess they'd created. Hurting families that had already suffered enough pain to last several lifetimes.

And mostly, I was tired of the defeat lining Aspen's beautiful face.

Before either of us could say anything else, a heavy knock came at the front door, followed by Trey shouting for me as he pushed inside.

Aspen made an irritated noise and pulled away from me. I chuckled, echoing the sentiment as I laced our fingers together and led us into the living room, where Trey waited on the couch.

"Make yourself at home," I said with an eye roll.

I had a feeling I wouldn't be getting sleep anytime soon, so I went into the kitchen to put coffee on.

"What's yours is mine, little brother."

"No it's not."

Cutting to the chase, Trey asked, "Why am I here?"

Aspen lifted her phone off the coffee table, where it had been abandoned a few hours before when I'd gotten home from work, wisely powered it off, and handed it to Trey.

"We think my phone may be bugged," she said.

Trey lifted a brow, eyes darting between us. "What makes you say that?"

Aspen and I shared a look, but before we could respond, the front door pushed open again, and Lane stepped inside.

"What's going on?"

"They were about to tell me why they think Aspen's phone has been bugged," Trey told him.

Lane's expression shifted from brotherly concern to cop mode in an instant.

I looked to Aspen. "You want to show him, or should I?"

"Show me what?"

She ignored him and said, "I will," then disappeared down the hall. A moment later, she reappeared with the notebook and reluctantly handed it over to Lane.

"During the course of every investigation, I keep a notebook. Thoughts, random tidbits of information that don't mean anything at the time but could pop off later, weird things that happen. That"—she nodded at the one in his hand—"is the one for this case."

"And this matters to me, why?"

"The day I picked my car up from the impound lot, I found a note under my windshield wiper. It's tucked in the back there, but I also wrote down what it said in case it ever got lost. I've also been getting creepy emails."

"What does this have to do with me?" Trey asked, almost bored.

"The fire at the Lees' house wasn't an accident," Aspen said.

"No shit," Lane muttered, and I cut him a glare that told him to shut the fuck up or he'd find my fist in his face.

"You asked me in our very first conversation how I knew about the case," she told Lane.

"And you said a concerned citizen, who I now know was Leigh Lee."

"Still wondering what this has to do with me."

Aspen glared at Trey, then kicked out, knocking his booted foot off my coffee table with her bare one. Lane and I choked on our laughter.

"No one but Crew knew I'd spoken to the Lee family," she finally told him. "But somehow, I don't think the killer lighting their home on fire was a coincidence."

Lane flipped through the notebook, pausing every so often to read a passage before moving on. Trey's attention was fixed on the device in his hand.

"Can you run diagnostics on it or something and see if it's been tapped?" I asked.

"Of course," he said. "Though I'm not sure how they would've…"

He trailed off, mumbling things to himself that made no sense to me.

"Do you mind if I take photos of this?" Lane asked Aspen.

"Take the whole thing."

"I'm going to need to see those emails too."

"Sure," she said, retreating to the office to print them.

"I can see the wheels spinning in both of your heads," I said to my brothers. "Tell me what you think we're dealing with here."

"I think it's likely this fucker has been keeping tabs on her," Trey said.

"It's an obsession," Lane agreed.

"But *why*?"

Though as soon as I asked, the reason occurred to me.

"She's the one that got away," Lane said, taking the words right out of my head. "This guy never had a vic survive until her. So it's become a fixation. He's taunting her, and taunting us because we still can't nail him down, even with a survivor."

"The fire at the Lees' is an escalation though, right?"

Trey nodded. "He's getting bolder. The spiral out of control is coming, and when it does, we have to be ready."

"She doesn't leave my sight when I'm off shift," I said. "But…I'm gonna need help when I'm working. Or maybe I can take some furlough. Chief Madden will understand…"

I trailed off, mind whirring with a to-do list to square the firehouse away for me to take some time off, but Lane held up his hand.

"Not happening, baby brother."

"Why not? She needs protection."

"And I'm not disputing that. But you can't take time off. We need to act like it's business as usual or this guy will spook and we'll never catch him."

"Okay, fair enough. So what do you propose?"

My brothers shared a look, something unspoken passing between them, and when Trey turned to me with a shit-eating grin, I'd already opened my mouth to protest.

"She can stay at the ranch."

I blinked in surprise. "Oh. That wasn't what I thought you were going to say."

Trey scoffed. "You thought I was going to suggest she bunk with me? Fuck no." He held his hands up in surrender. "Learned my lesson, brother. She's all yours."

"You're damn right."

We all whirled on Aspen, who stood at the mouth of the hall, a sheaf of papers in her hand.

"My girl," I grinned.

"I'm not opposed to staying at the ranch though," she said,

looking at me, and I breathed a sigh of relief that this wasn't going to be a fight. "So long as you come with me."

I groaned, and my brothers laughed, Lane slapping a hand down on my shoulder.

"Have fun with that," he said, then accepted the stack of emails from Aspen, shuffling through them. There were more than I expected. "God, this fucker is sick."

"Do I want to know?"

Aspen shook her head. "There's one in there that came from a different email address than the rest. Could be from someone other than the killer."

Lane's brows pinched. "What do you mean?"

She moved to his side and took the papers, flipping through until she came to the one she wanted and pulled it from the stack, holding it out to him.

I joined Lane, and Trey stood to read over his shoulder.

FROM: imwatchingu@email.com
TO: aspen@mckayinvestigates.com

SUBJECT: Can you help her?

The first is the key
Crowned the prom queen
Face forever locked in a scream
But who could the killer be?

"I'm so confused," Trey said.

"Me too," I agreed.

"Don't you see?" Aspen asked. "'*The first is key, crowned the prom queen*'? They're obviously talking about Vicky Lee. She was the first victim, and was crowned prom queen the night she died."

"So we find out *why* Vicky was killed, and we catch our killer?" Lane asked.

Aspen hitched a shoulder up in a shrug. "You tell me, Sheriff."

I grinned. Damn she was sexy talking about murder investigations. I'd already have her over my shoulder on the way to bed if my brothers weren't here. The look Aspen gave me told me she had the exact same idea.

"Where are we at on Missy Plano?" I asked Lane, mostly to distract myself.

"I've been unable to make contact. General consensus is that she's out of town. Left with some high rolling tourist a few weeks ago and hasn't come back yet."

Fuck. We really needed to interview her. I had this gut feeling she had information that could change things for this investigation. That feeling grew even stronger now that we knew Vicky Lee was likely the key to unraveling this entire thing.

"Can I borrow your computer?" Trey asked Aspen. "I want to run diagnostics on that too. Maybe it's not your phone that's been compromised, but your computer. I have no idea *how* they would've accomplished it, but we need to exhaust all possibilities."

Aspen cursed. "I didn't even consider that."

Trey smiled. "That's why they pay me the big bucks."

I rolled my eyes as Aspen once again disappeared. "You own your own company."

"And my clients pay me the big bucks for shit I'm doing for you guys for free."

Fair enough.

Lane slapped our older brother on the back. "And we appreciate you for it. Take that shit home and run your little tests. I'm going back to the station."

"What're you going to do?"

"Dust this note for fingerprints," he said, flipping to the back of Aspen's notebook where the scrap of paper with that first message rested. "Then give an FBI friend of mine a call. We were in the academy together, and now she works out of Boise, so this is all well within her jurisdiction anyway. It's about time I loop her in on these new developments."

I nodded, grateful. Having more eyes on this meant higher chances of catching the sicko responsible, which put us one step closer to putting this entire mess behind us. I craved those days, when Aspen and I could start our life together without this shit hanging over our heads.

After Aspen returned and handed off her laptop to Trey, I gathered her in another hug, not caring that my brothers were in the room.

"How do you feel?" I asked.

"Lighter," she said. "If that makes sense."

I hummed in agreement as she tipped her head back, mouth waiting. I captured it and murmured against her lips, "Asking for help ain't all bad."

"No, baby. It's definitely not."

thirty-four

. . .

ASPEN

ONE OF CREW'S brothers cleared his throat, and I reluctantly peeled away from him, reminding myself we had things to accomplish and sex was sadly missing from the list.

"Hate to break up the love fest—"

"No you don't," Crew cut Lane off.

"—but can we do a quick interview before I leave?" Lane asked me, ignoring Crew's interruption.

"About what?"

"That day on the street when you received this," he said, holding up the email in question. "Do you remember who was around? What were you doing?"

I glanced at Crew, and he dipped his chin slightly, encouraging me.

"Actually…have you ever heard of a cognitive interview?"

"Sure," Lane said. "You want to do one?"

"Yeah, but not about that day on the street. We can talk that out, but I *remember* that. I want to try to access my missing hours between the abduction and fire."

Lane blinked in surprise, but nodded. "Yeah, of course."

Trey moved from the couch to one of the armchairs, apparently not ready to leave quite yet. Crew settled into the spot he'd vacated first, then let me curl up into his side. If I was about to relive a piece of my trauma, I needed him holding me together. Lane pulled out his phone and set it to record, going through his pre-interview spiel, detailing why we were here.

"Tell me what happened that day on the street," he started, handing over my notebook to help jog my memory.

Squeezing my eyes shut, I transported myself back, then popped them open and scanned the pages of my notes, looking for the right one. When I found it, I tapped my finger to the passage and read aloud.

"The man holding his young daughter's hand. The woman in a smart suit, phone pressed to her ear as she ate up the sidewalk. The two women, clearly mother and daughter, exiting the diner with take-out containers in their hands. The man standing on the corner a block ahead, hat pulled low over his face, shoulders hunched as he waited for a car to pass so he could cross the street." I looked up to find all three men hanging on my every word. "I followed that last guy."

Lane sighed. "Of course you did. Any luck?"

I shook my head. "Nah. He'd disappeared by the time I got to the corner of the next block."

"Which direction?"

"Uhh…left?"

Trey snorted, and Crew socked him in the arm.

"Sorry, I realize that's not helpful. But I don't exactly have the lay of the land to be more specific."

"You were on Cassia, right?" Crew asked. "In front of the pizza parlor."

"Right."

"Which direction did the man head from there?" I pointed to the left, and Lane stated that for the record. "How many blocks ahead did he go?"

"He was already ahead of me by a block, so he went one further."

"The parlor is in the middle of the block between Ash and Juniper. Two blocks to the west would put you at Walnut. Another left turn would have him heading south."

"It's all a crapshoot, though," Trey argued. "That's all residential that way. He could've disappeared into a home and we'd never know better."

"We canvassed after the dumpster fire that night and nothing popped."

"And it wouldn't," Trey piped in. "This guy isn't going to come to the door with his wrists held together and say, 'Hey, yeah, it was me. Take me away.'"

As annoying as he was, Trey had a point.

"We'll circle back to this," Lane said. "Now let's focus on the night you were abducted and the events after."

My heart rate kicked up, and Crew wrapped his arms tighter around me.

"It's okay, little phoenix," he murmured. "Nothing can hurt you."

I nodded, swallowing around the lump that had lodged in my throat.

"You already told me about your abduction, so I won't make you replay that," Lane started, and I shot him a grateful smile. "Close your eyes for me and relax. Like Crew said, nothing can hurt you. You're safe here."

My eyelids fluttered closed, though my hand found Crew's and squeezed tightly.

"Do you remember waking up prior to the fire?"

Instead of trying to force it, I let my memories come to me, gliding forward like waves on a shore, rolling gently to the forefront of my brain before receding when they weren't what I was looking for.

An image appeared, blurry at first but sharpening by the second.

"I did," I gasped, eyes still shut. "I was in some sort of vehicle. A van, if I had to guess. The walls were grey and stripped down to the metal, as was the floor."

"That's great, Aspen. Then what happened?"

"We came to a stop a bit later," I said, the images coming quicker now, almost too fast for me to make sense of them, my pulse ticking up with them. "My captor opened the back doors— it had to have been a van."

"Could you see anything that would help identify them?"

I shook my head. "It was dark, and they were all dressed in black and…backlit?"

Why were they backlit? Lane repeated the question as though he'd plucked it right from my brain.

"I think…there was some sort of house behind them? But I can't see anything else. Not like a spotlight. More like the glow of a lamp or something."

"Could be a cabin in the woods," Trey mused. "There are all sorts of hunting shacks on the outskirts of the county."

"That would make a lot of sense," Lane agreed. "Somewhere quiet and out of the way to keep her until they figured out what to do with her."

Crew's hand smoothed up and down my arm. "You're doing amazing, baby."

My eyes remained closed. "Before they got me out of the van," I told Lane, "they tased me and knocked me out again."

"You had to have woken up again."

I squeezed my lids tighter together, trying to hold onto the crystal clear images, but my memory had once again gone hazy. "I'm sorry," I said, popping my eyes open. "There's nothing until I literally woke up on fire."

Crew inhaled sharply, his grip on me tightening. "You didn't tell me that."

"It's why the burns are localized and weren't worse. I came to, realized what was happening, and rolled across the floor to put them out." Tears streamed down my face. Fuck, I thought I'd gotten past this, but reliving even a fraction of the time I'd spent captive was…a lot. "I'm just glad it worked."

"And then I came for you," Crew said, pressing a kiss to my hair. "I'll *always* come for you."

Lane was quiet, though he stopped the recording and tapped around on the phone screen, then held it out to me. Trey merely watched us all with a contemplative expression.

"Flip through those three photos and let me know if this man looks familiar to you. Could he be the guy from the street—or the one who took you?"

I squinted at the screen. The man in the photos was dressed similarly to the man I'd seen on the street, though there was no hood up to shield his face from the security cameras. And honestly, in a small, blue collar town such as this, that wasn't abnormal. These were hardworking, dusty boots and Carhartt kind of men, not prissy, suits and thousand dollar loafers city boys. The man also wore a ball cap with some company logo I couldn't read in the dim and grainy picture.

"I can't be sure," I said. "They aren't the best photos. I mean, maybe? The height appears to be about right. I didn't get a look at the guy's face on the street or when I was taken, though."

"What are those from?" Crew asked.

"Stills from depot footage," Lane said, and Crew nodded like that meant something to him. For me, he clarified. "It's where all the county vehicles gas up and have maintenance done. Fire trucks, ambulances, police cruisers, the road crews, etcetera. This guy owns a landscaping company and has for years. The diesel fuel Crew and his guys noticed at the incident sites got me thinking, so I ran some things down. He's the right age to have been around when Vicky and Roger were killed, he's big enough to handle hauling bodies around, and he'd have access to all kinds of places like the Lees' home and Mack's shop thanks to his job —especially since he'd just bought it."

Crew practically shoved me away in his haste to get up. "You can't be serious."

"It's the best lead we've got," Lane said as he stood, though I could tell he wasn't happy about it.

I was missing something here.

"You're fucking insane," Trey muttered. "There's no goddamn way."

Crew vigorously nodded. "Agreed."

"I want to think you're both right, but I have a job to do."

"Will someone tell me what the fuck is going on?" I asked, rising to my feet. Crew and Lane shared an unreadable look but didn't speak, so I turned to the third brother. "Trey?"

He ignored me in favor of shooting Lane a pleading glance. "You really think it's him?"

Lane shrugged slightly. "I have to explore every possibility."

Trey finally moved, getting off the couch and stalking toward the door, disappearing without a word.

"Crew?" I pleaded. "Who is this man?"

"This man…his name is Ward Saunders. His daughter, Wyatt, is Trey's best friend, and his wife has worked at the school for probably three decades. She started as a teacher, but has been the principal for the last twenty or so years."

thirty-five

. . .

ASPEN

ICE SLID DOWN MY SPINE.

The principal's *husband?* And the father of Trey's best friend? That explained his pained expression and wordless retreat.

Fucking hell.

I didn't realize I'd spoken the words aloud until Lane said, "Yeah. So this should be fun."

"You're going to interview him now?" Crew asked.

"Yep. I was about to head over there before you called earlier, actually."

"I'm coming with," my man said, and Lane gave him a curt nod.

They headed for the door, but I stopped them.

"Wait, what about me?"

Lane's smile was brittle, like his facial muscles didn't want to cooperate. "Oh, you're coming too, little one."

On the way into town, Lane glanced at me in the rearview and said, "I don't need to tell you we need to handle this carefully, right?"

I shook my head. "I'm no stranger to interviews, Sheriff."

"Just let me do the talking and we'll be fine."

"Then why are we even coming along?" Crew asked.

"I want Aspen to get a read on Ward, see if you have any sort of reaction to him. And you're here because—"

"I go where Aspen goes," he growled at his brother.

Lane laughed and shook his head, but didn't disagree. "Yes, because I knew you'd raise holy hell if I tried to take Aspen along without you."

We chatted idly the rest of the drive, my attention out the window as we navigated through the neighborhood. It took me a moment, but with a jolt, I suddenly recognized it as the one I'd had my meltdown in the day I got out of the hospital. I didn't feel anything as we rolled along the streets, no sense of foreboding or those bad "woo-woo" vibes I often got during an investigation. The neighborhood was clean and quiet, a classic residential area.

Was it harboring a dark secret?

I couldn't say for sure.

Eventually, we pulled up in front of a gorgeous two-story ranch-style home with impeccable landscaping. Set atop a small hill, stone steps were cut into the incline, marking a path up to the front door. The driveway was level with the street but sloped up to the garage, which was attached to the house via a breezeway.

"Damn, this is beautiful," I mused unhelpfully.

"I can't believe we have to do this," Crew said, scrubbing a hand over his face.

"Not exactly my idea of a good time either," Lane agreed. "Goes to show that sometimes you don't know what people are hiding behind closed doors."

After another beat in which we all gathered our courage, we got out and made our way up the path. I stuffed my hands in my pockets so the guys wouldn't see them shaking as Lane approached and knocked on the door.

My entire body stiffened as I braced for the moment it would open, wondering if I was about to come face to face with my attacker. Would I even know if he was it?

Instead of a man, a gorgeous woman with strawberry blonde hair opened the door, her brows drawing together in confusion. Too young to be Mrs. Saunders, so I had to assume this was the daughter. My God, she was tall. Categorically, I was tiny, but this woman made me feel like an ant. At her feet, a gorgeous blue merle Australian Shepherd pranced around and yipped excitedly.

"Lane? Crew?"

"Hey, Wy," Lane said. "Your dad home?"

Wyatt scanned Lane up and down, no doubt taking in the uniform. "I take it this isn't a social call?"

"Afraid not."

Her blue eyes narrowed on me. "And who is this?"

"Aspen," I supplied, sticking my hand out. "Aspen McKay."

Wyatt's own palm flew to her mouth. "You're the one from the fire."

"Yeah," I shrugged. Honestly, what else was I supposed to say to that?

Hey, yeah, that was me. And by the way, we think your dad is the one responsible!

Absolutely fucking not.

"Aspen, this is Wyatt Saunders," Crew supplied, though I'd already figured that out.

Wyatt didn't acknowledge him, returning her attention to Lane. "Is this about her?"

A stiff nod was all he gave her. "Can we come in?"

Wyatt appeared as though she wanted to say no but ultimately stepped aside with a sigh and admitted us into the house.

"Who's at the door, Wy?" a deep voice called from inside.

Wyatt led us into a sunken living room that branched off the entryway. To the right was an open plan kitchen and dining room. A large man with broad shoulders, salt-and-pepper scruff, and wavy hair that was more grey than black sat on a couch in front of the television, watching *Jeopardy!*. When we entered, he paused it and shifted forward to stand.

Fuck, he was tall too. Nearly as tall as Crew and Lane, which put him a few inches over six feet. And he looked strong enough to have hauled me around like a rag doll.

I'd be damned if I could pin him as the man who attacked me, though.

I had this idea in my mind that when I set eyes on that person, I would know it deep in my bones. Like a flesh memory activated by being in his presence again.

But nothing happened. My heart didn't race, my body didn't seize with fear. As far as I was concerned, he was a normal man and not a crazed killer.

I took that as a good sign. Maybe this would be nothing more than a horrible misunderstanding.

Lane watched us closely, eyes darting back and forth. Subtly, I shook my head.

"Sheriff?" the man said.

"Hey, Ward. Mind if I ask you a few questions?"

"Regarding?"

Lane jerked his head at me as he withdrew his trusty notebook from his pocket. "This is Aspen McKay. She was the one Crew saved in the shop fire a few months ago."

Ward nodded. "I remember seeing your picture in the paper. Nice to see you out and about."

I cringed. Had I mentioned I'd been front-page news? Public photos of me in recent years didn't exist, so they'd used my head-shot from my *Sun Times* days to accompany the article and a large picture of the burned-out shop.

At least I didn't look like a gremlin.

"Thanks," I said awkwardly.

"Now what is this really about?" Ward asked suspiciously.

Next to him, Wyatt's arms were crossed over her chest. "You don't think…"

Lane put his hands up placatingly. "This is a routine interview, Ward. Nothing to be worried about. All I need to know is where you were on April twenty-second and twenty-third."

Ward's mouth gaped like a fish as he searched for something to say. In the course of my career, both as a journalist and private investigator, I'd seen this type of reaction before. He wasn't grasping at straws, trying to find a way out of being caught in a lie. He was genuinely shocked, knocked on his ass by the question and that he'd found himself in this situation.

I considered myself somewhat of a professional at reading people, and I knew right then this was not the person responsible for killing all of those people and attempting to murder me.

"On Friday, we had dinner here," Wyatt said, stepping in to save her father. "After, we went out to the Swallow for drinks and to watch the Rockies game."

Lane glanced at me, but that piece of information, that he'd been in the area at the time I'd been taken, didn't change my mind. Again, I shook my head.

"What about Saturday?"

Ward recovered at last, clearing his throat before he spoke.

"I was at a couple job sites," he said. "First, planting flowers at the community center with the ladies from the council, and then I had to go out to Rauschs' place for spring maintenance and to prep for the new pool they're putting in this summer."

Lane blinked, eyebrows flicking upward, as he jotted that down. "And that night?"

"He was here all night," Wyatt chimed in. "I came over for dinner again, and we watched the Rockies *again*." Her teeth were clenched, and I couldn't imagine how uncomfortable and infuriating this had to be for her. "I went a little too hard on the beer, so I slept in my old room."

The words rang true, but I didn't like the way she refused to look at Lane when she spoke, like she was hiding something.

Was it possible she knew more than she was letting on? Was I reading this entire situation wrong? Had that fire burned away my sixth sense for reading people?

I didn't think so, but Lane picked up on that thread.

"He could've snuck out when you were asleep," he pointed out.

"Not possible," she assured him. "I'm a light sleeper, and I would've heard him disarming the security system."

Wait. If they had a security system…

"That one of Trey's?" Lane asked, pointing his pen at the keypad mounted on the wall in the entryway.

"You know it is," Wyatt said with an eye roll.

"Put it in for free," Ward added, puffing his chest out proudly, glancing between Lane and Crew. "Good man, your brother."

"He's something," Crew mumbled, only loud enough for me to hear.

Lane gave them a curt nod and closed his notebook, then extended a hand to Ward, who accepted it reluctantly.

"Sorry about this, Ward," the sheriff said. "I'll confirm with Trey that the system was armed all night, and we'll put this all behind us."

"No problem, Sheriff. I understand you're just doing your job," Ward assured him as he led us back to the door.

We'd only been in the house for about ten minutes, but I was grateful to be leaving. The air here was charged with something I couldn't name. While I didn't catch any bad vibes from Ward, something about the way Wyatt acted told me maybe we needed to dig a little deeper.

Once we were back in Lane's cruiser, Crew released a sigh. "Well, that was a bust."

"I'm not so sure," I said, closing my eyes and replaying the entire interview over in my mind.

"You caught that too, huh?" Lane asked, and I could hear the smile in his voice.

I popped my eyes open to see Crew shift in his seat, his baby blues shifting between me and his brother. "Caught what?"

Lane put the car in gear and pulled away from the curb, and my attention remained locked on the house until we turned the corner and it disappeared from view.

When Lane spoke again, his tone was edged with excitement, like he was a search dog that had picked up a trail.

"Wyatt Saunders knows something."

thirty-six

. . .

CREW

"WHAT DO YOU MEAN, Wyatt knows something?"

"She was fidgety," Aspen provided.

"And she refused to look me in the eye. Telltale signs that someone is lying."

I gaped at my brother. "Wyatt Saunders wouldn't hurt a fly. You're telling me you think *she* is responsible?"

"Of course not," Lane assured me. "First of all, she's not nearly old enough. But what I am saying is that she's keeping something from me, and I intend to find out what it is." He shifted to glance at Aspen in the rearview. "You feel anything in there other than Wyatt being shady?"

"No. In my gut, I don't think Ward was the one who attacked me, but I've been wrong before."

The end of that statement piqued my interest enough that I shifted around in my seat to look at her. "What do you mean?"

Her shoulders raised and lowered dramatically as she heaved a sigh, gnawing on her bottom lip, almost like she didn't want to tell me.

"Is this about the Bullough story?" Lane asked.

Aspen nodded, giving into a shiver, like the name elicited

memories she had no desire to revisit. "The story that cost me my career—and almost my life."

Wisely, though I had a thousand things I wanted to say, questions I wanted to ask, Lane and I kept our mouths shut and let Aspen proceed at her own pace.

"Bullough Enterprises was a venture capitalist firm in Chicago. About six months before I left everything behind, I got an anonymous tip that they were skimming from their investors. According to my source, it wasn't anything crazy at that point. A few hundred thousand here and there. But it had the makings of an elaborate Ponzi scheme. If I could prove it, that kind of story could make my career. I had aspirations outside of Chicago, you know? So I started digging."

"What happened?" I pressed gently when she was silent for a few minutes.

"As it turned out, the CEO had a number of vices. The bulk of his money went up his nose, down the drain at illegal poker games, or to high-priced call girls. He found himself with some bad debts across the three extracurriculars and needed to raise money fast."

"So he started stealing from his clients," Lane supplied. I cut him a confused glance and he added, "I looked into Aspen. Read her articles." He met her eyes in the mirror again. "You're very talented."

"Thank you."

"So what happened?" I asked her. "Seems like you got the scoop."

"I was also beaten within an inch of my life to drop it and forget everything I knew too."

"Fucking hell, Aspen."

This woman—she was stronger than even I knew.

"I was followed home from the office one day," she continued, tone even and emotionless, like she couldn't allow herself to get worked up. The detachment was necessary for the sake of her mental health, a tactic I understood well. "These two goons shoved their way into my apartment and beat the shit out of me. Four broken ribs, collapsed lung, severe concussion, bruises all over my body. I only survived because they left my phone. They *let* me call for help." She lifted her hand to her forehead, trailing her pointer finger along the silvery scar that cut across the skin at her hairline "My souvenir."

"But you wrote the story anyway."

She nodded, swallowing hard. "My editor forced me to. He sat at my bedside while I recovered, typing the words I dictated to him when the pounding in my head became too much to stare at the screen any longer. He was fucking relentless, so leaving it all behind was pretty effortless. How could I keep working for a man who valued getting the story over my health?"

"You did the right thing," Lane murmured. "And for what it's worth, I'm sorry I tried to drive you out of town when you got out of the hospital. Unlike that guy, I actually was looking out for your wellbeing."

Aspen gave him a small smile. "I know. You're not a total asshole."

"Only kind of," I teased.

The joking eased the somber mood in the cab of the SUV considerably, but still my mind spun. Aspen had been through so much, way more than I'd known about, and the fresh information only made me fall that much harder for her.

She was so fucking strong, so brave in the face of all she'd endured, never balking from the fight to find this killer despite the fact that she was one of his victims.

Aspen McKay was magnificent, and I was goddamn lucky to call her mine.

Silence blanketed the car as we all turned our attention inward. I replayed the interview, still having difficulty wrapping my mind around it all. Even *considering* Ward Saunders as a suspect was, to me, farfetched. I didn't care if circumstances and fucking body type made him look good for it. I'd known that man and his family my entire life. Mrs. Saunders had been Owen and Trey's teacher, then my, Lane, the twins, and Aria's principal. She'd worked for the school for as long as I'd been alive.

Wyatt used to run around the ranch with us, she and Trey as thick as thieves, always getting up to mischief. Secretly, or maybe not so secretly, my entire family thought they'd end up together, married with a few babies by now. But they shocked the hell out of us by going their separate ways after high school. I knew they were still close, but we all had to accept—Mama most of all—that they were merely friends.

The point was, the family was as well respected in this town as any other. There was no fucking way Ward Saunders was responsible for hurting my girl and killing all those others.

"Uhh, Crew?" my brother asked, penetrating the haze of my swirling thoughts.

"Yeah?"

"Your phone, baby," Aspen said from the backseat.

The incessant beeping of a security alarm registered then, and I slipped my phone out of my pocket to find the screen blazing red with alerts.

Before I could make sense of them, it rang with an incoming call from Trey.

"You good?" he asked when I answered.

"We're just leaving the Saunders'. What the fuck is going on?"

"Looks like the system was breached. I'm headed over there right now."

"We'll meet you there," I said, then hung up. To Lane, I added, "Lights and sirens, Sheriff. Let's go."

Lane didn't have to be told twice.

We skidded to a stop in my gravel drive next to Trey's truck a short while later, and I pushed out of the SUV into a cloud of dust, leaving my brother and Aspen behind. The front door was open, the keypad for the security system bleating on the wall.

"Trey?" I called.

"Office!"

Fuck. That couldn't be good.

I was proved right a moment later when I entered the room to find it in complete disarray. The murder wall had been destroyed, torn corners of pages clinging uselessly to the tacks. My computer was a heap of twisted metal, glass, and wires on the floor, smashed irreparably.

A gasp behind me had me turning to Aspen, who stood in the doorway with her hand covering her mouth, eyes wide. Lane hovered behind her, jaw clenched as his eyes swept the space.

"Everyone out," he barked.

"What? Why?" I asked.

"It's a crime scene now, baby bro," Trey said with a hand on my shoulder, steering me from the room. Lane was already on his radio, calling deputies and CSI as he stomped back outside. A minute later, he returned with yellow crime scene tape, barricading the door to the office with a few strips before ushering us all back to the driveway. Then he placed another across the front door.

Trey's vehicle was outfitted with a mobile command center, and I stood next to him, hand cradling Aspen's, as he tapped away on his laptop, pulling up the feed from the cameras on my property.

"See anything?" I asked.

He pressed a few more keys then angled the screen toward me.

I watched the playback from the camera mounted on a tree in the yard. For several moments, everything was still. Then, a figure entered the frame. They were cloaked head to toe in black, their face obscured by a mask. An oversized coat with the hood pulled up hid their body type, making it impossible to determine anything about them.

They strolled right up to my front door like they owned the place, fiddled with the handle until it popped open, and disappeared inside. Less than five minutes later, they returned, the sheaf of papers they'd stolen from my office clasped in their gloved hands, and disappeared from view.

"That's it?" I asked.

"We don't have cameras inside," he reminded me. "And the footage from the ones mounted to the exterior of the house and garage don't catch anything else of use. This guy is a fucking ghost." Then he grinned. "The good news is, it's not Ward."

"Fuck!" I screamed, yanking my hand from Aspen's and shoving my hands through my hair, tugging until sharp pain bloomed on my scalp.

A hand settled against my spine briefly before Aspen's touch snaked around, coming to rest against my stomach as she pressed her face into my back. I calmed, if only a fraction.

"Guess it's a good thing we're moving to the ranch for the foreseeable future," she said quietly into my skin.

I let out a chuckle, more tension easing from my shoulders as I did, then spun to embrace her properly.

"Guess so."

LANE LET us in the house long enough to pack a few bags of necessities, and by the time we loaded into my truck to head for the ranch, my property was crawling with cops.

Deciding I needed the fresh air and freedom of the backroads, I eased us onto the two-track that cut across ranch land instead of around it, rolling the windows down as we bumped along. Riley Green crooned softly from the speakers, the sun was shining, and my girl was at my side. Despite the fact that the comfort and safety of my home had been violated, I was living the dream.

"I can't believe this is all ranch land," Aspen said, her hand out the window, riding the wind.

"It's the largest privately owned acreage in the state," I admitted.

She looked at me then. "What do you do with it all?"

"Not much, honestly. There are grazing pastures for the dairy cows, fields of soybeans Mama uses for the self-care products she sells, hay we harvest for the cattle and horses. Otherwise, it's untamed wilderness. We've got herds of wild horses, buffalo and bison, moose, deer, and all sorts of other wild animals."

"So why haven't you sold any of the land off?"

"Because the only people rich enough to purchase the kind of acreage we'd even consider parting with are developers who want to grade the land and build on it. My brothers and I refuse to let that happen in our lifetimes. Consider it a…privately owned wildlife sanctuary."

Aspen nodded. "Fair enough."

As we continued our trek, I pointed out places that had been scenes of mischief in my and my siblings' youth. The place where I'd gotten in the accident that ultimately led to my addiction. The stretch of river that Aria had fallen into once before she could swim and nearly drowned before we caught her at the next bend. The field that still had a bonfire pit scorched in the center from all the parties we'd held out there over the years.

"Your souls are woven into the fabric of this land," Aspen said, a soft smile on her lips. "Your roots are planted so deep there's no you without the land, and vice versa. It's a beautiful thing."

She said it like someone who didn't have a connection of her own to any place that truly mattered to her, so I reached over the center console and placed my hand on her thigh, squeezing gently.

"You can put down roots right alongside mine, little phoenix."

thirty-seven

. . .

ASPEN

"TO WHAT DO I owe the pleasure?" Birdie asked when Crew and I trudged up the front steps a half hour later.

"We're moving in," he said.

Her brow creased. "For how long? And why?"

"To be determined. My house was just broken into, and we need a safe place to land for a while."

Birdie's mouth opened and closed a few times while she grappled with what to say. Ultimately, she snapped it shut and ushered us inside.

"I don't need to tell you where to go," she told her son as we stood in the foyer, my hands empty because Crew insisted on carrying all of our stuff. "And I suppose you'll be sharing a room."

"Yep," Crew said cheerfully as he started for the stairs, and I trailed after him.

The old farmhouse was sizable, and my eyes drank in every little detail as we made our way through the living quarters. This was the first time I'd been up here, and I was in awe of how spacious it all felt.

"My parents added on once they started having more kids

than there were bedrooms," Crew said. "Even so, growing up, we all shared rooms, except Aria. I bunked with Lane until he'd gone off to college." He jerked his chin at another set of stairs leading up to a third level, and I followed him up. "This is it."

I blinked in surprise, excepting some sort of teenage boy special, a time capsule maintained as an ode to the children Crew and his brothers had once been, but the room was immaculate. There was a king-sized bed topped with a plush white comforter and mountain of pillows. Gauzy curtains bracketed the windows, and an antique dresser was pushed up against one wall. Two night stands rested on either side of the bed.

"It's gorgeous," I breathed, then narrowed my eyes at Crew. "Did your mom help you decorate your house?"

He snorted as he dropped our bags near a door in the corner, which I assumed was a closet. "Of course she did. You should've seen this place ten years ago. There used to be two full beds in here. We each had a dresser, but shared the closet, which usually led to arguments when one of us would take up more space than the other.

"Sounds…cozy," I smirked.

"Once Lane left for college, I had the whole place to myself. I started using his bed as a catchall for laundry I didn't feel like folding, filled his dresser with all my drug paraphernalia, and snuck out to parties through the window."

He moved over to it and I joined him, peering outside at the gentle slope of the roof and the tree beyond. The branches were spaced perfectly for easy climbing.

"You little rascal."

"That's actually my horse's name," Crew chuckled.

I wrapped my arms around him and tucked my hands into his back pockets, giving his ass a squeeze. "Appropriate," I murmured, rising onto my tiptoes to press my mouth to the column of his throat, working my way upward until he bent to greet me. "Tell me, hotshot. How many girls have you had in this room?"

Skating his hand along my neck and notching his thumb under my chin, he tilted my head backward until I met that crystal blue gaze. "None."

Blinking in surprise, I fisted my hands in his shirt, drawing him closer until his pelvis pressed into me, the thick length of his cock digging into my stomach through his jeans. "Not a single one?" I questioned.

"I didn't get my rocks off in this house, Aspen. I found my pleasure elsewhere, usually in some corner at a party, both of us high out of our minds."

I didn't like the image that painted in my mind, and I darted my eyes away lest he saw the jealousy surely taking over my expression.

"Hey, no," he said, forcing my attention back to him. "I was a dumb kid, and that was a long time ago." His free hand came to rest over my heart, which tripped and sped under his touch. "You're all I want now. Forever, if you'll have me."

The flare of envy died in a flash, replaced by passion, desire, and security. I believed every word he said because he continued to show me how much he meant them, day in and day out. Like my life, I trusted him with my equally fragile and precious heart.

"I'll take it under advisement," I murmured a moment before he crashed his mouth to mine.

"What do you say, little phoenix? You going to let me fuck you under my mama's roof?" he asked against my mouth. His roving hands slipped down my sides, grabbing healthy handfuls of my ass. In a beat, I was off my feet, my legs winding around his waist in a move that was now second nature. Instead of taking me to the bed, though, he perched me on the edge of the dresser.

"Yes, please," I whispered, my breath stolen by the way he looked at me.

There was such reverence there, in his eyes and in his gentle touch as he reached for the button of my jeans, flipping it open and drawing down the fly. I leveraged myself up when he gripped the waistband, dragging them and my panties over my hips and thighs, peeling them off and discarding them behind him.

"Can you be quiet?"

"I—I can try," I stuttered as his thumb brushed through my slit, making my thighs quake.

"Goddamnit, woman. How are you always so fucking wet for me?" he asked as he sucked his finger into his mouth.

"Take a look in the mirror, hotshot. You'll figure it out."

Crew grinned, that panty-melting smile a prime fucking example of why I was a horny mess around him at all times.

"I think there's more to it than that." His caress moved north from my thigh to my neck, pressure from his fingers against the sides of my windpipe eliciting a desperate gasp from me. "I think, for the first time in your life, you feel safe. In the bedroom, out of it. Mind, body, soul. It all fucking belongs to me, Aspen, and you know I'll take care of you like my life depends on it —*because it does.*"

The thumb of his free hand toyed with my clit, glancing strokes against the nub as his palm remained against my neck.

"Now be a good girl and stay quiet while I fuck your perfect cunt with my fingers."

All I could do was nod. I was beyond words anyway. The pleasure this man brought me was unlike anything I'd ever experienced before, like something about his touch altered me on a chemical level, heightening everything he did. The gentle petting of my clit turned to insistent pressure as he slid two of those thick fingers into my pussy, and I threw my head back, ignoring the pain as it collided with the wall, my back arching, hips angling him deeper.

"God, Aspen. The way your cunt takes me. Fucking perfect. Take your shirt off, baby. Let me see those tits."

I fumbled with the hem, awkwardly wrenching it from my body and adding it to the growing pile on the floor. I hadn't bothered with a bra, and my eyes popped open to watch Crew's darken to that stormy sea blue I loved so much. I'd always been self-conscious about my boobs—until Crew. Now, I knew my body was perfect, because it was perfect for *him*. Thanks to him, I no longer flinched at the sight or feel of my burn marks, the shiny skin that was still pink and would take years to fully turn the white of old scars. Crew loved me, and I knew he would until we were old and grey.

A grumble emanated from his chest, the pressure on my throat increasing slightly.

"You have no idea how perfect you are," he murmured, leaning close to draw the lobe of my ear, lined with golden studs of various shapes and sizes, between his teeth.

The amalgamation of sensations was nearly too much to stand. My tight nipples brushing against the fabric of his cotton tee. My slightly restricted airway making me lightheaded. The erogenous zone he'd unlocked by playing with my ear. And of course, the fingers in my pussy. I was a ball of unspent desire, gasping little whimpers leaving me as I wordlessly begged Crew for more, my hips swiveling against his palm, searching for friction on my clit.

"Needy little slut," he chuckled, pressing a rough kiss to my cheek.

"Please," I hissed.

"Damn do I love when you beg."

He rewarded me with a third finger, stretching me almost uncomfortably. Despite all the times we'd fucked in the last month, it still took me a moment to adjust to his size—fingers and cock alike. But the sting quickly soothed to a wave of thigh-quaking ecstasy as he curled those fingers against the perfect spot and pressed his palm harder to my clit. I began to rock back and forth on the dresser, neither of us giving a fuck as it thumped metronomically into the wall as I sought my release.

My orgasm coiled tighter and tighter in my core, lightning sparking under my skin. Pulse racing, breathing erratic, heart rate climbing. Every muscle in my body clenched in preparation, but I held on, even as Crew's fingers sped up, driving me higher and higher.

"Let go," he demanded. "*Let-fucking-go*, Aspen."

I shattered.

Crew's hands left me in an instant as he dropped to his knees in time for me to squirt all over his face. I white-knuckled the edges of the dresser as I spasmed, gasping for air, anchoring myself to this reality while I lost myself in the pure bliss he'd driven me to.

Through heavily lidded eyes, my vision hazy from the force of my climax, I watched him between my thighs, mouth open, catching my cum on his tongue, his cheeks and chin glistening. At last, the aftershocks ceased, and I sagged, chest heaving.

"Jesus Christ," I breathed.

"That was certainly a religious experience," he agreed, swiping a hand over his face. "I feel like you just baptized me."

I choked on a laugh, and he gathered me into his arms, carrying me to the bed.

He tried to move away, but I locked my arms and legs around him like a monkey, keeping him with me.

"I need you."

"You've got me, baby. Think I better show you how much I love you after I finger fucked you like you're my personal little slut."

"I liked it," I promised. "And I *know* you love me."

He disentangled himself from my hold and moved to where he'd dropped our bags earlier, rifling through his duffel and coming back to me.

"That was me fucking you to remind you your body belongs

to me, Aspen. Now let me make love to you to remind us both your heart does too."

"As long as yours is mine."

"*All* of it is yours. The very breath in my lungs, the heartbeat in my chest, the blood in my veins. Every single piece of me belongs to you now."

"I love you too," I grinned. "Now tell me what's in your hand."

He uncurled his fingers, revealing a bright purple ring, another nestled inside it, with a little tube on one side, a small cylinder peeking out either end. There was also a separate device that looked like a button. "How do you feel about trying a cock ring?"

"Yes please," I said eagerly. I'd never seen one in person, but I understood the purpose. The pressure around his cock would make him last longer, and the little cylinder on the one side would vibrate against his shaft and hit my clit with each inward thrust.

Crew quickly shed his clothes, and every single time I saw him naked was like the first time. I'd never tire of the perfection of his body, nor would the surreality that he was *all mine* ever wear off.

"You're drooling," he teased, swiping a broad thumb against my bottom lip. I nipped at it, and he pulled back. I watched raptly as he fit the ring around himself, the smaller ring nestled at the base of his dick while the larger one wrapped his balls. He pressed the button atop the remote, and a faint buzz filled the air between us. Crew sucked in a breath, clenching his teeth.

"Goddamnit, that feels good."

Reaching for him, I wrapped a hand around his length, a tingling sensation shooting up my arm. I tugged him forward until the head bumped my entrance, toes curling in anticipation as the vibration lit up my pussy, still sensitive from my previous orgasm.

With aching slowness, Crew pushed inside, filling me so completely there was nothing but him. His forehead dropped to mine, both of us swearing and huffing out laughs.

"I love you," he murmured as he retreated all the way to the tip before thrusting back in.

My hands cupped his face, eyes wide open and locked on his. "And I love you."

Crew's pace was unhurried, languidly rocking us together, and I relished it. The duality of this man, calling me a needy little slut one minute then making sweet love to me the next. The connection I felt to him only grew stronger with each delicious glide of his cock in and out of my sex. I arched to meet him, the vibrator of the ring trapped between us each time we came together, delivering luscious waves of pleasure to my clit.

But I needed more.

I let Crew's face go to bring my hands to his back, scraping my nails down his muscles, softly at first but with increasing pressure.

"Fuck me like you mean it, hotshot," I begged, sinking my fingertips into his ass and holding him to me when he bottomed out inside, swiveling my hips against the little bullet, gasping when goosebumps broke out across my skin.

"Hold on," he warned a moment before he withdrew and slammed home. I anchored myself to his shoulders, hooking my heels together at the base of his spine.

Crew was relentless as he took me over and over, our bodies coated in sweat, writhing together atop the once-pristine comforter of the bed. He rocked back onto his knees and pushed on my thighs, holding me down and wide open and he pounded into me, the bullet slapping against my clit in time to his rapid thrusts. Sweet and slow Crew was wonderful, but unhinged, reckless Crew was a goddamn sight to behold. That curled lock of hair falling over his forehead, every single muscle in his body straining, bunching and flexing as he drove us both to the edge.

His sexy moans increased in volume to match mine as I clamped tighter and tighter around him.

I blinked, and I was flying, breaking into a thousand tiny pieces that floated above my corporeal body. Crew roared his own release, his hips stuttering as he spurted inside, prolonging the aftershocks rolling endlessly through me.

At last, I came back to myself, Crew's face hovering over mine, my favorite sexy, sated grin on his face as he bent to kiss me. I met him weakly, my limbs wrung out and limp.

After a beat, he withdrew from me and got off the bed, pausing to power off and remove the cock ring before walking to the closet and returning a moment later with a dry washcloth. Gently, he cleaned me up, then reclined beside me, fingertips drawing patterns on my stomach.

"You okay?"

"Better than," I promised.

"Good."

Lifting my head, our lips met softly. I tilted my face to deepen it, apparently ready for round two—or was it three?—but a knock came at the door.

"If you're hungry, you better come eat before the ranch hands get here!" Birdie shouted through.

"Oh, God," I groaned, covering my face as my cheeks heated. "Do you think she…?"

Crew shrugged, unperturbed by the idea that his mom had heard us having sex. "Does it matter?"

"I suppose not," I giggled as I pulled away from him.

Crew caught me and gave me a final, hard kiss. A promise of all the things he still wanted to do to me.

Then we quickly got dressed and freshened up before heading downstairs for lunch.

thirty-eight

. . .

CREW

LIFE on the ranch was surprisingly enjoyable considering the fact that me and my…girlfriend? had moved in with my mother despite being in our thirties.

Aspen adjusted well, and I supposed it helped that she was used to uprooting her life and moving from place to place at the drop of a hat. Even on mornings when I didn't have to work, and we could sleep in—or spend those hours lazily exploring each other's bodies—she was routinely up before me. I'd always find her in the kitchen, helping Mama prep meals for the ranch hands. Then we'd venture outside, either heading to the barn so Aspen could learn more about Finn's rescue operation, or down to the dude ranch with West, where she'd jump at the chance to help turnover cabins for the next set of guests.

I'd known she wasn't afraid to get her hands dirty, but I thought there was more to it than that. Most likely, she was trying to keep herself busy. If she stopped moving, she'd think about all the things that had gone wrong since she'd arrived in town—and she'd run. So I let her do her thing, let her burn off that anxious energy during the day and reward her hard work with orgasms at night.

We spent the Fourth of July on the ranch, surrounded by family—both blood and found. Each of my brothers, Mama, Aria, Aspen, and I pitched in to put together an impressive buffet-style spread of summer staples for the ranch hands and their families to enjoy. There were lawn games, pony rides for the littles in the corral under the intense supervision of Finn, and Mama's signature margaritas flowing endlessly for the adults. We ended the night with an impressive fireworks show curated by West, who had blocked off reservations for his cabins to let ranch hands who lived off the property to stay the night.

The day was perfect, and things on the investigative front had been eerily quiet since the break-in at my house two weeks earlier, so it made sense that not three days later, something finally popped.

I'd been on shift the night before, so when the ringing of my phone dragged me from sleep, I swore heartily.

Blindly, I groped around on the nightstand for the infernal device, answering without looking at the screen.

"You're still sleeping?" Lane asked.

"What time is it?"

"Nearly four."

"Jesus," I breathed, rubbing the thumb and pointer of my free hand into my eyes before blinking them open.

Lane *tsk*ed. "Get up, baby bro. We've got work to do."

"You do realize I worked last night, hence the reason I'm still sleeping. *And* I'm not a cop."

"I'm going to interview Missy Plano today," he supplied. "Thought you'd want to come along."

Fuck yeah I did.

Since the day Chris had passed along Missy's name, Lane and the department had attempted to contact her several times with no luck.

"She's back in town?"

"Johns saw her at the Swallow last night."

"You call ahead?"

My brother snorted. "Hell no. We're showing up unannounced."

I grinned. I loved me an ambush.

"I'll meet you at the station in a half hour."

Lane hung up without another word, and I quickly shot Aspen a text, asking where she was and to meet me upstairs, knowing that'd be faster than searching her out myself.

Five minutes later, the door creaked open, and there my girl stood. By then, I'd managed to sit up and scoot to the end of the bed to wait for her. Wordlessly, I opened my arms, and she came to me, tucking herself between my thighs, my face coming to rest against her chest.

Aspen giggled, her fingers sifting softly through my hair.

"Good morning," I murmured, then titled my head up for a kiss, which she obliged with a happy little hum I'd never tire of.

"You slept late."

My palms skated down her sides, following the contours of her body until I cupped her ass. "Guess all those nights worshiping my girl finally caught up to me."

Aspen sighed as I kneaded her flesh, sagging against me for only a moment before pressing my shoulders and stepping away.

"As much as I love and appreciate it, we don't have time for any more worshiping right now."

"Oh, we don't?"

"It's almost dinner time," she explained.

"Why don't we convince Mama to take the night off from cooking?" I asked. "Lane called, and Missy Plano is back in town. We're going to interview her."

"I want to come."

"Later," I smirked.

Aspen socked me in the shoulder, packing a surprising punch for someone so small.

"Crew."

"Not on this one, little phoenix. If she's connected to these murders in any way, I don't want you anywhere near her."

Aspen's lower lip jutted out in a pout, an expression that would normally have me on my knees, ready to give her whatever she wanted.

But not this time.

I'd already taken too many chances with her safety, and I'd never forgive myself if she got hurt because of me.

Reaching for her, I brought my hand to her face and my thumb to that lip, brushing against it before cupping her cheek. "I'm sorry, baby, but the answer is still no."

She huffed out a sigh but said, "Fine."

"I'll call you the second we leave the interview, and I'll tell you everything when I get home."

"Bring Lane too," she said. "I don't want you to leave anything out."

"Deal."

<hr>

AS PROMISED, I rolled to a stop in front of the sheriff's department a half hour later. Lane was already waiting in his cruiser, so I got out and locked my truck before hopping into his passenger seat. But Lane didn't pull away immediately, and I found out why a beat later when Trey opened the rear door and got in behind him.

"He's coming too?"

Lane shrugged. "It's a family field trip."

"So how do you want to play this?" I asked Lane as he navigated across town, toward the trailer park where Missy lived.

"I want you to keep your mouths shut and let me do my job."

I opened mine to protest, but Lane cut me with a glare. "Both of you are here as a courtesy. Neither of you are cops, and neither of you have any power. I'm letting *you* ride along, Crew, because for one, you're deeply involved in this case on a personal and professional level, having worked the fire that nearly took your girl out. For two, I could use the backup."

"If you wanted backup, I feel like the former Army Rangers might've been better suited," Trey quipped from the back.

"They're busy, so I'm stuck with you two idiots."

"What about your deputies?"

"My department is spread a little thin at the moment dealing with other shit."

"Other shit like what?" I prompted.

"None of your business."

I knew better than to push, so I let it drop, and we proceeded the rest of the way to Missy's in silence.

The trailer park was well-kept, and Missy's home was no exception. The exterior was robin's egg-blue with a bay window jutting out at one end, the windows and doors trimmed in crisp white. The front porch was painted a dove grey and lined with fragrant white roses. The pathway stones were free from moss, weeds, and dirt, and the grass of the postage stamp yard was bright green and recently mowed.

"Cute little place," I remarked.

"To hide the dirty shit that she gets up to behind closed doors," Lane muttered, and Trey snickered.

When we reached the landing and Lane knocked, faint music filtered through the door, and a voice called, "One minute please!"

As promised, the inner door popped open a moment later, revealing through the screen a woman around Mama's age, her bleach-blonde hair teased to high heaven and wavy like she'd used one of those crimping tools I'd seen my sister wield a time or two. Her eyes were lined in heavy, dark kohl, her lips unnaturally plump and painted a glossy pink. A Fleetwood Mac tee hung off her shoulder, tight denim pants that flared out from the knee encased her legs, and each movement of her arms sent her collection of bangles colliding and jangling. Her feet were bare, toes painted black to match her short nails.

Missy cocked a hip, a coy smile appearing on her mouth. "Well, well. To what do I owe the pleasure, Sheriff?" Her attention turned to me. "Captain." Then to Trey. "Coach."

I didn't appreciate the way her grey eyes dragged over me like I was a piece of meat she wanted to sink her teeth into.

Unperturbed by the assessment, Lane merely said, "Mind if we come in? We were hoping to ask you a few questions."

"Regarding?"

"The Prom Night Arsonist."

Missy sucked in a gasp that hissed sharply through her teeth and said, "I've been wondering when you'd make your way to little old me."

When she opened the screen door to admit us, me and my brothers shared a quick glance, excited energy dancing under my skin.

She knows something.

Her home was decorated as the woman was dressed: like the seventies had thrown up on every wall and piece of furniture. Framed band posters hung in the living space, the bay window I'd noticed outside was lined with shaggy pillows, and macrame curtains covered the windows. A wicker stand in the corner held a record player, the disk and needle spinning and filling the space with the sounds of "The Chain."

She directed us to a sofa that looked straight out of *The Brady Bunch*, my brothers and I barely fitting shoulder to shoulder across it, with me sandwiched uncomfortably in the middle.

"Can I get you fine gentleman anything to drink?" she asked as she moved into the kitchen. The rooms were painted a creamy beige color, giving the whole thing a sepia-toned vibe, aided by the haze of cigarette smoke hanging in the air, like we'd stepped back in time.

I could only imagine what her bedroom looked like. Likely some *Austin Powers*-type shit, with psychedelic patterns and a round bed.

"This isn't a social call, Ms. Plano."

She waved a hand at him, giggling lightly. "Please, Sheriff. Call me Mel or Missy."

"Fine, *Missy*," Lane gritted out. "Please come take a seat."

"If you insist," she said, damn near gliding across the space to the armchair across from us.

"We have reason to believe you've got information that could help us catch the Prom Night Arsonist."

"*Moi?*" she asked in a horrible French accent, placing a hand on her chest. "Who would say such a thing?"

"The *who* doesn't matter so much as the *why*."

"You were a senior with Vicky Lee and Roger Stanhope, right?"

Lane nudged me with his shoulder, a silent reminder of his earlier directive: *keep my mouth shut*. But we didn't have time to sit here and dance around the matter at hand. I was merely cutting to the chase.

"I was…" she said slowly.

"Anything weird happen that night that you can remember?" Lane asked.

She snorted. "You mean other than two of my classmates being burned alive? Nope, can't think of anything."

Her flippancy grated on me. This was fucking serious. People had *died*.

"Did you have any personal connection to the victims?"

"It's a small town. Of course I did."

"I mean…intimately."

"Not with Vicky," she said slyly.

"So you were intimate with Stanhope?"

I'd been so focused on Missy that I hadn't noticed Lane had taken out his phone and started recording the conversation, the device balanced on his knee. Missy, however, had her eyes glued to it.

Coming back to herself, she leaned over to a side table and lifted a gold case—a cigarette holder. She withdrew a smoke and lit it up. After a few drags, she finally spoke again.

"He and Vicky were constantly on and off. It's always a grey area when you're that age, you know? We're all aware we're not destined forever with our high school sweethearts." She paused, as if recognizing whose company she was keeping, and added, "Your parents not included, of course. Birdie and Jase were soulmates. But around prom happened to be one of those times Vicky and Roger were off. So Roger and I got a bit hot and heavy. We had an understanding."

"What kind of understanding?"

She hitched a bony shoulder, blowing a stream of smoke out her nose like a dragon. "It was just sex. Emotions messed everything up, so we were having fun. Nothing more. Plus, I think he always *thought* he'd end up with Vicky, and the back and forth of their relationship was only growing pains."

"Do you remember if they went to prom together? Were they back on by then?"

"Nah," she said, reclining in her chair, grinning.

"Did you go with him?"

"I didn't."

"Then who?" Trey asked before Lane could, taking the words right out of my mouth. The three of us leaned forward, and my breath stalled in my lungs as I waited for her answer.

That gut feeling that we were onto something, that whatever Missy was about to say would change everything, was back with a vengeance, twisting my stomach into knots.

She smirked. "Roger went to prom with Kelly McAllister."

"McAllister, McAllister," Lane chanted quietly. "Why does that name sound so familiar?"

It didn't ring any bells with me, but Trey caught on almost immediately.

"McAllister," he said softly, his tone so full of pain that my head whipped in his direction, "is Kelly Saunders' maiden name."

thirty-nine

. . .

CREW

"WHAT A FUCKING MESS," Lane grumbled as he steered us into his office at the station.

"It's not possible."

Trey was clearly in shock, moving like a zombie since we'd left Missy's, but I was inclined to agree with him. There was no fucking way.

"Trey," Lane said gently, using that tone I'd often heard him adopt with families of accident victims. "The writing is on the wall."

"No!" I insisted, and Trey nodded. "That's even more ludicrous than our killer being Ward."

"Take your feelings about the family out of it and look at it logically," Lane implored us both. "Aspen and I both thought Wyatt knew more than she was letting on the day we interviewed Ward. And while Aspen didn't get any bad vibes from him, I wasn't entirely convinced. I thought maybe Ward was a sneaky tech genius and had managed to dupe the system."

"Not possible," Trey muttered, some life returning to him. "For starters, the security logs are iron-clad. No offense to Ward, but he's not smart enough to manipulate the system like that. No one in that family is. Hell, it's *my* software, and I'm not even smart enough to do it."

"Which means Ward and Wyatt were telling the truth. But there's a third member of that family, and after the interview with Missy, it makes perfect sense."

"I think you're reaching," I told Lane. "There's no fucking way Mrs. Saunders is responsible for forty years' worth of serial killings."

Lane shrugged. "The evidence says otherwise."

"What evidence?" Trey shouted, shooting from his seat. "You've got the town whore telling us Kelly went to prom with Roger and some bad vibes from the Ward interview. Quite frankly, you're jumping to conclusions, and I won't allow it."

Trey's chest rose and fell rapidly as he stared down at Lane, who blinked in shock at the outburst. Before Lane could respond, though, his phone rang.

"My FBI friend," he explained before he answered. "Hey, Addison. Heads up, you're on speaker and two of my brothers are here with me."

"Hey, Lane. Hey, other Lawless brothers."

Trey and I mumbled greetings, and Lane said, "What've you got?"

"So, the team and I took a look at all the files you sent over, both the police reports and incident reports from the fire department. And after consulting with a few colleagues at Quantico, we've built a profile. I'm emailing everything over, so take some time to review it, and give me a call if you've got any questions."

On cue, Lane's computer pinged with an incoming email. "Thanks a lot, Addison. I owe you one."

"A beer next time I'm down that way."

"Deal," Lane grinned then hung up.

Trey and I were on the edges of our seats while Lane navigated to the email and scanned the contents.

"HA!" he shouted.

The chair next to me creaked, and I looked over to see Trey had gripped it tight enough to bleach his knuckles, the wood groaning with the force.

"No," he said.

Lane gathered himself as he looked at our older brother. "I wanted to be wrong."

"About what?" I asked. "Tell me what the fuck that profile says."

"'Based on the information provided to this office courtesy of the Dusk Valley Sheriff's Department and Dusk Valley Fire Department, we have built the following profile of the so-called "Prom Night Arsonist." We believe we're dealing with a female, likely in her late fifties in accordance with the date of the first kill. This killer is…'"

I stopped listening after that, though Lane continued to read, mostly to himself.

Fuck. Mrs. Saunders? That was…*insane.* The FBI had to be wrong.

Trey, who was pacing the small stretch of office at the side of Lane's desk, stilled, and Lane shut up, all three of our heads whipping to the door when a knock sounded against it.

"Yeah?" he hollered, and the desk sergeant pushed inside.

"Sorry to interrupt, boss, but there's someone here to see you."

"Did you get a name?" Lane asked, pinching the bridge of his nose in irritation.

"She said her name is Wyatt, and that you'd know why she was here."

Trey dropped back into his chair heavily, like his legs had completely given out on him, and I felt the blood drain from my face as surely as it had his.

"You can watch from the viewing room," Lane told us as he moved from behind the desk, straightening his tie as he went to bring Wyatt back to interrogation, leaving us momentarily alone in his office.

"You don't have to go," I told Trey. "We'll relay everything."

"That's my best friend," he choked out. "Of course I'm going to be there. I just—"

He cut himself off and exhaled sharply, hand raking down his face.

"Yeah," I said in understanding, because I got what he hadn't spoken.

This was a lot.

"But hey," I continued. "It's possible she's here on something totally unrelated."

Trey shot me a death glare, and I held my hands up in surrender as we finally left the office and made our way to the viewing room of the first interrogation room.

And not a moment too soon.

"What can I do for you today, Wy?" Lane asked. He sat with his back to the one-way glass, giving us a direct line of sight to Wyatt, and my heart sank.

Her face was splotchy, eyes red-rimmed and puffy, like she'd been crying a long time. She'd placed her hands on the cool metal table in front of her, wringing her fingers together nervously. The rigid set of her spine and how she refused to look Lane in the eye made it obvious she wanted to be anywhere but here.

"I lied to you that day you came to talk to Dad," she rasped. "Well, no. I didn't lie so much as I didn't tell you everything."

Lane remained quiet, giving Wyatt the space to continue.

"Mom—" Wyatt choked on the word, and fresh tears splashed down her cheeks. Trey's hand found my shoulder, fingers digging in. Either he was trying to stop himself from going to her, or he was merely holding himself up.

Likely both.

"What about your mom?" Lane asked softly.

"She's been…scarce as of late. She's usually around so much in the summer to make up for working so hard during the school year, but since classes let out, and even before then actually, I feel like I've hardly seen her. She's been…cagey anytime we ask what she's been up to. But she seems weirdly happy?" Wyatt dropped her face into her hands. "I'm not making any sense, am I?"

"Your mom has access to your dad's work trucks, doesn't she?"

Wyatt nodded.

"I'm going to have you review some footage from the security cameras at the depot. It's not the best, but no one knows your parents as well as you, and I'm hoping you'll be able to clear some things up for us."

Wyatt lifted her head and nodded.

Lane left the room briefly, shooting us a look to stay put as he walked past, then returned a minute later with an iPad. Re-entering interrogation, he slid his chair around next to Wyatt, set it up in front of them, and pressed play on the footage.

There was no sound, but I could see the images reflected on the mirror—a legitimate mirror this time—behind them, watching as he sped through the frames until a truck with Ward's company logo pulled up to the pump, the driver facing away from the camera mounted to the depot lobby. I couldn't read the timestamp, but the artificial lighting overhead indicated late in the evening or very early in the morning.

Almost as though the person driving that pickup chose a time when very few people, if anyone at all, would be around.

Head down and hood up, someone got out of the vehicle, moved to the back, and pulled a gas can out of the bed. They brought it to the pump, inserted a credit card to get it running, and filled the can before returning it to the bed and driving away.

Wyatt was openly weeping, shaking her head as if she couldn't believe it, but Lane made no move to comfort her.

"You know who that is."

Lane wasn't asking, but Wyatt nodded, breathing deeply in an attempt to marshal her sobs.

"It's not one of the guys who works for your dad by any chance?"

Wyatt shook her head, then reached for the iPad. "May I?" she choked out.

"Be my guest," Lane said.

Wyatt rewound the video to the moment when the person stuck their credit card into the pump and paused it. Then she zoomed in on the screen until a sliver of the person's wrist between the sleeve of their sweatshirt and the edge of the glove was visible.

Wordlessly, Wyatt twisted her own wrist to reveal the word written there.

Always.

"I'd know that tattoo anywhere."

"Fuck!" Trey screamed, and Wyatt's head whipped up.

"Trey?" she asked.

Lane glared at us through the glass as I attempted to hold Trey back.

To Wyatt, Lane said, "Do you have any idea where she is right now?"

"No." The word was so quiet, I could barely hear her. "I haven't seen her since the day you, Crew, and Aspen came to the house. She came home that evening, ate dinner with us like everything was normal. When we told her you guys had been by, she didn't really react, which I suppose was a reaction for her." Another sob wracked her body. "Aspen. Oh my God, Aspen. That poor woman. All those poor women." She was crying hard enough now that there was no way she could speak.

Trey jerked free from my grasp, and I let him go. A beat later, the door to the interrogation room burst open, and he crossed the room to gather Wyatt in his arms. Both of them shook with the force of her sobs.

I joined Lane in the hallway.

"I'm going to head home," I told him. "I need eyes on Aspen. Keep me posted."

Lane nodded. "Be safe."

"Always am." I saluted him and raced for the door.

This time of year, the sun stayed up for hours, so the sky was still brightly lit by the time I stepped outside, but the shadows were lengthening. The second I was behind the wheel of my truck, I dialed Aspen.

"Hey, hotshot."

My shoulders relaxed, some of the tension of the last few hours bleeding away. "Hi, baby."

"You okay?"

"I've got a lot to tell you," I answered noncommittally. "You still okay with pizza for dinner?"

"Yep. Your mom told the ranch hands they had to fend for themselves tonight, but Finn and West are here. Will Lane and Trey be joining us?"

"Ahh…no."

"Ominous."

I chuckled. "You have no fucking idea. I'll swing by Mozzy's and grab some take-and-bakes. Have Mama fire up the oven, and I'll be home in twenty minutes or so."

"Be careful, baby," she warned.

"I love you too," I quipped and hung up.

Every single parking space on Cassia was taken, so I drove around to the alley and steered into the grass on the side, leaving my truck running as I entered through the back door. The wait was longer than I would've liked but after fifteen minutes, I headed out with three pies balanced in my hands.

I never saw the hit coming.

I was stunned enough that I stumbled, dropping the boxes of

pizza. Before I could react, a cold, blunt object pressed into the back of my head, and a distorted voice said, "Keep your mouth shut and I won't blow your brains out right here."

Still dazed from the blow, I wisely didn't move. The barrel dug in harder as the person shoved me forward, toward a white panel van parked nose-to-nose with my truck. We went around back, where the doors were open.

"Get in," the voice said.

I crawled in. The moment I was fully inside, but before I could turn to get a look at whoever the fuck this was, they reached out and pressed something to my neck.

First, there was a sting, then a jolt that reverberated through my entire body.

And then, there was nothing but blackness.

forty

. . .

ASPEN

"WHAT'S THE MATTER, DEAR?"

Birdie's voice startled me enough that I yelped, then slapped my hand over my face in embarrassment. I'd been standing at the windows in the den—the ones that faced the driveway— willing Crew's truck to come rolling down the gravel and ease the twisting in my gut.

"I'm so sorry," I told her, then flicked my wrist to check my watch. "But…Crew should've been home by now. My calls are going straight to voicemail."

Forty minutes had passed since he'd called to say he'd be home in twenty, and something about his tardiness wasn't sitting right with me.

"I can feel it too," Birdie whispered, gathering my hand in hers. "Something is wrong."

"What makes you say that?"

She pressed her free palm to her heart. "A mother always knows."

I sighed in relief that I wouldn't have to try to explain this nagging sensation tugging at my heart. Birdie merely withdrew her phone from the pocket of the apron she perpetually wore

366

and dialed a number. The ringing filled the silence between us, and a deep voice answered a moment later.

"Hey, Mama," he said, and I recognized it instantly as Lane. "Sorry, but I'm not going to be able to make dinner. Things are moving in this case, and I'll be stuck at the department until further notice."

"Have you seen Crew?"

"Not since he left here about forty minutes or so ago."

Birdie put the phone on speaker, and I said, "Hey, Lane? It's Aspen. Look, it's probably nothing, but he called me when he left there. Said he was going to get pizza from Mozzy's and head home."

"Fuck," Lane breathed. "I'm assuming you tried calling him?"

"Yes. They're going right to his voicemail."

"Trey and I will go check it out."

"Be careful, baby," Birdie told her son, echoing the last words I'd spoken to Crew.

"I'll call you when I know something."

Aria entered the room as Birdie ended the call and said, "Was that Lane? Is he coming out for dinner? And speaking of, where the heck is Crew with the pizza?"

"Finn? West?" Birdie called, ignoring Aria's questions.

The twins appeared in the den a moment later, and the training they received during years of active duty with the Rangers must've alerted them to the fact that something was wrong.

Finn opened his mouth, but Birdie shot him a pleading look, eyes bouncing from him to Aria, who missed the entire exchange thanks to something on her phone holding her attention.

"C'mon, Ari," West said, placing his hands on his sister's shoulders. "Let's see if we can scrounge up a snack."

"But…the pizza."

"Crew is taking ages, and I'm starving. Aren't you starving?"

Her reply was lost to distance as he steered her toward the kitchen on the other side of the house.

"What's going on?" Finn asked the second Aria was out of earshot.

"We don't know yet," Birdie answered honestly. "But Aspen and I both have a bad feeling something happened to Crew."

"Did you call Lane?"

Birdie nodded. "He and Trey were still at the station, but they're going to check it out."

"Why would Trey be at the station?" Finn asked, looking at me.

"Your guess is as good as mine, but if I had to make one, I'd say something popped on the Prom Night Arsonist case. Trey's been helping out on some surveillance matters, so maybe they decided to loop him in."

"Okay, back up," Finn said, taking my hands and leading me to the sectional, where he sat and pulled me down next to him. "I think it's time to loop *me* in."

"Me too," West said, reappearing with a carton of yogurt in his hand.

"Where's Aria?"

West shrugged. "Got a call, so she went upstairs."

"Good," Finn said, turning back to me. "Now spill."

I told them everything I knew, everything I could remember, from the moment I arrived in town to the conversation with Crew after he'd left the station not an hour ago.

As soon as I finished my spiel, my phone rang with Lane's name on the readout.

"Did you find him?"

"Is my mom with you?"

"Finn and West too."

"Good then I only have to say this once." His voice shook, and I braced for the impact of his news. I'd only known the sheriff a few short months, but he was unflappable. If he was worked up, the news was distressing.

"Crew is gone."

Birdie sucked in a breath, and my heart dropped right to my feet. I was trembling so badly that I dropped my phone, and one of the twins scooped it up. I didn't pay attention to which, not as my vision blurred with tears. Pain pricked the flesh of my arm, and looked down to find Birdie holding onto me for dear life.

"What do you mean, *gone?*" Finn asked.

"I mean, his truck is parked behind Mozzy's, still running, and there are three pizzas lying on the ground like they'd been dropped there. We spoke to the counter staff, and he was here probably twenty minutes ago. The place is crazy busy right now, so he must've had to wait in line for a while."

"But he's still gone."

"No sign of him, Finny," Lane confirmed, the pain and fear in his voice penetrating my own haze.

"West and I are on our way."

"I'm pulling security footage from here and heading to Trey's. He's already there, so that's where I need you."

"Done," Finn said. "See you soon."

"Bring Aspen."

"What? Why?"

"I don't want her out of our sight. Hell, bring Mom and Aria too."

"Absolutely not," Birdie said, her tone waterlogged with unshed tears. "Send some ranch hands up here to keep an eye out, but I'm not dragging your sister into this. We're as safe as can be here. This sicko isn't after us."

"Fine," Lane conceded. "Only Aspen then."

"Wouldn't I be safe here?" I argued.

"I need your help with this," the sheriff said, shocking the hell out of all of us.

We'd come so far since I first arrived in town, from Lane trying to drive me away to him folding me into the investigation. I had no idea what would happen with me and Crew in the future—the possibility that he wouldn't return safely wasn't one I would ever entertain—but somehow, I knew these people had made me part of their family. The type of family I'd so desperately craved, where every success and failure wasn't measured against the accomplishments of a dead sister. Where I could live my life freely, without someone hovering over my shoulder, attempting to dictate every move I made.

I loved these people, almost as much as I loved Crew.

We mobilized quickly after that, Finn and West both seemingly having plans in place for if they needed to be away from the ranch for any length of time. A couple phone calls had everything in motion. Several ranch hands came up to the house to hang out with Birdie, who immediately disappeared into the kitchen, saying cooking would soothe her, and Aria had yet to reappear.

Finn, West, and I piled into Finn's dusty, black ranch truck and headed toward Trey's. I tried to distract myself on the drive there by taking in the scenery. This was a side of the ranch I'd never seen before, and it never ceased to amaze me exactly how much land the Lawless family owned. We were in mid-summer now, and everything was so lush and green, with pops of colors from the wildflowers that sprouted up all over the place. The distant craggy mountaintops were capped in white.

"This place is beautiful," I said to the twins.

West turned to me and grinned. "Now you know why we all came back."

"Except Owen."

"Yeah, well…our biggest brother was always destined for more than this small town could provide. And after spending years providing for us, he deserved to carve out his own slice of happy. His wife is great, and so is her family. I doubt he misses us much."

Finn scoffed. "Speak for yourself. I *know* he misses me."

"Maybe in your dreams," West shot back, shoving his twin's shoulder lightly.

I loved that they could joke and tease despite the high emotions obviously coursing through each of us. Somehow, it put me more at ease, like the situation wasn't yet so dire that they became stoic and tense.

Fifteen minutes later, we pulled up to what could only be described as a compound. A wood and metal gate blocked the roadway, disappearing on either side into the trees. I had to assume it fenced in a sizable chunk of Trey's property. After Finn sent Trey a text, it slid sideways to admit us.

Trey's house was as gorgeous as Crew's and the ranch, but vastly different in style. It looked like three large wooden rectangles stacked, one staggered on top of another, the walls long expanses of glass, likely the kind where outsiders couldn't see in, but anyone inside could see out. Finn parked on the concrete pad in front of the garage door, which opened as we got out. The twins proceeded inside, me trailing along, turning my head to watch as we were closed inside. A door on the back wall stood open, and I followed Finn and West through it.

I didn't have time to appreciate the interior architecture of Trey's home as the twins disappeared through another doorway. I paused in the threshold, taking it all in.

The brothers joked about Trey's "little" private security firm, but there was nothing small about the operation taking up the room. Innumerable monitors blanketed one wall, servers beeped and blinked, and in the center of it all sat Trey, rapidly typing away at a keyboard.

Lane stood off to one side and, to my surprise, Wyatt Saunders hovered on a stool in the corner, her shoulders curved inward, hair hanging limply around her face.

"What the fuck is going on?" I blurted.

Neither Trey nor Wyatt moved, but Lane pushed off the wall

and ushered me and the twins back out of the room, closing the door behind him. He led us down a short hall into Trey's kitchen. Finn and West made themselves comfortable at two of the six stools that bellied up to the massive white granite island, so I followed their lead and sat down.

"It appears as though Kelly Saunders is the Prom Night Arsonist," Lane said without preamble.

The twins silently cursed, and I asked, "Wyatt's mother?"

Lane nodded. "It makes sense now why we both thought she wasn't telling us everything in that interview with Ward. Right family, wrong parent."

"But…how?"

Lane shook his head. "Obviously, we're not in possession of all the details, but I had an FBI friend in Boise look over the cases. Her team came up with a profile that fits Kelly perfectly. It seems Kelly's senior prom was the trigger, and she's been reenacting that night for four decades."

My mind spun with the possibilities. What could have happened that night to drive a woman—a seemingly normal woman with a beautiful family and home, and a community who greatly respected her—to kill twelve people?

I hadn't realized I'd asked the question out loud until West said, "The human mind is a funny thing."

"I doubt we'll get the answers we're after until we bring her in for questioning."

"And Crew?" I asked, voice catching on his name.

"We think she has him."

"And I repeat…*how*? He's a tall, athletic man in the prime of his life. There's no way she could've knocked him out and muscled him into a vehicle the way she did me."

"You were tased," Lane reminded me. "That's likely what happened here."

"I—fuck," I breathed, pulling on my hair.

A warm hand settled on my shoulder, and I turned my head to look at West.

"We'll find him, little one. He's our baby brother. I promise you we'll stop at nothing to bring him home safe and sound."

The smile I gave him was quick and didn't reach my eyes, but I was trying. It wouldn't do Crew any good if I fell apart. For his sake, I needed to keep a clear head and my eyes on the prize.

"Where do we start?" I asked the three of them.

"Trey is running some things down for us, but so far nothing actionable has come up."

I rose from my seat and shuffled back toward Trey's command center. When we entered, Trey and Wyatt had their heads bent together, speaking in hushed tones that cut off abruptly at our appearance.

Lane wasn't about to let that slide.

"In case you've forgotten, big brother," he said to Trey, "I'm the only one of us in this room with a badge and authority to take legal action to get Crew back. If either of you know something, I suggest you tell me now."

"He was just consoling me," Wyatt said quickly. "This is…a lot."

Lane's shoulders relaxed a fraction.

"For what it's worth, Wy, I really am sorry."

Her cheeks twitched at the edges of her smile. "Me too."

Lane pulled up an extra chair and sat. "Is there anything you can tell us about her and her movements? Does she own any vehicles besides the Jeep? Any vacation properties where she could be holding Crew?"

Wyatt shook her head. "Not that I'm aware of."

"I've run her name through all the databases," Trey supplied. "There's nothing registered or titled to her."

"What about Wyatt or Ward?"

"Again, nothing."

"None of your dad's work vehicles are missing, are they?" Lane asked her.

"Not that I'm aware of, but Dad would know better."

"You haven't looped him in?"

"I didn't want to worry him."

"Wy," Trey said softly. "I hate to break it to you, but…there's *a lot* to worry about. And we need to know if he can provide any information you haven't been able to."

She nodded as though Trey's words made perfect sense. I supposed, to her, from the mouth of her best friend, they did. The blow was softened because he cared about her, and he knew how badly this was hurting her.

"I'll go call him," she said, rising from her stool and waving her phone around.

When she disappeared, Lane shot West a look, and he slipped out after her.

"There has to be something we're missing," Finn said, leaning over Trey's shoulder to study the monitors. They displayed a dizzying amount of information, from camera feeds and building schematics to open documents and a large photograph of who I assumed was Kelly Saunders.

"Holy shit."

"Aspen?" Lane asked when I didn't elaborate.

"I've seen her before. Quite a few times. She was…they were there that night."

"Gonna need more than that."

Wild horses couldn't have dragged my gaze away from that screen, away from the face of the woman who I knew deep in my bones had tried to kill me and spent the better part of the last few months tormenting me.

"She and Wyatt were at the Swallow the night I was abducted," I said numbly. "I bumped into her. That's how I ended up wearing my beer. They disappeared into the crowd, and I left not long after. I was almost to my car in the parking lot when I was taken."

"When else?" Lane prompted.

"The day I picked up Black Betty from impound, when I found that note under the windshield. I had a bit of a breakdown right there in the middle of their neighborhood." I glanced up at Lane. "I recognized it that day we went to interview Ward. She was out walking the dog and stopped to check on me. I thought…"

I shook my head. I thought she was a kind citizen making sure I was okay and keeping her neighborhood free of any creeps. After all, I'd been a stranger around here back then.

"It doesn't matter what I thought."

"Did you see her anymore after that?"

"The day on the street when I got that email about someone watching me. She and Wyatt were coming out of the diner."

"I remember that," a voice said from the doorway, and we turned to find Wyatt and West had returned. "She was so distracted by something on her phone. We stood in the middle of the sidewalk for like five minutes while I tried to nudge her toward the car."

Before I could blink, Wyatt approached me, wrapping her tall frame around my much smaller one and pulling me into a hug. I stiffened slightly against the uninvited contact, but eventually relaxed and slipped my arms around her waist. I figured she needed it more than I did. I'd had plenty of time to come to terms with what happened to me. Giving a face to my attacker didn't change the work I'd done to restore my mental health since then—work only accomplished with the help of Crew.

But I felt for Wyatt, whose nightmare was only beginning.

"I am so fucking sorry, Aspen," she murmured. "If I had known—"

I cut her off by pulling away, shaking my head. "There's

nothing you could've done. She fooled everyone, including her own family. Don't beat yourself up about it."

Though tears continued to track down her pretty face, she nodded once.

"Did you get in touch with your dad?" Lane asked.

"I did. He said all the company vehicles are accounted for." The sheriff cursed, but Wyatt continued. "He did, however, remind me that when my grandma passed, she left Mom a cabin out in the woods. We stopped going there when I was younger, so we both assumed she'd sold it. But…"

"But what if she hadn't," I finished, grinning, and Trey's fingers were already going to town on his keyboard.

"Grandma McAllister, right?"

"Yes," Wyatt said. "Susan McAllister."

A few more keystrokes then: "Bingo."

Lane approached his older brother and the wall of screens. "You got something?"

"I checked through county records," Trey said, speaking quickly. "The last deed of record is old as shit. There haven't been any changes since 1985, when Susan added Kelly to the title."

"Mom couldn't have been more than eighteen," Wyatt said.

Trey hummed in agreement. "And your grandma died in…"

Wyatt screwed her face up, thinking. "It had to have been the early nineties. I remember her, but only vaguely."

"Where the hell is this place?" West piped up.

"Moss Township," Trey said.

"Northwest corner of the county," Finn supplied before Trey could pull up a map. "There's nothing out there as far as I know."

"Good," West grinned. "That'll make it easy for us to sneak in and get Crew back."

My own smile unfurled, matching the energy of his.

Nearly three months ago, Crew Lawless had saved my life and turned it upside in the best way possible.

Now, it was my turn to save his.

forty-one

. . .

CREW

THE IMPACT of my body on a hard surface jolted me to consciousness and knocked the air from my lungs. While I struggled to regain my breath, I took a beat to take stock of myself. A sack of some sort had been placed over my head, though the material was thin enough to tell the sky was still light. I hadn't been out long then. My wrists were bound together in front of me, but my ankles were free.

A strike to my side had me groaning in pain.

"Get up and walk."

The voice was no longer distorted, and I should've been ready for it. After all the information Wyatt had spilled at the sheriff's department, I should've been prepared for the voice of my abductor to be a woman—to be Mrs. Saunders.

I wasn't. If I hadn't already been prone on the ground, the sound would've taken me out at the knees.

That boot found my ribs again, and with a grunt and some careful maneuvering, I heaved to standing, breathing hard and squeezing my eyes shut as my head spun.

Some blunt instrument—likely that fucking gun again—pressed into my spine, urging me on, so I tentatively shuffled forward. I strained my ears for an auditory indication of where we were. The only thing I heard was the soft swish of grass beneath my feet and crickets chirping, which led me to believe we were likely far from town. I continued moving forward, and without warning, my boots collided with some uneven surface, sending me sprawling. Unable to break my fall with my hands, I twisted to the side. My shoulder took the brunt of the impact, and I hissed as I felt the joint pop out of place.

Shifting my knees under myself without further aggravating my shoulder wasn't an easy task, but I managed. Once I sank back on my haunches, I tried to get my bearings. The air around me had shifted, becoming overly warm and stale, like I'd entered some sort of building. It didn't feel like a wide open space like a warehouse would, though, so I guessed we were somewhere smaller, like a home or a cabin.

"Where am I?" I asked. "What do you plan to do with me?"

"You don't get to ask questions," the woman snarled.

Once again, a sharp sting in my neck accompanied a sizzle through my body, and the world blacked out.

WHEN I CAME TO AGAIN, the sack had been removed from my head, but my arms were still bound.

And I was no longer alone.

"Parker?" I croaked.

The boy sat against the exterior wall of what I could see now was an older log cabin, the chinking uneven and yellowed with age. His wrists were zip tied together, and he had the thousand-yard stare and trembling limbs of someone in shock. A quick scan of his body didn't reveal any obvious wounds, which I considered a good sign.

I cleared my throat and said his name again. This time, the

boy's head moved slowly in my direction. He was looking at me, but I could tell he wasn't really *seeing* me.

"Parker, what are you doing here? What happened?"

"I don't know."

"What's the last thing you remember?"

He squeezed his eyes shut, and my heart cracked as tears leaked free and spilled down his cheeks.

"Walking home from work. I picked up a summer job as a dishwasher at the diner," he explained. "Gary pays me under the table, and it keeps me out of trouble, you know?"

A slight smile curved his lips, and I nodded.

"That fucking park, man," the kid said, dropping the expletive like a well-practiced swearer instead of a sixteen-year-old boy. "I always cut across it. And this person came out of nowhere —completely blindsided me. I tried to get away, but then there was this pain in my neck and a weird current through my body. Next thing I knew, I was waking up here."

"You were tased," I explained calmly, though nothing about my current mood was *calm*.

Coming after me was one thing. I was a grown man who had spent the last three months investigating this case and playing host to the one woman that escaped the clutches of death at Mrs. Saunders' hands.

Going after an innocent kid and dragging him into this mess was unforgivable.

Think, Crew. Think, I silently willed myself. There had to be a way out of this. A way to save myself and Parker.

First and foremost, I needed to get the fuck out of the restraint around my wrists.

I got to my feet as carefully as I could, my shoulder screaming in pain with each movement, and took stock of the cabin. My first order of business was, obviously, to check the door. Unsurprisingly, it was locked tight from the outside, and no amount of yanking on it mattered. The windows were all painted and nailed shut.

Nearly a perfect square, with the walls at the front and back a little longer than the sides, the structure couldn't have been more than six hundred square feet. Parker and I were in a small living space that held an ancient couch, reminding me of the one in Missy Plano's house, and a heavily nicked and scarred coffee table. The most modern part was the combination TV and VCR that rested on a squat hutch against the wall where Parker leaned.

In the opposite corner was a tiny kitchen, the counters and upper cabinets arranged in an L-shape. A fridge stood about as tall as my chest next to a two burner gas stove, and the microwave was so old it had a dial instead of buttons.

Beside the kitchen was a walled off bathroom with a toilet, standing shower, and pedestal sink. A set of narrow stairs led to a loft above.

I moved toward the kitchen, using my left hand—my good arm—to pull open drawers and cabinets, searching for something to cut me and Parker free. Unsurprisingly, Mrs. Saunders had cleared the place out, leaving nothing to be found but crumbs, dust, and mouse poop.

That was fine. I was a big, strong dude, right? It would fucking hurt, but I could break myself free. Then I could help Parker. Heading back into the living room, I braced my foot on the edge of the coffee table, mentally psyching myself up.

"What're you doing?" Parker asked, rising to his feet.

"I'm going to snap the zip tie."

"How?"

"I should be able to strike my wrists against my knee and, with enough force, put enough pressure on the weakest point"—I indicated the spot where the tie came together—"to break it." I tried to smile reassuringly at him, but it probably looked more like a grimace. "Wish me luck."

The kid chuckled softly. "Good luck."

Taking a deep breath, I knew I'd have to move quickly and surely, both in deference to my dislocated shoulder and to get enough momentum. On the count of three, I quickly raised my arms up, gritting my teeth against the shooting pain radiating down my right one, and swung them down, hard and sure, tensing and driving my knee up into the blow simultaneously.

With a satisfying *snap*, I was free.

"Holy shit!" Parker crowed. "You did it!"

This time, my grin was genuine.

"Your turn."

Parker's expression sobered instantly.

"I'm not sure I'm strong enough."

"It's not about strength," I assured him. "It's about timing and force and angles."

Parker snorted. "I'm shit at all that stuff."

"You can do it," I promised.

Together, we took a few practice swings, with me correcting his form where needed.

"Keep your arms slightly bent and tensed," I told him. "The last thing we need is you dislocating an elbow on top of my dislocated shoulder."

He followed each of my directions perfectly, and when I was certain he was ready, I instructed him to give it a shot.

"Will you count down?" he asked.

"Sure. You ready?" He nodded. "Okay. Three...two... one...go!"

His arms arced high and swung down. He squeezed his eyes shut as he braced for impact, doing everything I told him exactly as I'd explained.

Another beautiful *snap* echoed through the room, and the plastic tie fell to the floor.

"I did it! I did it!" Parker danced around in place, chanting the three words over and over. Hooking my good arm around his neck, I hauled him in for a hug.

"Fuck yeah you did. Now what do you say we get the hell out of here?"

"I'm afraid I can't allow that."

Parker and I startled at the new voice, turning to the door. In all the commotion and excitement, we'd missed Mrs. Saunders coming inside. She set a bright orange gas can at her feet, then folded her arms over her chest and stared us down.

"Mrs. Saunders?" Parker asked, eyes wide, tone completely disbelieving.

Yeah, buddy. Me too.

God, I'd *known*, and still nothing could've prepared me for her appearance. The black clothing, gloved hands, menacing expression. Gone was the teacher and high school principal who led the school with kindness and grace—although the crossed arms was a stance I'd personally seen from her numerous times before.

"You should stop working out so much," she said to me, her tone full of malice. "You're looking awfully disproportionate. I suppose that explains why you're all brawn and no brains. Letting a little woman like me get the drop on you."

She smirked proudly, like she'd somehow bested me.

I snorted. "You knocked me over the head, tased me, and threatened me with a gun. You had an unfair advantage."

"Whatever," she said flippantly. "You're still here, and you're still going to die. My final kills before I ride off into the sunset, never to be seen or heard from again."

"But...why?" I asked.

"Because I can," she said simply.

"There's gotta be more to it than that."

"You think I *wanted* this?" she asked, sweeping her arm out to encompass the whole scene. "You think I wanted to be born with this weird mental mutation that gets off on setting fires and killing people? No, but we all make do with the hand we've been dealt."

"What happened on your prom night all those years ago?"

I knew if I kept her talking, it would give me time to figure a way out of this. My life wasn't the only one on the line, and Parker was counting on me. I'd at least had a chance to *live*, but he was only a kid, and he deserved the chance to escape and experience all the shit I already had.

Well, maybe not all of it.

"Made the connection, did you? Figured out my little riddle? I'll admit, that first email I sent to Miss McKay was a bit impulsive, but I loved toying with her so much I couldn't help myself."

I blinked in surprise. Aspen had thought that riddle had come from someone unconnected to the killer. We should've known that was merely another way Mrs. Saunders taunted her.

"Roger Stanhope was my best friend, did you know that?" I shook my head, but she wasn't even looking at me, eyes focused in some middle distance, here but not really *here*. "Trey and Wyatt remind me a lot of us…or what we could've been if he hadn't gone and fucked everything up."

"Trey and Wyatt aren't together. They never have been."

Mrs. Saunders snorted. "You think I don't see the way they look at each other? It's honestly a matter of time now. She's going to need someone in the aftermath of all of this, and you and I both know Trey will be there to pick up the pieces."

Hard to argue with that.

Parker, seemingly tired of standing around, sank to the floor and started toying with his shoe laces. Mrs. Saunders didn't even spare him a glance.

"It was supposed to be me and Roger. He was my best friend, yes, but I loved him so much more than that—and he loved me. Vicky and all the other tramps he got with were distractions. A way to pass the time of our high school years until we could move away from this godforsaken town and start our lives together. When he asked me to prom, I knew the time had finally come. It kills me every day that he's dead—that we never got that chance."

"*You* killed him," I reminded her, following Parker's lead and taking a seat on the arm of the couch. Might as well be comfortable while I listened to the psychobabble.

"Only because I *had* to! He betrayed me." She inhaled a deep breath, her eyes fluttered closed as she transported herself back forty years. "That night should've been the first night of the rest of our lives. I was going to give him my virginity, remind him my heart and body belonged to him, and his to me. We were going to move to California after graduation. Get married, have babies. There was a *plan*. And he ruined it when he couldn't stay away from that slut. Vicky Lee."

She spat her name with four decades worth of venom, like she couldn't get past her hatred of the girl despite being the reason she was dead. You'd think a gunshot wound to the head and setting her body on fire would've been enough to take the edge off, but apparently not.

"I was coming out of the ladies room after freshening up when I saw them sneak out together. They were laughing, holding hands, stealing kisses between steps out the door. Their stupid prom king and queen crowns shone on their hair. The way he looked at her…I realized then he'd never look at me that way.

"And if I couldn't have him, no one could."

I couldn't help but snort. What a fucking cliché. Parker cut me a glare, a silent plea to be quiet, but Mrs. Saunders was so lost in giving her killer monologue that she didn't even notice us anymore.

"I followed them up to the ridge, watched as they steamed up the windows of his car. I was so furious, you know?" The rhetorical question was accompanied by a burst of manic laughter, and poor Parker curled further into a ball, putting his head down as though that would protect him from the madness. "Roger was *mine*. But then this strange sense of calm came over me, and what I had to do became perfectly clear. I'd taken Daddy's truck to the dance because Roger wanted to hang out with his buddies before, so we agreed to meet there. And Daddy's shotgun was hidden beneath the seat as always. So I took it out and approached. God, you should've seen the looks on their faces when I tapped on the window with that barrel pointed right at their heads."

She sighed, as though savoring the memory, and nausea roiled in my gut. This woman was fucking insane.

"Roger rolled down the window, but before he could speak, before he could try to spew some pretty bullshit to get me to back down, I blew a fucking hole in his face. Vicky was screaming her head off, coated in Roger's blood, and I fired on her too.

"But that wasn't enough, you know? They were dead *and it still wasn't enough*. So I took the pack of cigarettes sitting in the cupholder—Roger was a Marlboro man—lit every single one, and dropped them on the seats and floors. Then I waited and watched as it burned and burned and burned. That fire was the most beautiful thing I'd ever seen. The fucking *power* I felt. A few days later when the story ran in the paper, accompanied by a tip line where the police were asking for information, I knew I'd gotten away with it, and I knew once would never be enough."

The blue-green depths of Mrs. Saunders' eyes met mine, the same shade as her daughter's, swirling with excitement.

"Twelve seemed to do the trick. I wanted to go for thirteen, but Miss McKay managed to survive. You see, Crew…that's why you have to die. Your life for hers. It's a bit poetic, since you were the one who saved her."

"What about Parker? He didn't do anything wrong."

"He narced," she said, a single shoulder rising and falling in a half shrug. "What's that old saying? Snitches get stitches? Or in this case, little boys who go and tattle to the police get burned alive."

"Please," Parker gasped, getting to his feet and shuffling over to her before falling to his knees in front of her, hands clasped, begging. "Please, Mrs. Saunders. You don't want to kill me. It's not like they figured you out from what I told them."

Mrs. Saunders seemed to consider that, cocking her head to the side and regarding him. Then she glanced up at me.

"You know, he has a point. How *did* you figure it out?"

I grinned, baring all my teeth. "Missy Plano. And your daughter."

forty-two

. . .

ASPEN

AFTER WYATT'S reveal about the cabin, the guys spent nearly an hour studying severely outdated aerial images of the property—the only ones they could get their hands on—trying to decide the best course of action for approaching and extracting Crew safely.

Finally, Lane had enough.

"You fuckers seem to think you have any say in how this goes down. Listen to me very carefully," he said, looking each of his brothers in the eye individually. "*You. Don't.* I'm calling my team in. We'll meet out there and brief them on scene before going in. What I say goes. Understood?"

The brothers made noises of agreement, and Trey said to the twins, "You two can raid my stash."

The three of them disappeared, and I turned to the sheriff.

"What about me? If you think I'm standing here like some wife watching her husband go off to war, you're sadly mistaken."

"Same here," Wyatt piped up.

Lane grimaced. "You can both ride along. But you stay in the car. If I see either of you within a hundred yards of the scene, I'll charge you with obstruction."

Wyatt nodded, and I held up my hands in surrender.

Honestly, I believed him, and getting involved wasn't high on my list of priorities. I merely wanted to be nearby when Crew came out. Still, as we loaded up, Lane, Trey, and Wyatt in the sheriff's SUV, me and the twins in Finn's truck, I wished I had my gun, or at the very least my taser. The guys were heavily armed and outfitted with Kevlar vests, and though I'd be out of the line of fire, I envied that level of protection.

There was nothing calming about knowing we were walking into a showdown.

"I made you a promise we'd get Crew out safely, Aspen," West reminded me. "Trust us to make good on it. You forget, Finn and I are ex-Rangers. We used to head into situations under a lot more pressure than this."

Finn held his fist out, and his twin bumped it. "Almost makes me miss the old days," he said.

West chuckled. "The old days like sleeping in the dirt and surviving on MREs?"

"Hey, that chicken and rice wasn't all bad."

"The chili mac started to grow on me after a while too."

As they lost themselves to reminiscing on the old days, I couldn't stop my mind from spinning out of control with all possible outcomes of this raid. Would we get to Crew in time? Would Kelly Saunders get away again?

What the fuck would I do if Crew didn't come out in one piece?

The thought didn't bear entertaining.

He *would* come home. I'd accept nothing less.

It felt like hours had passed by the time we rolled to a stop at the mouth of a narrow drive that snaked back into the woods. Darkness had fully descended, though the moon was bright overhead. Numerous vehicles sat idling, blocking any potential escape routes, all headlights turned off. The red shine of Lane's taillights gave the scene an eerie glow. Finn put the truck in park, turned to give me a reassuring smile, and got out.

West said, "Stay put. We'll be back soon," before following him to where Lane stood, circled by what appeared to be the entire Dusk Valley Sheriff's Department as he talked them through the plan.

Lane's hands moved through the air, pointing at his men and sending them off in different directions until only he and his brothers remained. Finn had left the truck running, so I rolled down the window, straining to hear their conversation.

"I go in first," Lane was saying. "Trey, I want you on the battering ram. Twins, you cover me. It's going to be fucking melee once the smoke bombs and flash-bangs go off, so keep it tight. It's one woman against all of us. We get Crew out, and we take Kelly dead or alive."

I winced, hoping Wyatt wasn't listening.

"Let's go then," West said, his bright teeth flashing in the dark.

My heart squeezed as they shared a quick group hug, and I heard murmurs of, "Lawless for life," before they took off down the drive in a single file line.

As soon as they disappeared, I got out of Finn's truck and approached the cruiser. Wyatt stepped out to meet me.

"You coming with?" I asked.

"What about staying put and obstruction of justice?"

I shrugged. "I don't give a fuck. That's my man down there."

Wyatt nodded. "And my mom. I know she's done some really fucked up and horrible things, but…"

"I get it, and I don't hold it against you." Then I jerked my chin toward the drive. "Let's go."

As silently as we could, Wyatt and I followed the silty two-track that wound through the towering pines. Maybe fifty feet ahead of us, the treeline broke open to a small clearing in which a log cabin sat in the center. Lights were on inside, and a white panel van that damn near glowed in the darkness was parked nearby.

Brushing my finger over my lips to encourage Wyatt to stay quiet, I crooked that same digit and crept closer. The Lawless brothers had fanned out across the lawn, guns trained on the cabin, waiting for Lane's men to get into position on the other three sides. From here, it appeared the only point of entry was the front door, with windows on at least two of the other sides, plus a small porthole nestled in the center of the gabled roof.

Across the way, a light blinked once, twice before extinguishing. The same pattern repeated from the opposite direction. Some sort of signal, then, to which Lane responded in kind.

The forest went abruptly still, as though the plants, trees, and critters understood something was about to happen.

Nature was bracing, and my breath caught in my chest as I did too.

A shout rent the stillness.

"Crew, take cover!"

And then…all hell broke loose.

forty-three

. . .

CREW

"YOUR DAUGHTER."

Those two words seemed to momentarily stun Mrs. Saunders, who gasped dramatically in their wake.

"That little bitch," she hissed. "Missy has always been a cunt, but my daughter…I thought I raised her better."

Before I could use her momentary distraction to my and Parker's advantage and take her out, she bent and lifted the gas can, then disappeared up the stairs.

My eyes scanned the area in desperation. There had to be *something*, some way out.

"What are we going to do?" Parker choked out between sobs.

"Stay calm, Parker, and follow my lead."

"What lead?" he hissed.

Good question.

Mrs. Saunders began descending, the can upended in her wake, splashing gasoline on the steps as she went.

Wordlessly, she moved into the kitchen, dumping more gas across the counters and appliances, doing the same in the bathroom before returning to face me and Parker as she emptied the rest of it on the ancient couch and tossed the can to the side.

"It seems my daughter has thrown a wrench in my plans, but all is not lost."

I didn't understand, couldn't see how she could possibly get out of this without lighting herself on fire as well. She reached into her back pocket to withdraw something, likely matches if she planned to torch this place.

I was proved wrong in a hurry.

Mrs. Saunders waved a nice little six-shot revolver around, the gun she'd threatened me with earlier, carelessly oscillating the barrel between my and Parker's heads.

"I was really hoping I wouldn't have to use this," she said, tone almost resigned. "Shooting people is so…messy and personal." With her other hand, she produced a lighter. "I much prefer the snap and crackle of flames, which I can enjoy from afar. But unfortunately, desperate times and all that. So here's what's going to happen. You two are going to stand at that wall." She gestured to the one farthest away from the door. "If you move before I'm outside, I won't hesitate to shoot you."

Mentally, I weighed my options. I'd had no time to check if there was something upstairs I could use to leverage the windows or door open. At the very least, I could probably smash the windows out with the coffee table or microwave, right?

It came down to a simple question: did I like my chances better against a bullet or a fire?

The answer was simple. I walked into fire every day.

When I didn't speak or move, Parker came to my side, and I shifted him slightly behind me so I could shield him with my body if need be.

Then Mrs. Saunders grinned. "It's a shame Miss McKay couldn't join us. She'll forever be the one that got away, but I suppose as her lover, the pain she'll suffer over your loss will have to do."

This woman was absolutely sick in the head, completely deluded into thinking what she was doing was right. All because some guy scorned her at a meaningless high school dance? Seriously, I was sitting here right now, listening to this fucking psychobabble because a boneheaded teenage guy who was only capable of thinking with his dick had ditched her at her prom.

I couldn't have made that shit up if I tried.

And the more I thought about it, the angrier I got.

Anger made people do stupid shit. There was a whole television series about what people did when they snapped.

My and Parker's best chance was to take her out before she could light this place up. Eventually, my brothers would find us.

As though I'd conjured them, a voice carried to us from outside. Deep and distinctly belonging to Trey.

"Crew, take cover!"

My body understood the words far sooner than my mind did, and I jumped on Parker and rolled us both, hiding behind the sofa as the window we'd been standing in front of shattered, followed by the rest in the cabin. A moment later, several *bangs* echoed through the room, accompanied by flashes of light and clouds of smoke.

I did my best to cover my face, shielding my eyes with my forearm and tugging my shirt over my nose and mouth. At my side, Parker choked and coughed.

A beat later, I heard the telltale sound of the entrance being breached, the door slamming back into the wall, and the room filled with shouting voices—*my brothers*.

Before I could react or stumble toward those voices I knew meant safety, I was hauled upright, though I remained on my knees, that goddamn gun once again pressed into my skull. Parker stared up at me with wide, panicked eyes, though he wisely scrambled away from us. Finn grabbed him by the collar of his shirt and dragged him to his feet, then shoved him in the direction of the door. With a final glance in my direction, Parker stumbled out into the night.

He would live, and the realization relaxed my shoulders a fraction.

But there was still the matter of the fucking gun being held against my head and this cabin being doused in gasoline.

"Let him go, Kelly," Lane warned.

"Stay back or I'll bury a bullet in his brain," Mrs. Saunders seethed from behind me, her voice hoarse, and she coughed to clear it.

My eyes watered heavily from the smoke bombs, blurring my vision, but I could tell we were surrounded. Not just by my brothers, but likely the entire sheriff's department. She wasn't getting out of this unscathed. It remained to be seen whether I would or not.

I needed to do something to help my chances, but once again, my damn mouth ran away with me.

"Little too up close and personal for you, don't you think?"

I spoke loud enough to be heard over the commotion, and the barrel dug harder against my head before it disappeared entirely. By the time I turned to face her, Mrs. Saunders—*Kelly*, I reminded myself; she was going to try to kill me either way—was in the kitchen, standing at the stove.

Cranking the knobs on the burners all the way up.

"Fuck," I breathed, glancing over my shoulder, eyeing each of my brothers, who now stood spread around the small space, in turn. "It's gonna blow. Bail out!"

"Not without you!" West protested.

"I'll be right behind you! Just go!"

"How sweet," Kelly mocked. "Always gotta be the hero, protecting your brothers from suffering the same fate as you. But what about all the times you weren't a hero, Crew? What about those years you lost to drugs and alcohol? Don't you think you'd be doing your family a favor if you died right here? Personally, I do. It's honestly a shame the drugs didn't take you those years ago."

There was a time, back before Chief Madden saved my life, before I got my shit together and found the fire service, that Kelly's words would've hit home. They would've burrowed their way under my skin and bred like maggots, crawling into all of my darkest parts and festering. Back then, I'd believed they were true, that maybe the world—especially my family—would be better off without dealing with my constant fuckups.

But I'd healed and grown a lot in the intervening years, and I knew without a doubt there was nothing I could do that would make my family stop loving me. And I reminded myself that I went to work every day and saved lives—like Aspen's.

And my girl? The woman who had blown into town and flipped my entire life on its head in the best possible way…I knew she'd never forgive me if I died at the hands of the same sicko she'd survived.

A look over my shoulder confirmed my brothers had retreated, and I hoped they were backed up far enough to be out of the blast zone. The liquid gasoline combined with the unlit stove burners was going to blow the roof off this place—literally —the second a flame came near any of it.

As slowly as possible, I started taking steps backward in the direction of the door. Kelly watched me curiously, flipping the lid of the lighter open and closed. When the cool night air from the open doorway caressed my back, I spoke.

"I think the only one dying tonight will be you."

As I turned and booked it out into the night, Kelly screamed in frustration, and the ignition switch on the lighter echoed in the space between us. The woman clearly didn't give a fuck about surviving this anymore, not when surviving meant spending the rest of her miserable existence in prison. She just wanted to take me out in the process.

No fucking way was I letting that happen. For my mom, my brothers and sister, for *Aspen*, I had to *live*.

I raced outside, my head snapping up as someone shouted my name.

Even in the dark and across what had to be a couple hundred feet through a copse of trees, I recognized my girl immediately. I corrected course slightly, making for her. I knew everything would be okay if I could reach her…

A *boom* shook me to my very core.

My ears hollowed out, all sound suddenly vacuumed from the world.

Suddenly, I was flying, then landing in a heap. Sharp, unending pain bloomed across my entire body.

And then, blissfully, I was aware of nothing at all.

forty-four

. . .

ASPEN

SCREAMING his name had accomplished absolutely nothing as Crew raced from the cabin before the explosion.

The blast still tossed him through the air like a rag doll. As soon as the air rushed past where I stood, ripping at my hair and clothes, hot and dry, I rushed for him. He wasn't moving, his pulse was weak and thready, and his entire face was covered in blood from a wide gash across his forehead.

But he was alive—for the time being.

I refused to leave his side as paramedics rolled in. Lane must've called them ahead of time, and they arrived not a moment too soon. Sutton Rausch's partner, some twit whose name I didn't bother to learn, tried to shove me out of the way, and I nearly decked him. Sutton calmed everyone down and allowed me to stay with Crew while she worked on him in the back as we headed to the hospital. I was far from next of kin, but none of the brothers protested when I climbed up into the ambulance.

As Sutton checked his vitals, she spoke to me, keeping me updated on what exactly she was doing and why.

"Due to the fact that he hasn't regained consciousness with

prodding, we're taking him to Boise," she said, almost conversationally. "That cut in his head is pretty nasty, and palpating the rest of his skull revealed a pretty gnarly bump on the back. Though his pupils are responsive, I made the call to take him to the city where there's a legitimate trauma center. We're going to get him the best care possible, okay?"

I could only nod, words eluding me as she continued to work on him. First, she bandaged his head, though the white gauze was soaked with a red splotch in minutes. She slipped an oxygen mask over his face and hooked him up to an IV.

Still, Crew remained unconscious, and I continued to silently cry.

I couldn't lose him. I simply wouldn't survive it.

As we pulled up to the emergency entrance, Sutton's partner —Thomas, I heard someone say—came around back to help unload Crew. Doctors and nurses swarmed the gurney, and before she got out, Sutton paused to squeeze my hand.

"He's going to be okay."

I nodded, giving her a wobbly smile, but I wasn't sure I believed her.

Numbly, I shuffled inside behind them, not paying any attention to where I was going, and a woman in scrubs stopped me as I tried to follow past the doors to the trauma bays.

"I'm sorry, miss. We can't let you back there."

"But that's my—"

My *what?* Fresh tears fell. Crew and I had never taken a second to define what exactly we were. All I knew was that he was the love of my life, and that had to give me some privileges where his medical care was concerned, right?

The woman gave me a sad smile and directed me to the glass walled waiting room, settling me in a chair and kneeling in front of me.

"The doctor will be out to give you an update when he has

one," she assured me. "I'm going to bring you some water. Is there anyone you want me to call for you?"

"I—"

Didn't get to finish that sentence as the cavalry appeared, the brothers filing into the room in order of age: Trey, Lane, Finn, West. Additionally, a teenage boy was with them, tall and gangly-limbed with a mop of curly, dirty blond hair. The twins sat on either side of me, simultaneously reaching for my hands. Trey and Lane took seats in the row across from us, the boy between them.

"Who's the kid?" I asked.

"Oh, this is Parker," Lane said, placing a hand on his shoulder. "He's the one responsible for the dumpster fire."

Parker groaned. "I thought we let that go."

"Never."

"Brooooooooo," Parker said, dragging out the word dramatically. "I almost got burned alive. Cut me some slack."

"Fair enough," Lane murmured, then to me said, "Any news?"

"They just arrived," the nurse answered for me. "The team is examining him now. As I was telling Miss…"

"Aspen," I croaked. "His girlfriend."

To hell with it. The man was mine in every sense of the word, the least I could do was call myself his girlfriend.

"Aspen," she nodded. "I was telling Aspen that the doctor will be out with updates when the care team has more info."

"So…we wait," Finn said.

She shot him an apologetic smile, turning and pointing to a hall that branched off the intake area in the opposite direction of the ER. "Feel free to use the cafeteria for drinks and snacks while you're here."

The guys murmured their thank-yous, and the nurse left us alone.

"Did someone call Mom?" West asked.

"I did on the way here," Trey supplied. "She and Ari probably aren't too far behind us."

As though the words had conjured them, Birdie and Aria rushed into the lobby, and I watched as Birdie approached the desk, her voice carrying to us as she asked for news on her son.

"I've got it," Lane said, rising to his feet to greet his mother.

I could hear Aria's sobs from here, though they muffled as Lane folded her and their mom into a hug, murmuring to them.

All I could do was put my hands in my face and weep.

***

"CREW LAWLESS'S FAMILY?"

My head snapped up. I must've fallen asleep because my neck ached from resting at an uncomfortable angle for too long, and a scratchy hospital blanket someone had thrown over me drifted to the ground when I shot to my feet.

"That's us."

"He's stable," the doctor began, and a collective sigh of relief echoed from us all. "He suffered trauma to his skull, both some sort of blow to the back and the gash on his forehead, which I closed with stitches. There wasn't a brain bleed that we could find, and there's only minor swelling. He's also got a few broken ribs, a dislocated right shoulder, which we have reset, and deep bone bruising to his right hip. He's going to be in significant pain and completely immobile for some time. We'll be keeping him for observation for a few days, but I don't see any reason why he won't make a full recovery."

"Is he awake?" Birdie asked. "Can we see him?"

"He's not awake yet. We've got him pretty heavily sedated. But a few of you can go back and sit with him if you'd like."

"Mom and Aspen," Trey said automatically. "Then we can rotate after that."

I shot Trey a grateful smile, then grabbed Birdie's proffered hand, following the doctor out and into the emergency department.

"It's not up to me to tell a doctor how to do his job," Birdie whispered, "but I don't like the words 'heavily sedated' very much. Not with his history."

"That makes two of us. Let's check on him, then we can make the team aware of his previous addiction issues."

Birdie nodded, and we proceeded forward, locked arm in arm.

That cloying, antiseptic smell hung in the air, and I had to force myself to keep my feet moving. Being back here—even if it wasn't the same hospital from either of my previous ordeals—brought up all kinds of bad memories. In that moment, I vowed to find a therapist at the first opportunity to work through my lingering issues, but this wasn't about me. This was about being there for Crew. Hand still gripping Birdie's tightly—honestly, I couldn't tell which of us was keeping which upright and moving—we entered Crew's room.

The first thing I noticed was how small he appeared. This larger-than-life man, the one who'd stolen my heart and saved me in more ways than even he knew, had his arm wrapped in a sling, heavy white gauze wrapped around his head, an IV line snaking from the hand of his bad arm.

And it was all my fault.

Birdie let me go and moved to his bedside, gently brushing his hair off his forehead, leaning in to press a kiss there.

"My baby boy," she murmured. "You got yourself into a real mess this time."

"I—" I started, unsure what I'd been about to say. Fuck, this was harder than I thought it'd be. I hadn't balked at getting into the ambulance with him, so why was this tripping me up?

Birdie's gaze snapped to where I stood, suspended in the doorway, unable to cross the threshold. As if sensing that, she walked back over to me, guiding me to Crew's side.

"It's okay," she whispered. "He's going to be okay, honey. You're going to get that time together. Right now, he needs you here with him. Even if he's not awake, I believe he can sense us. Talk to him. Give him your strength."

She pressed a kiss to my temple, holding me for a beat and allowing me to soak up all that motherly warmth. Then she gave Crew's hand a squeeze and left me alone with him.

No one else appeared to take her place, so I had to assume she was giving me and Crew the space I needed for me to get some things off my chest. To share with him what was in my heart.

So I did what she suggested, I pulled up a chair, cradled Crew's hand in mine, and talked.

I told him anything and everything I could think of, from stories of my childhood and how much I'd idolized my sister, how much I missed her, to dreams of what I thought our future should look like. An hour passed in a blink, and my throat was raw from endless talking.

"I never planned on you, you know," I said, smiling through my tears, eyelids fluttering closed against my blurred vision. "This was only supposed to be another stop, another map dot and a pat on the back for a job well done. But this case was the best thing that ever happened to me, because it brought me to *you*."

"Despite almost dying?"

My eyes flew open, landing on the gorgeous blue depths of Crew's.

I choked on a sob. "Despite almost dying," I agreed. Rising to my feet, I bent over him and dropped a gentle kiss to his forehead, murmuring against his skin, "God, you scared me."

"How long have I been out?" he asked, his voice rough and pained.

"About twelve hours."

The sun beyond the hospital had long since risen, though Crew's curtains remained closed.

He tried to shift on the bed, instantly hissing in pain. "Fuck. Everything hurts."

"That's to be expected," a new voice intoned, and I jerked my head around to face the doctor.

"Let's hear it then."

The doctor's voice remained flat as he detailed all of Crew's injuries, and another curse slipped past my man's lips when he finished.

Honestly, I was right there with him.

"If Kelly wasn't already dead…" I muttered.

Ignoring the doctor for the moment, Crew glanced at me. "She didn't make it out?"

I pursed my lips as if to say, *get real*. "*You* barely made it out." Gesturing to his body, I said, "Did you think you were here for fun?"

"What even happened? The last thing I remember was telling my brothers to bail and take Parker with them. Oh my God," he started, jerking upright before ultimately falling back with a groan of pain, eyes squeezed shut. "Is Parker okay?"

"Parker is fine, you fool," I assured him. "But you were thrown probably fifty feet through the air."

He grimaced, using the arm not in a sling to try to shift himself into a more comfortable position. "Explains why my entire body feels like a giant bruise."

"We can up your morphine dosage——" the doctor began. Honestly, I'd forgotten he was there.

Crew quickly cut him off with a shouted, "No!"

The doctor blinked in surprise. "Mr. Lawless, you've suffered a lot of trauma. Recovery will be incredibly painful regardless, but at least let us make you more comfortable."

"I'm a recovering drug addict," Crew gritted out. "I can't…I don't even like taking Tylenol."

"But you will take it?" Crew nodded. "Okay, I'll prescribe you the highest dosage we've got and advise my support staff that you don't get anything harder than that. And I appreciate your candor. In the interest of full disclosure, you should know that drip"—he indicated to the line in Crew's hand—"is definitely not Tylenol."

Crew moved like he was going to rip the IV out, but I clasped his hand, holding it at his side.

"Can you get a nurse in here to replace it, please?"

The doctor sighed like he didn't appreciate being ordered around by a patient's family, but wisely left the room without a word.

A half hour later, his line was changed out, the drip replaced with the promised Tylenol, and Crew's entire family had crowded into the room. I reclined in my chair, never more than a foot from him. Hell, I barely even let go of his hand. His mom, brothers, and sister chattered around us, tossing stories and insults around like we were crowded around the family dinner table instead of a hospital bed.

Honestly, though, I didn't mind.

The sense of normalcy was exactly what we needed after three months of everything *but*.

Crew's grip tightened around my fingers, and I glanced at him, melting when he smiled at me. His discomfort was obvious on every line of his gorgeous face, but that smile was like the sun shining after an endless winter. Blinding and beautiful.

"I love you, little phoenix," he murmured, only loud enough for me to hear.

"I love you more, hotshot."

epilogue

. . .

CREW

ONE MONTH LATER

"I'M STILL NOT CONVINCED this is a smart idea," Aspen said warily as she eyed the massive horse in front of her.

"C'mon, little phoenix. Rascal is an old softie, aren't you buddy?" I cooed, scratching the patch of white between his eyes. He nickered lightly, nipping at my hand with his lips.

Aspen's gaze narrowed on me. "This is the same horse you fell off that ultimately led to you becoming a drug addict. Forgive me if I don't exactly trust him."

"Well you're going to have to start."

"We should've gone riding before this," she muttered. "I have no idea what I'm doing."

"You know how to ride me, right?" I winked when she whirled on me. "The concept is the same. It's all in the hips."

"You filthy man."

"You love me."

"God knows why."

"Quit stalling and get that fine ass up there," I said, placing a hand on the small of her back, nudging her closer to the steps that would get her high enough to swing onto Rascal's back without my help.

Even I was going to use them, something I hadn't had to do since I was a kid. I wasn't completely healed from my ordeal, and as a tradeoff for letting me out of the house today, I had to promise Aspen I'd take it easy where I could.

Plus, my shoulder wasn't strong enough to hoist me into the saddle without some assistance.

Standing nearby to catch her if she fell or if Rascal got spooked—though I knew he wouldn't; I was merely humoring her—I kept my hands on Aspen's hips to steady her as she stuck her left boot into the stirrup, one hand on the pommel and the other on the cantle, exactly as I'd shown her. Momentarily, I was distracted by her ass, the light denim of her cut-off shorts stretched tight across the globes. Her hamstrings popped along the backs of her thighs, her calves tensed above the edges of her ankle-height Lucchese boots. Her arms were bare in her flowy black tank, the sides dipping low enough to tease the side of her boob and the edges of her new tattoo. She'd been working with my artist in Boise to cover her burn scars, and they were about halfway done.

That tantalizing peek got me hard.

My little city girl was going country, and I was as obsessed with her today as I had been the first time I saw her.

"Crew?" she prompted, and I blinked furiously, shaking my head.

With a count to three and a forceful push off her right foot, Aspen swung up and landed softly in the saddle.

Her excited grin was wide and infectious as she looked down at me. "I did it!"

"Of course you did, baby."

"Your turn," she said, scooting forward a bit to make room for me.

Getting onto Rascal was all muscle memory for me, even

with those muscles screaming from a month of disuse. I groaned as I settled in behind Aspen, who looked over her shoulder at me, eyes bright with worry.

"You okay?"

I wrapped my arms around her to grab the reins, and her back relaxed into my chest.

"Better than," I assured her. "I'm with you."

"Charmer," she teased, an *oof* leaving her as I kicked Rascal in the side, urging him forward into an easy trot.

Could we have taken the truck or an ATV to reach the spot I wanted to bring Aspen? Of course, and it would've been a lot easier on my body. But horseback was the best way to see the ranch, and it had been too long since I'd spent any quality time with Rascal, thanks to the uproar the last few months had caused in my life.

I wanted to feel the wind against my face and the sunshine on my skin. September was right around the corner, and though the days were still hot as hell, the nights had begun to cool considerably, allowing me and Aspen to sleep with the windows open.

A month had passed since the showdown with Kelly Saunders. A month in which I'd essentially been a captive in my own home save for the occasional trips to therapy for both my physical and mental health, and the ranch. Aspen and I had settled into a bit of a routine while I convalesced, but I was more than excited to be cleared for work. Hopefully sometime in the next week or so.

With my and Parker's statements, the Prom Night Arsonist case had officially closed, providing a sense of peace to all the victim's families. It rankled a number of them that Kelly hadn't lived to be served justice for her crimes, but I knew Aspen considered her death a fair trade.

In the past four weeks, she'd only left my side for a total of three days, long enough to fly to Denver, pack up her office and apartment, terminate her lease, and ship everything here.

My girl was finally putting down roots—with me.

I grinned remembering the day I asked her to stay.

"What's this?" she asked.

"A key to my house. Well…our house," I amended. I could feel my cheeks heating as I watched her stare at the pristine silver key dangling from the ring looped around my finger.

"Crew…"

"Will you stay?" I asked, my tone borderline begging, which I wasn't above doing. I'd get on my goddamn knees for this woman—and had, numerous times. "You can go off on your investigations as often as you want, as long as you always come back to me. As long as Dusk Valley is home."

Aspen shook her head, though she climbed onto my lap to straddle me on the couch. Closing her tiny fist around my hand and the key, she brought them between us and kissed my knuckles.

"Home is you, *Crew. Wherever you are, that's where I want to be."*

Those were the sweetest words I'd ever heard.

After my ordeal, I also encouraged her to contact her parents, reminding her we never knew when our time was up, and how shitty she'd feel if she lost one of them without ever speaking to them again. The conversations were short and stilted at first, but she'd managed to open up to them in a way she hadn't before, and I think it all went a long way toward repairing the damage done in the wake of Lola's death.

Therapy had a lot to do with it. Once a week, we drove up to Boise to meet with our respective therapists. Personally, I'd been making incredible strides in dealing with some repressed feelings regarding my addiction, and Aspen had been able to come to terms with the fact that all the bad things that happened to her were not her fault. She'd also started writing a book detailing the case and our part in it all, which she was calling *The Shadows of Dusk Valley*.

We were healing together, which only made our relationship stronger.

I was about to make the damn thing permanent if she'd have me.

Oh yes, I had an ulterior motive for taking this ride today.

The sun dipped toward the horizon as we crested the final hill, which flattened into a grassy plateau that overlooked the valley. In the distance, town was visible, the water tower jutting up toward the sky. Aspen and I dismounted, and I led Rascal over to a stand of trees, draping his rein over a low-hanging branch and offering him an apple as a thank you for getting us up here safely.

Then I took the basket I'd hooked on the side of the saddle and led Aspen to the center of the field. The country grasses were tall enough to brush Aspen's knees, mingling and twining in the breeze with vibrant and numerous wildflowers. Setting down the basket, I shook out the blanket I'd tucked through its handles and placed it on the ground.

Aspen sat as I knelt and laid out the spread.

"Crew Lawless, did you have your mama make all this?" she teased once everything was unpacked.

I grinned sheepishly. We both knew I was a more than capable cook, but I wasn't above asking Mama for help when the need arose. There were sandwiches, a tub of potato salad, crunchy homemade dill pickles kept safe in a jar, and thick slices of Mama's cheesecake for dessert.

"Maybe."

Aspen unwrapped the wax paper from one of Mama's turkey clubs and sniffed, sighing happily before taking a big bite. Around the mouthful of food, she said, "I ain't mad."

All I could do was chuckle and shake my head as I settled next to her with my own sandwich. We chatted idly about nothing while we ate, and when we were finished, I cleared up the garbage. Before we tucked into the cheesecake, I withdrew two individual sized bottles of sparkling white grape juice from the basket, handing one to her.

"Fancy," she giggled.

"It was the best I could do under the circumstances."

"What are we toasting?" she asked.

I took a moment to study her, to brand this moment into my memory for the rest of my life. I never wanted to forget the way the fading sunlight glowed on her skin, or how the sky behind her head was a gorgeous ombre from pale orange at the horizon to deep purple high above. How brightly her cinnamon eyes shone, glinting with what could only be described as pure happiness and love.

Love for *me*.

This woman was my entire fucking world.

The scene was something out of a dream, a fantasy miraculously and magically brought to life, which was the only thing that could explain Aspen McKay being here with me.

"We're toasting to us, my love. We've been through hell and back to get here, but there isn't anyone else I'd rather have by my side as we tackle all life throws at us."

Aspen grinned, leaning in for a kiss, and I greeted her hungrily.

In deference to my injuries, we also hadn't had sex in nearly a month, and I was a man starved.

Her hands came up to my shirt, fisting the olive-colored material and dragging me closer as our tongues tangled, our lips sliding together and breaking apart, teasing and taunting, waiting to see which of us would break first.

I'd never get tired of the way she tasted, like love and light, safety and serenity. She was my soft place to land, my partner in crime, my best friend and the love of my life. There wasn't a damn thing I wouldn't do for her. Hell, I'd take a fucking bullet or walk headfirst into the flames for her if she asked, and I knew the feeling was mutual.

Reaching up to cup her chin, I pulled back, both of us gasping for breath.

Aspen whined, chasing after me, managing to steal another kiss before I leaned away.

"Why'd you stop?"

"Because I need to ask you something."

"If the question is do I want to have sex right here, the answer is *yes*."

I chuckled. "Different question, but hold onto that response."

Shifting so I could reach into my front pocket of my jeans, my fingers closed around the tiny piece of jewelry.

"You've had that in there this whole time?" she gasped when I presented the ring.

"You're too sneaky for me to get away with carrying a ring box around," I grinned.

Aspen damn near knocked me over and she threw herself at me. I caught her around the waist, settling her so she straddled my lap.

"Ask me then!"

"Hold your horses."

"Technically, that's your horse," she said, pointing over my shoulder at Rascal.

"Aspen…" I warned.

"Sorry," she murmured, though her ear-to-ear grin said she was anything but.

"I've known there was something between us from the very first time I laid eyes on you in the fire station. While every day since hasn't always been easy, they've been wonderful and thrilling and so full of joy and love because of *you*. I can't imagine living the rest of my life without you by my side. And maybe people will say we're moving faster than a normal relationship should, but nothing about us or the hell we've walked together is normal. And I don't want it to be, because then it wouldn't be ours. I love you with every fiber of my being. Everything I have and everything that I am is yours. Until my last breath, you own me. Will you continue to make me the luckiest man alive and marry me?"

The air whooshed out of me as I landed on my back, Aspen's smiling face hovering above me as she peppered my face with kisses, punctuating each one with a single word.

"*Yes.*"

acknowledgements

Tackling a new subgenre of romance was such a daunting task for me, but I knew if I could figure it out, the story would be special—and I was right. There are a number of people to thank for making this one a possibility and a reality.

Always, always, always, the first thank you goes to my family. Mom, Dad, Sissy, Granny J and Grandpa Vic, my aunts, uncles, cousins, etc.: I'm so lucky to have y'all in my corner. Your support and pride keeps me going.

To my angels, Grammy and Grumpy. Being here without you never gets easier, but I can feel you with me every day, in everything I do.

Mer—there's nothing I can say at this point that I haven't already. Just know I'm so blessed to know you and call you my best friend. I couldn't do any of this without you.

To my incredible beta readers, Erika and Maggie, THANK YOU. Your feedback was invaluable, and I truly appreciate all of your help.

To my content team! You guys are the BEST.

To all of my author friends who have been there for me through all of the ups and downs, I'm so lucky to know you.

To Sarah, for the gorgeous covers. You always manage to take my vision and make it ever better than I could've dreamed. And to Lindee for sharing literally THOUSANDS of photos with me until I found the perfect couple to represent Crew and Aspen.

To my readers, who continue to show up for me. I will never take y'all for granted.

also by amanda chaperon

Dusk Valley Series
Fire Fight

Love on the Vine Series
Wine or Lose
Pour Decisions
Perfect Pairing
A Vine Mess

Pregame Series
Every Rule Worth Breaking
A Heart Worth Finding

about the author

Amanda Chaperon realized her passion for books and writing at a young age. Growing up, she was rarely found without a book in her hands, a hobby she carried into adulthood and which ultimately gave her the confidence to begin writing her own stories. She writes what she loves to read: heartfelt, passionate characters, lots of steam, and always a happily ever after.

Amanda lives in Michigan with her Golden Retriever, Gryffin. When she's not writing or reading, she can be found hanging out with her niece and nephew.